on
A
he
he
ses

in
Her
d),

reading, watching Formula 1 on TV and hanging out with friends, dancing, yoga, wine and chocolate.

If you're interested in being part of #TeamSueMoorcroft you can find more information at www.suemoorcroft.com/street-team. If you prefer to sign up to receive news of Sue and her books, go to www.suemoorcroft.com and click on 'Newsletter'. You can follow @SueMoorcroft on Twitter, @SueMoorcroftAuthor on Instagram, or Facebook.com/sue.moorcroft.3 and Facebook.com/SueMoorcroftAuthor.

A SUMMER TO REMEMBER

Sue Moorcroft writes award-winning contemporary fiction of life and love. The Little Village Christmas and A Christmas Gift were Sunday Times bestsellers and The Christmas Promise went to #1 in the Kindle chart. She also writes short stories, serials, articles, columns, courses and writing 'how to'.

An army child, Sue was born in Germany then lived in Cyprus, Malta and the UK and still loves to travel. Her other loves include writing (the best job in the world), reading, watching Formula 1 on TV and hanging out with friends.

A Summer to Remember

Sue Moorcroft

avon.

AVON

A division of HarperCollins*Publishers*
1 London Bridge Street,
London SE1 9GF

www.harpercollins.co.uk

A Paperback Original 2019

1

First published in Great Britain by
HarperCollins*Publishers* 2019

Copyright © Sue Moorcroft 2019

Sue Moorcroft asserts the moral right to
be identified as the author of this work

A catalogue record for this book is
available from the British Library

ISBN-13: 978-0-00-832176-5

Typeset in Sabon LT Std by
Palimpsest Book Production Ltd, Falkirk, Stirlingshire

Th   r

Acknowledgements

A *Summer to Remember* is my fourteenth full-length novel and was the most difficult to write. I'm not sure why. I loved taking my story to north Norfolk and creating a brand-new village in the form of Nelson's Bar. The characters came willingly into my head and we worked well together, but . . . the story took a bit of taming. When I felt the book was finally in shape, my editor, agent and beta reader all gave *A Summer to Remember* a hugely positive reception and I breathed an enormous sigh of relief.

As if to underline the novel's individuality, for once I involved comparatively few people in my research:

I'm greatly indebted to fellow author and Romantic Novelists' Association member Liam Livings. We didn't know each other very well when I approached Liam for help. A mutual friend suggested I contact him when I was struggling with what Harry and Rory's happy ending would look like. I didn't want to be trite or to dismiss their issues and I very much wanted to make their story thread feel real. Liam wrote me long emails, providing lots to think about and options to mull over. It's entirely down to him that things worked out as they did for Harry and Rory, and I'm as grateful to Liam as they are.

Paul Matthews advised me on the making of bespoke guitars even though, apparently, he didn't realise he was being interviewed. You can see his own fabulous creations on his Instagram feed @turnedoutalright.

Mandy Hull shared with me her knowledge of buildings insurance as it relates to subsidence.

My thanks to the many Facebook friends who entered into long and fascinating threads about Parish Meetings, Parish Councils, Village Meetings and Village Halls. I had no idea there was so much to know or how much work is involved.

I'm also grateful to the unknown man whose video conferencing software caught him in 'the act'. His face wasn't in shot but he probably wasn't pleased that the story found its way onto Twitter. If he ever discovers I put his embarrassment in my book, I hope he forgives me.

The rest of the material in *A Summer to Remember* came from my own knowledge, internet research and a glorious and happy time spent in north Norfolk. If you were around Hunstanton, Thornham, Titchwell and the salt marshes you might have seen a happy novelist roaming around in a heatwave, taking photos. A pub garden bathed in a vermillion sunset ranks highly in my places to pore over leaflets, books and maps with a glass of wine.

Mark West made time in his busy life to beta read my manuscript with his usual good humour and valuable commentary. As I get to the end of each book I ask him if he's free to read it and he always replies, 'Of *course*!'

The members of my wonderful street team, Team Sue Moorcroft, constantly offer support in so many ways. Thank you! I feel privileged that so many lovely people make time to spread their appreciation of my writing. A special shout out goes to Manda Jane Ward for naming the village of Nelson's Bar.

No acknowledgements page would be complete without me expressing my unending appreciation of my agent, Juliet Pickering and the team at Blake Friedmann Literary, Film & TV Agency, and my editor Helen Huthwaite and her colleagues at Avon Books. It's such a pleasure to work with each and every one of these outstanding people.

Lastly, of course, thank you to my wonderful readers, especially those who follow me on social media and write lovely reviews. Every book is for you.

Prologue

Six years ago

At the front of Thornham church, best man Aaron stood beside his bridegroom brother, Lee, who gently vibrated with nerves. The church organist floated background music onto the still summer air above the congregation, the vicar looked thoughtful, and they all awaited the bride, Alice.

Lee was welcome to high-maintenance Princess Alice, spoiled to death by her long-widowed mother, Sally, Aaron thought. Personally, he preferred her down-to-earth, brightly intelligent cousin Clancy, the only bridesmaid Alice had wanted. To joke Lee out of his obvious state of nerves he leaned in close to murmur, 'I hope all the stories about the best man and bridesmaid are true, by the way.'

Lee managed a smile. 'Your tongue's been hanging out since last weekend.'

'Guilty.' Aaron had been in a constant state of awareness since Clancy had hopped out of her car, one that looked too red and sporty for the tiny Norfolk village of Nelson's Bar.

'Alice and Clancy's mums are identical twins.' Lee moved the conversation to his favourite subject: Alice. 'It's why the girls look more like sisters than cousins.'

It was true that they shared chestnut hair and green eyes, but, as Aaron was quick to point out, 'They're really different personalities.' He and Clancy had been flirting all week, sharing jokes about the pre-wedding hoopla, and after last night's rehearsal dinner hosted by Aaron's parents at De Silva House, the flirting had culminated in a long, deep, hot kiss in the dark reaches of the garden. Her body, wedged against his, had driven him crazy as she nibbled along his jawline. Then Lee had come looking for him with some annoying best-man task – there seemed to be thousands – and Clancy had made a silent-scream face, before whispering, 'Tomorrow. After the wedding.'

Aaron could not *wait* for this wedding to be over . . .

A stir at the back of the church and the vicar in his white robes stepped forward expectantly. Finally! Aaron turned, his gaze filled with the sight of Clancy Moss walking up the aisle towards him, her dress of muted green flowing around her like water.

He began to smile . . . until, beside him, Lee made a strangled noise of distress. Then Aaron realised that everything about the picture Clancy made was wrong. She scurried instead of taking stately, bridesmaid steps. There was no bouquet. No *bride*. And no answering smile as she arrived breathlessly in front of the vicar.

She glanced at Aaron, before laying her hand on his brother's arm, her voice shaking with emotion. 'I'm sorry, Lee. I can't find Alice. Her mum had left for the church and Alice and I both went to our rooms for last-minute things but . . . when I looked for her, her wedding dress was back on its hanger. And her car was gone.'

Aaron swung around to look at his brother.

And Lee crumbled right before his eyes.

Chapter One

Now

Clancy had driven for three hours and it felt like someone else's hands on the steering wheel. Someone dream-driving her BMW away from London and the apartment in Chalk Farm she'd shared with Will. She hadn't paused for a cup of coffee or a comfort break, not wanting to leave the car unattended. It was stuffed with her possessions and she'd lost so much she just couldn't lose anything else.

Now she took a left from the A149 at the sign for Nelson's Bar, which might sound like a pub but was named for Horatio, Lord Nelson, born along the coast in Burnham Thorpe. The bar of land on which the village stood bisected the salt marshes as it thrust out to sea.

The car purred through a belt of pinewood, the land rising like a ski slope until she burst out into sunlight, feeling for an instant as if all she could see was blue sky. Then the road plunged and cornered between two hedgerows. And she was there.

She drew up at the side of Long Lane and switched off

the engine. Silence. Through a smeared windscreen she gazed at the homes peeping at her over hedges clothed in early summer green.

Nelson's Bar. She'd been here only once before, for the week of Alice's wedding – or not-wedding, as it turned out – but Roundhouse Row was just as she remembered it. Alice and Lee had lived in number one, the Roundhouse itself, a cylinder of white and red chalk stone with an occasional accent of flint, wearing its conical terracotta roof like a hat with windows.

Clancy climbed from the car and stretched. The salt-scented breeze filled her lungs so easily that it was as if a giant rubber band had dropped from around her chest.

She clicked open the garden gate and fished out the Roundhouse key. It turned smoothly and her footsteps echoed on worn red quarry tiles as she stepped inside the enclosed porch and then through the inner door. She paused to take in the ground floor, its central staircase cradled by hefty oak beams and posts.

Almost as the front door clunked shut behind her she caught the opening of the door in the opposite wall. 'Hello?' called a man's voice, and Aaron De Silva rounded the stairs, dark curls longer than she remembered and tousled around his face, the line of his jaw shaded more heavily with stubble, T-shirt and jeans speckled with grass clippings.

Six-plus years shrank to nothing.

He stopped short. 'Clancy?' He sounded stunned.

Silent seconds passed and Clancy was aware of more between them than the empty floor space. One fevered kiss. One blazing row. Years of carefully polite emails.

Aaron blinked. 'Am I supposed to understand what's going on? Your last email said you had someone for the caretaker job. Did you feel the need to escort her here personally?' He glanced behind her, as if expecting to see another person.

She had to strangle a laugh at his almost comical expression of dismay. 'No.' She made her voice firm. 'Because I'm taking the job myself. I need a change of scene.'

His dark brows snapped together. '*You?*' There was nothing comical about his expression now. It was more . . . horrified.

The urge to laugh vanished. Instead, Clancy suddenly felt clammy and unsteady. She blinked to clear her vision. Maybe her earlier dream-like sensations had been something to do with a failure to eat today. And possibly yesterday. She swallowed and her voice sank to a whisper. 'Sorry. I should have checked with you.' She tried to think of somewhere else she could go but her thoughts refused to co-operate. She'd found herself struggling with decisions recently. That's what the others at IsVid had said, Monty, Asila, Tracey – even Will. It was the shock. She wasn't functioning, they'd told her in varying degrees of kindness when she'd risen in the middle of a meeting with a client and gone home. In Monty's opinion it had constituted 'a breakdown' and he'd wanted her to get psychiatric help.

Enraged, she'd snapped a refusal. 'I simply recognised the reaching of a personal limit. I've emailed the client and apologised. They understand.'

'And what did you think you were doing when you sent out that newsletter making your personal relationship with Will public? It made us a laughing stock,' Monty had thundered on.

Clancy had hardly been able to believe her ears. 'Don't you think what Will did and your shitty, callous reaction

7

was more to the point? I know IsVid is important to you, Monty, but don't I deserve any support?'

Asila and Tracey had tried to cut across Monty's reply, beginning a gentler conversation about whether Clancy should take time out. She closed her eyes, remembering how Monty had brushed them aside with, 'Frankly, I'm not sure how we can go on working together after your chaotic reaction to what's happened, Clancy.'

As the others had fallen silent Clancy had gasped, 'You want *me* to leave?' Will had stood by, looking haunted, but hadn't contradicted Monty. And neither had Asila or Tracey, though their eyes had filled with compassion. The scene had grown ugly with rage and pain, and Clancy had stormed home. Except that it was no longer home. It was an apartment she'd shared for three years with Will and where she'd spent untold hours planning the wedding they'd now never have with its colour theme of grey and duck-egg blue. She'd already agreed to move out.

Then Aaron's email had arrived on her phone with a *ting*!

Clancy,
Did you get my message about the caretaker at the cottages? In case it went astray:
    Evelyn, who's lived at the Roundhouse in exchange for administering the two tenanted cottages and servicing the three holiday lets has left suddenly and we need to fill her position.
    Shall I advertise?
Aaron

The relief had been astronomical. Without questioning the wisdom of her impulsive action, the fact that she'd parted from Aaron on bad terms and had never been back to Nelson's Bar, her reply had flown from her typing fingers.

> *I know someone who wants the job with the accommodation, which will save you the bother of advertising. She'll arrive tomorrow.*
> *Clancy*

For the past six years, since Alice had jilted Lee and Aaron had bought Lee out of the property, she'd looked after Alice's half of Roundhouse Row with a tiny fragment of her capabilities. A part-time caretaking job would be a breeze; a summer in Norfolk would help her heal. She'd wilfully ignored Aaron's astounded reply: *TOMORROW??? What about references??? Or me being able to chat with this person?* And, later, *Clancy! Please reply!* She'd put her phone on 'do not disturb' in case he broke the tacit agreement of only communicating via email, and rang.

And that's how she'd ended up sitting amongst boxes last night, packing recklessly for a low-effort life change and a place to lick her wounds. She'd been able to look into Will's mortified face and say with manufactured indifference, 'I have somewhere to go. You needn't worry.' She'd handed him the white leather file emblazoned with *September Wedding* in silver. 'You'll find everything in here that you need to cancel our wedding. It's only fair that you take responsibility as you're the one to find someone new.' Then she'd completed her packing with the images of wedding dresses and morning suits swimming in the tears in her eyes, remembering, now she was about to return to Nelson's Bar, Alice's wedding day.

Clancy was getting an agonising taste of what Lee must

have felt. Surely Alice couldn't truly have imagined Lee's pain at being left at the altar like that? Or she would have arranged some gentler way of withdrawing from the marriage.

Now, with Lee's brother Aaron looking on, she swallowed convulsively against empty-stomach nausea. The fluttering in her ears grew louder and cold sweat gathered on her face. Ever the pragmatist, she murmured, 'I think I should sit down.'

And she did. The room rushed past her and the floor flew up to hit her, hard.

She heard Aaron exclaim, then a warm hand guided her head down towards her knees and his voice seemed to come from far away. 'Are you ill?'

Politely, she replied, 'I'm OK. I just missed breakfast.' Cautiously, she eased away from him and lifted her head. The room only spun slightly. And that might have been because she'd been suddenly engulfed in the memory of the last time Aaron had touched her. It hadn't occurred to her that he'd still affect her.

'How about you come and sit on the bench outside for some fresh air,' he suggested gruffly. 'I brought coffee stuff. I'll make some.'

'Perfect, thank you.' She managed to roll to her knees and then to her feet, aware of him hovering at her elbow as she struggled across to the back door and out to a black-painted bench on the edge of the circular patio. Vaguely, she took in a cardboard box half full of weeds and a spade and fork lying on the grass beside a dog bowl of water. A mower waited on a half-cut lawn speckled with daisies, the scent of new-mown grass increasing her nausea. She lowered herself until the wooden slats felt firm beneath her as a big, dark grey dog jumped up from a sun-splashed patch of lawn, beating his tail and holding his head awkwardly cocked as he regarded her.

'Oh, bless, he only has one eye!' she said, automatically extending her hand to be sniffed.

'He's a rescue. I took him because I could call him Nelson and he'd fit right in here. Will you be all right for two minutes?' Aaron was already stepping away.

She nodded carefully and the myriad colours of the garden made her vision spin like a colour wheel. Shutting her eyes helped, especially when Nelson lodged his head on her leg as if in comfort, and when Aaron returned she was able to half-open her eyes again.

'Here,' he murmured, proffering a mug of milky coffee and a cereal bar.

Shakily, she took them. 'Thank you.'

Clancy sipped and nibbled her way through the small repast, Aaron beside her in not-very-companionable silence.

Aaron had seated himself so he could observe Clancy until her coffee cup was empty and Nelson was nosing the wrapper from the cereal bar on the lawn. The breeze stirred her streaky chestnut fringe and flipped the ends of her hair from her shoulders. What had happened to her? She looked like a pale echo of the sleek, beautiful, mythical creature who'd once flashed into his life and out again.

He'd never apologised for the things he'd said – shouted – when Alice had all but destroyed his brother. He'd been too taken up with Lee, who'd stopped eating, acting, at only twenty-eight years old, as if his life was over.

'I'm surprised you want to move here,' he said, trying to focus on the present. 'Nelson's Bar's a far cry from London. I can't imagine wanting to live in a city, the sky only showing between the huge buildings you spend your life in, breathing stale air and looking out of windows that don't open, but it's what you're used to.'

She shrugged.

'The caretaker's job involves changing beds and cleaning up after guests,' he persisted. Then, though he knew because she'd once told him all about it, eyes shining with enthusiasm, and it was in her email sign-off, he asked, 'What is it you usually do?'

Her lips barely moved. 'All the hard shit.'

'Oh.' Odd answer. 'I thought it was film making.'

A robin flew down to perch on the handle of his spade and tilt its head to inspect them before flitting off again. Clancy watched it go. 'IsVid provides video content and video-based services. Websites. YouTube. Raw footage. Editing. Effects. Five of us built it up. The others are the creatives and the people people. I excel at what nobody else wants to do, like writing privacy policies and terms and conditions for us and our clients, working on their internet safety, adhering to law and legislation, writing agreements and contracts.'

'Oh,' he repeated. 'That does sound like hard shit.'

'There were compensations, like money and satisfaction. But I've left the agency. Or I'm taking time out.' Then she added, 'But nobody expects me back.'

He managed not to say 'oh', this time. 'OK,' he said instead, as Clancy wasn't showing any immediate signs of turning tail for London. 'As you know, numbers two and three Roundhouse Row have long-term tenants, Dilys and Ernie. For them the caretaker acts as agent to the landlord – arranging maintenance and checking the rent arrives, paying whatever bills the landlord's responsible for and negotiating any rent rises. Numbers four, five and six, the holiday cottages, can be let out for any number of nights from two up. The caretaker changes bed linen and towels and does the laundry, cleans the houses and does the gardens.'

'Why don't you do the garden? You're a gardener.' She'd turned to look at him, her head tilted much as the inquisitive robin's had been.

'Because I work full time for my landscape gardening business.' He knew she knew that. It was as if making the polite enquiries of strangers would erase the night they'd got hot and heavy.

Her turn to reply, 'Oh.' She scooped back her hair as the breeze tried to blow it into her face and she turned her gaze to the circular flower beds he'd been working on. Alice had thought it amusing to create as many circles in and around her circular house as possible. Even the garden shed was circular because Lee, besotted, had made it for her. 'You're doing this garden now,' Clancy pointed out.

'Because Evelyn found a boyfriend and hightailed it to live with him in Wales.' He went on with the caretaker's job description. 'You'd also handle bookings. A lot come through a tourism website; they ring you with the details. A few come directly by post or phone. You sort out guests' gripes, answer questions, solve problems and basically do whatever comes up. I'm afraid that if you're at home, tenants and guests consider you on duty. Evelyn left the book inside the Roundhouse. I'll show it to you.'

'Book?'

'The one with bookings in.' It was a fat, dog-eared volume Evelyn had kept up-to-date and in which she'd left copious notes for her successor.

'You make bookings in an actual book?' She almost smiled. 'There's no booking software?'

Slowly, he relaxed. This was it. Her sticking point. The indisputable fact he could share with her in good conscience and let it send her back to the city. He stretched his legs and crossed them at the ankle. 'No booking software. The village is an internet "not spot" with ancient phone lines and poor-to-non-existent mobile signal. Look,' he said, feeling magnanimous now he realised there was no way a city girl used to being permanently plugged in could exist in an environment where information technology was rendered virtually – ha, ha – useless. 'I suppose being involved with the cottages peripherally hasn't given you a clear picture of life in Nelson's Bar.'

He encompassed the row of cottages joined to the Roundhouse with a wave of his arm. 'The rental cottages are the only real holiday homes in the entire village, though there is a B&B, which has a bar about six feet by six and, outside, a few tables with umbrellas. We have no church, no shop, no pub or coffee shop. The Norfolk Coast Path bypasses us and although north Norfolk is popular with walkers, most don't tackle the hill climb to get up here.' He sat back, giving her the opportunity to hum and haw, to backtrack on her intention to live in the back of beyond.

But then Clancy's breath left her in a long, slow, peaceful sigh. 'Sounds perfect,' she said.

Chapter Two

Clancy knew her answer had surprised Aaron from the way his brows clicked down over his eyes. 'Seriously?' he asked stiffly. From within the Roundhouse, a phone began to ring and he rose from the bench, disappearing indoors to answer it. Then he reappeared. 'That was my girlfriend. She knew I was working here and I'm late to meet her.' He paused, checking his watch. 'I'll come back in a couple of hours. We need to finish this conversation.'

'Fine.' Clancy wondered whether he was expecting her to think twice in his absence.

She watched him pack the garden tools into the shed and click his fingers to his enormous dog. Every word Aaron had spoken had increased Clancy's belief that Nelson's Bar was exactly what she needed. He might as well have said, 'Here's a quiet, safe backwater where you can get your head straight. The job's a doddle for someone with organisational skills.'

Clancy Moss, however temporarily exhausted, thrived on challenges, and the ability to adapt had been bred into her. With engineers for parents, she'd been brought up in Belize, various parts of Africa, Dubai, Hong Kong . . . sometimes in company compounds or city apartments but also in remote villages. She'd attended company schools, boarding school, local schools and international schools. She'd even, at times, attended Alice's school, and had loved the feeling of having a settled home with Alice and Aunt Sally while her parents vanished into a part of Africa considered unsuitable for their daughter. Boarding school and its dull routines and restrictions came a poor second to sharing escapades with Alice and being spoiled by her aunt.

Once she'd come to the UK for uni she'd tried to re-create that feeling of belonging. She'd thought she'd found it with Will but now . . . Now she'd been pushed into the painful break from Will and her colleagues – she wasn't sure whether it was still logical to call them friends – she needed to regroup.

OK, so, food first. Just to confirm what Aaron had said, she took out her phone. *No service.* So she'd just drive to Hunstanton and find a supermarket. Then she'd—

'Yoohoo!' came a creaky female voice. 'Do you mind if I come into the garden? Hope not, because I'm in.' The voice trembled a laugh.

Surprised into rising and facing the direction the voice had come from, Clancy had to grab the back of the bench as her head swam anew. A short, rotund woman with a dandelion clock of white hair and a sweet smile shuffled around the house. 'Are you are our new Evelyn? I'm Dilys, from number two. I thought I'd say hello.' By now Dilys was standing in front of Clancy, daisy-strewn wellies peeping from beneath a rose-splashed skirt. Her eyebrows bobbed enquiringly.

'I'm taking the caretaker's job, yes.' It was impossible

not to return Dilys's smile; it was so twinkly and warm. 'I was just wondering where I could find a supermarket. Or furniture shops. Aaron had to rush off before he could tell me.' She supposed she was lucky that she had money in the bank but she hadn't really bargained for the hassle of furnishing the Roundhouse when she decided to launch herself towards Nelson's Bar.

Dilys's grey eyes twinkled as she turned and let herself down stiffly onto the bench beside Clancy. 'Furniture? I expect he'll just bring the other stuff back. They stored it up at De Silva House – Aaron's parents' place – because Evelyn had her own.'

Clancy suppressed a wriggle of hurt that Aaron hadn't mentioned something that, clearly, would make her life easier. Evidently, he didn't want her here. So what? She'd been unwanted by people much closer and more important to her than Aaron De Silva. Her ex-fiancé and work colleagues, for example. And with her parents it had always only been fifty-fifty.

She shoved those negative thoughts away with a bright, 'Was it Alice and Lee's furniture? I'm Alice's cousin, Clancy.'

Dilys beamed. 'Her cousin! How is Alice? I never hear from her.'

'I think she's OK,' Clancy answered carefully. After jilting Lee, Alice had made no bones about preferring to be invisible to anyone at Nelson's Bar and had wheedled unashamedly to get Clancy to represent Alice's interest in Roundhouse Row. 'I'm on the move all the time anyway and you're so good at stuff. Don't make me interact with judgy big bro Aaron, puhleeeeease, Clancee.' Clancy had sighed and said yes. People often said yes to Alice. Maybe it was because she just seemed to expect it, but also it

17

was her pretty smile, the swish of her stylishly cut hair, or the way she had of linking arms as if to demonstrate how much she liked you.

And, wherever Clancy had been in the world, Alice had always sent letters, cards, messages, demands to know where Clancy was and what she was doing, requests for postcards or photos or to know when Clancy was going to come and live with them again. Whatever Alice's faults, she and Clancy had a bond.

These days it was Alice's travelling the bond had to survive, rather than Clancy's. The only time they'd seen each other in the last six years was when Aunt Sally had died suddenly four years ago. Alice had reappeared for the funeral, white-faced and red-eyed over the loss of her mother. Then she'd sold the family home in Warwickshire and vanished again, her travel fund firmly bolstered by her inheritance.

None of this needed to be shared with Clancy's new neighbour, so she just said, 'Dilys, could you point me at a supermarket, please? I need supplies.'

Dilys's face shifted its wrinkles into a delighted grin. 'Can I show you instead? I don't drive any more so it's a boon for me to get a ride into Hunstanton. Tell you what,' she swept on. 'How about I trade you lunch? I've made vegetable soup and I was just about to have some.'

Warmth stole into Clancy's heart at such a friendly offer. 'What a brilliant trade. Thank you.'

She followed her to the next-door cottage, assailed by a deliciously oniony fragrance as Dilys opened the door. 'Welcome to number two,' she said. 'It's not as big as the Roundhouse but it's been my home since I've been on my own. Take a seat at the table, lovie, and I'll dish up.'

It seemed only seconds before Clancy was dipping chunks of bread into thick vegetable soup and sipping tea, looking around her. Dilys's kitchen was full of . . . stuff. Heaps of fabric and wool teetered, jars of buttons or bowls of beads glowed with colour.

'I'm a crafter,' Dilys explained, following Clancy's gaze. 'Whatever I see or find I make into something else. It used to drive my poor husband mad. Still, it doesn't concern him, not now he's gone.'

'I'm sorry,' Clancy said automatically.

'I still see him of course,' Dilys continued, slurping up a soup-sodden square of bread.

Clancy paused. 'Oh?' She considered herself far too down-to-earth to believe in the supernatural but Dilys sounded so confident that she asked, 'Where?'

Dilys put down her spoon in her empty bowl with a sigh of satisfaction. 'In the garden. He lives next door.' She burst out laughing.

Clancy laughed too, laying down her spoon, though she'd eaten only half her lunch. 'I thought you meant he was a ghost!'

'Not him.' Dilys was still grinning. 'We can't share a house but we can't do without each other completely.'

Finishing the industrial-strength tea and feeling ten times better for food inside her and the hand of friendship Dilys seemed to have no hesitation in extending, Clancy went out to empty her car boot ready for their shopping.

They set off for the supermarket, Dilys exclaiming over the comfort of the car's leather interior. Clancy was instantly plunged into a host of memories of Will helping her choose the car less than a year ago. It had been a symbol of the success of IsVid and now she was glad she'd chosen to spend the money that way rather than doing something sensible like paying a chunk off the mortgage. Resolutely, she shoved the thought away. 'I forgot to look how big the freezer at the Roundhouse is.' She slowed the car as she turned right onto the A149 and immediately came up behind a car towing a caravan.

'There's a good, capacious freezer,' pronounced Dilys. 'Capacious was the answer to the nine-letter word puzzle in the paper yesterday.'

Clancy tried not to be distracted by the energetic pinging of the phone in her pocket now they'd left the village and, presumably, picked up a signal. 'Are you a puzzler? I like Sudoku and crosswords.' They passed the rest of the journey amicably chatting about why cryptic crosswords were so much more fun than the 'easy' counterparts, which neither of them actually found easy, until they reached Hunstanton, where, entranced by the dancing blue sea on their right, Clancy had to concentrate to follow Dilys's directions past the formal gardens and through the busy traffic to the centre of town.

When she'd parked at Tesco's, she stole a quick look at the alerts now showing on the screen of her phone: Tracey and Asila both asking if she was OK. After a moment's deliberation, she tucked the phone away again because she didn't know how to reply. Was she OK? She could've said, *Fine except for my relationship ending and my co-directors wanting me out of the business*, but as they were two of those directors it would be a) aggressive b) whiney c) pointless. It would be more fruitful to devote her time to providing herself with what she needed in order to *be* OK.

As well as filling a trolley with food and household items, she discovered that seaside supermarkets sold things like wetsuits for children, buckets and spades . . . and

20

airbeds. Just in case Aaron truly intended leaving her without a bed for the night, she bought a lilac-coloured one for less than a tenner and Dilys offered to lend her a duvet. She hadn't wanted to bring constant reminders of Will in the form of things they'd shared so new bedclothes would be on her shopping list once she had a permanent bed sorted.

It was late afternoon when they arrived back at the Roundhouse. Clancy helped Dilys into number two with her shopping and collected in return a single duvet in a bold, bright patchwork cover, then carried her own purchases indoors to join the bags and boxes she'd brought from London.

She halted. London was no longer her home.

The echoing emptiness of the Roundhouse seemed to catch her suddenly beneath the breastbone, the only sounds her own breathing and muted birdsong outdoors. 'You can do this,' she told herself aloud. 'This is not the first time you've moved house and begun again.' So she set to, dividing the shopping between fridge, freezer and cupboards. Kitchen units had been fitted along a section of the curved wall and into an island unit too. As she worked, she wished she'd asked Aaron exactly when he'd be back. Dilys probably had his landline number but there was no reply when Clancy popped out to knock on her door.

OK. Back to the Roundhouse. She walked a slow circle around the ground floor, remembering how Alice and Lee had set the space out in segments: sofas, a coffee table and footstools beside the panelling screen; then a circular dining table with chairs, and the space beneath the stairs filled with oak and glass cabinets built by Lee.

Next, she trod up the wooden staircase to the three

wedge-shaped bedrooms and two bathrooms on the first floor. All three bedrooms were carpeted so it felt less echoey. In the master bedroom she stood on tiptoe to catch glimpses of a hazy blue-grey sea between trees and houses. Woolly white clouds dotted a paintbox-blue sky. Nelson's Bar was high above the waves on its headland but she remembered Alice showing her the way down to a small beach.

She turned to survey the master bedroom without much enthusiasm. It had been Alice and Lee's. Across the landing, the second bedroom's view was of the lane and the house across the road. She turned and strode up the next flight of stairs to the loft, where she'd slept on her only visit, opening the door with a teeny-tiny – but welcome – sense of familiarity.

The space she walked into was conical with room to stand straight only in the middle or by the window dormers. Beyond the rooftops, she could see the sea from one window and the pinewoods from the other. She stood for a long time, gazing over the village. Gardens and trees between the houses. The peaceful sound of seagulls and the occasional car engine.

The sun lit the room, danced on the distant sea and warmed her heart.

Feeling something approaching enthusiasm, she ran downstairs for the airbed and duvet. By the time the bed was inflated she was red-faced and puffing, but she smiled as she cast the patchwork quilt over it.

Her temporary bed in her new room and new home. So there was no real furniture! Nobody who really knew her would think she'd be put off by a little thing like that.

Chapter Three

In the morning, Aaron's conscience prodded him awake ridiculously early, considering it was Sunday.

He hadn't meant to leave Clancy Moss alone in an unfurnished house yesterday.

He'd met Genevieve at his end-terrace flint cottage in Potato Hall Row on the edge of the village near the cliffs, and found her worrying aloud about where to go while builders repaired her own cottage. It was a tricky subject. He was all too aware that she was fishing to move in with him and he was beginning to resent it. They might have been together for a year or so but he liked his life in Nelson's Bar as it was. He was content with his own company, creating gardens, soil between his fingers, the scent of grass on the air, blossom in spring, crinkling leaves and the promise of frost when autumn came. Nature's glorious, ever-changing landscape. OK, he didn't have much of a relationship history – serial monogamy interspersed with happy singledom – maybe his brother's public dumping had had something to do with that.

But that was his choice.

As it happened, while he'd been trying hard not to tackle the issue of where Genevieve was going to spend the months the builder needed to underpin her house, Aaron's mum Yvonne had telephoned. 'Aunt Norma's broken her ankle on a day trip to King's Lynn, and bumped her head. She's got to stay in hospital overnight. Your dad's on shift at the hotel—'

Knowing his mother's car control in times of stress, Aaron immediately offered, 'I'll drive you.' His great-aunt had looked after him and Lee a lot when they were little so Yvonne could work. He'd apologised to Genevieve and was soon driving his mother out of the village, noticing the absence of Clancy's car outside the Roundhouse and sparing a moment to wonder whether she'd decided to head home to London already.

He had little opportunity to examine his reaction to that possibility during the hassly fifty-minute journey as Yvonne alternately worried aloud about her aunt and reproved him for the disreputable interior of his double-cab pickup, littered with notes, plans of gardens and empty crisp packets.

Once at the Queen Elizabeth Hospital, they found Aunt Norma had concussion. Queasy and quiet, she looked unlike her usual noisy, feisty self. Yvonne croaked, 'Oh, Auntie! You poor thing!' and became quite tearful.

They stayed on, requesting information of nurses and buying Aunt Norma magazines from the hospital shop. Her normally bright eyes were closed against queasiness and she didn't tease anyone or ask awkward questions, so they knew she had to be feeling pretty rubbish.

Finally, after she'd fallen asleep, Aaron and Yvonne went out into a dark and breezy evening. Yvonne was inclined to sniff and Aaron gave her a reassuring hug before they got into his truck, her loose curls blowing into his face.

It wasn't until he was nosing his pickup into the mad traffic on the huge roundabout on the outskirts of King's Lynn that Clancy Moss returned to the forefront of his mind with an uncomfortable jolt. He should have made some effort to check whether she'd definitely left. He had the landline number of the house but the clock on the dash of his truck read 22:47 – too late to ring.

When, eventually, he'd driven his yawning mother past the Roundhouse, the place was in darkness, but the smart blue BMW was once again parked outside the front gate. He drove on, feeling like a git. Spending a night in an empty house couldn't be comfortable.

As he was feeling no better about himself this morning, he let Nelson out into the garden, pausing to enjoy the view of the glittering, restless sea and wonder why anyone would live anywhere other than Nelson's Bar, then passed half an hour strumming one of his favourite guitars on the garden bench. It always put his soul at peace.

When it was nine o'clock, mindful that yesterday Clancy hadn't seemed to be looking after herself, he stuffed four cereal bars in his pockets, called Nelson and snicked on his lead, then stepped out into the early summer sunshine. He strode past the rest of Potato Hall Row, mainly flint cottages edged with red brick. Nelson's feathery tail waved as the king-sized canine sniffed hedges and gateposts. They made their way down the curve of Long Lane to the Roundhouse.

The scent of clipped privet was strong on the air as he passed 3 Roundhouse Row where Ernie could be seen sweeping up hedge trimmings. 'Aaron!' Ernie hailed him at max volume. 'Do we have a new Evelyn? Dilys says we

25

have but nobody's told me.' He waved towards the blue BMW parked in the lane and leaned on the broom handle, shaggy grey eyebrows knitting above the bridge of his nose.

Aaron met Ernie's scowl with a smile. There was no point trading Ernie grump for grump. He couldn't help but attack every subject like a threat any more than Aunt Norma could help tripping on uneven pavements. 'Possibly,' he replied.

Ernie revolved on the spot as Aaron attempted to carry on by. 'And she's Alice's cousin? Come to represent the family interests, has she?'

Aaron shrugged, managing to sidestep Ernie on the second attempt. 'Hard to say. Hedge is looking great, Ernie.' Ernie was instantly distracted, beaming with pride as he patted his manicured privet, and Aaron escaped. Dilys must have met Clancy, which was like telling the whole village, and Aunt Norma had the same knitting and sewing mates. It was no doubt only because she was in hospital that he hadn't already received an indignant phone call about a member of Alice's family living in the Roundhouse.

He broke into a jog, determined to pass Dilys's cottage without being collared again but, thankfully, her red gingham curtains were drawn and he was able to slip through the gate to the Roundhouse.

It was no use checking for drawn curtains there as every window was presently bare. His conscience gave him another prod. He gave the outer front door a gentle knock. If she was upstairs asleep – on what? – she would be unlikely to be disturbed by it and—

A brisk rattle, then the porch door swung open and Clancy stood in the opening wearing jeans and a T-shirt.

Her chestnut hair fell poker-straight and glossy to her shoulders, the fringe framing those direct green eyes.

'Oh, good, it's you,' she said, beckoning him in. The smell of coffee and the red mug and bowl he could see in the sink as he followed her suggested she'd had breakfast. 'I've found the bookings book in a kitchen drawer,' she began as she strode ahead. 'Can I get access to the Roundhouse Row bank account? Or do I come through you to check payments received? Evelyn's notes don't cover that.' By now she'd reached the place on the kitchen island where the bookings book and a few piles of paper were all neatly arranged. She glanced down at the big dog beside Aaron. 'Morning, Nelson.'

Nelson waved his tail. Evidently, he didn't know her well enough to perform his greeting dance.

'But first—' Aaron broke in, taken aback to realise the dreary, droopy ghost Clancy he'd met yesterday had vanished, leaving in its place a Clancy much more like the sparky woman he remembered.

'"But first" let's get the Roundhouse furniture out of storage?' she finished for him, her honeyed tones belying her steely expression. 'It's high on my list, but not high on yours, evidently, as you didn't bother coming back yesterday, regardless of whether I had anything to sleep on.'

Aaron felt a smile tug at his mouth. He didn't want it to, but something amused him about her obvious satisfaction in possessing knowledge he'd failed to share. 'But *first*,' he repeated firmly, 'I need to apologise for abandoning you yesterday. There was a small family emergency.' He explained about Aunt Norma.

Instantly, concern filled Clancy's eyes. 'Your family comes first, of course. I can manage on an airbed for another couple of nights if necessary.'

An airbed. He caught his mouth this time before it grinned at her resourcefulness. 'I'm relieved you didn't have to sleep on the floor. Can we sit down for a few minutes?'

She looked ostentatiously around the space about them, still devoid of furniture. 'On what?'

This time he didn't trouble to hide his smile, not minding points being scored over him when it was done with such elegance. 'The garden bench worked perfectly yesterday.'

He led the way out, letting Nelson off to sniff around. Clancy sat down and waited for him to begin, apparently content to watch a blackbird hopping about a gnarly apple tree as if choosing the perfect perch from which to sing.

'I'm glad you feel that family comes first,' he began carefully, joining her on the bench, 'because I don't think you being here's a good thing.'

Her hair swung around her face as she turned to regard him, the sun picking out glittering flecks of gold in her eyes. 'Why's that?'

'Leaving aside the fact that I don't think you realise what it's like living in such a tiny, out-of-the-way place as Nelson's Bar, you have to consider my family.'

She tilted her head. 'Why's that?' she repeated.

Aaron began to feel less amused. It might be better – for her as well as him – if he was more direct. 'Lee was nearly destroyed by Alice. He was heartsick for so long that we were afraid for him. As you know, Alice agreed that I could buy his half of the Roundhouse and Roundhouse Row to enable him to move away and make a new start, but he's living in the village again and you'll be a reminder.' He paused, then went on, feeling she might as well know the truth. 'To give you an idea of the level of antipathy in my family, they refer to Alice as "Awful

Alice".' He sat forward, leaning his elbows on his thighs, giving her a level look. 'There's resentment, Clancy.'

Clancy leaned forward to prop her elbows on her thighs and give him a level look of her own. 'You may be your brother's keeper, but I'm afraid I'm not my cousin's.'

'I didn't say I was Lee's keeper,' he interrupted, stung.

Clancy overrode him in the same level but firm voice. 'What Awful Alice did was nothing to do with me, which I'm sure Lee's mature enough to realise.'

He decided to become yet more direct. 'Personally, I thought of your cousin as Princess Alice, not too worried about what anybody else wanted, expecting her wishes to be paramount even when she was crying for the moon.' He ignored the way her eyes widened at this candid appraisal. 'Even if you're not like that, I'm pretty confident Lee would prefer you to consider his feelings in this and return to your life in London. And – friendly warning – he won't be alone in that.'

Her gaze didn't waver, though she made a tiny movement, as if somewhere deep inside she flinched. 'You're mixing up opinion with fact. Anyway, I can't go back. Lee's not the only one things have gone wrong for. My fiancé – ex, now – has got someone else, Renée, who I suspect he's moving into our apartment pretty much as we speak. I'm being shoved out of the business I worked long and hard to help build so, as well as having nowhere to live, I have no job. I represent Alice's interests and therefore I appoint myself as caretaker.'

Her voice softened. 'I think Alice will want me to have the job. She and I – there's a special relationship. I haven't seen her for a while, but that doesn't matter. That's how it's always been because my parents towed me around the world or they put me in boarding school or left me with

Alice and Aunt Sally, when, despite your assessment of her character, she shared her home, her life, her friends and even her mother with me without hesitation. Now I'm based in the UK and she's the one travelling I'm pretty certain she'd support my wish to come to Nelson's Bar. But we can ask her, if you like.' Her expression clouded. 'I'm genuinely sorry you don't want me here, and I can see you might think that with my history I should be inured to just cheerfully packing up and shoving off somewhere where I'm less of an inconvenience. But I need a new home, at least for now. And this is it.' Her voice wavered and she clamped her lips shut on the end of the sentence.

In the silence, the blackbird began to sing beautifully fluting notes. Nelson lifted his head as if searching for the source of the sound with his one eye.

Aaron stared at Clancy, shaken to his plummeting core. He should have recognised the trouble he'd seen in her eyes yesterday. He'd watched Lee battling similar heart-wrenching grief. *Now* he understood why she had arrived looking so ill, why abandoning her in an empty house hadn't made her turn tail. Clancy was in a mess. And, judging from the way her fingers were folded around each other so hard that her knuckles were white, her composure was only a very thin skin deep.

Aaron had never been able to kick people while they were down and rarely refused to give help where it was needed – leaving aside the current uncomfortable situation with Genevieve. Nelson was only one in a succession of badly off animals he'd adopted at one time or another. He dragged up a breath from the pit of his lungs and let it out in a gusty sigh. 'OK. I'll get my truck. We'll fetch the furniture.'

A noisy swallow, then she replied, simply, 'Thank you. May I walk along with you?'

'Of course,' he muttered.

She locked up the Roundhouse with city-dweller punctiliousness. They began up Long Lane through the dappled sunlight created by laburnum trees, the last of their yellow blossoms floating down around them. They headed into the village before swinging towards the north side of the headland. May was mild this year and the sunshine stroked Aaron's skin with warm hands. 'I live further up the lane in Potato Hall Row,' he volunteered. Having made the decision not to hurl further impediments in Clancy's way – though he wasn't particularly looking forward to the little chat he'd soon need to have with his family – he went on: 'Long Lane loops right around this side of the village as far as the B&B and The Green, towards the furthest point of the headland. Then Marshview Road takes over and comes back round.' He swept his arm in a long U-shape.

Clancy's hair blew in a sudden gust of wind and she smiled faintly, as if enjoying the freshness of the air. 'Alice took me around the village a couple of times when I was here before but I don't remember much. Do your parents live somewhere near here?'

'Frenchmen's Way. This turning we're coming up to.'

Neither of them said anything about the shared kiss in his parents' garden one night, a long time ago, as they passed the opening to Frenchmen's Way. Long Lane continued to bear right and slope upwards. Clancy strode out beside him. 'Are your parents going to mind me being with you to pick up the furniture? Or Lee? Perhaps, to follow the alliterative style of Awful Alice,' she went on ruminatively, 'they'll call me Crappy Clancy.'

'They won't be there,' he admitted frankly, at the same time wishing he hadn't told her about the Awful Alice thing. 'Dad's at work and Lee's taken Mum shopping before my great-aunt comes home. Aunt Norma lives in an annexe at De Silva House.'

'That's nice.' Clancy sounded genuinely touched at this sign of family love. 'Oh, look! Those flint cottages are so pretty.'

'That's Potato Hall Row,' he answered. 'Mine's the furthest one, the one with the workshop attached.'

She nodded absently. 'How have you and I emailed so regularly if there's no internet in the village?'

He was thrown by the sudden question and was sure, from the way she watched him out of the corner of her eye, that he was meant to be. 'I have satellite broadband.'

'Ah,' she said, raising her eyebrows. 'So the thing about *no* internet was fake news. How about no pub, no shop . . .?'

'There is no pub or shop,' he said defensively, though he wasn't sure whether she was teasing him or was actually annoyed. 'There are a few places in the village with satellite broadband, but you can't get it everywhere because of the conservation area, listed buildings, and even preservation orders on trees that block the signal.'

'Oh. I see the issue.' She frowned. 'As one of the owners of Roundhouse Row, couldn't you share your internet access with the caretaker?'

'I could,' he admitted. 'Evelyn wasn't keen on learning to do things online so it didn't come up. So many people ask to hook up with it that I suppose I've become wary of reaching my data limit before the end of the month. People are always asking to "just borrow" my connection. I change my password a lot.

'Here's the truck,' he added unnecessarily as he stopped beside the big silver pickup with *De Silva Landscaping* on the side. He beeped it open.

'But,' Clancy began again. She was interrupted by Genevieve suddenly rounding the side of his house, waving energetically, the breeze making her long blonde hair wave too. Nelson yanked at his lead so Aaron let him bound over to fling himself at her, not sure how he felt about Gen's unscheduled appearance. It was new and not particularly welcome for her to hang around him so much. Before she'd tried to solve her housing issue by moving their relationship up a level, she'd been a warm, fun, independent girlfriend who'd seemed as content as Aaron to include a relationship in her life but not make it the be-all and end-all.

'There you are!' Genevieve fussed Nelson but looked at Aaron as she spoke, as if she was talking to a little boy who'd wandered off. 'You're out early. I heard about your aunt and came to see if I could help.' Then she looked at Clancy with a half-smile of enquiry.

'The village grapevine hasn't taken long with the news about Aunt Norma's ankle,' he said drily. 'She'll be OK. This is Clancy Moss. She's going to move into the Roundhouse and take Evelyn's job.'

Genevieve's smile broadened. 'Oh, the Clancy who's Alice's cousin? Maybe we met when you were here for . . . anyway, welcome to Nelson's Bar. Are you moving from very far away?'

Clancy sent Aaron a glance, as if divining that Genevieve had been going to say *for Lee's wedding* and noting that she'd thought better of it. 'From London. We're just going to pick up the furniture from Aaron's parents' house.' Clancy smiled pleasantly and didn't remark on Genevieve knowing Alice. Everyone knew everyone in Nelson's Bar.

Genevieve immediately hurried to join them at the truck. 'I'll help you.' And before Aaron could react, she'd ushered Nelson into the back seat of the cab and taken her customary spot in the front.

'Thank you,' said Clancy politely, climbing into the back alongside the dog. Aaron suspected that Clancy took refuge in absolute courtesy when she didn't want people to read her too accurately.

He took the driver's seat and Genevieve twisted round as Aaron turned in the road, telling Clancy about her favourite subject: waking up one day to a substantial crack in her kitchen wall and discovering the ground was subsiding around the foundations of her cottage. 'There must have been water leaking underground for ages, the builder thinks.'

Reaching De Silva House in less than a minute, Aaron reversed up to the double doors in the storage area beneath Aunt Norma's flat, and they all climbed out of the truck.

Aaron turned to Clancy. 'You'll appreciate that Lee long ago disposed of his half of their furniture.' He hauled one of the doors open with a rumble and a creak to reveal a dim interior of sheets flung over large objects.

They began removing dust sheets – disturbing a lot of dust – and assessed what lay beneath. 'Two beds, a sofa and chairs, a couple of tables and a cabinet. Might as well take it all.' Aaron indicated a stack of boxes. 'These came from the Roundhouse too.' The boxes contained crockery and kitchen equipment, books and ornaments. Then came Alice's things. Clothes and shoes. Dusty make-up. An outdated laptop and a jumble of pens and paperwork.

Clancy stared at it all. 'I hadn't thought about what happened to Alice's things. I suppose I ought to take them rather than leave them to inconvenience your parents.'

Genevieve came to peer over her shoulder. 'Where is Alice these days, anyway? Can't you send them to her? We were quite friendly when she lived here but now I never hear from her at all.'

'I have an email address. I don't actually know where she is,' said Clancy absently, folding the flaps of the box closed again. 'She moves around a lot.'

Genevieve sounded fascinated. 'How mysterious she became! Did she really just sneak out while you were on the phone that day?'

'If you don't mind taking the boxes, that would be great,' Aaron interrupted. He was beginning to wish Genevieve hadn't tagged along on this expedition. He could do without the village rehashing 'poor Lee being jilted', especially now Lee was living locally again.

Clancy rose, dusting off the knees of her jeans. 'Let's get everything to the Roundhouse and then I can let you two get on with your Sunday.'

Genevieve smiled and patted Aaron's bum as she passed, as if to emphasise their closeness. 'I'll lay a couple of the dust sheets in the bed of the truck. If I know you it'll be filled with grass and soil.'

Aaron suppressed a snippy remark about the function of the truck being to transport lawn mowers and plants and merely said, 'Thanks.'

It didn't take them too long to load up and Genevieve chattered happily to Clancy as they drove down to the Roundhouse, and all through the process of unloading.

Conversely, Aaron found himself working in silent frustration, especially when Genevieve giggled madly at having to squeeze and wiggle the springy mattress through the door at the top of the second flight of stairs, Clancy apparently having chosen the loft as her bedroom.

At that point Clancy called a halt. 'Thank you both. I can manage from here. Would you like a cuppa before you head off?'

Genevieve blew her hair out of her face. 'Love one! And Nelson adores a saucer of coffee if there's enough going.' She'd obviously taken to Clancy and when she'd settled beside her on the sofa Genevieve returned to her preoccupation with her housing issues. 'Not being able to live in my place during the building works is going to be a nightmare. I've got a whopping excess of a thousand pounds to pay so I've nothing spare for rent.'

Clancy blew her coffee. 'Your insurance company wouldn't expect you to live under a hedge. They should meet a reasonable rent.'

Aaron paused. He didn't remember this point being aired before.

But Genevieve was quick with an answer. 'There's nowhere available to rent in the village, but the main thing is that I'll save loads on the utility bills if I can find someone to stay with, which will mean I can afford the thousand pounds.'

Aaron began drinking again. That was true. Genevieve didn't have a well-paid job and, accordingly, only modest savings.

But Clancy hadn't finished exploring the subject. 'That could work in your favour because if there's nowhere to rent in Nelson's Bar, they should let you move into the village B&B instead. A B&B rate being inclusive, the utilities won't come into it so you'll save just the same.' She glanced at Genevieve with a faint smile. 'I interned with an insurance giant when I was doing my MBA.'

'Oh,' said Genevieve, smile fading. 'I *suppose* I could see if the insurance company will wear it.' Cheeks suddenly rosy, she kept her gaze away from Aaron's.

'I don't think they have a choice, but I'm happy to talk to them for you if you encounter resistance. You've helped me today.' Clancy began to smile. But then she looked from Genevieve to Aaron and back and whatever she read in their body language caused doubt to flicker in her eyes.

Genevieve drained her coffee. 'Thank you. It seems my knotty problem isn't a knotty problem after all. I should have known to ask the insurance company about alternatives.'

Aaron rose, as awkward for Genevieve's obvious discomfort as it was possible to feel at the same time as being so relieved his whole spine flexed. He wanted to hug both women: Clancy in jubilation for resolving the Genevieve situation without apparently trying . . . but Genevieve in consolation because he felt guilty. It was really tough to disappoint someone you were fond of. But now she had no reason to pressure him he hoped Gen would return to her old independence and their relationship could revert to the easy-going thing it used to be.

He became aware of Gen's eyes on him, as if she were reading his mind, seeing and being hurt by his relief, so he hunted for a neutral subject. 'Clancy, are you starting work tomorrow? It might be a good idea for us to run through things in more detail.'

Clancy nodded. 'That would be great.'

They arranged a time for first thing tomorrow, Monday, then Aaron and Genevieve said their goodbyes, Nelson stretching and shaking in preparation for leaving.

Outside, the sky had become inky and big drops of rain had begun to spatter the dust of the lane as Aaron opened the passenger door of the truck. 'Gen, I'm giving Mum a ride to visit Aunt Norma. Fancy coming along?'

Genevieve was standing still, staring up Droody Road

towards the centre of the village. 'I think I'd better go home and examine my insurance policy,' she said, all signs of her earlier vivaciousness gone.

As he had so often lately, Aaron experienced an uneasy feeling of guilt, which prompted resentment that he felt it. 'Want me to ask Mum and Dad if you can store your furniture with them if Clancy's B&B idea works out?' He winced, conscious he'd called it Clancy's idea as if to distance himself from it.

She shook her head, still not looking at him and ignoring the rain pattering on the leaves of nearby trees. 'If the insurance will pay for the B&B then they'll pay for my furniture storage.'

'OK. Hop in. I'll give you a lift home. It's going to pour down.' He clicked his fingers to tell Nelson to jump in the back seat. Big, hairy dogs took a lot of drying.

Genevieve did look at him this time. 'It's only half a mile. I'll walk. Clancy's pretty, isn't she?'

He nodded, because he'd have been blind not to notice that. There was something in Genevieve's expression that he didn't particularly like. Jealousy? Suspicion? He was reasonably certain that he'd never told her about the episode in the darkness of his parents' garden but had she picked up some lingering vibe between him and Clancy?

She began to turn away, and suddenly he found himself commenting, probably more bluntly than he should, 'You don't seem very happy that Clancy might have solved your accommodation issue.' He hesitated, trying to find a way to put into non-contentious words something that had been bothering him. 'You've always loved your cottage so much. I know it will be a wrench to leave it, even temporarily.' *So why angle to move in with me and make it sound permanent?* was his subtext.

She sighed and answered. 'Yes. But I suppose the problem has made me face things I hadn't realised existed. It's ended up being more about my future than about four walls . . . hasn't it?' Then she began striding away from him, her hair flying, head up as if she were confronting something other than the rain on her face. She didn't offer him a kiss goodbye.

And Aaron didn't mind that she hadn't. He watched her go and knew they'd just acknowledged that the subsidence had been the cause of cracks in more than her cottage walls.

He drove to De Silva House, a solid, red-brick Victorian, the home still echoing in his imagination with childhood games shared with Lee in the tall rooms or the sprawling garden. Five granite steps swept up to the black front door, bay trees like sentries on either side, and each gracious bay window gleamed in the emerging sunshine. His father's car was absent but Lee's van was outside, indicating that Lee and their mum had returned from shopping.

Aaron found them in the kitchen. Four-year-old Daisy was helping put the shopping away by darting about to grab whatever caught her eye and getting under the feet of adults. It occurred to him that Daisy's existence was something he hadn't mentioned to Clancy. Probably just as well. She didn't need additional emotional pressure right now.

'Uncle Aaron!' Daisy bellowed when she saw him, smile wide and arms out in the certainty of a good welcome.

'Oof!' He caught her in mid-air and swung her up. 'Crazy Daisy!'

'I want to say hello to Nelson,' she said, trying to scramble down the instant she was up.

'Sure thing.' He set her carefully on her feet. 'In fact, I

think he wants you to take him in the garden and play tug o' war with his rope toy.'

'Yeah! I know where it is, don't I, Granny? It's in the utility room. C'mon, Nelson!' She flew towards the next room, Nelson cantering gamely after.

'Back garden only,' Lee called after them. He turned to Aaron. 'Want a beer?'

Aaron ignored his mother's slight eye-roll and accepted. Though he'd been much more relaxed and carefree when he was younger, Lee had become a solemn man who took single fatherhood seriously, pragmatic about living with his parents until his place in Northamptonshire was sold. A beer or two with Aaron might be the social highlight of his week, particularly as Yvonne would be busy with Aunt Norma and less available for babysitting.

'Thanks.' Aaron took the proffered beer along with a seat at the table. 'I've come to mention the new caretaker at Roundhouse Row. To everybody,' he added.

Yvonne, busy stacking tins of soup in a cupboard, glanced over her shoulder. 'I didn't think you'd advertised.'

'It became unnecessary.' His words seemed to ring in his own ears as he added, 'Clancy Moss has taken the position herself.'

Lee, who'd been making for another chair, halted.

Yvonne dropped a tin of soup with a clang. 'Why on earth do you want her to do it?' she demanded.

Aaron's eyes remained on Lee. 'I would have avoided it if I could.'

Although he'd paled, Lee remained composed. 'OK, thanks for telling me.' He looked at the bottle in his hand and then around the kitchen as if suddenly struggling to remember where he was or what he was doing. 'I'll just go and check Daisy's OK.'

When the back door had closed behind him, Yvonne rounded on Aaron, pink and damp-eyed. 'This won't be good for Lee. Can you stop her?'

Aaron sighed. 'No. She has as much say in it as I do.' He deliberated over how much to reveal. 'She's not here to make trouble, Mum. From what she told me, she's had a hard time of it and hasn't got many places to go. Lee seemed to take it OK. Let's not make a big deal out of it, in case he gets anxious.'

Yvonne gazed at him, eyes dark with worry. 'We certainly don't want that.'

Chapter Four

On Monday morning Clancy awoke in an unfamiliar bed in the only-slightly familiar room and the memory of why she was there crashed in on her.

Will.

Renée.

Will with Renée. The images of them together flashed before her eyes.

Stop it! she told herself sternly. She was in a *new* bed in her *new* room. She had a *new* life in a tiny jewel of a village high up above the sea. A wedge of sunlight sliced through the dormer window onto the floor, as if tempting her to get up and warm her feet on the wooden boards. Once that was accomplished, getting on with the day became easier.

First job when she got downstairs: sit down and write a shopping list.

Bedclothes
Towels
Curtains (downstairs and loft)

A rap at the front door made her drop her pen and jump up to answer, expecting it to be Aaron, though it was fifteen minutes earlier than they'd arranged. But when she threw the door open it was to find a woman standing there, her curls dancing in the breeze. 'Hello, Clancy. I thought it best if we cleared the air.'

Clancy stepped back, feeling her cheeks heating up. 'Oh! Mrs De Silva. Yvonne. Come in.' The De Silvas must truly still be harbouring ill-feeling towards Alice and her family if air-clearing had to be done.

Yvonne looked strained and pinched. She stepped inside, her gaze roaming around the big echoing space of the ground floor in which the few pieces of furniture now in Clancy's care were almost lost. She wasted no time getting down to business. 'Are you absolutely sure about living here?' Her hair was untidy. Not the tousled look her son carried off so well, but more the bedhead style of someone who hadn't been able to wait to come and air her concerns.

Clancy had been about to offer her a cup of tea, but Yvonne's words made her suspect it wasn't going to be a long visit. 'Nearly sure,' she answered, honestly.

'I see.' Yvonne gazed at Clancy, her dark eyes tired. 'I won't beat about the bush. I'm worried. When Alice left so cruelly Lee was so hurt . . . I was terrified at the way he crashed, emotionally. I thought he'd end up in either the psychiatric ward or the morgue. It destroys you to see your child that way and know someone else is responsible.'

'Of course,' Clancy said softly.

Yvonne sighed and seated herself at the kitchen table. 'Fergus says I have to remember you aren't Alice.' She ran a hand through her hair. 'But humans want someone to blame when things go wrong.'

Clancy tried to laugh, but, as much for Alice as herself,

it tried to turn into a sob in her throat. 'I'd heard villages were friendly places.'

Embarrassment crept across Yvonne's face. 'I'm sorry. You must think I'm a horror. But Lee . . . I thought he'd made such progress when he came back here to live a few months ago. Then Aaron told us about you turning up, and the look on Lee's face—' She had to stop to swallow.

Her own throat aching, Clancy nodded. She'd liked Yvonne before and understood she was only paying this visit because, in her eyes, one of her children was being threatened. For an instant she was tempted to cave in. Say, 'OK, I'll find somewhere else. I've certainly done it before. I could go out to Namibia where my parents are working on a new school. Or find out where Alice is and see if I can join her . . .'

But, then, into her mind flashed more of the memories she'd managed to shove away, earlier. That awful afternoon in the conference room. Asila, Monty, Tracey . . . and Will, looking absolutely wretched, as if, she remembered thinking, *she'd* been the one to cheat. Monty saying, 'I appreciate you didn't like the way we wanted to handle things but we were only thinking of IsVid.'

'But it's not fair to let people think it was *me*—!'

'It's not personal,' Monty had snapped. 'All our livelihoods are tied up in IsVid.'

But it had felt personal. Her friends . . . Asila, so petite that it always looked as if her glorious black hair would pull her over, eyes filled with tears. Jon 'Monty' Montagu regarding Clancy angrily through his glasses. Tracey, big, cushiony Tracey, troubled but resolute, though it had been in her arms Clancy had wept in pain and humiliation when Will's infidelity had come to light in such an excruciatingly public way.

44

Clancy remembered gasping as if plunged into ice water. She, the victim, was being sacrificed for the business.

She'd had little choice but to go – though not before she'd told them a couple of financial truths about what her leaving meant, ending coldly, 'You don't think I'm going to just *give* you my share of the business, do you? A fifth of everything you're guarding so blindly is mine.' That had taken them aback, especially Will, judging from his stark expression. She hadn't been able to withhold a parting shot. 'Next time you cheat on someone, Will, you need to think where it leaves everyone financially.' Then she'd stared Monty down. 'No pat answer for that one?' But she'd known lots of things were more important than money. *Lots.* She'd lost Will, her best friends and her work.

And she was not about to be the loser again.

'I can only tell you what I told Aaron,' she said to Yvonne, making her voice sympathetic. 'I need somewhere to be and something to do. I'm sorry Lee was hurt – and I know how he feels – but I didn't hurt him.' Clancy manufactured a smile. 'At least I'll be doing a great job for your other son's investment. I'm going to caretake the hell out of Roundhouse Row.'

Yvonne sighed, murmuring enigmatically, 'You strike me as that kind. Thank you for being frank, at least.' She rose, and so did Clancy – just as the door-knocker clattered again. Clancy opened up to reveal Aaron on the doorstep.

His brows clanged down when his gaze lit on Yvonne. 'Mum? I didn't expect to find you here.'

His mother lifted her chin. 'I wanted to speak to Clancy.'

'Really?' His eyes flicked Clancy's way and he said to her, 'Be with you in a minute.' He began to close the door with himself and his mother on the outside.

'Just come in when you're ready,' Clancy muttered, returning to the kitchen table and her list. She'd added gardening gloves by the time Aaron stepped indoors.

He was still frowning. 'I had no idea Mum planned to call on you. I hope she didn't—' he hesitated '—make you uncomfortable.'

She wrote down coffee pod machine and sat back. 'I hope we came to an understanding.'

'Right.' He looked as if he wasn't sure he wanted to know what that meant and took the chair beside hers. 'Shall we get straight down to business? You've read Evelyn's notes, you said?'

'And the information sheet she puts out for guests. I now know that the village was named to celebrate Nelson's victory at Waterloo, his being born just along the coast at Burnham Thorpe, this headland being a bar, or spit, of land.'

A smile tugged at the corner of his mouth. '"Nelson's Spit" wouldn't have sounded as picturesque, would it? There's also a story that he was conceived here, but how anybody thinks they know that I have no idea.' He glanced at his watch and moved the subject on to Clancy's duties and the joys of 'changeover days' when one set of guests would leave by 10 a.m. and the next move in after 3 p.m.

After they'd discussed Evelyn's notes, Aaron sat back. 'You've met Dilys, I hear. Shall we see whether Ernie's in? He's feeling left out.' He hesitated. 'I ought to warn you that he's becoming rather . . . blunt.'

'Thanks for the heads up.' Clancy followed Aaron out of the front door to the next-door-but-one house and between clipped hedges to the front door. When he rang the bell it was answered by a rather fierce-looking man with sticking-up grey hair and a pendulous bottom lip.

'I'm Ernie Romain,' he said, sticking out a hand to shake Clancy's. 'You're our new Evelyn.'

'Clancy Moss,' she said. 'I'm doing the job Evelyn used to do, yes.' Then, thinking that she ought to demonstrate her willingness to be approached, added, 'Just let me know if you have any issues with the cottage.'

'Come in,' he said, as if she hadn't spoken. He turned on his heel and disappeared into the house.

Aaron sighed but when Clancy stepped through the green front door into a tiny hall with stripy wallpaper, he followed. In the kitchen they found Ernie, who obviously had an impressive turn of speed despite his age, already switching on a kettle, an open jar of Maxwell House standing beside three mugs. The kitchen was the same size and shape as Dilys's but clean and bare.

'Only a quick one for me.' Aaron took a seat at the table. 'I'm supposed to be terracing a garden in Titchwell.'

'She's better-looking than Evelyn,' Ernie answered, evidently in a different conversation in his head.

Clancy caught an apologetic glance from Aaron and found herself grinning. 'Have you lived here long, Ernie?' she asked, in an effort to turn to safer topics before he enlarged on his opinion of hers or Evelyn's looks.

The kettle boiled and Ernie poured the water into the mugs, stirring vigorously. 'Since I lost my wife. Soon be ten years she's been gone and still a pain in the arse.' He stuck a sugar jar and a carton of milk on the table too.

Clancy might have been thrown by this if Dilys hadn't already explained their novel living arrangements.

'She said you're Alice's cousin,' he added suddenly, peering at Clancy. 'Where's Alice got to? She was a gal,

47

she was.' Ernie snorted a laugh. 'Always up to something. Always got some plan afoot. Pretty little dot. She and me got on like a house on fire.'

'Good! I've always got on with her, too.' Clancy was glad someone had something positive to say about Alice.

'You look a bit like her. But she was a cow, pissing off like that,' Ernie added, his fond tone belying the caustic nature of his words. He fell to drinking his coffee meditatively.

Oh dear, the positivity hadn't lasted long. 'Er, well, I'm looking forward to exploring the village soon. For one reason or another I've been stuck in the Roundhouse pretty much since I got here. Evelyn left maps she gave the guests—'

'Maps?' Ernie bellowed a laugh, his eyebrows beetling incredulously. 'If you need a map to find your way round Nelson's Bar you must be brainless.'

Aaron cleared his throat and, finding the elderly man's bluntness uncomfortable judging by his pained expression, managed to keep him talking about Roundhouse Row until they'd finished their coffee and could leave.

'Sorry about Ernie,' Aaron apologised as soon as they were out of earshot in the lane. 'He just turns his thoughts to words, no matter how inappropriate or blunt.'

Clancy shrugged. 'I'm sure we'll get used to each other.' Then, as Aaron took out the keys to his truck, she recalled something that had bothered her last night. 'By the way, I'm sorry if I somehow said the wrong thing to you and Genevieve yesterday. The atmosphere got a bit . . .' She let the sentence tail away rather than say 'weird'.

He scuffed a booted toe in the dust of the lane. 'It was kind of you to share your knowledge. Gen's been knocked off balance by what's happening to her home.'

When he said no more, Clancy ventured, 'She seems nice.'

'She is,' he acknowledged, but he sounded rueful. His brown eyes looked very dark in the sunshine; almost black.

Clancy backed away a step. 'OK. Good. Well, thanks for clueing me in about my new job.'

He took a couple of steps in the other direction, towards his truck. 'If you have any questions, just call me on my landline or mobile – I can normally get a signal if I'm out of the village. Or you can leave a message.'

'Sure.' With a final smile goodbye, Clancy slipped indoors through the porch, wondering whether she was just being ultra-sensitive . . . or whether she'd read something in Aaron's awkward manner that did not bode well for Genevieve.

Chapter Five

Despite Ernie's guffaws, Clancy did pick up a map of Nelson's Bar out of the folder Evelyn had left. She would have liked Evelyn, she was sure, judging by the neat way she'd left everything.

The hand-drawn map showed that most of the village nestled between Long Lane and Marshview Road, curling together as they neared the tip of the headland and met Droody Road running through the middle. The shape they made looked a little like a heart with an arrow through it, she thought fancifully. Where the three roads met a building was marked 'The Duke of Bronte B&B' after which Evelyn had written, '(The Duke of Bronte being Lord Nelson's secondary title)'. Side roads such as Frenchmen's Way, Trader's Place and The Green led off the main thoroughfares, and the hill leading to the village was prosaically named Long Climb.

As she'd already walked up Long Lane as far as Aaron's place, Clancy decided to begin with Marshview Road, as it would lead her towards what was marked on the map as Zig-zag Path leading to Zig-zag Beach, which she remembered as the short stretch of sand where Alice had once taken her.

She stepped outside, the map tucked in her pocket. Once she'd left the shelter of the lane the wind pounced on her, whipping her hair about and making her zip up her fleece. Many of the cottages, sunbathing behind hedges as she passed along Marshview Road, were built of the red and white chalk she was fast getting used to. Between them she was able to catch glimpses of the sea, blue and enticing, each wave sporting a jaunty white frill.

After a few minutes, she reached a small but well-worn footpath to the right, between a hedge and a fence, with a sign saying *To Zig-zag Path*. Following it, Clancy soon arrived on the scrubby, undulating grassland of the clifftop. The footpath became a vague line where the soil showed through the grass, leading to where a white handrail was poised at the cliff edge and gulls wheeled and called mournfully above.

Exhilarated, hair thrashing more wildly than ever, Clancy strode to the handrail that marked the beginning of Zig-zag Path, pausing to drink in the full glory of the view. Sea, sea, sea, right to the curved horizon. Catching the sun's rays and tossing them into a million dancing lights, the waves ran constantly, restlessly inshore. To catch sight of the swaying reed beds and winding creeks of the salt marsh between Nelson's Bar and Brancaster she had to swivel to her right and look almost behind her. The Nelson's Bar headland seemed to have erupted through the gentle, flat scenery all around it, right out into the sea.

At Clancy's feet the handrail zigged and zagged steeply down, out of sight after the first few sharp bends. She gave in to its lure, her feet slapping the ground as she followed it down, the sea closer with every step, the hiss and crash of the waves louder.

At last she reached Zig-zag Beach, a triangle of pale sand gritty with countless broken seashells. For several minutes she watched as the waves chased each other up the beach almost to the high tide mark of tossed seaweed, then fell back with a disappointed *tshhhhhh* into the giant blue and white canvas of the sea. The gulls called to her like lost souls, riding the wind on their perfect wings, then they moved off as if realising she had no food to share.

It didn't take her long to explore the beach, turning pungent heaps of kelp with her toe, shells crunching beneath the soles of her trainers, but as she breathed in the briny air she was filled with a oneness with the place, almost a feeling of belonging. Or just longing?

Finally, she began back up the path.

She'd toiled to the halfway point, the muscles of her calves pulling, when she was surprised by sounds from behind her and two panting teenaged lads in dripping board shorts jogged up to overtake her.

'Hello. 'Scuse,' said the lead boy, sprinkling chilly seawater as he passed. His dark curls were a bit like Aaron's. The second boy's hair was slicked back against his head. He grinned, and puffed past her too.

'Hello,' she said to their departing backs. Where the hell had they appeared from? Intrigued, she followed as their bare feet picked a way through grit and stones until, at the top of the path, they swung right. Clancy was just able to keep them in sight as they ran a hundred yards to where there was a dip in the clifftop, pausing to confer as they backed away from the edge.

Then, with Tarzan yells, they sprinted right off the top

of the cliff, arms windmilling for balance as they plummeted from view.

Shocked into action, Clancy broke into a run, hardly feeling her feet touch ground until she reached the spot where the boys had vanished. Cautiously, she peered over the cliff edge, almost dizzy with relief – or at the way the sea swirled below – to see two heads bobbing in the waves.

'Are you OK?' she yelled, only half-believing anyone could jump that far and not be crippled by the force of hitting the water. Faces turned up towards her and an arm waved. Reassured that they'd survived their mad leap, she waved back as they turned to swim through the frothing sea and out of sight around a fold in the cliff.

She hovered restlessly, assuming they'd be swimming to Zig-zag Beach but, unable to be certain, poised to get help if they never appeared.

It must have been a good ten minutes before she could smile and relax as they puffed into sight, doing their tiptoe jog over the inhospitable ground. 'You scared the life out of me,' she called, pulling what she hoped was a comical face. They were about eighteen, she judged, old enough to resent reproof.

The dark, curly-haired one wore a big grin. 'We're all right. We're cliff jumping.'

Clancy glanced at their launching point. 'Isn't it dangerous?'

'We're all right,' he repeated. 'This is The Leap. The tide doesn't go out far enough here to be a problem. Wanna try it?' His grin widened.

'Erm, I didn't bring my swim things.' Clancy pulled a petrified face, making both lads laugh. 'I'm Clancy, by the way. I've moved into the Roundhouse.'

'Oh, yeah? I'm Harry,' said the dark one.

'Rory,' added the other, speaking for the first time.

Harry beckoned Clancy closer to the cliff edge. 'The Leap's quite easy. You need to avoid those rocks there. That's why we take a run at it, so we jump over them.'

She stared at the sea breaking over the dark jagged rocks then sucking restlessly away. It seemed a long way down. 'Doesn't it hurt?'

Rory was beginning to shiver. 'Depends. You don't want to belly-flop.'

'No, I don't,' Clancy admitted frankly. Then she stood back to spectate while they retreated twenty or thirty yards from the cliff edge before beginning a new charge to the accompaniment of blood-curdling yells. They hurtled confidently into thin air, their trajectory arcing well out past the rocks. They hit the water in explosions of spray, bobbing back to the surface a few seconds later. Then they struck out towards the fold in the cliffs, once again vanishing from view.

This time, Clancy whiled away their absence by studying her surroundings. She was at the furthest point of the headland now so the sea surrounded her on three sides and the salt marshes were out of view. Out to sea, a couple of white-sailed yachts leaned over in the wind and she watched them skipping atop the waves. Inland, the edge of the village was only a hundred yards away. A few tables stood outside a comparatively large building of brown stone, though the parasols stuck through the tables were furled against the wind. The B&B, she realised. It must have a fantastic sea view. She glanced back to check the progress of the two white yachts. It was a shame the Roundhouse was on the landward side of the village. She could look at a view like this all day.

Then some kind of inner alarm went off and she swung

around sharply, her gaze flying to the top of Zig-zag Path. Where were Harry and Rory? They'd had more than enough time to climb back up. She cast around for any sign of them. What she presumed were their clothes were heaped beneath a nearby tree so they hadn't got past her while she'd been daydreaming.

She hurried to the cliff edge. Nothing. Almost running now, she went back as far as Zig-zag Path and craned over the handrail, hoping to catch a glimpse of wet teenagers jogging back up.

Nothing.

Breath heaving in her chest, she ran back to The Leap, harbouring dubious thoughts about jumping in after them. She was a strong swimmer but throwing herself fully clothed into an unknown sea in the hope of rescuing two lads bigger than she was seemed foolhardy. Panic bubbled in her chest. Should she ring the coastguard? Instinct made her pat her pockets before she remembered abandoning her phone at home as it was so useless in the village. She could sprint to the B&B. They'd have a landline and it must be staffed by locals, people who'd know what to do.

Then, finally, faintly, she heard youthful laughter and turned to see them running up the clifftop towards her, grinning and nudging one another in, she imagined, glee. Relief coursed through her. The little ratbags had been trying to wind her up, probably hanging on to a rock somewhere, hoping she'd still be waiting around for their reappearance and laughing up their sleeves – if they'd been wearing any.

She determined not to give them the pleasure of detecting her erstwhile panic. They were teenagers. Winding up adults was what they did. So, 'Going in again?' was all she said, gaining a little satisfaction at their evident disappointment that she wasn't going to shout at them.

They looked at each other and shrugged and nodded. They ran at the clifftop again, Clancy taking up her vantage point to watch their screaming, euphoric flight down to the dancing waves so far below. Once she'd seen them safely bob to the surface she waved goodbye and made her way across the scrubby grass towards the Duke of Bronte B&B. Evelyn's notes had said the B&B and Roundhouse Row occasionally sent each other business.

As she approached the lawn in front of the building someone came out and sat down at one of the two tables, a hot drink in one hand and a plate in the other. Clancy paused as she recognised Genevieve's flowing blonde hair.

A middle-aged woman followed, depositing condiments on the table then pausing to chat as Clancy started forward again. Both women looked up at her approach and she found herself slipping into her business persona, giving Genevieve a warm hello and then extending her hand to the other woman. 'Hi, I'm Clancy. I've moved into the Roundhouse and I'll be looking after the cottages.'

The woman beamed. She had a round face with a chin to spare and her small dark eyes almost disappeared when she smiled. 'I'm Kaz. Me and my husband Oli run the B&B. Welcome to Nelson's Bar.' Her smile broadened. 'We have a tiny bar indoors and that's called Nelson's Bar too. An old girlfriend of Horatio Nelson lived here, legend has it.'

It seemed there was no end to Nelson's connections with the village. They chatted for several minutes and then Clancy became conscious of a rumbling tummy and indicated the salad before Genevieve. 'That looks good. I didn't realise you did lunches.'

Kaz beamed anew. 'We do whatever people want if it means business for us. Gen's got a ham salad there but I can also offer you cheese or tuna, or any of those things in a sandwich. If people give me a bit of notice I can usually offer jacket potatoes or omelettes too.'

After ordering a ham salad and a cup of tea, which sent Kaz bustling indoors, Clancy hovered beside Genevieve. 'May I join you?'

Immediately, Genevieve nodded. 'Sit down. It'll be nice to chat.'

Relieved, Clancy took the seat opposite. 'Sorry if I was a know-all about your insurance situation. I'm one of those annoying people who see a puzzle and try and solve it.'

Genevieve shrugged, pulling her hair back into a pony-tail as she prepared to eat. Her blondeness looked natural, fitting well with her milky skin and blue eyes. 'I rang the insurance company and you were exactly right. I was just making arrangements with Kaz to move in here for a couple of months. You've provided her with a guaranteed guest, which is good for business, and me with a summer of being looked after.'

Clancy didn't think she sounded super-thrilled, but smiled and began a polite getting-to-know-you conversation. Genevieve, she discovered, was a nursery nurse in a kids' club in Hunstanton where holidaymakers could leave children for a couple of hours' play. 'Monday and Tuesday are my days off this week so I'm using them to get organised for the builders to move into my poor little cottage.' Tears shone in her eyes for a moment. Then, as Kaz appeared with Clancy's lunch, 'In fact, I think I deserve a glass of wine. Fancy joining me?'

As Kaz had paused hopefully Clancy immediately fell

in with the suggestion. 'Wonderful idea.' They ordered large glasses, red for Clancy and rosé for Genevieve.

The salad proved to be a rainbow confection of leaves, tomatoes and peppers with cheese and thick-cut ham.

'So, what's brought you to Nelson's Bar?' Genevieve asked, as Clancy began her meal. 'Did you decide you needed to be more on the spot to look after your cousin's interests when Evelyn left?'

'Not at all,' said Clancy hastily, not wanting that version of events to get back to Aaron. 'I really, really needed a change. In fact,' she added honestly, 'I needed somewhere to live and a job.'

Kaz popped out with two glasses of wine, both glowing with colour in the afternoon sun. Clancy gave her time to bustle off before she carried on. 'Up until about ten weeks ago I thought I was getting married. To Will. He's the sort of man everyone describes as "lovely" so it was a big shock when I found out that he'd met someone else. We worked together too.'

Genevieve paused, her wine poised just short of her lips. 'Was working together still tenable? After?'

Clancy sighed. 'We tried. Will managed OK, but I . . . didn't. It became obvious one of us had to leave and it seemed as if everyone wanted it to be me.'

'But that's not fair!' Genevieve exclaimed.

The warmth of sisterly solidarity stole over Clancy. 'Agreed. And I could question the legality, if I wanted to.' It had crossed her mind often, sitting alone in the Roundhouse and feeling betrayed. 'But, anyway. Roundhouse Row needed a new caretaker, and filling the position got me out of two unpleasant situations in one go. Now I'm in Nelson's Bar, while Will moves his new girlfriend into our apartment.' She chose not to admit that

58

Will was mainly moving Renée in because of the financial knot Clancy had tied him up in, which had pretty much bound him to the apartment, at least for now.

Genevieve's eyes had been getting bigger and bigger. 'I can see you're Alice's cousin.'

'Really?' Clancy turned to look at the other woman. 'So you knew her well?'

'We were friendly enough to go out for a drink together, until she . . . Well, neither of you are frightened of making big changes to your lives, are you? Your relationship ends and you just move on.'

Clancy polished off a couple of gulps of wine thinking there had been no 'just' about her moving on. 'A woman doesn't have to be defined by the love of a man, or the loss of a man. I do regret that I closed my eyes to warning signs, never challenged Will on why he was spending so much time elsewhere. I was complacent, which put my fate in his hands and set me up for a nasty fall. But I deserve better and I'm getting used to being single.' She held aloft her wine to invite Genevieve to clink glasses.

Genevieve obliged. 'Until you meet someone new?' she queried with a grin.

Clancy batted the idea away. 'I'm in no hurry for that, believe me.'

Chapter Six

It had been good to get a full day's work in, Aaron thought, as he drove into the village late on Tuesday afternoon. He'd just about finished planting out the terraces in Titchwell. A heatwave was predicted and he was already anticipating customers not watering their gardens and then blaming him for dead plants and lawns with gaping cracks.

He was due to pick his mum up to collect Aunt Norma from King's Lynn hospital and wanted to be at the ward at seven when it opened. Then he was meeting Genevieve later.

A quick stop at home to shower and grab a sandwich, then he set out again for De Silva House. Yvonne was uncharacteristically quiet when she climbed into his truck.

On the journey, through Hunstanton and on to King's Lynn, Aaron tried to get the conversation going but his mother replied only absently, even to his enquiries about Daisy. He settled for concentrating on the traffic and listening to Capital FM.

Aunt Norma was ready when they arrived, a plaster cast on her ankle and a livid bruise on her temple. The nurse who organised her discharge said she was being sent home with a walking frame. 'Bloody thing,' Aunt Norma called it. Aaron brought the truck up close and settled her into the front seat and she wasn't much more talkative than Yvonne while Aaron negotiated the overcrowded traffic system out of King's Lynn.

It was only as they were on the more open road that she shifted her plastered foot irritably and demanded, 'Aaron, what are you doing allowing Awful Alice's cousin to park herself in the village?'

Aaron glanced across at her. 'Clancy? I couldn't do much to stop it. She acts for Alice. And I don't suppose she even gets paid for that,' he added, realising he'd never before thought of it. He received an income stream from the rental but all Clancy saw was the profits vanish, half in his direction and half in her cousin's. 'I told her about Evelyn leaving and suddenly she was moving in.'

Aunt Norma sniffed. 'But what about Lee? How does he feel?'

His great-aunt was old and just out of hospital so Aaron kept his own tone level. 'You'll have to ask Lee. I hope that now he's moved on with his life he'll be OK with Clancy. She didn't ask Alice to—'

'You seem to be on her side,' Aunt Norma commented sadly. She was known for being pretty forthright in her views.

He glanced at the old lady again as he continued to trail the car in front, wishing the traffic would speed up. 'I'm not taking sides,' he said quietly. 'Alice treated Lee shamefully and I was as worried about him as anyone. I tried to persuade Clancy the job wasn't for her but I failed.' Then, when neither his mother nor aunt replied, he added, 'If Lee has an issue with the way I've handled things then he's welcome to raise the subject but I'm not going on a witch hunt. Life's been pretty crap to Clancy, from what she's told me.'

Aunt Norma sniffed again. 'There's no need to say crap.'

Aaron swallowed his laughter. Was he thirty-six or thirteen?

It was turned nine when he'd eventually helped Aunt Norma into her annexe at his parents' place, driving up the slope, walking beside her as she puffed her way up the ramp that delivered her to the first floor. 'Thank you, Aaron,' she said stiffly. 'You get off now.'

Aaron kissed her soft cheek and said she could call him if she needed anything. His mother gave him a hug, then Aaron took Aunt Norma at her word and left.

Once home, he released Nelson from the confines of the kitchen, rubbing the hairy head as Nelson reared up on his hind legs and pawed the air with whimpers of joy. 'Come on, you silly hound. Let's give you a run.' He walked a circuit of the clifftop, watching the scrubby trees waving, throwing the ball so Nelson covered plenty of ground, then whistled him so they could turn off to Genevieve's home in Trader's Place.

When he arrived at The Mimosas, a pretty name that seemed to him to be trying to compensate for the less-than-pretty brick-built cottage, it was to find Genevieve three-quarters of the way down a bottle of wine, sitting out in her garden in the twilight looking balefully at the corner of her home, propped up for safety until the builders began the necessary dismantling, underpinning and rebuilding.

'Hey,' he said, pulling up a mismatched garden chair to join her, leaning down to brush her lips with his. 'Feeling down in the dumps about the cottage?'

'Yup,' she answered flatly, putting down her wine glass to accept Nelson's panting, pawing expressions of adoration. 'Amongst other things. Like, whether we've got a future.'

Aaron had been about to go and get himself a wine glass but instead he dropped into the chair in surprise at this opening gambit. 'Where did that come from?'

She sighed, still tousling Nelson's grey hairy ears. He'd taken up station with his head on her lap and looked well happy with the situation. 'I've been thinking about it ever since Clancy came up with the idea of me moving into the B&B. You were so relieved! You obviously don't want me to move in with you.' Her eyes glittered in the fading light.

He put his hand over hers, feeling bad that she'd read him so accurately and it had hurt her. 'But you love your cottage.'

She shrugged. 'Does that mean I'm forced to live alone in it for the rest of my life?'

'Well, no,' he acknowledged. 'But we'd never talked about living together and suddenly you were hinting that we should, and as if it would become a permanent thing. Taking such a major step out of expediency, because your cottage needs work—'

'—is *not* happening,' she finished for him, her voice tight with tears, forehead furrowing with misery. She gulped a mouthful of wine.

'I didn't put it like that—'

But she wasn't listening to him, just gazing at the sagging corner of her house as if it held all the answers. 'We've been together a year. To be absolutely clear – do you ever foresee us taking our relationship to the next level?'

'Hey,' he said gently, patting the hand that lay unresponsive under his. 'What's going on? I feel as if I've missed half a conversation.'

'Do you ever foresee us making our relationship more committed?' she insisted.

'I don't discount it,' he answered carefully, as she was clearly intent on making him lay all his cards on the table. 'We've had a great relationship and, if you're asking me to be honest, then I'm happy as we are.'

She turned to face him. 'Clancy says women shouldn't be defined by the love of a man, but I'm going to ask you. Do you love me? And *yes* or *no* are the only acceptable answers.'

Aaron tried to get a grip on the conversation, which felt as out of control as a kite in a hurricane. He hated upsetting Gen but that familiar prickle of resentment at being made to feel the bad guy was there too. He made his voice gentle. 'Backing me into a corner isn't going to help this situation.'

Slowly, her blonde hair lifting on the evening breeze, Genevieve upended the wine bottle over her glass, watching it fill almost to the brim. 'So that's a *no* then.'

'I didn't say that!' He'd never asked himself whether he loved Genevieve, or any past girlfriends. He'd never wanted to settle down before he was thirty and then, when he was exactly that age, what happened to Lee had made him wary. Lee had given his whole heart to Alice and she'd ripped it up and tossed it over her shoulder as she shook the dust of Nelson's Bar from her feet.

Genevieve went on as if he hadn't spoken. 'I feel as if you've been playing me along.'

Once more, he was taken aback. 'I didn't realise we had different expectations, that's all.'

'I'm thirty-four. It didn't occur to you that I'd want children?' Her eyes were huge with unshed tears.

He decided there was no right answer to that because

it had, in fact, been in the back of his mind, but not in a positive way. 'I'm sorry you're upset,' he said.

'So am I,' she responded slowly. 'I deserve more than a man who neither loves me nor sees a future with me.' Tears began to leak from the corners of her eyes. 'I obviously feel more than you and I don't want to spoil the memories of what we've had for the last year. Let's not bicker or blame. Let's part as friends, both of us free of unrealistic expectations.' Then, as Aaron sat, stunned into silence, she gave a half-laugh, half-sob. 'I think you should go now, before I make a bigger idiot of myself than I already have.'

'Are you sure this is what you want?' he asked, rising uncertainly to his feet. Genevieve just looked away and shooed him with a wave of her hand. Aaron had little choice but to click his fingers to Nelson and leave for home, his thoughts circling madly.

How had he just gone from being cautious about his relationship moving too fast to it exploding in his face?

And . . . how much did he mind?

Chapter Seven

To: Clancy Moss
From: William Martin
21 May

Dear Clancy,
Just writing to confirm that the company will
continue paying you dividends – in the short term –
and I've today paid what we agreed as rent for your
half of the apartment. I'd like to think these financial
arrangements are interim. When the dust's settled
we'll be able to put lasting proposals to you. You'll
probably know more about what you want the future
to look like by then too.

Is it possible for you to tell one of us you're OK?
If you feel the need for a complete communication
break then we'll try to understand but we're
concerned. I hope you can take that in the spirit
it's meant.

Will hadn't signed the email. Clancy supposed he hadn't known how. Kisses were no longer appropriate and *Kind regards* plain odd when a few short months ago they'd been deciding the menu for their wedding breakfast. In those days, the apartment had been the settled home she'd waited all her life for. Will was her forever man.

She sat back and sighed, the noise and bustle of a busy Hunstanton café surrounding her. Dilys and Ernie, who'd leapt at the opportunity of grabbing a lift into 'Hunny', were running errands while Clancy emailed her parents to update them on the past weeks, though the remote village in Namibia where Brenda and Gerry Moss were working was almost as technology-deprived as Nelson's Bar. There, all communications were via satellite and easily affected by weather.

Luckily, Clancy's superpower had always been not needing parental support.

As she'd tried to make good her intention to throw herself into her new life, the week had sped by without her moving out of the village and into a signal or Wi-Fi area. She hadn't liked to press Aaron about using his satellite broadband, especially when it wasn't for Roundhouse Row matters. Instead, she'd readied the rentals for occupation, including mowing lawns and tidying borders, and found her feet with the paperwork side of her caretaking duties. She'd also cooked more than she'd had time for in London, and a couple of times invited Dilys and Ernie to share the results.

But now she felt guilty, especially when she thought of those texts from Asila and Tracey, which she'd ignored. She replied to Will quickly, noting his comments on financial arrangements. Then she began another message.

To: Asila Memon, Jon Montagu, Tracey Murland,
William Martin
From: Clancy Moss
25 May

Just to let you know I'm OK. I didn't deliberately
blank your texts/emails but I'm staying somewhere
that doesn't have mobile signal or broadband.

She thought of the years they'd worked together from
the first idea, which had been Monty's, making enthusiastic
plans over takeaways at kitchen tables, beginning with
rented equipment in a tiny enterprise zone, building their
client list and their reputation and eventually moving to
the offices in Islington. Until Will got caught with his pants
down she'd considered it her life. After reflecting on their
years as friends as well as colleagues she added, *Hope*
you're all OK.

Then she began a new email.

To: Alice Nettles
From: Clancy Moss
25 May
Subject: Nelson's Bar

Alice, just to update you:

Clancy spent twenty minutes explaining how she'd come
to move into the Roundhouse.

Then she rounded off:

As I've been looking after things for you I didn't
think you'd object, but I thought I'd tell you I'm here.

68

*Are you still in the US? Are you having fun? Send
me a lovely long catch-up. I haven't even seen you
on Insta lately.*

*It's funny being in Nelson's Bar without you, living
in the Roundhouse where you used to live with Lee,
but it's a sweet village.*

After adding love and kisses, she shut down and went
off to stow her laptop in the car and shop for readymade
curtains, thinking of Alice and wondering if her travelling
days would ever end. Funny how they'd become the
antithesis of each other. Alice had spent her early years
in England but had developed itchy feet. Clancy, with
travel-bug parents, had been relieved to come to the UK
and put down roots, roots that had eventually come to
mean Will and IsVid. She wondered what she'd find to
replace them.

It was late afternoon by the time she drove Dilys and
Ernie back to Nelson's Bar, thinking how odd it was
they lived apart when they seemed to get on. Then Ernie
told Dilys she was very wrinkly and she snapped at him
to shut up, and she thought maybe they knew what they
were doing after all. As they came into the village, they
passed a tall figure walking a big dog and Ernie and
Dilys broke off their argument to exclaim, 'There's
Aaron!'

Clancy drove carefully around the pair while Ernie and
Dilys waved out of the car windows.

As she parked outside the Roundhouse, Dilys said, 'It's
the village meeting at De Silva House later. Are you coming,
Clancy?'

Clancy pressed the button that opened the boot so they
could access their shopping. 'I don't think so.' She didn't

know anything about the meeting but it didn't sound appealing.

Dilys pulled herself out of the car. 'Official village matters are dealt with by the Village Committee through Parish Meetings, but this is a village meeting, which is sort of unofficial.'

Clancy shook her head as she opened her door and hopped out with more agility than Dilys. She'd done pro bono work with a rural charity and had heard enough about the intricacies of Parish Councils, Village Councils and Parish Meetings to feel them best avoided – and that was without considering her prospective welcome at De Silva House. 'I don't think I'd have anything to contribute.'

'You would!' Dilys cried, sounding disappointed. 'It's about improving the village. I want to get internet and you know about it.'

'No more than many people who've used the internet on a regular basis,' Clancy replied firmly. 'We'd better get our shopping in. Come for coffee tomorrow and you can tell me about the meeting then.'

'What good's that?' Dilys, instead of taking her bags from Clancy, planted her fists on her hips. Then her face brightened as she looked over Clancy's shoulder. 'Aaron! Come and tell Clancy about the village meeting.'

Clancy turned to see Aaron bearing down on them, Nelson with his ears back and tail wagging. Aaron glanced at Clancy.

'Do you want to come to the meeting?' he asked in much the way he might have said: 'Do you *want* to eat worms?' Stubble darkened his jaw as if he hadn't shaved for a couple of days.

'No,' answered Clancy obligingly, though nettled at his

70

tone, which she assumed sprang from the fact that the meeting would take place in his parents' home. It was as if someone had arranged for her to be permanently in the wrong. Will began an affair with Renée; Clancy was asked to leave IsVid. Alice did a runner on her wedding day? Clancy should be kept at arm's length.

Dilys seemed unaware of the undercurrents. 'We need the internet. We need to be able to order groceries to come to our houses, and do our banking without having to go into Hunny.' She clapped Clancy on the shoulder. 'This girl, she knows all about it. She should tell everyone.'

Aaron looked anywhere but at Clancy. 'Um . . . you could always give the information to me to be shared with the meeting.'

It was so obvious he hoped Clancy would go for that option that she nodded. 'OK. As it happens, I have a little understanding of the problem of connectivity in rural areas because I once worked with a rural charity client.' She drew a breath and delivered a rapid stream of facts about the need for affordable, fast broadband for working from home, networking, advertising, education and socialising. 'Unfortunately, the commercial reality is that big providers are not necessarily interested in small communities,' she ended. 'Good luck.'

Then she deposited Dilys and Ernie's shopping on their respective doorsteps; returned for her own bags, offered the three still standing in the lane a goodbye smile and sailed indoors.

It was after a couple of hours of hanging curtains that Clancy realised she was short of curtain hooks. Knowing she'd bought plenty, she trotted out to check her car boot. Sure enough, two packs had found their way into a corner and she had to move to the offside of the vehicle and stretch in to reclaim them.

She'd just straightened up when a white van rounded the bend and came flying up the lane, forcing her to leap out of its way. She dropped the packs in the dust in her fright. As she retrieved them, muttering under her breath, she heard the sound of the van halting and a door opening and closing.

'Sorry,' came a male voice. 'I took the bend too quickly.'

Clancy met the man's awkward gaze with a sense of shock.

'Clancy,' he murmured, when she remained speechless, 'I thought it was you.'

His hair was lighter and straighter than Aaron's and his face less animated but Clancy knew him too. She looked into his eyes – also lighter than Aaron's – and was shocked. He looked so weary, and more like five years older than his brother than two years younger. 'Hello, Lee. I'm glad to see you.' She would have been gladder to see him with the boyish grin he used to wear.

His smile looked to be an effort. 'But perhaps not at such speed? I'm late for a thing at my parents' house but I didn't mean to mow you down.'

'Don't worry, you missed.'

An awkward pause, Clancy absorbing the fact that she'd said she was glad to see Lee but he hadn't returned the compliment. In fact, he was regarding her in the way a child might regard a spoonful of medicine – unpleasant but unavoidable.

She decided to try a gentle tackle on the elephant in the lane. 'I hope me being around doesn't bring back bad memories. I just . . . needed somewhere to go.'

He looked struck as he digested this. 'I suppose I did

72

the same.' Then he patted her shoulder awkwardly, returned to his vehicle and drove away.

She returned to the Roundhouse thinking sombrely that life just beat some people up. She'd continue to fight against becoming one of them.

The summer sky had taken on a navy blue hue between box hedges and chalk cottages when Aaron arrived, unannounced, at Clancy's door, Nelson sporting a doggy grin, at his side.

'Got a minute to chat?' Aaron asked, by way of greeting.

Conscious that he owned half the building she was living in and so, presumably, didn't really need to ask, she decided to be civilised and invite him in for coffee. 'Good meeting?' she asked politely, as she took down mugs. They'd been Alice's and were plain white with Royal Doulton on the bottom. Alice was nothing if not aspirational.

Aaron had helped himself to a seat at the kitchen table, dark eyes on her as she tried to remember how to work her new coffee machine. 'I suppose so,' he answered. 'The usual stuff: the school in Thornham closed in the eighties – that always gets an airing – so we need young couples to stay in the village and increase the population. We should have a village hall but no one knows how to come up with the money. Kaz at the B&B wants more tourism and is worried about the future of the business. Obviously, wanting Roundhouse Row to be as full as possible, I agreed with her, not least because the B&B is in our literature as somewhere our guests might get a meal, but some villagers huffed and puffed about not wanting Nelson's Bar "overrun with tourists".'

'Three holiday rentals and one B&B won't attract

enough tourists to "overrun" will they?' In view of her current occupation, Clancy felt an affinity with Kaz and Oli. Kaz had seemed very nice if – understandably, it seemed – a little preoccupied with business.

'Unlikely,' Aaron agreed drily. 'And those same people want the B&B there when they fancy lunch on the lawn or somewhere local for friends and relatives to stay. Ernie says the B&B needs a bigger bar so more than five people can get in at a time – nobody disagreed with that one. And, as you knew she would, Dilys took the position that Nelson's Bar needs the internet and Ernie boomed out that the internet's full of viruses and crooks.'

The coffee machine hissed and began to emit the unmistakeable coffee-is-nigh fragrance. Clancy gave him the first cup – with a splash in a saucer for Nelson – and popped in a coffee pod for the second. 'The B&B seems a big part of the village.'

He gave a short laugh. 'It would certainly be a worry if it came under threat. I had a chat with Kaz and Oli afterwards, trying to remember all the points about rural communities that you'd fired at me. Anyway,' he went on, before she could ask more, 'I've come to apologise. And explain.' He'd propped his chin on his fist.

'Go on then,' she said, intrigued. The second coffee ready, she scooped it up and joined him at the table.

He ran a fingertip moodily around the rim of his mug. 'I'm not impressed with myself. I deliberately made you feel unwelcome to go to the meeting.'

'I got that.'

He closed his eyes for a moment. 'Which makes it worse. I'm sure it felt personal but, really, it wasn't.'

'It was because of Lee,' she supplied.

The dark eyes flicked open, looking wary. 'Yes. You

74

probably think I'm way exceeding my protectiveness but—'

'I've seen him,' she put in, remembering the fragility in Lee's eyes. 'He stopped to say hello.' She told Aaron about the meeting, adding, 'I couldn't get over the change in him. He looks a genuinely troubled soul. I have to admit that at first I was stung that you so obviously wanted to keep me away from De Silva House and impatient if Lee was still rotting inside about what Alice did, but he looks so . . . beaten.'

Aaron's shoulders relaxed a notch. 'Thank you for saying that but it proves how misguided I was to try and protect him, when he chose to meet the issue head-on.' He inhaled the steam of his coffee before taking an appreciative swig. 'I'm guilty of excessive big-brotherliness – but I don't think you have siblings, do you?'

'I'm an only child,' Clancy agreed slowly, 'but did you know that because our mothers are identical twins, the DNA profiles of Alice and me are more like half-sisters than cousins?'

He lowered his coffee cup, looking struck. 'Maybe Lee told me that once. Does it make a difference?'

'I think so. I feel closer to her than my few cousins on Dad's side, which allows me a glimmer of insight into why your family closes ranks around Lee.' Clancy still had to push aside a pinprick of hurt though. 'It's more about Lee than it is about me.'

'Yeah.' But he was frowning again. 'But you're just as entitled to a safe haven.'

'Oh.' The pinprick of hurt blossomed suddenly into warmth. 'Thank you.' Feeling in charity with him, she broke out a packet of chocolate Hobnobs, which led to more coffee making as neither of them really had enough of the first cup left to allow dunking. Nelson jumped up hopefully when he heard the packet rustle but lay down again with a sigh when none of the bounty came his way.

Clancy resumed her seat and tried a less contentious subject. 'I saw Genevieve at the B&B. It sounds as if her insurance company are playing ball OK. She's moving into the B&B soon, isn't she?'

He shrugged. 'Think so.' He dunked a Hobnob and popped it into his mouth whole. After he'd chewed and swallowed he added, 'She ended things between us.'

'Oh!' Clancy paused. So much for less contentious subjects. 'I'm sorry.'

'Thanks,' he said moodily. 'I think we were moving through the relationship at different speeds, but there's something about being dumped, isn't there?'

'Yes.' Her stomach gave the familiar lurch when she thought of Will. Will and Renée. 'And when it's a nice person who does the dumping, you wonder what that says about you.'

His gaze flew to her face and he cursed under his breath. 'Sorry. I wasn't thinking. I didn't mean to—'

'It's OK.' She buried her face in her coffee mug. Moving away from everything she knew had provided lots of distractions. Will had moved on in a brutally permanent way and so must she.

Aaron selected another Hobnob. 'Actually, Genevieve quoted you. Something about women not being defined by men.'

'I did say that, but I was talking about myself, not her.' She began to add something about his love life being none of her business, but then stuttered to a halt when the memory of their kiss in the garden flashed into her mind. That had been a tiny bit of his love life, and it had certainly been her business. Did he ever think of that when he was at De Silva House? Ever look at the nook just beyond the garden arbour . . . ? 'I hope nothing I said influenced her decision,' she ended.

Something flickered in his eyes, as if he were reading her mind. After a pause, he said, 'I don't think so. I was feeling that Genevieve was trying to manoeuvre me into asking her to move in. I didn't want that – or not yet, anyway. When you came up with the B&B information, it got me out of that situation and apparently I let my relief show.'

Clancy's face heated up. 'If I interfered, it was totally unwittingly—'

He waved her words aside. 'I'm not blaming you. Gen began demanding answers and I handled it badly. I was honest, I suppose, but not particularly gentle. She asked me if I loved her and I sort of became paralysed. So she ended things. I hate that me not wanting to commit definitely – or indefinitely – caused her pain but I can't force feelings I don't have.' He dunked another biscuit.

Clancy froze. His words had jolted her heart into an uncomfortable rhythm. 'You feel bad because you can't care for her as much as she wants you to?' she clarified.

'Basically.' He popped the biscuit into his mouth.

She felt clammy. 'Why *should* you share your home with someone if you don't want to?'

He nodded as he swallowed. 'That's it. I live alone because I like it that way.'

A sigh slipped out from somewhere deep within her heart. 'That must be how Will felt too. Have you got someone else?' She was probably getting all up in his business even voicing the question but he was being pretty open with her.

His hand froze over the biscuit packet, his black eyebrows up in his hairline. 'No! I haven't cheated.'

'That's a significant difference.' Now Aaron had provided the key to the puzzle she felt compelled to share what it unlocked. 'Will does love someone else. Her name's Renée. He's loved her for years but she married a friend of his so he presumed it was hopeless. Then she came back into his life as an employee of an IsVid client. She was single again and his old feelings flooded back.' She stopped to ease the tightness in her throat with a gulp of coffee. 'He didn't know how to tell me . . . so he kept quiet. I thought it was from malice but what if he couldn't tell me out of affection? I found out about Renée in a particularly horrible way, but he couldn't help how he felt about her and he couldn't help how he felt about me.' She suddenly realised that Aaron had abandoned the biscuits in favour of holding her hand.

'That's crappy for you,' he said feelingly.

'For him too,' she acknowledged for the first time. She'd punished Will for something he couldn't help; was punishing him still.

Aaron seemed at a loss for an answer. When they'd sat in silence for several minutes, she got a hold of herself and introduced a new subject, one unlikely to lead to as much heart-searching as the last. 'Do you know a couple of teenagers called Harry and Rory?' Her voice came out reedy and she battled to make it sound normal as she explained how she'd met them. 'They had me really worried when they didn't come straight back up to the clifftop.'

Aaron grinned ruefully, accepting her change of topic. 'Harry Drew's my second cousin's son. He's a live wire all right. I expect they hid out on Secret Beach to give you a scare.'

She screwed up her forehead. 'The beach at the foot of Zig-zag Path? I ran back to look and I couldn't see them.' She remembered the minutes of worry that she'd have to take action when it felt as if a wrong choice could mean the difference between life and death.

'That's Zig-zag Beach,' Aaron said. 'If you go off The Leap, which most of us have tried at some time, between where you land and Zig-zag Beach there's a tiny cove that disappears at high tide. We call it Secret Beach. You can swim to Secret Beach from Zig-zag Beach if you don't want to go off The Leap – which is about as high as those boards the Olympic divers go off, so not recommended for poor swimmers or anyone of a nervous disposition.'

Glad to focus on a nice safe emotion like indignation, Clancy withdrew her hand from his large, warm one. 'The little gits! I was running backwards and forwards like an idiot.'

'Yes, they're pranksters. They have too much time on their hands.'

They chatted about the village for a little longer, then Aaron rose, clicking his fingers and interrupting Nelson's snooze on the sofa, which he'd crept onto when no one was looking.

She accompanied them to the door. 'It's a shame everyone focuses on the negatives of this village. No village hall, no pub, nothing for youngsters. But it's beautiful! You have the sea on your doorstep, the salt marshes either side, flint and chalk cottages, pretty gardens and a real community. My stress levels dropped the moment I drove into Nelson's Bar. Although that wasn't hard at the time,' she added fairly.

He smiled down as he opened the front door and the

sea breeze romped in to blow his hair forward over his face. 'You should be the village's PR officer.'

'PR came into everything at IsVid. Except writing terms and conditions or privacy policies.' She sighed, wondering how everyone was getting on without her. *Without her*. Her heart flinched.

Hoping it didn't show, she stooped to ruffle Nelson's fur. 'I was thinking today that I've never had a dog.'

Aaron moved out into the porch. 'I don't suppose you'd like to practise on Nelson tomorrow? Mum has him if I'm working somewhere I can't take him, which is much of the time. With Aunt Norma being on that walking frame it might be awkward though. He tends to get up on his hind legs to greet people and might bowl her over.'

'I could,' Clancy said impulsively, liking the idea of a bit of a dog-share. 'The garden here's secure, isn't it?'

'It is. Are you sure? I was half-joking, really.' He looked from Nelson to Clancy and back again.

She was gathering enthusiasm for the idea though, envisaging walking around the leafy lanes with the big dog beside her and having something – someone? – to talk to in the Roundhouse. 'Of course! At least, let's try it. Bring him tomorrow and see if he settles. What kind of dog is he, anyway?'

Aaron regarded his pooch gravely and Nelson flattened his ears and grinned. 'He looks like a wolf, stands on hind legs like a meerkat and plays on his back like a bear cub. He's just a Nelson.' After they'd made arrangements for the next day, Aaron stepped out into the dusky evening and left. Clancy stayed at the door, watching.

She felt a sudden prickle run over her skin. She wasn't watching the way Aaron's body moved so easily under his clothes, was she?

No, she told herself, stepping back indoors. She was admiring the grace of her new borrow-dog loping at his side.

Obviously.

Chapter Eight

The next Saturday was the first day of June. Aaron had agreed to drive Aunt Norma to Hunstanton because she wanted to attend a craft fair at the Artisans' Hall. Dilys and three of her crafting buddies had already cadged a lift with Clancy so they could 'fleece a few tourists'. Aaron suspected Aunt Norma, a sporadic crafter of handmade cards, would enjoy the gossip with her friends more than the actual business of selling her products. It also crossed his mind that she might welcome the chance to take a look at the latter-day Clancy.

Aaron picked Aunt Norma up at eight-thirty, helping her down the ramp from the annexe, pausing to chat with Daisy and Yvonne, who were going to pick daisies on the clifftop as it was much too early for blackberries. Aaron stowed his great-aunt's folding chair along with her box of merchandise. He drove the truck out of the village between the chalk cottages with red-tiled roofs, swooping down Long Climb beneath the pines, and queued to turn onto the A149.

'Dilys says Clancy's been dog-sitting Nelson this week,'

Aunt Norma began. In his peripheral vision, he saw her glance his way.

'She kindly offered because I was worried about Nelson bowling you over.' Aaron managed to pull out into the traffic without risk to life or limb.

'Seems she kindly offered a lift to Dilys and the others today, too,' Norma went on. 'Seems she makes a habit of kindly offering.'

Raindrops began falling on the windscreen. Puttering through Holme and into Old Hunstanton, Aaron chose not to hear the combatant undertone. 'Yes, I've found her to be the opposite of Alice in lots of ways. By the way,' he added deliberately, 'I'm afraid I let slip that we call her cousin Awful Alice so she's quite expecting you to call her Crappy Clancy.'

There was a short, shocked silence. 'Have you given her the idea we're rude?' Norma sounded scandalised, just as he'd intended her to feel. Then she added, 'Don't say crap.'

The Artisans' Hall was set back from the seafront in prime tourist shopping territory. In the car park they found Dilys and the other crafters, Irene, Pat and Eunice, unloading boxes and bags from Clancy's car. Aunt Norma wound down her window and called, 'Glad to see this rain! Bring the tourists in off the beach.' She nodded in Clancy's direction. Clancy sent her a quick smile and nodded back.

Aaron extended his role from chauffeuring to delivery-man, ferrying the boxes of cards, pictures, quilts, embroidery and goodness-knew-what into the hall. Clancy helped until the crafter gang had begun to open the boxes then said brightly, 'If you're all set then I'll head off to catch up on my emails and stuff.'

She was gone before Aaron could answer. Maybe she

didn't care for Aunt Norma, from her fold-up chair, watching every move Clancy made.

Although it had originally been his intention to return home until the fair ended, Aaron made a late decision to enjoy Hunstanton for a few hours instead. The rain had stopped but dark clouds scudded over the sea as he sauntered along the main beach, watching the waves rearing up to smash their heads on the shore. It wasn't a beach he visited often as dogs were on the list of prohibitions posted on big notices up and down the promenade.

Alerted by loud music, he realised he was level with the funfair and was prompted by happy memories to cross the prom and jump up on the sea wall. When he and Lee had been children, a couple of goes on the rides had been a treat; as a teenager the fair had been a happy hunting ground for girls. Now he watched the dazzling colours of the waltzer and the gracious progress of the Ferris wheel, breathing in the evocative fragrance of suntan oil, candyfloss and hotdogs.

For a moment he thought he saw Clancy near the dodgem cars and prepared to jump down and cross to speak to her. It wasn't her, but once she was in his mind he took out his mobile phone – no problem with signal in Hunstanton – and sent her a text.

From Evelyn's notes Clancy understood that Saturdays, as changeover day, would be busy from now on. For now, however, she'd grabbed a table in a café called the Honeybee, a friendly-looking bee depicted buzzing across the top of every menu.

Her inbox had filled up as soon as she'd hooked up with the Wi-Fi and it gave her a strange sensation to see that Tracey, Asila and Monty had all replied to last week's email.

SO glad you're OK, said Asila.

Don't drop out of our lives entirely! pleaded Tracey.

And *Good news you're OK but wtf about no internet????* came from Jon 'Monty' Montagu.

Will had replied too. Her heart made a funny little misstep.

Clance,
I HATE how things are between us. I'm gutted I hurt
you but once I realised that it wasn't going to
work . . . well, it wasn't going to work. I think about
you every day and hope that sometime you'll forgive
me.

Clancy swallowed a lump in her throat at this unexpected change in tone. Part of her wanted to reply that, of course, marrying someone when you loved someone else was absolutely wrong and she was moving on with her life.

The other part was tempted to be mean and sarcastic. *It would have been a crowded marriage with three of us in it.* Or, perhaps, *I suppose you think that the nicer you are to me the easier I'll be on you when it comes to reckoning up the value of my share of the apartment and the business?*

Then she read the second paragraph:

I've thought long and hard about whether to say
this, but . . . here goes. I don't think I was the love
of your life.

Clancy read the bald statement several times, her heart thumping.

I think when you fall for the love of your life you'll be grateful that you and I didn't settle for each other. I hope you don't hate me for saying it.

For a few minutes, Clancy did think she hated Will. She certainly hated being forced to consider how he'd felt about Renée, that he'd risked everything, put himself in a highly uncomfortable situation, involved others, risked on their behalf . . . all for the love of his life. She tried to imagine herself ever risking everything for him.

After sipping her coffee and letting her heartbeat subside, she wrote:

I don't hate you. And then: *I'm glad you're happy. If things hadn't worked out for you with Renée after all . . .*

She let that comment hang, a not-so-subtle hint that she'd feel worse if the misery he'd put her through had been for nothing. She ended: *I've found a safe haven.* Apart from those who weren't keen on her because of Alice, she thought, clicking 'send' and remembering the suspicious way Aaron's Aunt Norma had stared at her at the Artisans' Hall.

She finished her coffee, giving the jumbled feelings about Will time to ease away while she read an email from her parents.

Well, we don't really know what to say, darling, though we can see why you wanted to get away from the apartment – if you're sure that leaving Will in possession was wise . . . ? Are you coping with

86

*all this OK on your own? One of us could fly back
for a visit, if you want.*

Clancy, who couldn't see what good a brief visit would
do her, replied bracingly that it was really just a matter
of coping with the fallout now. *You brought me up to be
independent,* she added, which couldn't be disputed.

The email she left till last was from the elusive Alice
Nettles herself.

*Hey, Clancy, it's weeks since I heard from you!
Are you seriously living in poky little Nelson's
Bar??? Can't believe it. London's much more you,
surely? Anyway, it's fine by me about the caretaker
job if you really want it. Maybe you should begin
advertising for your replacement straight away
though because I can't see you in the sticks for
more than a week. LOL
I LOVE America! There's always so much to do.*

She went on chattering about road trips to iconic places
like San Francisco's Golden Gate Bridge and the Strip in
Las Vegas, finishing with, *I hope you get on OK with Aaron.
Maybe he's improved with age. (Haha.)
Alice x*

In view of Las Vegas being seven hours behind the UK,
Clancy gave up her impulse to ring and hear Alice's voice.
She was just thinking of composing a jokey reply that at
least by taking the caretaker job she was getting paid for
some of the help she gave her cousin, when her phone
beeped to announce a text.

It was from Aaron. *Are you busy? Thought we might meet
for lunch.*

It catapulted her back to the present. She glanced at the time on her phone – nearly quarter to one. The café had filled up with chattering customers while she'd been busy mooning over the past and composing emails and now she noticed an empty feeling where her stomach should be. She'd so far occupied a table for half the morning at the Honeybee Café for the price of only two cups of coffee. She replied: *Yes, why not?* and gave him her location.

While she waited, she found the tourism website used by Roundhouse Row and studied its entry. Aaron arrived ten minutes later, running because summer rain was falling through sunrays struggling between the clouds. He fell in through the door, shaking raindrops from his hair and grinning when he saw her, attracting several looks from women as he crossed the room. 'Flaming June,' he said cheerfully, pulling out the other chair. 'They should be doing good business at the craft fair.'

They chatted desultorily as they made their choices from the menu and a girl in her late teens came to take their order. Then Clancy decided to tell him about hearing from Alice, without passing on the negative comment about Aaron.

As if to demonstrate feeling no more warmly about Alice, he raised his dark eyebrows. 'Did she ask anything about Lee?'

'No,' Clancy was able to say truthfully. 'I've only seen him once anyway, so I wouldn't have much to tell her.' She waited for him to try and give her a steer on what she should/shouldn't say to Alice concerning his brother.

Instead, he said idly, 'It's funny to think you're close. I see a family likeness appearance-wise, but not in personality.'

Clancy sat back to let the waitress lay their table with clean cutlery and cream napkins. Every table was full now and people were coming in out of the rain and looking disappointed. 'I don't suppose we are,' she agreed. 'But I miss her.'

His gaze found hers. 'I hadn't thought of that,' he said slowly.

'No, I don't suppose anybody here does think it.' She let out a sigh that stirred the edges of her paper napkin. 'Our lives have taken us in different directions. We talk via email or the phone but it's not the same. Our mums were the kind of twins who looked identical but were different under the skin – mine went out into the world; hers was a home lover. Alice was always envious of the travelling I'd done—' She hesitated.

'So she's taken every opportunity to travel herself since she did the runaway-bride trick,' he rejoined drily.

'It seems so.' Clancy sat back and smiled at the young waitress who was setting eggs Benedict before her and a bacon sandwich in front of Aaron, then she asked him about Hunstanton because it seemed a safer topic than Alice. He proved to have a fair knowledge of its history.

By the time they'd eaten, the sun was shining again. The pavements outside glistened and the tables began to empty. Aaron didn't immediately get up to leave. 'Do you mind if I run something past you, something to do with Genevieve? I don't want it to be horrible and awkward when we meet. It's such a small village that we're bound to trip over each other. I thought it would be easier if that first meeting was public but casual, so we've looked each other in the eye and said hello. What do you think?'

Clancy stared outside at people strolling by, the traffic moving slowly. He was being thoughtful, but there was an ache in the pit of her belly. Had Will felt the same when he'd written that email, trying to be kind to the woman who'd wanted to share his life? It was so close to being pitied that her skin crept.

'I think I'd want to get it over with as easily as possible.' She shuddered.

The lines of Aaron's face had begun to relax, but now he frowned. 'Is this upsetting you?'

She picked up her water glass and put it down again. 'Not the conversation.' Just the memory of a humiliation; the end of hers and Will's relationship had played out excruciatingly publicly.

After another moment, he went on. 'Friends are coming round tonight for a drink and pizza. I wondered about inviting her.'

Clancy was dubious. 'So long as you make it obvious that it's a gathering, not a reconciliation attempt, that *might* work. But neutral territory would be better.'

'There isn't much neutral territory in Nelson's Bar. There can't be many people who don't know one or both of us.' He fiddled with his napkin, folding it over and ironing in the fold with the side of his fist. 'Don't hesitate to tell me to bugger off if I'm overstepping the mark, but I wondered if you'd come too, to make sure Genevieve's not the only woman. You seem to get on with her OK.'

Clancy mused on his suggestion, quite tempted by the opportunity to meet more of the villagers. She had got on with Genevieve on the couple of occasions they'd met and evenings at the Roundhouse were solitary. She'd been made welcome to share a cup of cocoa with Dilys over a puzzle mag but going to someone's house and meeting people her own age was more appealing. 'OK,' she responded, before she could change her mind.

Aaron looked relieved. 'Thanks. You know which cottage it is, don't you? Come round the back because it's meant to clear up later this afternoon so we'll probably gather on the patio. Any time after seven-thirty.'

'That's a date,' said Clancy, feeling brighter. 'I don't mean a *date* date, obviously,' she added hastily.

He gave a rueful smile as he got up. 'Those certainly wouldn't be the right circumstances in which to face Gen for the first time.'

They laughed. Aaron went off on his own errands and Clancy turned back to her laptop but the idea of Will pitying her kept swooping around in her head, making it hard to concentrate. Almost as a counterpoint, the realisation that she was now free to date for the first time in over three years kept occurring to her too. Visions shimmered of being taken out to dinner in a pretty summer dress. White tablecloths. Candlelight. Maybe music.

If that happened, she decided, she could email Will and say: *You don't have to worry about me. I'm dating again.*

She filed that in her head under 'not yet'.

Sometime, she'd have to face Will again, and everyone at IsVid too. There were things to be sorted out.

She filed that under 'not yet', too.

Chapter Nine

Aaron wasn't looking forward to ringing Genevieve but she sounded OK when she answered. They exchanged awkward hellos.

He went straight to the point. 'I'm having a few people round for pizza tonight and wondered if you'd like to come. Clancy's coming. She doesn't know many people in the village yet.'

Genevieve took from that more than he'd meant her to, but it worked in his favour. 'And you don't want her to be the only girl? I suppose I could. She seems nice.'

'Great,' he said, relieved to get it over with so easily, then went up to shower before searching out plates and glasses. His freezer already held a variety of pizzas.

Several of his friends had already arrived by the time Clancy and Genevieve rounded the corner of the house together, including his noisy second cousin Jordy – the father of Harry who Clancy had met at The Leap – and Jordy's quiet wife, Anabelle. Aaron thought it likely that Genevieve had loitered outside until she saw Clancy coming so she was spared the ordeal of walking in alone.

Nelson welcomed both of them on his hind legs, honouring Clancy as a new source of walks and ball games and Genevieve as a long-beloved purveyor of coffee. After greeting Nelson, Genevieve's unhappy gaze flickered to Aaron. He waited for some pang of regret or hunger as, awkwardly, she offered her cheek to be kissed, but all he felt was a renewed urge to apologise – which was crazy when *she'd* dumped him.

Clancy's attention was on the sea that glittered in the evening sunshine. 'Wow! Look at that view. I hadn't realised your garden would be so close to the cliff edge. The sea's almost on your doorstep.'

Silently thanking her for breaking the awkward silence, Aaron made a show of peering out at the waves rolling towards them. 'If that lot arrives on my doorstep we're going to have to hope that Noah comes by in his ark.'

'And this garden! It looks like something from Japan.' Clancy gazed admiringly at the paving, the delicate-leaved acers in glowing greens and purples and the conifers Aaron controlled with close clipping, the ferns and the hostas. Pebbles and shale kept weeds down and slugs away. The only water was in a stone bowl for the birds but he felt the sea was near enough to qualify as part of the scene.

'Low maintenance,' he answered. 'When you garden all day, you want something easy at home.'

Jordy, who he'd primed to engage Genevieve in conversation if she looked at a loss, roared, 'Gen! Now you've finished with that sad loser, come over here and talk to me and Belly,' which wasn't exactly what Aaron had had in mind but did act as an ice-breaker, causing laughter and a reason for Genevieve to move further into the gathering, even if Anabelle winced at her name being mutilated into 'Belly'.

Genevieve knew everybody, of course, but for Clancy it was different. He drew her into conversation with three brothers he'd known ever since he could remember. Their parents had named them Michael, Nicholas and Richard but they were known universally as Mick, Nick and Rick. Nick was the same age as Aaron, Mick a couple of years older and Rick a couple younger. Compared to Jordy – roaring with laughter at his conversation with Genevieve – Mick, Nick and Rick were quiet and personable. Rick sometimes worked for Aaron when he had a job that needed another pair of hands. Clancy didn't show any signs of being intimidated by having new names hurled at her. She just smiled and fell easily into conversation.

'Can I hook up with your satellite Wi-Fi, Aaron?' Rick demanded, waving his phone. Good-naturedly, Aaron gave him the password, and, as he'd known they would, others whipped out their phones too. He retired to the kitchen to unwrap the pizzas and slide them into the oven. He'd change the password tomorrow or he'd have half the village lurking outside to hook up their devices.

The evening was breezy, as tended to be the case in Nelson's Bar, perched on its spit of land on the east coast of England, but the sunshine was warm enough to make up for it. They'd eat outside, Aaron decided, then move indoors when the sun went down.

When he stepped into the garden again once the pizzas were cooking, he saw Genevieve and Clancy talking together. Jordy had joined an all-male conversation – a loud one, as most of Jordy's tended to be – about some TV thriller Aaron hadn't got into. As he'd only had one small beer, he crossed to the drinks table to get another. It brought him close enough to Genevieve and Clancy to hear their conversation as he helped himself to a bottle and flipped off its lid.

'Thing is,' Clancy was saying, 'that I know my ex is feeling sorry for me.'

Aaron did a smart about turn before he could hear Genevieve's reply. That absolutely didn't sound like a conversation he wanted to be part of. He was feeling ridiculously on edge at being around his ex-girlfriend as it was.

In half an hour the pizzas were golden and bubbling. He sliced them up and each plate was fallen upon as soon as he carried it outside. 'Please don't feed pizza to the dog!' he called, knowing Nelson would make 'staaaaaarving' faces at everyone.

The pizza vanished and empty beer bottles began to outnumber full ones as the sun sank into the sea in a blaze of glory. Anabelle asked Aaron to play them something on his guitar. He'd left his acoustic in the sitting room so fetched it and played 'Duelling Banjoes' because that's all anyone ever seemed to ask for. Then he spotted Clancy watching the sunset as if it were a movie, her fascinated gaze fixed on the streaks of deep vermillion. The light made her chestnut hair appear redder and her white jeans look pink. As no one requested another song, Aaron stowed the guitar in the kitchen and moved up to stand at Clancy's side.

'I didn't know you played,' she commented.

'A bit,' he replied. 'This piece of coast gets some amazing sunsets. If you were on a boat out there the cliffs would look dark red.'

She didn't remove her gaze from the sky. 'I can't believe the colours.'

'I could take a pic of you with the sunset as the backdrop, if you like.'

She glanced his way as if assessing whether she should be reading anything into the offer, then fished for her phone and handed it to him. 'Thanks. I can email it to my parents.'

He took several shots, trying to make her laugh to get a natural result, capturing her streaky hair mirroring the fiery reflections in the sea. He'd just tapped in the password to his Wi-Fi into her phone for her when he was surprised at the sound of Lee's voice. He turned around and, sure enough, there was his brother, looking strained, but smiling.

'I thought you didn't have a babysitter?' Aaron gave his little brother a quick man-hug. He'd been sorry to learn that his parents and Aunt Norma had already made plans for this evening because he'd felt Lee could use a night off.

Lee returned the hug. 'The folks came home early. Daisy was already asleep so I thought I'd come up to join the party.' He halted. 'Hello again, Clancy.'

Aaron turned to follow his line of sight and saw Clancy regarding Lee. She returned his greeting and Lee stepped closer, Clancy looking like a cat prepared to flee, Lee like a dog not sure of his welcome.

With an effort, Aaron turned away to join another conversation. Sometimes being the elder brother meant protecting Lee for all he was worth or helping him when he was at rock bottom, but right now it meant leaving him to interact with someone who'd never done him any harm but nonetheless was a connection to bad memories.

As the evening slid into night, the light from the kitchen spilling onto the patio, Aaron found himself in an awkward conversation with Genevieve. 'Shall I go upstairs and pick up the stuff I left here? Or come another time?' she asked, her eyes guarded.

Aaron tried to say the right thing. 'Whenever suits you best.'

'If you don't care one way or another I'll come back another time, when there isn't half the village here to stare.' She tossed down the last of her wine and muttered, 'Bye.' Before he could protest, she stalked off around the side of the building and into the night.

Nettled at how he seemed to have ended up in the wrong, he drifted over to the furthest corner of the garden, looking out into a darkness punctuated by the winking pinpricks of boats running under lights.

'So Lee has a child?' He didn't need to turn to know who had spoken. He'd been aware of Clancy as she crossed to join him, her jacket fastened now, her hands in its pockets.

Behind them the party continued. Mick, Nick, Rick and Jordy were getting raucous and gales of masculine laughter rang out on the summer night. 'Yes – Daisy,' Aaron said. 'She's four.'

Her voice was stiff. 'So somewhere in the second year after Alice left, Lee fathered a child. Despite his broken heart?'

'They're the basic facts,' Aaron agreed carefully. He turned towards her, seeing the wariness on her face. He touched her hand, letting a couple of their fingers link. It felt important that he make contact, as if that would keep her there, listening. 'When he was living alone in Northamptonshire, isolated from his family, friends and Nelson's Bar, he did see women. Why shouldn't he? Women like him. Alice had crapped on him.' Mentally, he heard Aunt Norma sniffing, *'Don't say crap!'*

'Beth was a woman he saw for a couple of months,' he continued, 'but she got pregnant. It wasn't what they'd expected but they had a go at making a family for the baby. It proved a rocky road. Beth never located her maternal side and when they split up she wanted Lee to have Daisy. He's a good dad and he found a childminder and fought to keep her and his job.'

He paused, hoping she'd join the conversation.

'Sounds hard,' she conceded, after several moments.

'It was,' he agreed. She hadn't unlinked her fingers from his. It made him think of another summer night in a different garden, when all his senses had been tuned to Clancy, the shape of her against him, her heat, the shoulders and neck laid bare by a summer top. With an effort, he brought his mind back to the present. 'He decided to come back to Norfolk in time for Daisy to begin school here. He'll get his own place when the sale of his house in Northants goes through.'

For several moments, Clancy said nothing. One side of her face was visible in the light streaming from the house, the other in shadow.

'I expect it looks strange from your perspective,' Aaron went on, encouraged that she seemed to be weighing his words. 'You probably think I've made too much of Lee's fragility. I can only tell you how hyper-aware we all were of him questioning whether life was really worth the effort it takes to live and that we saw Daisy as someone for him to live *for*. Then—' he flicked a glance behind him to check nobody else was within earshot '—he said he wanted Daisy to know us all properly in case anything ever happened to him. We were terrified all over again. That's why we're hyper-protective of him, however faint a threat something seems.'

He waited. He'd opened his heart in a way he hadn't really done to anyone apart from his parents. Not Genevieve. Not a single one of his friends.

The wind ran its fingers through Clancy's hair. She was wearing make-up tonight, mascara and professional-looking eyeliner, and he thought it was the first time he'd seen it on her since she'd arrived in Nelson's Bar. She was beautiful without make-up, but with it she was much more sophisticated. He thought about her life in London and imagined her going out to swanky venues with her entrepreneurial colleagues and the unknown Will. In evening dress he'd bet she looked stunning. Perhaps even more stunning than she did biting her lip now and staring at him.

Aaron didn't get cities and why people wanted to live on top of one another like in a hive or a nest. But when he'd first met Clancy he'd been entranced by her city gloss, the things she talked about. It was lust or infatuation, a crush in other words, but it had given him a week of cloud nine, euphoria. Before it crashed.

He was pretty sure she'd react badly if he dipped his head and kissed her again now but that didn't stop him wanting to, even a non-swanky, non-city boy like him.

A gusty sigh escaped her. 'Thanks for helping me understand.' A pause drew out. He could almost see her ordering her thoughts. 'Did Lee never show what you call his "fragility" before Alice left?'

Aaron squeezed her fingers, pretty sure he knew what was coming. 'He was always much moodier than the rest of the family.' He went on even as she opened her mouth to speak. 'You're going to suggest that he might have suffered from depression if Alice had stayed, aren't you? I guess we'll never know for certain . . . because Alice *left*.

And Lee fell into a deep black hole he's never completely climbed out of.'

She nodded, slowly. Not long after that, she said her goodbyes and left, as if the little taste of the village social life had been enough.

Chapter Ten

Will

Want to be the one to tell you Renée and I got married yesterday. V quiet but I know my sis put pix on her Instagra . . .

Reading the partial WhatsApp message on the lock-screen of the silver iPhone in Aaron's hand sent a cold, slimy feeling sliding down his spine. His fingers itched to tap the notification and read on but that's what password protection and face recognition had been invented to prevent.

The phone was Clancy's.

He'd been holding it last night when Lee had arrived and he must have slipped it into his pocket out of habit. Hooked up to his satellite broadband, the phone was still receiving this morning and it wasn't until he'd seen that awful notification that he realised what he'd done.

So there went a lazy Sunday morning. He must return Clancy's property.

And only a monster, having read the first part of that message, would shove the phone at her and run.

He went downstairs to let Nelson outside, while he thought. The garden was a mess of empty beer cans and bottles left by those people who evidently couldn't be bothered to dump their empties in the box he'd provided. He gathered up the debris, grumbling under his breath. At least none of the bottles had smashed, a huge hazard for unwary paws.

Nelson sniffed around for pizza crumbs, bushy eyebrows twitching.

By the time Aaron had finished it was nine-forty-five. He tapped the home button on Clancy's phone again and took another guilty look at the shitty beginning to the message Will had sent. It had now been joined by an iMessage notification from someone called Asila, her avatar a pretty Asian woman with glasses. *Clancy, can you ring me ASAP, hon? xxx* Will's avatar was a well-groomed guy with stylish blond hair. Aaron pushed his fingers through his permanently ruffled curls self-consciously. He rocked an ungroomed look himself.

He put down Clancy's phone and rang the Roundhouse landline. The ring tone sounded a few times before Clancy answered, sounding faintly puzzled. Probably she hadn't given the number out. 'Hello?' she said, then, probably remembering that occasionally somebody telephoned to book. 'Roundhouse Row.'

'It's Aaron,' he said. 'I have your mobile phone. I must have stuck it into my pocket after taking the photo of you and the sunset. Sorry.'

'I thought that was probably what had happened.' She gave a small laugh. 'In the Nelson's Bar "not spot" I only use it for taking photos so I didn't miss it until this morning.'

It was nice to hear her laugh but he had a feeling he was about to be a mood changer. He cleared his throat. 'Um, thing is, I've got a silver iPhone too, so I tried to unlock it, thinking it was mine. It was only when I read the first part of a message on your lock-screen that I realised it wasn't.'

'OK.' She sounded so unconcerned that she obviously wasn't getting a subtext.

He had to be blunt. 'The message is a WhatsApp from Will and it's about something you need to know. Come up here and download the rest on my Wi-Fi if you want.'

Silence. Then he heard her take a long breath. 'I'm guessing it's nothing good?'

At that moment, there were few things he wanted less than to be asked to read what he could see of the message out. 'You should read it for yourself,' he said gruffly. 'I'll be in until about twelve-thirty, then I'm going to my parents' for lunch. Come round the back. I'll be in the garden or kitchen.'

'OK. I'll come up now.'

While he waited for her, he made coffee in his filter jug. He couldn't usually be bothered but she'd asked for filter coffee at the Honeybee Café yesterday at lunchtime. By the time he'd grabbed milk and sugar and carried it out to set on the table with her iPhone, Nelson was doing his greeting dance in front of Clancy, who'd paused just inside the garden to fuss him.

Make-up free this morning, her face was pale and freckles danced across the bridge of her nose. She was wearing shorts; not the buttock-grazing kind but short enough to draw Aaron's gaze.

'Coffee?' he offered, indicating the pot.

'Thanks.' As soon as she'd created her preferred concoction with milk and a half-spoon of sugar she picked up her phone from the table.

Aaron trained his gaze on the sea, blue and sparkling. 'Feel free to go off somewhere to check your messages. You'll get connectivity anywhere in the house and garden.'

'It's bad enough that I might want to be alone to read it, is it?' But she came to sit beside him on the garden bench, parking the coffee mug beside her. Her hair blew against his skin and it felt like being stroked with feathers.

He knew she was about to be hurt and he couldn't do anything about it. He revised his earlier reluctance to tell her what he knew. 'If you want, I can tell you the little bit I accidentally read.'

'No, I'll . . .' She dropped her gaze to her phone, regarding it as she might a venomous snake. Then she tapped and swiped at the screen, paused, and sat for several moments with her head bowed. 'So you read that Will has married Renée,' she said, her voice high and brittle.

He nodded, feeling almost sick on her behalf as she absorbed the blow. He hadn't felt this bad for another person since Alice left Lee waiting for her in church.

Nelson came up and propped his big shaggy head on Clancy's lap as if sensing she needed comfort.

Clancy stroked him behind the ears. Nelson's eye half-closed in pleasure. 'It was an impulse, apparently. Neither of them wanted to wait. He thought he'd better tell me. Didn't want me to find out by seeing it on his sister Mel's Instagram account.'

'Shit.' He winced. 'I suppose he had to tell you but . . . well, shit.'

'I certainly cut up rough when he kept me in the dark about accidentally falling in love with Renée so I suppose I can't complain about him coming clean now.' It was difficult to tell whether the noise she made was a giggle or a sob. 'I think it would be a good idea if I checked out Mel's Instagram and saw the wedding photos. Get all the pain over with at once. Would you mind if I sat here with you and did it? I feel a bit like a dog frightened by a storm.' As if to demonstrate how that felt, Nelson whined.

'I don't mind at all.'

Clancy fumbled again with her phone, scrolling shakily until, judging by the way she froze, she discovered what she was looking for. After what seemed like a long time she turned the screen so that Aaron could see. 'Renée looked very pretty.' She gasped another of those half-hysterical giggles. 'The last picture I saw of her was . . . accidental.'

Aaron took her hand, absolutely out of things to say. It seemed indecent to look as happy as Will and Renée did at the expense of the woman quivering beside him. The fair woman in the cream silk dress, beaming as she gazed adoringly at the well-groomed blond man from the WhatsApp message, wasn't a patch on Clancy, in his opinion. Though conventionally pretty, she was insipid, not striking or vivid, like Clancy. Intelligence didn't shimmer from speaking eyes; her hair didn't shine different colours as she moved.

'When it happened,' Clancy said drearily, 'it came as a total shock. I thought we were committed.'

'Planning to get married does sound like a commitment,' he observed, tightening his fingers on hers.

'I suppose I was doing most of the wedding planning.

All of it, really. Will must already have been dragging his feet but because I was so certain of the path we were on, I didn't take it in,' she admitted. 'Then one day we'd scheduled a conference call. Monty and I were in a hotel after a meeting in Leicester, two people from the client company were in their offices somewhere and Renée, also from the client company, was with Will in his office at IsVid. She was the client's in-house creative and they'd been working on video footage over the preceding weeks. I hadn't met her. He hadn't told me he'd once loved her from afar.'

When she paused, Aaron could hear only leaves stirring in the breeze and the hiss of waves breaking fifty yards below at the foot of the cliff. 'He and Renée got close?'

She laughed, a hard, ragged sound. 'Will somehow didn't realise – or forgot – that the conferencing software was already streaming from his computer. Monty hooked us all up and there was this extraordinary image on the screen. It was like watching sex through a letter box. You could just see a segment of a man standing up, his trousers sliding down and a wo-woman's legs over his arms.' She started rushing her words as if she had to get all this bad stuff out of her head. 'Monty started shouting at Will. The clients began to laugh, probably thinking some hacker had planted porn footage. But I knew what I was looking at. I'd heard Will's voice – how could I not know? And the things he said to her were things he'd said to me! The clients laughed harder than ever. Then Renée started saying, "Oh, no! Oh, no!" as she realised they were visible via the conference software. And their laughter stopped like a flick of a switch. They recognised her voice and realised it was live, I suppose.'

'Jeez,' Aaron said helplessly, trying to imagine how shitty it had felt.

Clancy flashed a glance at him. 'Monty apologised to everyone and ended the conference call. It's a bit of a blur after that. Monty drove me back to London. I was in shock. Will met me at home and confessed to being in love with Renée. He was horrified to have hurt me but said he was relieved the lies and subterfuge were over. So shock number two: it wasn't just a fling. We were both directors of IsVid, owned our apartment together, and we were supposed to be getting married. It was one hell of a heap of shit.'

'I can only imagine.' But so clearly that his heart bumped as if he'd experienced it with her.

Her voice dropped into a dull monotone. 'I was in a daze. At the limit of what I could cope with, I suppose. Monty got to hear that the clients – other than Renée, no doubt – had found the story about the video-conference-turned-porn-flick too good to keep to themselves. Our conferencing software saved automatically and the clients had access privileges to any call they were party to. Someone there made sure the footage was shared. I suppose Renée could have asked her HR department to investigate but decided it might not work in her favour.'

A shudder ran through her and he wished he could think of something comforting to say. He passed her coffee, holding the mug steady until he knew she'd got it so it wouldn't splash over her bare legs, though he wouldn't have minded splashing the hot coffee over the absent Will's lap.

'So.' She dragged out a sigh. 'Worried, he said, about our image, Monty came up with the excellent idea of saying it had been me Will was . . . with. Will and I had plans to marry, so it would downgrade the incident. Asila and Tracey told him not to be a moron and I should have let them stop him. Instead, I lost my sense of proportion and put out an IsVid newsletter saying the woman Will Martin had screwed on the desk during a video conference had not been me.'

'Oh.' Aaron cringed for her.

'Yeah.' She sat up a bit straighter. 'It wasn't seen to be normal behaviour. The newsletter got on social media and IsVid was tagged. Asila and Tracey suggested I took time out but Monty went further and said he didn't see how we could all continue to work together. And it wasn't Will, the one who had messed up, who was to leave! It was me. Monty said Will had "kept his composure". So that's what was important? Not ethics and loyalty, not slaving to make the business a success? It was composure.'

He was still holding her hand. 'Harsh.'

'I don't even remember everything I said now. I was distraught. Betrayed. I certainly didn't keep my composure.' With her free hand, she brought her coffee mug, still trembling, to her lips. 'So I tied them and Will up in a financial knot. You could say I was protecting myself or you could say I was being a vindictive bitch. Then I told Will he could sort out un-planning the wedding and I left for Nelson's Bar.'

Their clasped hands had somehow slipped down to her leg. Her skin felt chill, as if she'd gone into shock just telling him what had happened. 'Are they still in the financial knot?'

Absently, she nodded. 'I don't know why they didn't see the possible consequences before they asked me to "put the business first" by leaving it. The directors own equal shares and therefore receive equal dividends. I refused to sign a waiver so they have to keep paying me. Directors' homes secure borrowing at the bank so Will's in a tricky situation, as he has no alternative security. He suggested we sell the apartment to separate our finances. I said no. He asked that I sell out to Renée. I said no. Add to that: the others will have to raise the finance to buy me out and you see I left them in a right bloody mess.'

'Wow.' It had stretched his brain just to follow it all. He watched her drain her coffee and set the mug down. 'I don't know what to say . . . except that I'm truly sorry you've had to endure all this shit. What comes next?'

She shrugged, a world of trouble in her gaze. 'One day I think I'm punishing Will for something he couldn't help: falling in love with Renée. Next moment I hate him for letting me find out the way I did, for not keeping his attraction to her platonic until he'd reversed out of our relationship, for letting me be humiliated. Then I think I'm a horrible bitch . . . One day I suppose I'll break the cycle and know what to do.' She sighed. 'Will's last email said he wasn't the love of my life.'

He digested that. 'What do you think?'

She frowned out at the horizon, where the sea silvered just before it met the sky. 'We had something built up over time, on respect and sharing. Matching intellects, similar backgrounds.'

He nodded understandingly. 'I suppose Genevieve and I had all those things too.'

She frowned. 'But she wasn't the love of your life and so you didn't allow yourself to be railroaded.'

'True,' he acknowledged gently. 'She was manipulating

things to get a greater commitment; I was manipulating them to avoid it. If I could go back and be more honest sooner, I would. I hurt someone I was very fond of.'

'*Fond* of? She'd be hurt by that too.' She fell to watching nearby fronds of Black Dragon Grass dancing in the wind.

Aaron looked at her hand in his. It was small with a smattering of tiny freckles, her nails neat ovals. She probably wore gloves for the jobs around Roundhouse Row that might break them.

'I like your garden,' she said suddenly. 'When we were young, Alice and I used to say we'd have a garden centre one day.'

'I didn't know either of your interests lay in that direction,' he said, accepting that she needed a change of subject.

'They don't. It was just because of our surnames – Moss and Nettles. Do you garden in winter?'

'Some.' He thought of a way to provide her with a reason to stay if she wasn't ready to be on her own yet. 'But it's so restricted by the weather that I have a side business. Want to see?'

The sun caught her eyes as she glanced at him questioningly. 'Sounds interesting.'

'I think so.' He went to the kitchen door and took down a key from a hook then led her to his workshop on the side of the house, switching on the light as they entered.

She halted as she saw the parade of glossy instruments on the wall. 'Wow. Guitars! Lots of.' Then she looked around at his woodworking machinery, the router, a couple of electric saws, a pillar drill, and all the hand tools on racks or stands. 'You *make* them?'

'That's right. Some I make to commission, others I make for stock for anyone who wants to buy off the peg.' He lifted one down from the wall. 'I've nearly finished this. It's a Fender-style Jaguar in mahogany, sprayed British Racing Green. The action's a bit high. That means the strings aren't close to the fretboard. Some people don't like it in case when they're bending a string it slips under another, but it's less likely to buzz.' He put it back and took down another. 'I chose a natural finish for this one, so it's clear-lacquered rather than painted. It's semi-acoustic, which means it has a hollow body and doesn't have to be plugged in to play. The body's oak, the neck rosewood and the fretboard black walnut.'

'You played well last night.' Her pallor had warmed a touch.

'I think it would be almost impossible to make guitars if I wasn't at least competent. I wouldn't understand what I could do or why I was doing it.' He took her around each instrument, explaining which woods he'd used and where he'd got them, and that people often went for oak because it seemed a mark of quality but actually it was so brittle that it wasn't his favourite to work with. He played a couple of scales on a semi-acoustic so she could hear the notes drifting onto the air. Then his landline began to ring.

She glanced at the extension on the wall of the workshop. 'Don't ignore it on my account.'

'It'll be my mum, probably.' But when he answered the voice that came at him down the line was high-pitched and excited.

'Uncle Aaron, I haven't seen you for ages. It's nearly dinnertime, Granny says.'

Aaron grinned at the indignation in the passionate little

voice. 'I had a lot of tidying up to do this morning,' he fibbed. 'Tell Granny I'll be there.' After a little more chit-chat, he replaced the receiver, aware of a slight sense of disappointment that Clancy had moved to the door.

'It's time I went,' she said, making a valiant effort at a casual smile. 'Thank you for letting me use your Wi-Fi and for . . . listening.'

'You could come to Mum's with me for lunch,' he suggested. 'She never minds one more.'

'No thanks,' she said quickly. Then smiled apologetically. 'This is going to sound so ungracious as you've been so kind, but I don't want to go somewhere else I'm not wanted. Not today. I'd be awful company anyway. I'm going to go for a long walk and mutter to myself about the unfairness of life.'

'OK.' He'd feel much the same in her shoes. He busied himself with turning out the light and locking the work-shop door. 'If you want to stay here and use the Wi-Fi . . .?'

She screwed up her face. 'Like to reply to Will? No thanks. Wouldn't do to disturb the honeymoon.' Then she managed a smile. 'Thanks again. See you.' Hands in pockets, she began to back off.

Aaron clicked his fingers to Nelson. 'We'll walk with you till I turn off.'

She shrugged, but hovered while he found Nelson's lead and stopped him bouncing around with excitement long enough to clip it onto his collar. They walked together down Long Lane until they reached the turn to Frenchmen's Way.

Aaron paused, but Clancy carried on walking. 'Thanks again,' she threw over her shoulder. Evidently, she wasn't going to hang around long enough for him to re-invite her to lunch.

He watched her walking away, her chin at a defiant angle. If he hadn't just witnessed the pain she'd gone through he would have thought that she was completely comfortable in her own skin.

Chapter Eleven

Almost a fortnight after the pizza night in Aaron's garden, Clancy was still ordering herself, *'Don't think about Will and Renée's wedding'* but it was like that game 'Don't think of an elephant' when, of course, all you could then think about was an elephant.

An elephant would have been a relief. What had been floating before her eyes since she'd seen Mel's Instagram account were the beaming faces of two people who hadn't been able to wait to tie the knot. Will in an unfamiliar suit, Renée in an ivory silk dress, not quite a wedding dress but adequate when dressed up with flowers and an elaborate up-do.

It made Clancy remember her own wedding dress which was, presumably, still in Tracey's spare room where she'd hung it so Will wouldn't invoke bad luck by seeing it before the supposed big day. Cue hollow laughter.

The erstwhile plans for her emphatically-not-going-to-happen wedding taunted her. Cream bouquet and button-holes, duck-egg cravats. Morning suits in pewter grey. Reception at the Gladstone Library in Whitehall Place . . .

Much better to think of elephants.

Two of the three holiday cottages were occupied just now, but the guests had gone off in their cars. She spent the morning mowing the lawns and was weeding the front patch at number four Roundhouse Row, deciding which were weeds and which were plants by drawing on her memories of helping Aunt Sally in her garden. She was enjoying the scent of damp earth, when Aaron's cousin Jordy strolled up hailing her as if he'd known her for years. 'Got a minute? I want to ask you something.'

Jordy seemed to wear a permanent cocky grin. Older than Aaron, his dark curly hair was shot with silver and shone as if he used an oily product on it. She'd liked his quiet wife, Anabelle, when she'd met her at Aaron's, but hadn't been able to snatch much conversation with her. Jordy had been so loud. Clancy straightened up, still holding her trowel. 'Ask away,' she said politely.

'It's Harry,' he began, folding his arms and frowning. 'My son, Harry Drew.'

'I've met him,' Clancy acknowledged cautiously. She wasn't a parent and wasn't sure whether Jordy was likely to complain if she said she'd seen Harry and his friend Rory cliff jumping and hadn't immediately brought it to Jordy's attention. She vaguely remembered a saying about it taking a village to bring up a child – which sounded ridiculous because surely a child ought to be brought up by its parents? – and wondered whether there was some Nelson's Bar etiquette she'd transgressed.

'He says you're quite cool,' Jordy said, settling himself comfortably on the front step. 'Trouble is, the little bugger thinks he knows better than I do about university. He's got a place at Leicester but he says he's not sure he wants

115

to go. But there's not much here for kids. I want him to get to uni and meet girls. He spends a ton of time with young Rory but Rory's not the brightest button in the box. You're a smart cookie. What do you think?'

'I don't know either of you very well, so I'm not sure,' Clancy offered apologetically, gazing at the crafty-looking man who'd appeared just as she'd been failing for the hundredth time to stop thinking about Will and weddings, the do-anything-for-love thing he'd crashed into with Renée. 'Maybe Harry would rather get a job? He can always go to uni later.'

Jordy gave a short laugh. 'Then why hasn't he tried to get a job this summer instead of lazing about? His mother says maybe he needs a gap year but I think it might turn into a gap thirty years or so.' His white teeth flashed. 'You've been to university. I asked Aaron and he said you'd got a Master's degree.'

'Lots of people have,' she assured him, slightly surprised Aaron had remembered something that had been mentioned in passing when she was talking to Genevieve about insurance. 'I honestly don't know what I can tell Harry. Or you.'

'Oh.' Jordy looked disappointed. 'Only it causes a lot of acrimony between me and his mum. Won't you even talk to him?' He sounded injured.

'If he has any specific questions I can help with, of course,' she agreed. 'But isn't it up to him what he does with his life?'

'You wouldn't say that if you were footing the bill.' Jordy sighed as he got up and said his farewells, leaving Clancy bemused but relieved that the meeting was over. She might mention it to Aaron when she saw him. If she saw him. Nelson hadn't needed a dog-sitter for the past couple of weeks as the owners of the big house where Aaron and one of the Mick/Nick/Rick brothers were apparently creating a knot garden were in Nice for a month. Nelson was welcome in their absence.

She hoped Aaron wasn't avoiding her because she'd been such a wimp that she couldn't open the message from Will without someone there to hold her hand. Literally. He might be sick to death of emotional females after his break-up with Genevieve.

Clancy had moved next door to number five when Kaz from the B&B arrived. The sun had come out and she'd scraped her hair back in a butterfly clasp.

'You're here!' Kaz beamed over the fence, the apples of her cheeks rosy in the sunshine. 'I was just going to call at the Roundhouse and invite you for lunch.'

'Um, what an unexpected pleasure,' Clancy said tentatively, straightening up with a handful of bindweed. If most people invited you for lunch you could take it at face value but she'd found that when the inviter ran a commercial establishment you might find yourself paying £50 for an event put on by a business networking group.

Kaz looked taken aback at her tepid response. 'You don't have to but we thought if we gave you lunch at the Duke of Bronte we could pick your brains.'

Clancy, remembering that the Duke of Bronte was the real name of the B&B and feeling she'd sounded ungrateful said, 'Sounds lovely. When were you thinking?'

Kaz looked at her watch. 'It's quarter to twelve so if we wander up there now we'll be just right.'

Taken aback, Clancy gazed down at her jeans, a gentle shade of green at the bottom hem and brown at the knees. 'I need a shower and—'

Kaz batted that idea away with a *pshaw*. 'You always look gorgeous. Oli wants to meet you and he's got to meet the bank manager at three.' She didn't actually say, 'So look lively!' but she made little beckoning motions and began to back down the garden path.

'OK. If you don't mind.' Clancy shrugged. She couldn't imagine going to lunch in London in gardening clothes but life was pretty informal in Nelson's Bar. Also, in London, the nearest thing she had to a garden was a jardinière in the bay window of the lounge, a circle of black wrought iron supporting five pot plants. They'd found it at an antique fair during a weekend in the Cotswolds, a weekend of togetherness and laughter containing no hint that Will had once loved another woman hopelessly – more than he loved Clancy. And that one day that woman would reappear, so would the love, and Will would act on it.

She put away her gardening tools and turned her mind to enjoying the stroll up Droody Road, the tang of salt heavy on the air. Droody Road had a pavement as befitted the main road in the centre of the village and some of the larger rendered houses were painted yellow, blue or pink. A couple, quite imposing, were built of beautiful red brick, mellow in the sunlight.

Kaz chatted nineteen to the dozen about alterations they were considering to the B&B and Clancy became interested, remembering Aaron intimating that he saw the B&B as an asset to the village. When they reached the stone building they paused to admire its gables and many windows, then Kaz seated Clancy on the lawn at a table with a pretty yellow parasol, saying, 'Just popping in for sarnies and fizz.'

When she reappeared minutes later it was with a

covered platter of sandwiches and a man in tow, who was carrying a tray. 'This is Oli, my husband.' Kaz beamed, which seemed her default expression, the breeze ruffling her brown hair. 'He talked to Aaron at the village meeting and Aaron mentioned you'd worked for a rural organisation.'

Clancy waited for Oli to put down an appetising-looking bottle of Prosecco and three glasses so they could shake hands, thinking that Aaron seemed to have talked about her quite a lot at the village meeting, what with first Jordy and then Kaz approaching her for information. Probably people were curious about a newcomer to the village and some would have known Alice. She wished that she'd visited Alice when she was living happily in the village with Lee, but Alice had always wanted to come to London and as it meant a longer visit, Alice finding it easier to get away from Roundhouse Row than Clancy did from IsVid, Clancy had agreed. Lee had occasionally come for the day but would leave Alice while he returned – usually with an air of relief – to Nelson's Bar.

'So I thought perhaps we could have a chinwag,' Oli pronounced, pulling the clingfilm off the platter and helping himself to two triangular sandwiches. 'Has Kaz told you we're thinking of extending?' The fizz frothed into the glasses as he poured it, sparkling in the sunshine. 'At the village meeting Ernie said we need a bigger bar and we're wondering if we *could* extend it; whether it would be worth the capital expenditure. We've got a modest dining room and the outdoor space in summer, but if we have a bar, the locals would have somewhere to socialise all year round. We don't want to miss a trick and let a proper pub move into the village.' Oli's thin hair kept lifting in the breeze, making him stroke it carefully back into place.

Clancy nodded, enjoying cheese sandwiches with a delicious chutney and gorgeous thick-cut ham with rocket.

'So when Aaron said who you'd worked for,' Kaz pronounced excitedly, producing a pad and pen from her pocket as if about to take an order, 'we thought you might know about funding. Whether there are alternatives to the bank.' Pen poised, she waited expectantly.

Oli looked at his watch as if hinting that time was pressing. 'Or grants.'

Evidently Clancy was expected to earn her lunch. She suddenly felt a fraud. 'It was a rural charity. I didn't work for it, it was just one of my clients. I only know a little bit and in the broadest terms. I think if you go to their website they'll have lots of information about projects like village halls but the accent was on communities, the not-for-profit sector. I don't know what help, if any, there is for commercial enterprise.'

With a frown, Oli took two more sandwiches. 'But the village can't afford a village hall. If we extended our bar it could be let out sometimes and be used for meetings and that.'

'But you'd still own it. The profits would go to you.' Clancy was sorry she couldn't provide the answers Kaz and Oli had obviously hoped for. 'I don't know any charities that support rural businesses.'

Kaz and Oli looked so disappointed that Clancy felt sorry for them, though she was surprised that anyone in business could be as naive as they seemed. As if reading her thoughts, Kaz sighed. 'This is our first time working for ourselves. Oli's uncle owned the B&B and he didn't have kids of his own so he left it to Oli in his will because

120

Oli was the only one out of his brothers and sisters who stayed in Nelson's Bar.'

'Wonderful of Uncle George,' Oli put in. 'I was sick and tired of driving into King's Lynn every day to work in a ghastly admin job. My company HR department was looking for people to take redundancy so I put my hand in the air and got a lump sum, which came in handy. The B&B had gone a bit downhill under Uncle George.'

'What money's left has to be looked after,' Kaz put in anxiously.

Oli reached out and gave her a sudden hug. 'Don't look so worried. We're not losing money or anything.'

'But we aren't earning a lot either,' Kaz said mournfully. But then she sighed. 'Really? Shall we show you the bar anyway?'

More out of curiosity than because she thought it was going to affect anything, Clancy agreed, following on into the B&B through a pair of oak doors, propped open, and across a cramped flagged area to the dining room. There, the walls were painted dark green and there was room for only six tables, all set with gleaming cutlery and white paper napkins. A door gave directly into the kitchen.

'Right.' Clancy nodded, thinking the room would look more spacious with lighter walls and less fussy brocade at the windows.

'And this is the bar.' Kaz led the way into a really small room. The actual bar itself was quite nice, a polished wooden counter with barley twist spindles supporting a glass rack above and gleaming optics on the wall behind, but it took up a third of the available space. Clancy almost knocked over a bar stool as she pirouetted to observe the profusion of prints of Admiral Horatio Lord Nelson on the walls – who was better-looking in his much-decorated uniform than Clancy had ever supposed – HMS Victory and even Nelson's column.

Oli straightened one of the picture frames carefully. 'I believe Horatio Nelson's dearest aunt lived in Nelson's Bar.'

Kaz sent him an incredulous look. 'She didn't!'

He gave an impish smile. 'She will when I go to the bank, if I think it will help sell them on the idea of our extension.'

He explained to Clancy which wall they'd need to break through, then they went outside again while he paced out what he saw as the projected building line, allowing not just for a larger bar but a bit on the dining room and kitchen too.

'How are we ever going to raise that much money?' Kaz fretted.

Then Genevieve emerged from the B&B and crossed the lawn, smiling. 'Do you mind if I join the party? I saw you from my room and boy are days off boring when you're not in your own home.'

'You come and sit down,' Kaz cried, her face transforming as if at the flick of a switch. Clancy recognised the professional face being slipped into place and ached for Kaz's worries.

The conversation turned to unexceptional things for a few minutes, then Clancy made a move to go. 'I'm going to make hay while the sun shines – or lawn clippings, anyway. Thank you for the lovely lunch. Sorry I couldn't be more helpful.' She didn't want to be specific about their conversation with Genevieve listening.

Oli scuffed his feet. 'Not sure what to do about my appointment now.'

The emotional water was getting deeper all the time and Clancy didn't want to find herself out of her depth. 'Why not go? The person you see might know something worthwhile.'

Oli thanked her and Clancy turned to go.

Genevieve pushed her hair back from her face. 'Can I walk along with you, Clancy?'

'Of course,' Clancy replied. They made their farewells to Kaz and Oli, then turned into Droody Road, headed for Roundhouse Row.

Genevieve heaved a sigh. 'Seen much of Aaron?'

Clancy guarded her tongue. 'Now and then.' She wondered if Genevieve was about to announce that she was going to try and repair the rift. If Aaron became reattached she'd have to be on her guard not to cry on his shoulder again. You couldn't go holding the hand of someone else's boyfriend, no matter how rocky and emotional you were feeling.

A couple of cars trundled by, one with Oli at the wheel. He parped his hooter and waved. They waved back.

Genevieve hooked her blonde hair behind her ears. 'Aaron wasn't that upset when I ended things, so he probably was surprised but not unhappy. Then he invited me to that pizza and beer thing at his house as if I was just a friend so that's probably what he wants to be.'

She waited expectantly, so that Clancy felt she had to contribute. 'It's between you two, isn't it?' she said neutrally.

Genevieve gave a little laugh. 'I thought you'd tell me to go out into the world and do something that didn't depend upon a man. I know we've had trouble catching up with the feminist movement up here in the sticks.'

'Of course I wouldn't! It's true I don't think we *need* men to make us happy but I totally accept that a man can make us very happy indeed. Or very unhappy.' Then because Clancy was finding the conversation tricky, she told Genevieve about Will's message about his marriage to Renée, which made Genevieve gaze open-mouthed and breathe, 'The *bastard*,' several times, which made Clancy feel a bit better.

The next morning, Saturday, Clancy had to wait for the holidaymakers from number five and number six to drive off and then carry in her pail of cleaning things, throw open the windows and strip the beds. She'd been in Nelson's Bar a month now and felt in the swing of things, quite enjoying a proper changeover day. It was like a mini spring clean, as if she was clearing metaphorical cobwebs away as well as real ones. This was the first time she'd had to do changeover on two properties in a day but the bookings book told her the time was not far off when she'd have to do three.

Singing under her breath, she completed her tasks, left the little welcome packs of milk, tea, butter and a loaf of bread, went back to the Roundhouse and stuffed the first load of laundry into the washing machine, scoffed a quick sandwich for lunch then knocked on Dilys's door. 'Want to go to Hunny?'

'Do I ever!' Dilys cried happily. 'Norma's here. Lee dropped her off. Can we take her? The doc's taken her zimmer away and given her crutches instead.'

Before she'd had time to reply, Ernie shot out of his front door and hurried to the hedge. 'Are we going to Hunny?' he demanded. As he was already clutching shopping bags, Clancy grinned and said yes. If she was going to have Norma along then there would at least be safety in numbers.

'I have to be back by four,' she cautioned. 'I'm having a TV delivered.'

Ernie wanted to know about the brand and size of the TV mainly, it seemed, so he could tell her that she should have bought something different. As they bickered amiably about it, Dilys vanished into her house, appearing a few minutes later. 'Here's Norma!'

Norma leaned on her crutches and looked at Clancy as if she expected something bad of her.

Clancy said, 'Good afternoon,' ultra-politely and Norma said, 'Good afternoon,' back, then she stick-stepped to Clancy's car as if against her better judgement.

Once in the back with Dilys, Ernie riding shotgun in the front with Clancy, Norma embarked on a conversation with Dilys about something called 'buttonorama', which seemed to be making pictures out of buttons and a small amount of embroidery. Ernie confided audibly to Clancy that she wasn't to mind about Norma because she sometimes got a stick up her jacksie.

While Clancy struggled not to laugh, Norma muttered something that sounded a lot like 'old git' under her breath.

In deference to Norma's lack of mobility and Clancy's schedule, it was decided that they'd make the supermarket their only stop today. 'But let's have a bit of cake at the coffee shop before we shop,' Dilys pleaded.

It suited Clancy, who settled down to check messages and email on her phone, leaving the three older folk to chat.

She opened an email from Will with a wriggle of anxiety but discovered it was only the same message she'd received by WhatsApp two weeks before. After a little thought, she clicked reply and returned *Congratulations*. It made her feel quite in control not to make a pithy comment, although she did wonder whether Will had managed to salvage anything financially from the deposits they'd already paid, so making his impulsive wedding into an economically sound one.

She wouldn't ask.

She'd just think it.

Then her phone rang, and *Alice* flashed up on the screen. Clancy answered with a little burst of gladness in her chest. 'Hey, stranger!'

Alice gurgled with laughter, her voice warm and familiar. 'I've been trying to call but I'm always getting the "not available" message.'

'Not much of a signal at Nelson's Bar,' Clancy acknowledged. 'How's everything with you?' She got up and moved away from the others. Alice was in a chatty mood, asking about Aunt Brenda and Uncle Gerry, Clancy's mum and dad, before moving the conversation on.

'Your emails have been making me think about Nelson's Bar and Roundhouse Row quite a bit. For the last few years I've been absorbing the income stream without much emotional engagement – or not once the hoo-ha over big bro Aaron buying Lee out was over.' She laughed again. 'What a pain in the arse he was over that, obsessing over details! Anyway, I thought it might be nice to have a catch-up about what's going on.'

Clancy frowned, puzzled. 'I told you in my first email that I was living in the Roundhouse and doing the caretaker's job because my engagement's off.'

'You're living in the Roundhouse itself?' Alice asked.

'Just like the last caretaker did,' Clancy confirmed. 'Is there a problem with that?'

'Not at all,' Alice replied. 'So you and Will are definitely over?'

Clancy snorted. 'He's married Renée, so my guess is yes.'

With a horrified gasp, Alice demanded full details and it was a while before Clancy ended the call and returned to her seat and went back to checking her messages, seeing one from Tracey saying: *I understand Will's contacted you. I hope you weren't too upset. It would be lovely to hear from you.* Then a sad face emoticon shedding a tear.

Clancy felt quite touched. Was her sense of betrayal becoming blunted? It was mid-June, four whole weeks since she'd packed up her life and sought sanctuary in Nelson's Bar. It seemed longer. She had a new routine. Knew new people, although not many of them very well yet and one or two – she glanced over at where Norma was holding forth to Ernie and Dilys – weren't madly friendly.

She was enjoying the pace of her new life. The only deadlines she had to meet were created by guests moving in and out of 4, 5 and 6 Roundhouse Row.

She tried to summon up the awful sensation of let-down she'd felt that afternoon the others had confronted her in the meeting room but it wouldn't quite fly into focus. Monty had been out of order but Asila and Tracey had been on her side when he'd wanted to 'leak' the lie that it had been Clancy on the table.

Now, she thought she could remember Tracey saying, 'Clance, we're all worried about you—' Clancy had the uncomfortable feeling she'd refused to listen.

She thought about the years they'd been together. Then she began a new email to Tracey.

Hi Tracey,

Sorry to be out of contact so much. Circumstances have dictated. Thanks for trying to warn me about Will and Renée's wedding. She paused to read that phrase again. The first shock was over now. *Will did tell me himself. It knocked me for six to start off with but it's over between us and I'm enjoying my new life.* She paused, wondering whether Will would ever have agreed to live somewhere as rural as Nelson's Bar. They'd once been in a pub debate about Londonites downsizing to the country and he'd said, 'By the time I'm forty I want to move to some shire or other and raise goats.' She hadn't been able to see it, then, and she couldn't now.

Would he have been happy with no phone signal? No London salon to trim his hair every four weeks?

She returned to the email, picturing big, comfy Tracey reading it in the little flat she shared with another woman on the Finchley Road. Or maybe she was eating brunch in a pavement café somewhere. Clancy went on. *Seeing Will's wedding pic on Instagram reminded me that I left my wedding dress, veil, shoes etc. with you. I'm sorry if they've been in your way. Are you still involved with those causes auctions? Please stick the whole lot in one, if so, and let a charity benefit.* She added a kiss to her sign-off feeling somehow lighter, and better disposed towards her old life than she had for some time.

After, as she pushed her shopping trolley around the supermarket aisles, she felt her phone buzz and discovered that Tracey had replied, thrilled to hear from her and hoping they could meet up as soon as Clancy returned to London.

Tracey thought she'd be going back.

Clancy realised she wasn't thinking in those terms.

London already felt as if it belonged in her past. Nelson's Bar felt like a safe haven.

It was like a wind of change had blown over her. And she welcomed it.

Chapter Twelve

The sun's fingers reached into the Roundhouse loft to prise up Clancy's eyelids early on Sunday morning.

She clambered out of bed to yawn at the dormer window. Over the village rooftops she could see a shining blue sea. On impulse, she flung off her nightshirt and wriggled into a green swim suit, shorts and T-shirt, grabbed a towel and set off for Zig-zag Beach. To start the day with a swim felt like a lovely seaside thing to do. She might swing by the B&B after and see if Kaz and Oli would provide a sausage sandwich for breakfast.

She strode up to Marshview Road, enjoying the early sunshine, and took the footpath to the clifftops, invigorated by the briny wind whipping her hair. The first view of the sea was glorious, the sun reflected in fragments on every wave. As she headed for Zig-zag Path, two youthful and familiar figures emerged from the top. The lead figure, Harry, caught sight of Clancy, and veered towards her, Rory following in his footsteps.

'You jumping?' Harry called, eyeing the towel beneath her arm.

Rory laughed. Both boys were shivering as they jogged on the spot, water glistening off their bodies, but it didn't stop them wearing big excited grins.

Clancy glanced in the direction of The Leap, an innocuous enough dip in the clifftop from here. 'I've never jumped off anything like that height. I was just going down to the beach.'

'It's awesome, like flying.' Harry shivered. 'Just take a run and jump in.'

'I'll watch you first,' she decided, not convinced. She put down her towel and stationed herself at the cliff edge at a point where she could see both run up and leap.

'Ready?' shouted Harry. Then, side by side, the lads sprinted across the grass yelling, '*Yeahhhhhhhh!*'

They thundered to the edge of the cliff and launched, their impetus sending them on a graceful arc that ended with a near-vertical plummet, spray flying up, silver and gold, as they crashed into the waves. Clancy held her breath until they bobbed to the surface of the glittering sea, shouting out their exhilaration, and then watched them swim out of sight, their laughter carried up to her on the breeze.

Filled with the compulsion to know the same short but thrilling flight, trembling with excitement and adventure, she took off her shorts and T-shirt and stacked them with her towel while she waited for the lads to reappear.

When they did, rubbing the goose bumps from their arms as they trotted over the grass, Harry roared his approval. 'She's going to do it!' and they took up station out of the flight path but on the cliff edge to watch her safely down.

Heart bouncing around her chest and knees not quite steady, hardly believing what she was about to do, Clancy

131

paced back to where she'd seen the boys begin their run-ups.

Slowly, she turned around to regard the sea and the two expectant faces.

'One,' she counted out loud, 'Two . . .' Then, because her heart felt as if it were going to beat itself out of her body added, 'two and a half . . .'

'Just friggin' jump!' Harry bellowed.

'Three!' Clancy exploded into action, arms pumping, feet flying, ignoring any discomfort to the soles of her feet in her race towards the cliff edge as Harry and Rory shouted, 'Go-go-go-go!' The edge approached at a frightening speed and her stomach lifted as if it had already hurled itself out into thin air.

And then she heard another voice. 'NO! Clancy! *No! NO!*'

Hazily, she realised Harry and Rory, too, had begun bellowing, 'Stop! Stop!'

With a heartbeat like a clap of thunder she tried to hurl herself to one side, skidding, bruising, scraping as she concentrated on sliding sideways, not over the edge to crash on the rocks below.

She squeaked to a stinging halt with one foot over the abyss but the rest of her safely on dry land and still high up above the sea.

Then Nelson was pouncing on her like a hot, hairy waggy-tailed missile and she could hear Aaron calling, 'NO! Nelson! *No!*'

Clancy covered her mouth against an enthusiastic canine tongue, crowing for breath and getting an unnerving close-up of Nelson's permanently shut eye.

'Are you OK?' Aaron arrived, skidding, gasping for breath, falling on his knees and dragging Nelson off her.

Harry and Rory jogged up too. 'Sorry, Aaron,' Harry said guiltily. 'I didn't see Nelson running after her.'

'Holy hell. Do you have to make everybody as bonkers as you are, Harry?' Aaron crashed down onto his back on the grass beside Clancy, clutching his chest. 'First I thought Nelson was going to follow you over then I thought you were both goners. Fuck. Thanks for managing to stop.' He coughed as he tried to suck air into his lungs.

Clancy lifted her arm to examine fiery pink grazes. 'I didn't see him either. Would he really have jumped?'

Aaron nodded, dried grass in his hair. 'Probably. He jumps with me from a rock beside Zig-zag Beach, but it's only about six feet. I've no idea if he'd have survived that drop.'

'Might not,' Harry said philosophically. 'But you can hold Nelson and we'll jump in with Clancy—'

'Better idea.' Aaron rolled to his feet, brushing grass off his backside, still breathing hard. 'Nobody jumps but I'll buy you all breakfast at the B&B.'

Clancy groaned as she accepted Aaron's hand to pull her upright. 'I've kind of lost my mojo for the sea today anyway.'

'OK.' Harry and Rory fell in with the idea cheerfully, drying themselves before pulling their clothes back on – severely ripped skinny jeans and ugly T-shirts.

Kaz was able to provide four full English breakfasts and soon they were all tucking into tasty sausages and thick-cut bacon with eggs that were crispy at the edges, just as Clancy liked them. Their host didn't seem as smiley as usual and Clancy wondered whether it was anything to do with Oli's reception at the bank. Kaz didn't mention it though, and Clancy felt she couldn't ask.

Aaron was just telling her of his bravado when he'd

first jumped The Leap himself, for a dare, when she noticed his attention wander and checked behind herself to see what he was looking at.

'Cosy!' Rory whispered at the same time, which made Harry turn and look too.

Genevieve had come to sit at another table with a man. He had his back to them but Clancy wouldn't have been able to see his face anyway – he had Genevieve stuck to it.

Clancy turned quickly back, glancing at Aaron. 'Oh.' She hesitated, trying to read his expression. 'Is this painful?' she murmured.

His eyebrows were up in his hairline but he smiled. 'Just unexpected.'

Harry and Rory had wolfed their food already and were studying the throbbing graze on Clancy's elbow admiringly. 'Bet that proper burns,' said Harry. 'Thanks for brekkie, Aaron.'

'Thanks,' Rory echoed, then the two jogged off across the headland, apparently ready for the day's next adventure.

Aaron shook his head ruefully. 'Harry's crazy. Bored to tears, obviously, and ripe for any mischief.' Then he took Clancy's arm in his tanned hands, turning it gently to scrutinise the graze. 'You ought to get the grit washed out of that.'

Gingerly, she took her arm back. 'I'll go home for a shower.'

Aaron sat back with the big mug of tea that had come with breakfast. 'I'm going to Keelmarsh House along the coast later this morning. Fancy coming? I've got permission to take photos of the knot garden I've been creating for my website. You could pose as a visitor to the hall, reading in the arbour or drifting artily along the pathways.'

'That would be fun,' Clancy said, thinking of a drive along the coast road and the chance to see how the other half lived. 'At IsVid we were always acting as extras for client videos.'

Aaron began to rise. 'The tourism site rang yesterday, all enthusiastic about our rewritten blurb for the cottages. Presumably that's your doing?'

Clancy grinned. 'Evelyn left the sign-in details so I bigged up the cottages for get-away-from-it-all breaks, free from the tyranny of the mobile phone and the internet. People feel too available these days. Colleagues not being able to get them on email, text, WhatsApp or direct messaging could sound like bliss.'

'Very smart,' Aaron agreed, then went into the B&B to pay for breakfast, calling, 'Hello!' to Genevieve and the man she was now holding hands with across the table, while Clancy set off for the Roundhouse, glad for Genevieve if she'd managed to move on.

After a shower to rinse out her grazes, though they stung like crazy, she'd just enough time to dry her hair and choose a summer dress long enough to cover her grazed knee, a lacy cardigan that would hide her grazed elbow and sandals that didn't press on her grazed toes. Light make-up, and she was ready when Aaron turned up in his truck.

His gaze glowed when he looked at her and Clancy was taken by surprise by a little spurt of heat.

When Aaron saw Clancy in a pale blue denim dress embroidered with poppies and daisies he was glad he'd changed into grey cotton trousers and a white short-sleeved shirt from what he termed 'the trendy shop' he frequented in King's Lynn.

At the truck, he tried to be smooth, opening the passenger door for her, only for her to burst out laughing when Nelson jumped from the back seat into the front and Aaron had to do some undignified tugging on the big dog's collar to persuade him back into the rear. Her smile burned itself into the back of Aaron's eyes when she murmured, 'Thanks,' and swung gracefully in.

Soon they were bowling along the A149 east through Titchwell then Brancaster, chalk or flint cottages edging the road. Clancy didn't seem to mind Nelson's hot breath down her neck as they threaded their way between hedgerows and through villages of chalkstone cottages. The road was busy, as befitted a sunny Sunday as tourist season began to build, but Aaron was in no hurry. Clancy's scent kept washing over him. He loved the way women smelled with their layers of scents, from shower gel to deodorant to moisturiser to make-up, and then possibly perfume on top. Clancy's fragrance today reminded him of the wild yellow genistra that edged the drive of Keelmarsh House.

She appeared relaxed, her hands clasped lightly in her lap. 'I had a visit from your cousin Jordy,' she said, stretching her bare legs out, the angry red graze on her knee just peeping at him from under the hem.

He shifted his gaze from her legs to the road. 'What did he want?' Jordy was a bit of a lad. His relationship with his wife was up and down and if he was about to start playing the field Aaron wasn't keen on the idea of Clancy being in the field Jordy played in.

'About Harry.' She went on to outline Jordy's concerns for Harry's future.

Aaron was pleasantly surprised. 'I thought he might have seen a YouTube video of Harry and Rory "surfing" in the back of a moving truck. Not my truck!' he added hastily. 'I hope Jordy isn't trying to browbeat Harry. Harry, for all his clowning around, hasn't found a way to stand up to his dad yet. Anabelle finds it hard too.'

'Jordy is a bit . . . assertive,' Clancy owned.

At Burnham Norton, Aaron slowed to turn left onto a back road that became ever narrower, the hedges wilder, then he turned left and halted in front a set of black electronic gates. He punched in the entry number and when the gates had shuddered aside he drove on up the drive of Keelmarsh House, wild white roses punctuating the yellow genistra on either side between great rocks of red chalkstone.

Clancy clasped her hands. 'Wow. This is like a grotto. I'm expecting to see elves.'

He laughed, keeping the truck to twenty miles per hour as the notice by the gate requested. 'Keep your eyes peeled but all I've seen here are deer. One of the builders working here says there are boar in the woods.'

She gave a tiny shudder. 'They can stay there.'

It took several minutes to traverse the green mile of drive. The knot garden being not far from the front of the hall, Aaron drove right up to the house, where the drive became a perfect gravel circle.

They got out of the truck with Nelson on the lead, poop bags in the attached pouch because canine calling cards on the lawns would not go down well with the permanent garden staff. However, apart from cocking his leg up the truck wheel as soon as he jumped out, Nelson behaved impeccably, trotting majestically at Aaron's side with his ears up and his gaze roving the landscape as if he'd heard the talk of deer and boar and fancied a snack.

Clancy gazed at the imposing brown stone house, drinking in the castle-like crenellations and the green

Virginia creeper making its way around the massive bay windows.

'It's built of carrstone,' Aaron told her, following her example and gazing up. 'Our local building materials are carrstone, white and red chalk and a bit of flint. I'd suggest the owners took the creeper down if they asked me, because it can damage the masonry. But they haven't asked me.'

'Tell me the owners are successful actors or musicians who come here to create their masterpieces!' She backed up a few steps, craning to take in the turret with gothic arched windows that looked to have come straight out of a fairy tale.

He grinned. 'Sorry to disappoint. He had an advertising agency in London and she was a merchant banker when you could make real dosh at it. I think they've gone off for the summer exhausted from keeping track of all their bank accounts.'

He swung his camera over one shoulder and led her back down the drive. 'A lot of the knot garden's young because it's not easy to move mature box hedging about, so it'll look quite different in ten years,' he explained. 'For now I've made use of lavender for edging with young box behind, ready to take over, and there are a lot of aromatic plants like marjoram and thyme. The miniature roses are quite mature, so they're already making a good impression visually.'

When they reached the knot garden, Clancy halted to admire it. The paved path formed a square with a circle laid within it. At the centre stood an obelisk. Above borders of lavender, butterflies flitted and bees buzzed, Nelson snapping at any that hovered too close. 'It's gorgeous,' she said. 'Is this what you've been doing for the last couple of weeks?'

'Re-doing really,' he admitted. 'The pathways were already here but I relayed the flags on fresh sand, adding shale in various places. The four yew pillars at the corners were OK to reshape. Just about everything else had to be done from scratch.'

He left Clancy to walk the circular path and branch off to approach the tall stone shape in the centre, tall, four-sided and pointy, while he took out his camera, one of those that looked professional but was actually point-and-shoot. 'Oh,' she breathed. 'It's a monument to the family members and household staff who died in the two World Wars.'

'Pretty sobering,' he agreed, trying a few shots of bees on lavender and close-ups of the shale and gravel, their colours brought out by the sun. He was pleased with the purplish slate shale beside the flowering lavender and tiny muted green leaves of thyme. Clancy was still reading the words inscribed on the obelisk, her head tilted. Her hair was glossy and bright in the sunshine, the blue of her dress contrasting beautifully with the yellow-green yews. Nelson stood beside her, gently waving his tail if she glanced at him. Aaron fired off about five frames, glad that Nelson had his good side to the camera. He didn't think anyone would be particularly sold on the sight of his permanently closed socket.

He began working through the shots he wanted, asking Clancy to stroll along paths, looking like a heroine on a book jacket walking towards her future, or watch butterflies pensively in the sun. Nelson settled down to sunbathe. Aaron produced a book from the truck and asked her to settle in the shade of the arbour at the very back of the knot garden and pretend to read. He'd borrowed it from his mother's store of notebooks, chosen for the highly stylised illustration of flowers on the cover – all from non-existent species, in his opinion.

Clancy could have been born to the task of ornamenting garden shots, propping a hand beneath her chin thoughtfully or hooking a foot behind the opposite ankle and looking studious. He took about ten times the shots he needed just because he was enjoying looking at her through the lens. 'I think I've got enough,' he said eventually, feeling regretful.

She closed the notebook with a snap. 'You haven't taken any video.'

He shrugged. 'I wouldn't know what to do with it.'

'But video content's such a powerful tool,' she said, looking shocked. 'Let me show you.' Taking out her phone, she directed him to walk away from her, looking down and right towards the lavender and a circular bed of clipped dark red hebe. Nelson obligingly jumped up at Aaron's approach and loped to meet him, hurdling the corner of the border like a deer.

Clancy tapped at her phone, beaming. 'What a fab spontaneous clip this will make. I've got iMovie so I can do some editing, just to show you.' She dropped back onto the bench in the shady arbour and worked over the screen for a couple of minutes.

Then she handed the phone to him. 'Look. A few seconds of moody video is great for websites or blogs. Do you have a YouTube channel? You can host it on there.'

Smiling at her enthusiasm, Aaron took the phone, warm from the sunshine and her hands, and she tucked her hair behind her ears to watch him press the triangular 'play' symbol. What he saw was himself in soft-focus, walking down the path, the sunshine slanting from behind the hall, easing into slow motion just as Nelson flew into shot like a professional photo bomber, gazing up with doggy adoration when Aaron stooped to scratch him behind the ears. 'That is amazing!' he said, glancing at her with respect.

'May I see your camera?' After investigating its functions, she got him to put the sprinklers on and took slow-mo of sunshine through the spray, explaining what she was doing so he could try it himself.

'Fantastic,' he said, when he'd viewed the end result.

'I wasn't one of the creatives at IsVid but we all had to know the basics,' she answered eagerly. The smile faded. Then it reappeared with an almost visible effort and she went on to suggest they end with a couple of fanciful shots, like with her sitting on the top of one of the stone columns of the arbour.

He took the photos from below, she tucking her dress artfully around her injured knee.

'It must be time for lunch,' he said finally, reaching up to help her down from her perch. Realising his intention too late, she half-fell, and he moved swiftly to catch her.

She landed so that they were toe-to-toe, his hands just above her hips.

For several moments the world went blank, as if an electric charge had shot up his arms and stopped his brain. Clancy gazed up at him, the sunlight highlighting each individual shade of gold and green in her irises.

'You're beautiful,' he heard himself say.

She laughed, but breathlessly.

Slowly, so she had time to turn away if she wanted, he dipped his head and brushed his lips to hers, leaning in as he came back for another taste, letting his hands move around her until they came together on her back. Her lips parted slightly under his and he let the kiss deepen, feeling as if she were questing, trying it out, deciding. Then he brought the kiss to a close before she could and smiled tentatively.

Her answering smile was equally unsure . . . like: 'OK, so that came out of nowhere.'

But she didn't complain and so he kissed her again, once, twice, softly. Then Nelson rushed up, nails clicking on the shale, and reared up on his hind legs as if to join in the fun. The waft of dog-breath definitely brought proceedings to a halt. Aaron grumbled, 'How to destroy a moment, Nelson. Get down!' and Clancy giggled.

'I wish I'd brought a picnic now.' He turned towards where the truck waited, handily close to a fountain Nelson could drink from. 'Near the woods is a wildlife meadow. It's full of wildflowers.' Although, when he thought of it, also full of bees and wasps. Probably deer droppings too. 'Is there anywhere in particular you'd like to eat?'

She shrugged. 'I don't know the area. Good seaside fish and chips would be lovely.'

He laughed. 'OK, let's go to the pub in Thornham, where Nelson's welcome. We can walk on the marshes after.' He was happy to extend their time together.

Once again they drove along the A149, past the cottages, churches and garden centres, tourists enjoying the early summer sun at the outdoor cafés.

Over lunch, he told her about his childhood, days out in Wells-next-the-Sea and crabbing on the quayside. 'I don't know what the attraction was,' he added. 'We always put the crabs back in the sea before we went home.'

Clancy cut into her crispy fish batter with the side of her fork. Her nails were painted with tiny silver flecks that glinted as she moved. 'We rarely got to the British seaside. It was more scuba diving in Belize or white-water rafting on African rivers. I took a few trips to Brighton or Hastings when I stopped travelling and came to the UK to go to uni so I've ticked the really big boxes like eating seaside rock.'

'Whelks, winkles, jellied eels?' he suggested.

She wrinkled her nose. She'd put on sunglasses and he caught his own reflection whenever she turned to look his way. 'I've eaten alligator in New Orleans. Are they anything like that?'

'I haven't eaten alligator so I don't know.' He looked around at the other wooden tables filled with tourists, chatting and smiling. He loved Norfolk. He knew its beaches and cliffs, salt marshes and largely flat landscape. 'I suppose I seem a real stay-at-home to you, born and brought up in the village I still live in. Working in a thirty-mile radius.'

She gazed at him. 'There's nothing wrong with that. I've lived in some wonderful places but also some pretty manky ones. I've had more inoculations than I can count. I changed school ten times and never kept friends until I came to the UK to live. I finally made what I thought were lasting friends but now they aren't really available to me,' she added. Then stopped.

He gave her hand a comforting squeeze.

She smiled and said, 'This is lovely,' indicating her golden fish and crispy chips.

Later, they walked down the road, past the church, and he showed her the way onto the salt marshes where a sign told them they were on the Norfolk Coast Path. She gazed at the enormous blue sky laced with strings of white cloud and the grasses taller than herself that waved and wove in the breeze. He pointed out phragmites, sea asters and golden samphire, though the samphire hadn't flowered yet. 'It's all glorious,' she breathed.

'I'll show you the harbour.' He'd taken her hand again as they strolled, Nelson trotting ahead along the track. It felt comfortable and right.

'There's a harbour?' She stopped to gaze at the miles of vegetation all around, the stunted shrubs and occasional dead tree that stood like planted driftwood.

'Not a big harbour,' he admitted. It actually consisted of one old building and a lot of landing stages with a picturesque wreck on one bank. The tide was out and the sea creek was mainly mud, sandpipers wading between the boats that lay on their sides.

He'd rarely seen her so relaxed. When she'd arrived in Nelson's Bar she'd been taut and unhappy, her eyes wary and letting him know how it felt to have nowhere else to go. Now she beamed and chattered as she explored the inlets and it gave him huge pleasure to be there with her.

She hadn't mentioned their kisses in the knot garden, though she'd been thoughtful on the drive between Keelmarsh and Thornham. He'd thought she was processing her feelings and hoped she'd conclude that they were both putting the past behind them and were free to enjoy each other's kisses. Maybe more.

Disturbing his thoughts, her phone beeped.

Her eyebrows popped up as she fished in her little bag, the phone beeping a second time. 'There's a signal here in the middle of the marsh?'

'Apparently.' Aaron watched her pause when she looked at the text bubble on her lock-screen. She tapped. Stared, her smile fading. He almost felt the tension shoot into her shoulders and back as, slowly, she put the phone away again.

'Are you OK?' he asked softly.

When she'd stared into space for a few moments and

his heart had sunk for the same length of time she responded, absently, 'Fine, thanks.'

Obviously, whatever messages she'd received had not contained joyful news.

On the walk back to Thornham village Clancy knew she wasn't behaving normally. Aaron was sending her wary glances. He was the first man for several years, apart from Will, who'd kissed her. She'd kissed him back, welcoming the heat that had flooded through her, the kind that had nothing to do with the bright sunshine. It had made her feel like herself again: alive and capable of feeling desire.

But the texts she'd just received seemed to have paralysed her vocal cords. They'd been from Will. The first had said: *I'm so excited! Do the second pregnancy test tonight so I can see it turn positive for myself!!! xxxxxxxxxx* Then a row of emoticons from smiles to excitement and hearts.

Almost instantly had followed: *Shit! Clancy, I am so fucking sorry. Msg wasn't meant for you. I am so, so, so sorry you would find out like this. Renée and I are having a baby. I am so sorry.*

She felt as if he'd picked her up and hurled her against a wall. Will was going to be a dad. With Renée. Kisses and smileys for Renée; so fucking sorry for Clancy.

Said it all really.

The walk back to the pub felt as if it took hours, not thirty minutes. Finally, they reached Aaron's silver truck, standing out amongst all the cars in the car park, and got in.

Aaron said something about his niece Daisy loving the marshes. He held the ignition key as if he could start a conversation with it.

Clancy made an effort to reply, her tongue feeling as if it were some new device she had to gain control of. 'I'm

145

sure she does.' She took a breath and turned to face him. 'Sorry I went weird on you. The texts were from Will.' Her throat felt so stiff and tight she was surprised the words could find a way through. She fumbled for her phone again and pulled up the texts so he could read them for himself.

His eyebrows shot up into his hair. 'That was a shitty way for you to find out.' He put a comforting hand on her leg.

Her voice, when it emerged, was husky. 'It was unexpectedly emotional.'

Aaron gave a humourless laugh. 'Traumatic, I should think. You found out about Will's infidelity in a particularly horrible and humiliating way, he told you about his marriage in case it escaped onto Instagram, and now—'

'I doubt if any of it was deliberate,' she cut in.

He said nothing, his thumb circling on her leg.

She turned to look at him. His skin had the healthy colour of an outdoorsman, his shoulders and chest naturally sculpted and, she knew from having been pressed against them, firm. 'You think he let me find out like this *on purpose?*' Her voice squeaked on the last two words.

Aaron shrugged. 'Or he's incredibly careless.'

'Will's a nice guy.' She put her hand over his where it lay on her thigh, because Aaron was a nice guy too and she was sorry about her shocked retreat into silence. They'd been having a lovely day till then.

'Does a nice guy cheat?' he murmured, as if to himself. 'Get caught with his pants down? Mix up his ex-fiancée and new wife *in the middle of* a conversation about pregnancy?'

Clancy thought hard, watching cars pass on the road. She felt slightly sick, as if there was an oil slick in her stomach. 'That day . . . he told me the relationship with Renée was like riding on the back of an enchanted dragon,' she said. 'Out of control but loving every moment. I said could he not have hopped off the dragon ride just long enough to tell me the wedding was off? He told me I wasn't romantic. You'd think, under the circumstances, that that would be the least of my worries but I was surprisingly hurt. I'd thought our relationship enduring because it was well nurtured and mature.'

'Like a plant you give exactly the right conditions to.' Aaron wasn't smiling but neither was he looking sour. He was just looking at her.

She tilted her head. 'But plants given perfect conditions still get blight?'

'Afraid so.' He gave her hand a squeeze. 'I can see what motivated you to tie Will in a financial knot. And your friends too.' He hesitated, obviously picking his words. 'If you don't mind me asking – what happens if your old company goes bust?'

Her anxiety turned to snakes in her stomach. 'Because of the financial knot?'

He shrugged. 'For any reason. But the financial knot seems a contender.'

She was quiet for a long time then, wrestling not just with her answer but why she hadn't thought of it before, her, the so-called pragmatist. The business world was harsh and she'd left IsVid in a situation.

'Sometimes,' he said, giving her hand a pat, 'business can be emotional. Take me and my share of Roundhouse Row. It would have been a sound business decision to let the Roundhouse out and pay someone to do the part-time caretaker's job.'

He smiled and she found herself grinning unwillingly

back. 'But you only have fifty per cent of the vote as to what happens to Roundhouse Row.'

'Ah,' he replied, taking back his hand and starting up the truck. 'But I had one hundred per cent of the ability to change the locks before anyone turned up with a key. I'm glad I didn't because when the new caretaker turned up, I realised she needed someone on her side.'

Chapter Thirteen

For the rest of June, Clancy worked at settling further into the routine of Nelson's Bar.

With extra business brought in since she'd posted the new advertising copy, the holiday cottages were booked almost entirely until the end of September. Changeover day became a challenge, all three cottages needing service. If guests stayed until the last possible minute before check-out she could have as little as four hours. At least weekend or midweek bookings were fewer, which meant one changeover a week rather than two, and she continued to cut lawns and weed borders while holidaymakers were out during the week.

Guests turning up at the Roundhouse door became a frequent occurrence. Sometimes it was to report a maintenance issue but most often it was to request clean sheets when children wet the bed – in which case Clancy made sure they could work the washing machine in their cottage too.

She dog-sat Nelson a couple of times, depending on whether Aaron could take him to work. Lee, along with his daughter Daisy, called one day to see if Nelson wanted to go with them to Zig-zag Beach. Daisy, who was an absolute poppet with a melting gaze, peeped at Clancy from beneath her fringe of baby-soft curls and said, 'Please would you come too?'

At least it made Lee, who had been looking uncomfortable about knocking on the door of a place that was once his home, laugh, and say, 'Blimey, Daise, she's only just met you!'

Seeing the little girl's face fall, Clancy said, 'How about if I just come for ten minutes? Because then I'll have jobs to get back to.' It seemed to work for Daisy, who asked if she could be 'Nelson's lead person' and trotted happily at the big dog's side, her head just level with his good eye. Though Lee was careful of Daisy as they passed beneath the colourful gardens of Marshview Road, scrunching up their eyes against the sun, once they got to the footpath to the clifftops he allowed her to go a few steps ahead, though well away from the cliff edge.

Lee was a lovely dad, Clancy decided. He always had a smile for Daisy, even when she sulked because Clancy left them on the beach to go home.

In the past two weeks, Clancy had seen Aaron only when they talked about the cottages or the dog. He'd withdrawn since the day she'd received the texts about Will and Renée's baby. Oh, he'd remained perfectly pleasant and polite as he drove her home but he hadn't suggested they stay out for dinner or tried to kiss her again. Well, OK, he did give her a peck on the cheek as he left her at her door but no red-blooded woman would consider that a *kiss*.

As she'd thanked him for the lovely day and stepped into the silence of the Roundhouse, she cursed Will's text and her reaction to it. She'd been enjoying the day, feeling a little like Sleeping Beauty because when Aaron had kissed her she had certainly woken up. And then she'd retreated into herself; Aaron had backed off, and she couldn't blame him. He'd taken her out for the day and then she'd turned moody over another man. And, deep inside, she hadn't *really* needed him to point out that Will's treatment of her was going from bad to worse. It was making her question even the years they'd supposedly been happy, before Renée launched herself back into his heart. It felt uncomfortably as if he'd settled for Clancy once he'd thought the love of his life was gone.

Last Sunday, while in Hunstanton with Dilys, she'd finally replied to Will's texts.

Congratulations to you and Renée. I very much hope you're enjoying your life as much as I'm enjoying mine. She could imagine him reading that last sentence and wondering whether she was having a lovely time or a horrible one, for her to wish him the same.

Alice hadn't emailed this week so Clancy left a chatty email for whenever her parents touched civilisation again, and then she did her shopping.

In the car on the way home, after they'd found a way to cram their bags in the boot of her Beemer, Ernie, as usual converting his thoughts into words uncensored, had said, 'I like you now, Clancy,' which had made her laugh even as a tear came to her eye.

The first half of July was quiet. Aaron phoned to say he was working at a house where the owners had two labradors and every day had become a playdate for Nelson. Aunt Norma was much steadier on her crutches now and he probably wouldn't have to call on Clancy to dog-sit much in the future.

Although she'd never become sick of her own company

before, increasingly Clancy found herself wandering next door to Dilys's house with a book of cryptic crosswords. Dilys would work on one of her crafting projects and Clancy would read out a clue like, 'Five letters – fish in a corner.'

Dilys would cry, 'Angle!' triumphantly, and Clancy would write it in. Luckily, she was faster than Dilys at Sudoku or her self-respect would have been completely shot.

She still enjoyed her solitary wanders along the clifftops – spangled with daisies and dandelions now – especially when she wanted to think, which she was doing a lot. On the last Friday in July she was just wondering if she'd ever get up the courage to actually jump from The Leap when she came upon Harry and Rory sprawled on the grass. Fully dressed rather than in their swim things, they were talking, their forearms over their eyes against the sun, which was beating down gloriously.

As she drew close she heard Harry say gloomily, 'You know what my dad's like. I just don't think I can.'

Not wanting to overhear anything she wasn't meant to, she called out to them. 'Not jumping today, guys?'

They sat up abruptly, blinking as the sunlight hit their eyes. Harry shrugged. 'Don't feel like it.'

Rory didn't even smile. Till now, Clancy hadn't taken as much notice of Rory as she had of Harry, probably because most of the time Harry spoke for them both. Now she saw that Rory's eyes were pink. She wondered whether she should just walk on, but a tiny spark of doubt made her pause. What if the boys were in trouble? They didn't strike her as the kind to always make low-risk decisions.

'Mind if I join you?' she asked.

After shooting a look at Rory, Harry said, 'Sure.'

Clancy tried to start a conversation but the boys weren't chatty. Finally, prompted by Rory's woebegone expression, she felt she had to say, 'I know it's nothing to do with me, but is something wrong? I'm quite good at puzzles and I might be able to help you figure it out.'

The lads gave matching shrugs. Then Harry looked at Rory, as if for permission, and muttered, 'My dad's pressuring me about uni.'

'And you don't want to go?' Clancy asked sympathetically, wriggling into a more comfortable spot because the dry grass was prickling through her cut-offs. 'I suppose loads of teenagers go through that kind of worry.'

Harry switched his gaze to the distant horizon where sea met sky. 'Yeah, that's it. Trouble is, I'm good at everything. I got ten GCSEs all A and A-star and four A levels, three As and a B. It's like ten people all shouting different instructions at once. It's paralysing. I can't think through all the noise to pick a subject.'

Rory lifted his head. 'You *do* know what you want to do. You want to do design. Conceptualise. I could never come up with ideas out of nowhere like you do.'

Harry flicked him a frowning glance.

Staring at Harry, Rory said, 'Tell her. She's not your dad. Tell her.'

Harry sat perfectly still.

Clancy knew she was missing something vital. 'You can tell me anything you like,' she said carefully, hoping she was right.

'Rory can't go to uni, he hasn't got the UCAS points,' Harry burst out. 'And I don't want to go without Rory.'

Rory gave Clancy a sad smile. 'I'm not clever. I went to college for bricklaying but I got stuck in this cycle of resits for GCSEs in maths and English 'cos I couldn't get the grade. They give you a scribe but I just get muddled. I got some BTECs though.'

'You're *dyslexic* and you like to work with your hands,' Harry snapped. 'It's different to being not clever.'

'Right.' Clancy felt sorry for them and didn't ask Rory why he hadn't got a job yet. They'd obviously been brought up so closely in this tiny community that they were like twins, reluctant to break away and face the world each on their own. 'Most people make new friends at uni—'

'I want to live with Rory,' Harry spat, flushing furiously. 'But Dad says it's no good Rory getting a job wherever I go to uni because they can't afford me to live out. It's more expensive. I'd have to live in halls, not with him.'

Clancy shut her mouth on what she was about to say next because she suddenly had an idea of what she'd been missing.

Rory looked at Harry but it was to Clancy he spoke, defiantly. 'We're a couple.'

Aaron sat on the bench on his patio alternately gazing out to sea and rubbing teak oil into the mahogany body of the guitar across his lap. Nelson lay full-length on the paving in the hot sun and twitched in his sleep. It was Sunday afternoon and, though it was a sight Aaron had seen a thousand times, he was fascinated by the white, curvy clouds that bounced over the sky, the sun dancing on the restless sea. It was windy – what a shock – and he wore a baseball cap back to front to keep his hair from his eyes.

Clancy was coming to see him. She'd left him a message on his answering machine. He wished that expecting her didn't make him feel like his insides were fizzing. He'd stayed away from her as much as he could since he'd realised just how not over her ex she was, despite the receptive way she'd greeted his kisses. He knew a little about rebound relationships from watching Lee. They sucked. Nobody got what they needed.

Aaron wasn't going to be Clancy's rebound. He refused.

One day, Clancy would do the disappearing thing, like Alice. What was there to keep her in Nelson's Bar? After the summer, when the sea breeze became a gale and sunshine became horizontal rain, what would she do then?

Obvious answer? Leave.

Aaron hadn't always been averse to summer romances. In his late teens, tourists coming and going from Hunstanton every week or two, he'd even squeezed several romances into one summer. But now that he was thirty-six, the appeal had gone from being able to see the end of the relationship right from the beginning.

He tipped a little more teak oil onto his cloth and returned to the long, uniform strokes that produced even coverage on the wood.

Being single didn't bother him. Sexual desire could be slaked in an evening or two around the clubs of Hunstanton, King's Lynn or Norwich. It was a whole hell of a lot safer than trying to move things on with Clancy.

Clancy, who, gazing at him with bright green eyes from beneath a poker-straight chestnut fringe, had looked amazing in her summer dress, laughing in the knot garden at Keelmarsh House, fairly skipping with enthusiasm as she taught him about videos and fanciful shots.

That Clancy he'd wanted so fiercely it had been all he could do to concentrate.

But London Clancy, leaving Clancy, still-in-love-with-her-ex Clancy . . . from her he had to protect himself.

Suddenly, Nelson launched himself out of a peaceful

155

snooze and into a flurry of barking, tail lashing as he welcomed a figure rounding the corner of the building.

It was flesh-and-blood Clancy.

She paused to fuss Nelson, who obligingly stood up on his hind legs so she didn't have to bend down, and smiled tentatively at Aaron. She was wearing jeans today, with a white hoodie that made her hair look especially bright.

His heart turned over and his lips took on a will of their own and smiled back.

'Is now a good time to chat?' She hovered closer and he invited her to join him with a nod in the direction of the vacant half of the patio bench.

He kept on working on the guitar because having it across his lap provided a buffer zone so she couldn't get close enough to brush against him. 'What can I help you with?' he asked easily.

She let herself down gracefully on the bench, stowing her bag at her feet. 'Gorgeous guitar.'

'It's a Telecaster-style hollow body,' he said, although he was pretty certain she hadn't come to talk about guitars.

Her shoulders lifted and sank on a big sigh. Then she turned to look at him. No fringe today, he noted absently, because she'd clipped it back. 'I feel as if I should have sent you an agenda before this meeting, so you had the chance to object,' she began. 'One subject's a bit tricky and could also be considered not my business.'

'Sounds intriguing.' Wary over her air of tension more than her joking mention of objections, he let his hands rest loosely on the guitar body, aware of the chunky shape beneath his fingers even when they were still.

'It concerns Harry Drew.' Her eyebrows gave a little shrug.

She looked so serious that he asked, 'I feel as if this is

going to concern something more significant than one of his pranks.'

'I don't think it's a prank unless he's an amazing actor.' She frowned thoughtfully. 'I've got their permission to tell you, hoping that you might be able to help, but Harry's adamant he doesn't want his dad to know. I know it's horrible when someone tries to get you to swear secrecy before you know what's going on but if I promise he hasn't done anything wrong, will you?'

'Swear secrecy or help?' he asked, wanting to be clear before he committed.

'The former to start with but the latter would be great,' she answered frankly. Her hood blew up behind her head and she pushed it back.

He nodded. 'OK.' He couldn't somehow imagine Clancy putting him in the position unless she was pretty sure he was safe to commit.

'Well.' Clancy clasped her hands between her knees. 'Apparently Jordy isn't very understanding with anybody whose sexual orientation is other than his own.'

'Ah.' Aaron felt a clunk of misgiving in his midriff. He could only think of one way this conversation was going to go now and it would explain a lot. The exclusive friendship. The way they dropped off the radar. Their sometimes silent communication. Harry's attitude to going to uni. 'Harry and Rory?' he asked slowly.

Relief flashed across Clancy's face. 'You'd guessed?'

'Not until you mentioned sexual orientation. Jordy being a bit of a dinosaur in that direction and the way Harry and Rory are always together suddenly made a new kind of sense. Wow.' He sat silently, trying to assimilate the information and project its likely consequences.

Clancy gave him the gist of a conversation she'd had

157

with the boys and Aaron listened intently. 'If Jordy's pressuring Harry to go away to uni and live in such a way that he can't share accommodation, then I'd imagine he has suspicions,' he said at the end. 'He's trying to separate them. He probably thinks it's a phase Harry will grow out of if he suddenly has a feast of girls around him.'

Clancy looked doubtful. 'If that's how he thinks then I can see why Harry's reluctant to tell him.'

'Yeah.' Aaron reflected for a bit longer, then sighed. 'Thanks. I'll have a think about it and talk to Harry. See if we can work anything out. Poor kid. Jordy can be overbearing and rigid and nobody's ever "come out" to the village, so far as I know.'

'It would be a solution if they both got jobs and moved away together,' Clancy mused. 'But Rory's fixed on Harry going to uni and not wasting his potential. Isn't life hard?' Clancy reached out and ran her fingers over the neck of the guitar, following the curve that would spend a lot of time resting in the soft part of its eventual owner's left hand.

Aaron watched her fingertip trace its contours and an entirely inappropriate image filtered into his mind. If he wasn't careful, life wasn't going to be the only thing that was hard. He made his mind switch tracks. 'I'll talk to Harry and Rory. See if I can come up with anything to help.'

Clancy removed her hand from the guitar and became brisk. 'Another thing I wanted to talk to you about is the videos from Keelmarsh House.' She foraged in the bag she'd left at her feet and brought out a thin Mac laptop. 'I've made them into several clips. I thought that I could hook up to your Wi-Fi and share them with you.'

'That would be great.' Aaron put away the guitar and

they spent the next hour at the kitchen table looking at what she'd done, her apologising for only knowing the basics of video editing.

'It looks incredibly professional to me,' he admitted. 'Really amazing.'

'I had an idea for your website headers.' She leaned over to his laptop and pulled up his website. 'Do you know if you can have animated headers? Because, look, we could flip the clip of you walking up the path and put it together with the clip of me wandering up the same path and it would draw the eye to a central point.'

'I can't do anything clever,' he owned up. But he signed in to his admin area and soon she was engrossed in trying to bring to fruition what she'd envisaged, tutting and looking up on Google things that were like a foreign language to him. By the time she'd finished he had an eye-catching, soft-focus, slow-motion active header and she'd earned herself a big glass of wine.

'Moving on to my last reason for being here,' she said, sipping the wine and reaching once more into her bag. 'Here's the up-to-date printout of our bookings till the end of September.' She unfolded the A4 sheets, which were now covered in blocks of red, green and orange to denote that the holiday cottages were almost completely full.

He reached out and took them, brushing fingers with her, her skin warm and soft. 'This is a bumper summer. You've probably increased the income by fifty per cent from last year. Thank you very much.'

She grinned, looking pleased. 'I used my social media channels to talk about the cottages too, so that's created some interest and I got a lot of shares. I think maybe later we ought to start pushing October half-term holiday as somewhere families can get away from it all. To bring in people from the end of September till then I thought about tweaking the website copy to mention birdwatching and the salt marshes. I don't know anything about those things,' she added contemplatively. 'But I'm sure I could glean enough from Google to write the copy.'

'So you're extending the season too? You're amazing.' He smiled and for several seconds their gazes locked. Aaron experienced that thing again where he seemed to lose control of his own actions. As if an unseen force was controlling him he turned his head and touched his lips to hers. Her lips parted and he began to stroke her tongue with his, loving the sweet smoothness and the prickling of awareness, the desire that seemed to cover every inch of his skin.

Then common sense poked its scabby hand between them, reminding Aaron of everything he'd decided about leaving Clancy alone, and he ended the kiss.

He looked into her face as he drew away, reading regret in her eyes and maybe a smidgen of hurt.

Her lips parted and she said exactly what he'd been expecting, sooner or later. 'I'm going back to London tomorrow.'

Chapter Fourteen

Clancy realised she'd spoken unguardedly when Aaron's arms dropped away from her.

'Ah,' he said, unsmiling. 'Hence today's meeting. These are your handover notes.' He tapped the printout she'd brought him.

'I'm only going until Friday!' she put in quickly, her heartbeat beginning to thud heavy and deep at his froideur. 'I'll be back for changeover day on Saturday.'

'Of course.' But the warmth had gone from his eyes.

'It's time I talked to Asila, Tracey, Monty and Will.' At the same time, she didn't actually want to see Will, which was tricky.

She knew she was being cowardly but the prospect of seeing him frightened her. She'd thought of it over and over during her clifftop walks. He'd done everything he could to make her fall out of love with him and their old relationship seemed to have taken on the unreal quality of having happened to another person but . . . what if she saw him and some remnants of her old feelings came flooding back? She'd despise herself for not remembering the all-encompassing betrayal that had shrivelled her heart a few short months ago.

Her thoughts circled endlessly around the way everything had come to a head within IsVid. More than once she'd been on the verge of letting things ride for another month, or till the end of summer, or the end of the year.

But, in her heart, she knew that the funds that had arrived in her bank account over the past ten or eleven weeks tied her to the past. She needed to move into her future.

What she'd done had to be undone, but it was going to be unpleasantly like walking over a minefield – and she'd laid the mines herself.

'I'll be back on Friday,' she repeated now, perhaps to emphasise this to herself. 'Apart from anything, there's a Parish Meeting in the evening and the chair, Megan, has asked if I'll say something about broadband so it can be officially minuted.'

He nodded, closing his laptop. 'It would certainly be helpful if you could tear yourself away from the bright lights to do the rest of the summer.'

She tilted her head. His reaction wasn't what it had been in her imagination. 'What happens at the end of the summer?' She was curious about his views because she'd begun to give the occasional thought to autumn and winter herself. If she stayed in Nelson's Bar then she needed to think about the future. She was enjoying being the caretaker at Roundhouse Row for now but suspected it might not fulfil her long term.

'Autumn and winter,' he replied with a smile that didn't light his eyes. 'Autumn can be great but winter's pretty bleak in Nelson's Bar, when the headland's enveloped in mist or deluged with rain. We're having such a great summer that winter will seem all the worse in comparison.'

Clancy's mouth went dry. She rose to her feet and shoved her laptop into her bag. 'Amazing so many people live in Nelson's Bar at all,' she said softly. 'You'd think that they'd choose to live somewhere more hospitable. Why do you stay?'

A long silence. Aaron gazed out of the kitchen window with a distant stare. 'I belong here.'

She drifted towards the door, her bag hard across her chest like a shield. 'What do you think happens to people who haven't lived all of their life in one spot, who feel they don't belong anywhere? Do they just keep moving from place to place? Forever? Or do they find somewhere they like and feel wanted, and call it home?'

Clancy didn't wait to see his reaction. She gave Nelson's turned-over ears a rub and let herself out into the late afternoon that smelled of salt and the honeysuckle climbing a trellis on the cottage wall. She didn't pause to admire the sea today but continued steadily out of the garden and onto the lane where sunflowers had grown tall enough in the sunshine to gaze over garden walls.

On Monday morning Clancy packed a small case and threw it in the boot of the BMW, still determined to tie up the ends of her old life, even though she got an unpleasant twirl in the pit of her stomach whenever she thought of it. Tracey had said she could sleep in her spare room, but Clancy had opted for a hotel. It would be neutral territory, and if Tracey hadn't got rid of Clancy's wedding dress yet then it would definitely be creepy to sleep in the same room as it.

She was touched when Dilys and Ernie came out to say goodbye.

Dilys gave her a hug and a fruitcake. 'Drive safely, duck.'

Ernie stood back, looking glum. 'Can't we have a slice? Her fruitcake's delicious.'

Clancy suddenly wanted to spend another half hour in the village. 'Shall we have a cup of tea too?' She'd built in plenty of dawdling time on the journey.

The cuppa and cake seemed to cheer them all up and Clancy wrapped up the depleted cake, waved to Dilys and Ernie as they vanished back into their respective homes, and made a second attempt to leave.

This time she was delayed by the sight of a male figure loitering by her car, silhouetted by the sun. For an instant her heart tingled, but then she saw how youthful the figure was and realised it was Harry. Like looking for the other magpie, she glanced about and spotted Rory sitting on the grass verge with a couple of backpacks. He got up and dusted off his shorts when he saw Clancy, his gaze fixed on her apprehensively.

'Hi, guys!' She expected they'd come to ask whether she'd talked to Aaron for them yet and she could spare another few minutes to reassure them that she had.

Harry, hands in pockets, shuffled closer. 'Aaron said you're going to London. Will you give us a lift?'

With a sudden rush of foreboding, Clancy glanced at the backpacks again. 'I'm not coming back till Friday.'

'That's OK,' Harry shot out.

Clancy gazed at Harry and Rory. Then at the backpacks, which, now she examined them properly, looked to be bursting at the seams. 'You're not running away, are you?' she asked in rising alarm.

Across the road, Rory fidgeted, as if not completely happy with how things were going down.

Harry turned a dull red, his eyes emitting sparks. 'We're

eighteen. Adults. If we choose to go to London then it's nobody else's business.'

Slowly, Clancy nodded. 'I suppose that's true, so I'll put the question another way. Do your families know you're going?'

Impatiently, Harry turned on his heel. 'C'mon,' he said to Rory, marching over and grabbing one of the backpacks. 'We'll walk to the main road and see how far we can hitch. It's summer – we can camp out if we don't get there tonight.'

'Hang on.' Clancy tried to sound as if her heart wasn't trotting in alarm at this development. 'You talked to Aaron yesterday, did you?'

Harry gave a jerky nod.

'What did he say? Does he know that you're going to London? And whether you're coming back?' Clancy tried to imagine Aaron being told a second time that someone was going to London, and whether he'd been as icy over the boys' plans as he had with hers.

It was Rory who answered. 'He talked to us about our options. Moving away together was one of them.'

'But like this?' Clancy pressed, pushing back her hair as a car blew past them down the lane and both boys raised an acknowledging hand at the driver.

'Look, we'll be all right. We'll hitch,' Harry said, as if being seen by the driver of the car had unsettled him. 'Sorry to ask. We're not your problem.'

Rory, obviously taking his cue, slid his arms into the straps of his backpack and hefted it onto his shoulders. He looked miserable. Harry looked pugnacious.

Clancy sighed. 'Come on. At least I can get you there safely.' And she beeped open her car, watching matching smiles break over Harry and Rory's faces while she fought a hollow feeling that she'd just complicated an already complicated week.

She used the journey to chat to Harry and Rory about their – sketchy, it turned out – plans. When they stopped for a comfort break, Clancy lingered in the ladies' long enough to ring Aaron and leave messages on his answering machine and his voicemail. 'It's Clancy. Harry and Rory were going to hitch to London so I decided it would be the lesser of two evils if I took them. They're making a big deal out of being eighteen and able to go where they want but they're babies in terms of worldliness. They've got just over a hundred pounds between them, which might get them into a hostel for a night or two I suppose, but they haven't got a clue where to find one. I don't know if I've done the right thing but it's obviously safer for them to be with me than hitching. Ring me when you can, please.' She had absolutely no idea of her next step if he didn't. Or even if he did.

Next, deciding that she could stand the financial hit, she rang the hotel where she was staying in Muswell Hill to see if she could book Harry and Rory a room, only to discover that owing to extra publicity around a big event at Alexandra Palace, the hotel was now full. She was reluctant to stash two eighteen-year-olds with, she surmised, limited street smarts, in some other hotel. The only way she'd have to keep in touch with them was a cheap pay-as-you-go phone that belonged to Rory. Smart phones weren't something Nelson's Bar parents prioritised as their kids had to leave the village to use them.

Once they were again bowling along towards the M11 she said, 'Thing is, I'm supposed to be meeting someone at six.' The 'someone' was Will, as she'd decided that settling things with him was easier (slightly) than settling the business concerns and she'd feel better once it was no longer hanging over her. Then a solution to the lads' accommodation issue flashed into her mind, somewhere they'd have someone around and it wouldn't involve her shelling out hundreds of pounds.

'But on the plus side,' she went on, grinning, 'I've just thought of somewhere to get you a bed for a couple of nights.'

'Ace!' breathed Harry.

'Awesome,' crowed Rory.

When Aaron got home and saw the red eye of the answering machine winking at him from the kitchen wall he ignored it. He didn't want to talk. He'd left his mobile at home today deliberately. Fuck everybody. 'Except you,' he said to Nelson, who'd flopped on the cool tiled floor after a sniff around the garden, where the late afternoon sunlight was gilding the edges of the acer leaves. Nelson waved his tail then put his nose on his paws and closed his eyes.

Aaron was tired, hot and fed up. All day he'd laboured in the kind of intense July sunshine that exhausted you if you were one of the tourists carpeting the beaches, let alone working in its full glare. His thoughts of Clancy had created a heaviness in his chest almost as great as the York stone he was hauling about to create a rockery for a couple of early retirees who'd bought a house in Old Hunstanton. They'd gone on and on about how lovely their life was on the East Coast compared to London, and actually he hadn't wanted to think of London. He wanted to think of Clancy there even less. He'd imagined her putting on her gorgeous city-girl persona and simply returning to her old life, thinking of the village with amused disbelief that she'd ever gone there.

167

Would she email him and un-appoint herself as caretaker just as readily as she'd appointed herself? The rocks got heavier, the sun hotter. He kept visualising that moody website header she'd created for him, their two figures walking on converging paths. Maybe she should have arranged them so they walked away from each other instead.

His iciness yesterday . . . He recognised that he'd been protecting himself, but had it been worth it? Not worth it? Strong? Weak? Intelligent? The stupidest step any clumsy man had ever taken concerning a beautiful, clever, vulnerable woman?

Yeah, that, probably.

It wasn't until he'd showered and eaten dinner in front of the TV that good sense reasserted itself and he listened to his messages.

The first was from the lady he'd worked for at Titchwell saying she'd given his number to a friend who wanted her garden terracing too.

The second was from the garage, confirming arrangements for his truck's MOT.

The third began, 'It's Clancy. Harry and Rory were going to hitch to London—' He listened to the rest in growing dismay. Jeez! Why had Clancy got involved? What was Jordy going to say? Then he sighed, hearing the worry in her voice and acknowledging that the boys really had put her between a rock and a hard place. The message had been left late morning and now it was evening. He returned the call without delay.

'Hello?' She sounded out of breath, even anticipatory, as if she'd hurried to reply. A hum of conversation in the background told him she was in a public place.

'Thanks for letting me know about Harry and Rory,'

he said softly. 'I'm glad you rang.' He didn't say whether he was glad because of the boys or just glad.

'It's been a bit tricky,' she answered guardedly. 'My first reaction was that it would be wrong to take them, but then it became obvious it would be wrong not to. If they'd gone with their plan – well, Harry's plan – to hitch, who knows what could happen. I'm super-conscious their absence from home is soon going to become obvious, but what do I do? I could get Jordy's home number from you and ring, but . . .'

'Harry's trusting you and he's eighteen,' Aaron finished for her. 'It's a delicate situation. I thought the discussion last night had gone well. We talked about their relationship and all the different ways they could proceed from here. I even offered to go with Harry when he told his parents, but Harry knows very well that he couldn't rely on Jordy to react like a sensible human being instead of a homophobe.' Aaron leaned against the wall, feeling reassured to hear her voice.

'So, do you have a view?' she asked now, breaking into his musings. 'I can't just let the boys' parents start panicking because their kids haven't come home. It's already past eight so they'll be wondering.'

'True.' He thought for several moments. 'How about I talk to Harry?'

'That would be great, but he'd need to ring you back,' she said carefully.

He got that certain conversations were best not conducted in public places. 'OK. Where are they right now? No, don't tell me,' he amended quickly. 'If I don't know then I can't tell anybody. But are you with them?'

'I am at the moment and I've been able to arrange a

169

bed for them for a few nights,' she added. 'Hopefully, Harry will speak to you in a bit.' She rang off.

Aaron began clearing up after his meal. A knock fell on his back door and Nelson jumped up in a whirl of woofs and claws skittering on the floor. When Aaron swung the door open, Genevieve stood framed in the doorway. 'Oh,' he said.

She smiled. 'Am I interrupting anything?' She looked at him uncertainly as Nelson fawned around her legs.

'No,' Aaron said, wrong-footed but deciding that ex-lover etiquette suggested he should be polite. 'Want a coffee?'

Her face lit up and she came in and sat down at the kitchen table as she used to.

'How are things going with your house?' he asked as he put the kettle on to boil. 'Nearly finished?'

Genevieve nodded. 'Yes. I suppose that's why I've called to see you, really. It's probably a bit sad—'

Aaron's landline began to ring. 'Sorry, I should have said I'm expecting a call,' he said, not able to let it go to his machine when he'd only just arranged with Clancy that Harry would call.

Genevieve smiled politely and picked up her cup.

It was Clancy. 'Harry's here.'

'Put him on, please.' He waited until he heard Harry's gruff greeting. 'Hey, Harry, you OK? I hear you're with Clancy? That's good. Have you told your parents where you are?'

'Not yet,' Harry replied reluctantly.

'I feel that's a minimum requirement,' Aaron said carefully, hoping he sounded sympathetic and like a shoulder to lean on rather than a condescending adult. 'They could call the police or anything. What about Rory?' Rory lived with his mother in a small house on The Green, not far from the B&B and where all the shrubs seemed to grow in one direction because of the wind. She was about as opposite to Jordy as it was possible to be, quiet, smiling and very much live-and-let-live.

'Rory hasn't told his mum either.' Harry sounded even more reluctant.

Aaron decided it was up to him to take a stance. 'OK, here's the deal. Clancy says you can use her phone to tell your parents that you're in London. It's up to you whether you tell them why or where but if she can't ring back and tell me they at least know that you're safe, I'll go round and tell them myself. I can't leave them worrying.'

'Shit.' The line became muffled as Harry conferred with someone, probably Rory. Then he returned. 'If you talk to Dad, what are you going to tell him?'

Aaron blew out his lips as he considered. 'That you're safe and in London with somewhere to stay tonight, and same for Rory's mum. I won't say more, partly because it's your decision but mainly because I think you ought to tell him yourself.'

Silence.

Eventually Harry's voice again, ungracious and sullen. 'I'll ring him. But, Aaron, there's a gay community down here, like there is most places apart from Nelson's Bar. We could come to live in London and just never tell Dad we're gay.'

'You could try it,' Aaron agreed sombrely, his heart going out to his young relative for having to face such decisions. 'You just have to think about how your parents would feel if they found out some other way.'

'Yeah.' Harry's sigh down the line was almost loud enough to make Aaron pull the phone away from his ear. 'OK, I'll think about it. Thanks. I'll ring home now.'

It was when he finally put the phone down that Aaron remembered Genevieve's presence and tried to recall whether his side of the conversation could have revealed its sensitive nature. But when he turned around, she'd gone. Damn. He'd been rude after all. He couldn't even kid himself that he'd been focused on the wellbeing of his young relative. The fact was that when he'd heard Clancy's voice on his answering machine everything else had just fallen away, even the bad mood he'd come home in.

He couldn't help that he felt something stirring for Clancy, and that all he felt for Genevieve was guilty regret.

Still, there was the man she'd been kissing outside the B&B – over breakfast, no less! Maybe that's why she'd called tonight, to mention it, not wanting there to be any difficulty between them as they each moved on with their lives. That would be a relief.

It wasn't until he was going to bed later that he saw an envelope on the doormat at the front door with *Aaron* written on the front.

Dear Aaron, he read, when he opened the note.

Under the circumstances, we've decided not to go ahead with the work on our garden, at least for now. We're sure you'll agree that it would be awkward and hope to see our deposit returned.
  Regards,
  Doreen and Francis Trent

Beneath the sign-off were their bank account details, neatly printed. Aaron stared at the notepaper. Doreen and Francis were Genevieve's aunt and uncle, and they were cancelling work he was due to begin in a couple of weeks.

It wasn't that he was short of work at this time of year, but he felt he was being chastised – and not very fairly, considering his only crime was not being able to feel what Genevieve wanted him to feel.

Ignoring the fact that it was stated clearly in his business terms and conditions that deposits were non-returnable, he logged onto his internet banking and returned Doreen and Francis's deposit. He briefly considered typing *WTF?* or *SHE ended it!* in the reference field but decided not to further alienate anyone and simply put *As requested* instead.

Genevieve was moving on, Aaron was moving on; least said, soonest mended.

Chapter Fifteen

Clancy had been dreading the meetings and confrontations awaiting her in London but Harry and Rory's situation was proving a useful distraction.

Will's wide-eyed expression was priceless to see she had two strapping teenage lads in tow when she turned up in the evening at the pub where they'd agreed to meet. It was a quiet pub, in Chalk Farm terms, but they looked suitably impressed at being in a London bar. 'These are my friends Harry and Rory,' she said briskly. 'I'll get the drinks.' She settled the lads at a nearby table with a couple of pints of lager. Nelson's Bar not having a proper pub hadn't stopped them getting familiar with beer.

It left Clancy free to take a deep breath and turn her full attention to Will. It had been more than two months since she'd seen him, and nearly five since he'd exploded her life by being caught with Renée. Since then, through carelessness or thoughtlessness, he'd let other, lesser missiles detonate too. *Oops, my wedding's on Instagram. Oh, dear, text regarding baby sent to wrong woman . . .*

And yet there had been those sneaking worries that when she saw him again something of their old life together would spring back into focus and cause her pain.

It had come more from her brain than from her heart. *You were supposed to be in love with him. You'd decided to spend your life with him. Can it have all gone?* But then, unbidden, a picture of Aaron's dark eyes swam into her imagination, a smile lurking in their depths.

The fears for this meeting gurgled away. Will's blond hair was as neat and fashionable as always and in his work uniform of untucked shirt and black trousers he looked familiar yet undeniably different, especially as he was growing a beard that was so blond it put Clancy in mind of fuzz on a gooseberry. 'How are you?' she asked him politely rather than an acid: 'So, how's married life? Have you bought any baby clothes?' Justified in jabbing at Will she might be but it wasn't the best way to get what she wanted from him. Her stomach was harbouring the odd butterfly but she'd called this meeting so she was going to keep control of it.

'Good,' he answered, casting a glance at Harry and Rory, then flashing a smile at her. He wiped his palms down the legs of his trousers. 'Good to see you.'

After a bolstering sip of wine she plunged straight in. 'Is Renée still in a position to buy my half of the apartment?'

'That is so what I was hoping you were here to ask!' Relief swept over Will's face. For the next hour they worked on the awkward business of easing apart the joint threads of their lives. Clancy began to relax. Now she was with Will she wasn't aware of much between them but memories. What he'd done still hurt but the stark fact was that what she'd thought was a solid relationship hadn't been enough for him. More to the point, it *shouldn't* have been enough for her, just because they fit together well. Will had been right – he hadn't been the love of her life.

When Aaron finally rang, Clancy easily put her conversation on pause while she talked to him. Then, while Harry borrowed her phone and went outside to make his calls, Rory in anxious attendance, it only remained for Clancy to wind things up with Will.

'I don't think we can plan any more until we meet with the others tomorrow afternoon,' she said brightly. 'Except one small thing. As I still own half of the apartment for now, I'd like Harry and Rory to have use of the second bedroom for a few days.'

Will's eyes widened, then scrunched closed in a long-suffering expression. 'Really?'

'Really,' she said firmly.

'But why? It's weird,' he protested, and, 'it's an imposition. I'll be uncomfortable.'

'Because they need somewhere safe to stay for a few days and they're good kids,' she replied coolly. She added, 'It was weird for me to see you having sex with Renée when I hooked up for a conference call. It was an imposition that you told me about your wedding in case I saw Mel's Instagram. I was miles more than uncomfortable when you "accidentally" messaged me instead of Renée about your baby. I think you owe me.'

Will flushed so deeply scarlet that it made Clancy wonder whether Aaron could have been right and that Will could have done those things to avoid looking her in the eye and telling her. 'Just for a few days, right?' he mumbled. 'It's a good job Renée's away.'

'A few days,' she agreed, unable to care too much about

Renée's feelings. What would happen if the lads declined to return to Nelson's Bar with Clancy on Friday was a worry for another day.

She was beginning to feel exhausted by the upheavals in her life, but Harry and Rory hadn't yet returned with her phone. Clancy passed the time telling Will a little about Nelson's Bar, finding herself nostalgic for its peace and quiet.

He looked bemused. 'Sounds lovely,' he said, in a voice that suggested it sounded anything but.

Finally, the lads reappeared, Harry looking so red-faced and mutinous that Clancy's, 'Did you speak to your family OK?' was barely necessary.

Harry nodded once and moved close to Rory. 'We just said we wanted a bit of time in London, hanging out. Dad ranted. I said I thought he wanted me to see more of life and we've never been to London. He said why sneak off, if that's all it was. But we didn't sneak. We just . . . took an opportunity.'

Rory, too, was unsmiling. 'Mum's not proper pleased that I took off without telling her, either.'

Clancy made sympathetic noises, not wanting to say anything that might appear to put her on the side of the parents. The only way she could think of to deal with the situation was to maintain friendly relations with the teenagers and keep in touch over the next couple of days. On the cusp of adulthood, if they just vanished into the streets of London she could do little to stop them. However, it would cause untold upset to their families if they did, so she said brightly, 'People get upset when they're worried. They know you're safe, that's the main thing.'

Then she explained what she'd arranged with Will regarding their accommodation.

'Won't you be there?' Harry asked, looking unsure.

'Well, as Will's my ex, that would be bizarre,' she said frankly. 'I've got Rory's number and you've got mine. How about I ring you tomorrow? We can meet up for a bite to eat after my meetings. Will you be OK during the day?'

The lads shrugged and said yes so she waved them off in the company of Will, who was wearing a long-suffering expression.

At her hotel, Clancy kept telling herself Harry and Rory were adults, that she'd come to live in the UK on her own at their age and that they were not in any way her responsibility. None of these things stopped her worrying whether she should have tried to switch hotels to one where she could get two rooms, and hang the expense.

In the morning, after a fitful night's sleep, she was on the phone to Rory by nine o'clock. 'I've just realised we could meet up this morning. My meeting's this afternoon.'

'It's OK.' Rory sounded young and excited. 'Will's given us an A to Z of London 'cos my phone can't run a map app and we're nearly at the tube station. He's going to show us how the underground system works. We want to go to Covent Garden and see the buskers.'

'That sounds great,' Clancy said, relief trickling through her at this demonstration that yes, eighteen *was* adult. And, evidently, Will was earning back his nice-guy credentials.

But that left her with a long morning to while away, alternately trying to read or watch TV, changing books, flicking channels, until it was time to go.

She'd agreed that the most sensible place for the meeting was in the IsVid offices in Islington but it was freaky to arrive outside the yellow-brick building not knowing the code to get in. She'd once been so very much part of the team.

Will came down to take her in the lift to the fifth floor where he said the others were waiting. She had to physically square her shoulders before entering the conference room. There was a noticeable hesitation before she, Asila and Tracey hugged each other and it felt as if the harsh words exchanged here in May hovered above them. Monty, who'd played the biggest role in Clancy's acrimonious departure, was stiff and non-huggy. Paradoxically, his palpable unease helped settle Clancy down. As she deliberately took the seat at the head of the table as if assuming authority, she patted his arm. 'Don't worry. I want things sorted out as much as anyone.'

Monty managed a wintry smile and began passing out coffee and tea from the drinks station at the side of the room.

It proved to be a long drawn-out meeting. Negotiating Clancy's exit package and funding it were not matters of a moment and the ball was slow to get rolling as everyone waited for everyone else to air their views. It was nearly six when they broke to digest what had eventually been discussed. Clancy's mind clanged with figures, with valuations, assets and liabilities.

She hadn't had much spare capacity to worry about Harry and Rory but it was still a relief to call Rory's phone and discover they'd found their way to the Thames and followed it as far as the Houses of Parliament.

Clancy relaxed. 'If you still want a meal, we could meet up outside Westminster tube station.' She was conscious that they could drain their collective purse rapidly in London.

'Wicked,' replied Rory. 'We're up for it.'

179

An hour later, she was watching them order pie and chips in St Stephen's Tavern and thirstily draining pints of lager.

Will was OK and the apartment was great, they told her. When they'd tried to offer him money for food, he'd waved it away as 'the least of his worries'. Renée was away all week, an arrangement Clancy strongly suspected to have been put in place once she knew Clancy was going to be around. No matter how convinced you were that all was fair in love and war, facing the person whose fiancé you'd stolen was probably uncomfortable. Renée wasn't to know that any impulse Clancy had once had towards making life difficult for her appeared to have faded and died, along with her feelings for Will.

After dinner, Harry asked, awkwardly, whether Clancy was able to help them find out about jobs in London and somewhere to live. Though alarmed at this indication that she might not be able to deliver the boys back to their families at the end of the week, Clancy took out her phone and they began searching the internet for *London jobs+ accommodation*.

The boys began optimistically enough. 'Look at this,' exclaimed Harry. 'Live-in housekeeper job for a music-industry professional spending two months in France. The salary's loads! Enough for both of us, seeing as we'd get room and board. We could share the job.'

'Not sure an employer would view it quite like that,' Clancy put in cautiously.

They dismissed that obstacle but became glum about the requirements for references and experience. Still, nothing ventured, nothing gained. Harry put together what he thought was a 'killer' email applying for the job and received, within the hour, a response saying that their application would be kept on file.

'Wonder how long before we get a proper answer?' Harry asked, grinning at Rory.

Clancy felt honour-bound to point out, gently, that 'application on file' almost always meant *no*.

'Oh.' Harry looked disappointed for only a minute. 'But, look, there's this job at a London club. A turndown attendant.'

'What's that?' Rory and Clancy asked in unison. Clancy was quite glad she didn't need to drive tonight because she was already on her second glass of wine.

'Erm, sort of housekeeper,' Harry decided, reading the job description. 'Let's both apply, Rory.'

By the time they'd – optimistically in Clancy's opinion – applied for a couple of other vacancies that came with accommodation, it was dusk outside and the lads were ready to move on. Clancy offered to stick with them, thinking dubiously that perhaps she should try and find them somewhere they might meet other gay couples of their age, preferably somewhere less lively than Soho, but they were resolute in their refusals.

'We had another look at the map and we want to walk over the bridge and along the South Bank to see the London Eye,' said Harry, waving the A to Z.

Rory was a little less cavalier about jettisoning Clancy. 'Thanks loads for dinner and the beer,' he said, pulling on Harry's arm to prevent him from dashing out into the evening with a brief goodbye. 'You've been amazin', bringing us to London and setting us up at Will's apartment.'

With only a small sinking feeling of sadness at hearing the place that had been her home for three years and she still half-owned referred to as 'Will's apartment', Clancy gave them each a hug, hanging on to them just long enough to get them to agree to meet her tomorrow evening too.

Then she returned to the tube and onward to her hotel, feeling zero inclination to call up any old friends to say she was in town. Maybe she'd disconnected too thoroughly while she'd been living in a tiny Norfolk village on a headland projecting out to sea.

By ten-thirty she'd hung up the work clothes that now felt less familiar than the jeans and T-shirt she wore to change beds at Roundhouse Row. A good book kept her mind from whirring on the subjects of business and relationships, past, present and possible until, finally, she fell asleep.

Wednesday brought another trip to IsVid to regroup over the tricky task of balancing what Clancy's share of the business was worth with what IsVid could realistically afford. Tensions mounted. Monty got angry – though with whom wasn't clear – and Will was upset and monosyllabic. Asila and Tracey emerged as the negotiators most likely to steer them all to a solution everybody could live with, especially when Monty lost his head sufficiently to explode at Clancy that she was ruining everything.

In return, Clancy lost touch with her professionalism for long enough to flash back: 'What a fucking injustice! Will destroys our relationship in a particularly painful way, you guys respond by asking *me* to leave, and I'm supposed to *give* you my share of the business I slaved over?'

Monty sat back, face tight. 'Don't worry. We've all shared our views with Will about his behaviour and the situation it's landed us in.'

'But not asked him to leave?' Clancy snapped. 'Because I committed the sin of letting my emotions show?' A red-faced Will sent Clancy a hurt look but she didn't care. Anger sloshed inside her like acid. 'If you can't find the necessary dosh, would you like me to return to work at IsVid? Is that it? Who, here, can honestly say that's a tenable solution?' She glared around the table.

Silence.

Tracey, looking pale and unhappy, touched Clancy's shoulder. 'We're all under stress but we can do this. Can't we?' She raised her eyebrows reprovingly at Monty, who mumbled, 'Let's get on with it, then,' as if it hadn't been him who'd ignited the flash of fury.

In the afternoon, the company accountants arrived and, eventually, in an atmosphere of exhaustion, a figure was reached that Clancy would accept for her shares in IsVid.

Hands were shaken.

Though formalities were yet to come, Clancy had no reason to stay on the IsVid premises. Dazed, she stepped outside onto the busy pavement. London was sweltering, the buildings seeming to huddle together to trap hot, polluted air around them. She looked wistfully at young women chattering by, bare brown arms swinging as they hurried towards whatever the evening held in store.

It had been a stressful day and the thought of making her way from Islington into central London in a crowded and overheated tube train made her feel oppressed. She was relieved to ring Rory's phone and discover the teenagers were at Will's place. Well, hers and Will's place really. But not really.

She gave them directions to meet her at a brasserie in Chalk Farm Road, uncaring that it had once been a favourite place for her and Will. She was halfway down a big glass of white wine, shoes kicked off beneath the table by the time the lads arrived. She hurriedly pressed send on the email she'd been composing to Aaron. *Don't want your family to worry, so emailing to say I'm still in touch with Harry and Rory.*

It was good to think of the cooling breezes of Nelson's Bar. And to think of Aaron too.

Harry and Rory had lost yesterday's ebullience. 'Nobody's interested in seeing us about any of the jobs we've applied for,' Harry said morosely, pulling out a chair to slump on. He made air quotes with his fingers. '"The ideal candidate will have experience of the working sector." How do you get experience if you can't get a job?'

Clancy made a sympathetic face. 'That's always been tricky.' She wished she could be more help because the lads were so likeable, yet so unworldly. She'd hate them to make a decision they'd later regret. Their obvious love for each other gave her a warm feeling around her own heart.

Rory leaned an elbow on the table. 'Getting a job with somewhere to live attached isn't going to happen. Harry, it's me holding you back. I think you should go to uni in Leicester like your dad wants.'

'I suppose,' Clancy said slowly, 'that lots of people do manage long-distance relationships—'

'*No!*' Harry almost shouted the word, eyes glittering. 'We're together. End of. Maybe we can find somewhere to live first? Then getting a job might be easier.'

So Clancy, who didn't really want to see their young love tested or them pining for each other, got out her phone and Harry stabbed and swiped while Rory watched dolefully, looking close to tears. The stumbling blocks to securing accommodation quickly proved to be not only references but a deposit too. Hostels began at what seemed a reasonable £10 a night, though the lads had only £80 of their original £100 plus now, which meant four nights. Hotels and apartments might as well have been on the moon, they were so far out of reach.

Harry slapped the table in frustration. 'It can't be impossible to move to London! How did you do it, Clancy?'

Clancy felt apologetic that it had been comparatively easy. 'I had money. My parents supported me through uni and I had holiday jobs. After uni, I interned until I got a job. Later, I helped start up a business. I wish I had a magic solution for you but the truth is that London's a hard and expensive place.'

'My parents won't give me money,' Harry snapped.

Clancy searched for the right approach. 'They're prepared to support you through university. That's not cheap.'

'*Just* . . . don't.' Harry's voice quivered.

After that, the meal was a quiet one. Harry's mood was suspiciously like a sulk and Rory kept blinking back tears.

Nobody wanted dessert and Clancy was just wondering what to do or say next when Aaron's name flashed up on her phone. She answered slightly breathlessly.

His voice was warm and deep. 'How's the trip going?'

'Progressing on the IsVid front,' she reported. 'Tricky, but no bloodshed.'

'That's good. It's hot as hell building rockeries. We've had an electrical storm but it hasn't broken the heatwave.'

Harry broke in impatiently. 'Is that Aaron? Can I talk to him, please? I'll put him on speaker so you can hear,

185

Rory,' he added, blithely disregarding phone etiquette in a restaurant. As he groaned to his cousin about their lack of progress in finding a job and/or somewhere to live, Clancy paid quickly, then ushered Harry and Rory outside and to a side street without Harry pausing in pouring out his woes.

'Would you tell Dad about me and Rory, if I asked you to?' he demanded, waving at Rory to be quiet when he tried to break in.

'I *would*,' Aaron agreed, his voice hollow through the phone speaker. 'But I'm not sure it would achieve anything because you'd have to face him sometime.'

Harry's shoulders sagged. 'Right.' He exchanged a look with Rory, then said abruptly, 'Thanks, Aaron. Don't say anything to Dad. I need to think more.' He ended the call and returned the phone to Clancy.

After offering subdued thanks for the meal, the boys went off to explore London further and Clancy returned to her hotel in Muswell Hill. Tracey had extended a hesitant invitation to drop in on her and her live-in, Roisin, this evening, but Clancy had pleaded a previous engagement, thinking wistfully of the past, the laughter they'd shared over meals Asila had cooked or in King's Cross brasseries, sharing tapas. Maybe they could rediscover some form of friendship when the dust settled on business matters – but not yet. The tension over the negotiating table was too present.

What she almost did about five times was ring Aaron back. Harry had commandeered the last phone call and her nerves were dancing with the need to know whether Aaron had only rung to speak to his young cousin. Or to speak to her.

*

186

Late on Thursday afternoon, a formal offer to buy Clancy Moss's shares in the business was presented by the remaining directors of IsVid.

Clancy formally accepted, ousting herself from a company she'd helped grow from its inception. Everyone looked relieved and Clancy managed a fairly natural smile. 'I'm sure IsVid will go from strength to strength.'

Asila and Tracey hugged Clancy and even Monty patted her shoulder.

Will hung back. 'Emotional,' he said unhappily. Sweat beaded his brow and made the front of his hair frizz.

Impulsively, Clancy gave him a hug too. 'Don't be. You've got a new life and so have I. I want you to be happy.'

Will gave her a rueful smile. 'I want that for you too.'

'Definitely,' she said firmly, releasing him. 'This week has helped me realise how much I've moved on.' To a tiny village on the cliffs above the sea where nothing much happened but where she seemed to have left a piece of her heart, judging by the way she kept thinking about the Roundhouse and Dilys and Ernie.

And Aaron.

'Thanks for not being difficult about Harry and Rory in the spare room,' she carried on, picking up her bag. 'They want this evening in London but I hope they'll come back with me tomorrow.'

Will's fair brows flew up. 'What do you mean, "hope"?'

'Did I say "hope"?' she said innocently, preferring not to think too much about what would happen if the lads refused to return with her or, indeed, had already melted into the streets of London, never to return to Nelson's Bar. 'We have plans to meet at my hotel in the morning.' Mentally, she crossed her fingers.

Another round of goodbyes and she left IsVid forever. She was happy to eat alone that evening because there was nobody whose company she really desired. Nobody in London, anyway.

Chapter Sixteen

On Friday morning, Clancy stowed her luggage in her car and settled down in the hotel coffee shop to meet Harry and Rory. As she had a few minutes to spare, she ordered a tall latte and hooked her laptop up to the Wi-Fi. Overnight an email had arrived from her parents.

It began without preamble. *We've been asked to stay another six months to a year to work on other infrastructure projects but don't know what to do. As we'd had everything set up for a September flight back for your wedding we left that in place, worried about you being alone to sort out the mess that little shit dropped you into. How's that going? We can come home if you'd like it. Let us know ASAP.*

Or why don't you come out here for a while? It's such a worthwhile project. We can't picture you in Nelson's Bar for long! What on earth do you do all day?

Mum and Dad

xxxx

Though her father's name appeared at the foot of the email, Clancy detected only the maternal voice. She could picture her mother typing furiously in the office in Namibia Clancy had only seen in photos.

As Harry and Rory hadn't appeared, she sent the reply she was pretty sure they were hoping for.

There's no need to return. Now the shock's worn off I realise marrying Will would have been a mistake. She gave them the gist of the financial unknotting she'd been busy with this week. *I love Nelson's Bar,* she went on, as she sipped her latte before it cooled, *and if that changes I'll move on.* She definitely didn't feel that way yet though.

She moved on to another email and it was only when she finished working through her inbox that she glanced at the clock on her computer and realised with an unpleasant jolt that it was eleven-thirty and Harry and Rory were now an hour late. Her stomach sank as she reached for her phone to call Rory.

It went to voicemail.

Should she ring Will? She hesitated. Will would, presumably, be at work, and she found she wasn't super-keen to warn him that the lads she'd 'hoped' would be in his spare room only until this morning might have unofficially extended their visit.

Just as she was concluding unhappily that she'd have to contact Aaron to report losing his cousin and ask for advice, relief flooded through her as she caught sight of Harry and Rory ambling across the hotel foyer. Each wore rumpled clothes, dazed expressions and, Clancy was able to verify when they dropped into the seats across from hers, a strong aroma of stale alcohol. They did, however, have their backpacks.

'Sorry,' Harry said, offering Clancy a goofy smile. 'We're pissed.'

'Oh.' Clancy studied their red eyes and loose movements. 'That's quite a feat in London when you have no money.'

Harry and Rory burst out laughing, leaning against one another in their mirth. 'It's all gone,' Harry crowed.

'Fantastic,' she muttered, and bought them hot buttered toast to try and soak some of the alcohol up, and hot chocolate, as each declared a hatred of coffee, while she sipped another latte.

'So, guys, I'm heading back to Nelson's Bar now,' she said, eventually, in between the boys bursting into loud guffaws at every excuse. 'How about you?' Beneath the table, she crossed her fingers. 'Will said you could only stay till Friday, so . . . ?'

Harry's smile faded. 'Yeah. Suppose we'd better go back. But we're not sticking in Nelson's Bar for long.' He jutted out his jaw.

'OK.' Not her immediate problem. Clancy glanced at the menu for prices and dropped enough money on the table to cover the bill. 'We're a bit late, so can we get going?'

The boys clambered unsteadily to their feet and followed her out to where her bright blue BMW shone in the morning sun.

'OK,' she said calmly, when she'd set her satnav for the Roundhouse. Nelson's Bar might not be blessed with a mobile signal or broadband but it had postcodes like anywhere else. 'Do you want to tell me your plans? Only if you want to, of course.'

From the back seat, Harry gave a noisy yawn. 'Will let us use his tablet and we looked up the gay community in London online. We got this link about the Bavage Trust, which is for gay young people, and we talked to one of their youth workers, Darren. He was cool. We met him in a café. He gave us booklets.'

Rory took advantage of another of Harry's yawns to get a word in. 'He made us feel like we're not alone. He said he could even sort us out with emergency accommodation in London if we were absolutely dead set on staying. But he thought it would be better to go home to think about our next move. He said some gay teenagers have to leave home when their parents find out but because we're not in that situation—'

'Yet!' Harry chimed in.

'—we didn't have to rush into anything.'

'So we went to this gay bar, one Darren said would be OK,' Harry put in wonderingly. 'It was awesome.'

'Oh?' Clancy had to keep some of her attention on the road because of the stop-start London traffic and proliferation of roundabouts, but she could see the lads in the back seat via the rear-view mirror. Harry's head was on Rory's shoulder and his eyes were closing. 'What made it awesome?'

Harry yawned again. 'Because we could hold hands. We could be together, like we want. We got talking to these kids who were exactly like us last year – one going to uni and the other not. The one going to uni got settled in halls then just moved his boyfriend in too. Nobody *checks*. So that's what we're gonna do. I don't know what we were obsessing about. I'll go, Rory will follow, and he'll get a job in Leicester. Darren's given us the contact details of the Leicester branch of the John Bavage Trust. We're sorted.'

Clancy beamed with pleasure for them as she tried to edge onto a roundabout, looking forward to the end of the A406 so she could take the M11 north. 'Wow. That's *amazing*. I'm thrilled you had such a positive experience.' But she felt a twinge of guilt too. 'I should have thought of youth workers. I'm afraid I've been caught up in sorting myself out. Well done you.'

Silence.

She glanced into her mirror again. Both boys' eyes were closed, Harry's mouth open and Rory's cheek pressed to the top of Harry's head.

She smiled, settling down behind the wheel. In less than three hours she would be in the Roundhouse. The responsibility she'd assumed for the slightly whiffy teenagers behind her would be over. She could stop worrying if whatever she did was the right thing.

She turned up the radio as Harry began to snore and headed to a tiny village on a bar of land between Holme-next-the-Sea and Titchwell.

They were on the A10 coming up to King's Lynn before either of the recumbent teenagers stirred.

It was Harry, always the most vocal, who suddenly demanded, 'Clancy, can you stop? I need a piss so bad.'

Rory whimpered at such a rude awakening, then mumbled in a small voice, 'I might have to puke.'

'Hang on to both,' Clancy urged. 'I'll pull off.' After a couple of minutes' tense silence and fidgeting from the back seat, a lay-by hove into view and she made a dive for it, grateful that at least lads were more equipped than girls for relieving bodily fluids behind a hedge.

The lads scrambled out, slamming the car doors and wafting in heated, fume-laden air. Clancy stretched comfortably, deciding not to leave the climate-controlled comfort of her car. Noisy vehicles roared past only feet away, masking any unfortunate sound effects. Then her phone began to ring and she pressed the button on the steering wheel to reply via the car's system.

'Hi. How's everything?' Aaron's voice filled the air around her. It made the hair on her neck stand up. After a slight hesitation he added, 'Are you still coming home today?'

A smile tugged at her lips at him calling Nelson's Bar 'home'. 'We're south of King's Lynn,' she replied. 'A lot will depend on traffic from here but I should be back in plenty of time for the Parish Meeting. The boys needed a comfort stop.' She told him about the drunken state of them this morning.

'At least they're with you. That's a relief.' Again a hesitation, as if he wasn't sure how to go on.

She decided the lads were a safe topic. 'I've been wondering what'll happen when I get them back to the village— Oh, heads up, they're about to get in the car and you're on speaker.'

'Got it,' Aaron replied easily. More slamming of doors, Harry grumbling about feeling crap, Rory leaning back and closing his eyes with a groan. A laugh in his voice, Aaron came over the speaker: 'What kind of state are you two in?'

Harry sat up. 'Hey, Aaron!' Then, more quietly, 'We're hungover and we'll be home soon,' as if both were equally dreadful.

Clancy restarted the car and indicated her intention to join the traffic.

Aaron's disembodied voice continued to float around the car's interior. 'I saw your parents last night, Harry. They're obviously worried about you and mystified about why you didn't let anyone know you were going to London.'

A car coming up behind flashed its lights and, waving her thanks, Clancy was able to pull away and resume their journey.

Harry vented a long sigh. 'Suppose they have a point.' He went on to sum up everything he and Rory had told Clancy that morning, adding, 'This Darren said that it was up to me how honest I was with my parents. When he came out to his family there was a massive row and he walked out, but then his boyfriend had the opposite experience and his parents were great and still are. Rory's mum will probably be OK. It's just Dad. Darren said I might have to be pragmatic.'

Aaron didn't try to dismiss Harry's concerns. 'In what way?'

A silence. Then Harry said gruffly, 'Not come out to them. Just go to Leicester and live there as I want to. As we want to.'

Aaron's turn to sigh. 'I can see why you'd make that decision.'

Harry sounded suddenly tearful. 'I don't know how they're going to be when I get home, even without . . . telling them.'

The worry in his voice made Clancy's heart ache for him as she drove. The threshold between childhood and adulthood could be a tricky place. She wanted to say, 'But Harry and Rory aren't doing anything *wrong*! Why should he be frightened to tell Jordy?' But it was an idealistic view. If Jordy disliked everyone who wasn't 'straight' then that was what had to be dealt with. Whether his prejudice sprang from ignorance or fear or upbringing, it was there.

Aaron answered Harry. 'He'll be glad to see you but cover it up with bluster, I expect. I could go along with you if you think it would help,' he added.

Harry was suddenly resolute. 'No, thanks. I'm eighteen. If I want to go to London for a few days then I will.'

Aaron didn't comment, though Clancy wondered

whether, like her, he was thinking, 'So why didn't you tell them you were going?' Instead, Aaron said his good-byes and Harry and Rory fell quiet as Clancy drove past King's Lynn, Hunstanton and Holme. Then she took the left towards Nelson's Bar, passing through the pinewood, the car's engine note changing as they hit Long Climb. The atmosphere became taut, and not just on the part of the boys. Clancy was unsettled too; hearing Aaron's voice without, once again, really being able to have a conversation with him herself, was like an itch she couldn't reach to scratch.

That day at Keelmarsh House, she'd been totally lit up by Aaron's kisses, but when Aaron had pulled back with a vengeance at her being so palpably knocked off balance by Will's text, it had been like a shower of icy water.

What next? The Parish Meeting this evening, of course, and tomorrow racing around the three holiday homes to change the beds and clean before the new guests arrived after 3 p.m., then she might take Dilys and Ernie to the supermarket, as it seemed to have become part of their weekend routine. On Sunday she could take a walk along the cliffs or call in at the B&B for lunch.

But her mind kept flying back to Aaron's kisses amongst the soft pastel colours of the knot garden he'd created. Her heart flipped at the overheated memory of shivering with desire. But her brain glared at her heart. *'Seriously? Only months ago it was all cancelled wedding plans and pity party yet now you're feeling like this? And you have no idea how he's feeling, what he thinks, what he wants. You're reading waaaaaay too much into a kiss or two. He's just out of a relationship himself and probably enjoying being free to kiss whoever he wants.'*

One last bend, then they were on the approach to the

Roundhouse. Clancy slowed the car and pulled up outside the garden gate. Then she caught sight of a tall man with dark tousled hair sitting on the step, his back against the front door, and her heart took zero notice of her brain and leapt so hard into her throat that it almost stopped her breathing.

Switching off the ignition, she took a steadying breath. Harry cried, 'There's Aaron. C'mon Rory.' By the time Clancy had opened her door and hopped out onto the dusty lane, Harry was already talking earnestly to Aaron, Rory's gaze on Harry's face, both boys sporting their backpacks on one shoulder.

'Maybe it would be good if you'd come with me after all,' Harry was saying as Clancy hovered. 'Dad thinks I'm eight, not eighteen and will start spouting all his usual bollocks. Let's go and get it over with.' He turned to Clancy. 'Thanks loads, Clancy. You've been amazing.' He gave her a big hug.

The warmth behind the gesture easily compensated for the aroma of hungover teenager. Gladly, she hugged him back. 'I hope everything works out for you.' As they disengaged she glanced at Aaron. His gaze was on her. It seemed to ask a question but she couldn't read what it was.

Then Rory gave her a hug too, quicker and more diffident than Harry's, obliging Clancy to look away. When she looked back, Aaron's attention was on Harry again.

Before he went off with Harry and Rory, though, he gave Clancy one last quick smile. 'So I'll see you at the Parish Meeting tonight?'

'I'll be there,' she agreed. She watched the three stride towards Droody Road, Harry jabbering away to Aaron, Rory watching and listening, as usual. Just before the curve in the lane took them out of sight, Aaron glanced over his shoulder. He was too far away for her to read his expression but she flushed to have been caught watching him.

Then Dilys popped out of number two wearing jaunty flowered trousers and a beaming smile. 'Hello, dear! It's been quiet without you. The washing machine at number five broke so I let them use mine, though it beats me why people want to do laundry while they're on holiday. Aaron got the engineer here this morning so at least the new guests tomorrow will have a working washer. Fancy a cuppa?'

Instantly, Clancy felt in the swim again, welcomed by the details of village life, absorbed into the fabric of the place. 'That would be lovely. Shall we have it in the garden? It's a gorgeous afternoon.' She turned her face to the breeze and took a good lungful of the now-familiar briny air. Whatever happened or didn't happen with Aaron, for now she could relax into the feeling of being home in Nelson's Bar, enjoying the simple pleasure of a drink with a neighbour. Feeling welcome and at home.

Chapter Seventeen

As Aaron left the Roundhouse behind, glad of the shade in leafy Droody Road, he decided not to tell Harry that it was Clancy he'd been waiting to see. Harry was obviously expecting a quarrel at home and that was of more immediate importance than Aaron's eyes being continually drawn to Clancy's glossy hair and bright eyes, the way the wind blew her top against her body.

Eighteen Harry might be but Jordy . . . well, all Harry's age meant to Jordy was that it was time he went to university. Aaron would do his best to support Harry, though Jordy, a holder of strong opinions he never hesitated to share, was perfectly capable of telling Aaron to butt out.

He stopped suddenly, realising his thoughts had carried him past the junction with The Green, the enclosure of carrstone cottages arranged around a square of grass where Rory lived. The boys had paused to talk quietly. Then, patting each other's shoulders in a gesture that wasn't quite an embrace, they parted, Rory heading off past a rambling rose bush of delicate pink tumbling over a wall, abuzz with insects in the late afternoon sun. Harry wore a scowl as he caught up with Aaron. They walked on together in silence to Trader's Place.

The front garden of the Drew family home was full of fuchsias, the dainty pink and purple flowers dancing in the breeze like ballerinas while a tangle of Russian Vine rioted up one corner of the house. Harry brushed past and threw open the side door to the house, letting it bang against the wall. He might as well have bellowed, 'Warning! Teenager in a strop.'

Jordy and Anabelle hurried out of the kitchen and met him in the hallway, Jordy wearing a pugnacious expression – which matched Harry's.

Anabelle, face creased with anxiety, got to their son first. 'What made you take off without saying anything like that? I was worried to death! Are you all right?' Her words hurried over each other as she pulled him in for a big hug, having to stand on tiptoes to press a kiss to his cheek.

Harry looked abashed. 'Sorry. It was a bit spur of the moment because Clancy was going to London and we could get a free lift.'

Jordy was ready with a sharp question. 'And you and that Rory just happened to have packed backpacks with you? What have you been up to?'

'Doing some thinking.' Harry shoved his backpack off his shoulder and let it thud onto the tiled hall floor. 'Doing some sightseeing. Having a bit of fun.' He folded his arms as if putting up a barrier.

'Hello, Aaron. Shall we sit down and have a cuppa?' suggested Anabelle, sending Jordy an apprehensive look.

Jordy, ignoring her, turned to Aaron, eyebrows raised in surprise. 'What are you doing here? You haven't been to London with him, have you?'

Aaron had prepared an answer as he'd walked to Trader's Place and used it to introduce something non-contentious to the conversation. 'I was waiting to talk to Clancy when Harry arrived so I walked along with him. Mum wants to know if you'll help at Aunt Norma's birthday barbecue in August. And yes, I'd love a cuppa, Anabelle, please.'

Remaining planted in front of the kitchen door as if stating that anybody who wanted a cuppa would have to go through him, Jordy waved Aaron's words away. 'That's bloody weeks off!' He returned his attention to his son. 'Don't you get ideas about loafing around in London with that Rory. You're going to university at the end of September.'

'Yep.' Triumph filtered into Harry's voice. 'Don't sweat, Dad. There's nothing to stress you about me going to London for a few days. It's you who keeps telling me there's a lot of the world outside Nelson's Bar. Clancy got us a spare room at her ex's place—'

'Why the hell should she involve herself?' Jordy grumbled. Then his red face creased slowly into a broad grin as what he'd just heard dawned on him. 'Good news that you're settled about uni, son. You're a clever lad and could have the world at your feet in a few years. Let's hear no more nonsense about going off somewhere with that Rory. Nice enough, he is, but bloody sawdust for brains.'

Harry's face had been relaxing into a smile too but at this he snatched up his backpack and sidled past Anabelle. 'He's dyslexic, not stupid.'

Two strides and he'd reached the foot of the stairs. In seconds he'd gone, leaving only an echo of thumping footsteps and an atmosphere behind him.

Anabelle's face sagged into lines of distress as she turned to her husband. 'Why'd you have to say that?'

Jordy snapped, 'Shut up, Belly. Do something useful and get Aaron the coffee you offered him.'

Aaron hastily interposed. 'Actually, I'll get one at home. I need a bite to eat before the Parish Meeting anyway.' Aaron gave Anabelle a hug and kissed her cheek, said bye to Jordy and made his escape, relieved his input hadn't really been needed.

It was only when he was halfway up the garden path that he realised there was someone a step behind him. He turned to see Jordy following. 'What's up?' Aaron asked, waiting for him to catch up.

'I just . . .' Jordy shifted from foot to foot, his brow furrowed above his eyes. 'Just bloody Harry and Anabelle, sometimes! He's getting big for his boots and she's just cooing over him.' He shook his head as if inviting disbelief at the load he had to carry.

Aaron felt his patience snap. 'I don't know what you want, Jordy. Harry's home safely and he's agreed to go to uni. Why not relax and enjoy it? Take him and Anabelle out for fish and chips to celebrate. Stop being a dick.'

Jordy scowled, gazing outwards instead of meeting Aaron's eye. 'Do you think there's anything wrong with Harry?' he asked abruptly.

'No,' Aaron answered truthfully and impatiently. 'Do you?'

'Dunno.' Finally, Jordy smiled ruefully. 'Maybe I'm worrying about nothing. I'll just be glad when he goes to uni and meets more girls. He's stuck in this bloody backwater where there are hardly any his age.'

'He'll meet whoever he meets,' Aaron replied enigmatically. 'He's an adult now, Jord.'

'And he needs to meet girls,' Jordy repeated determinedly. But then he clapped Aaron suddenly on the shoulder and flashed a smile. 'So you think Harry's OK, do you? Maybe I will take them both out to celebrate. You're right. Cheers, cuz.'

Parish Meetings were held wherever the Chair of the Parish Meetings decided. The present chair, Megan, had very stylishly had the ground floor of her red-brick house converted to open-plan, so recent meetings had taken place there, with people on sofas, dining chairs, footstools, borrowed chairs, garden chairs and perched on bar stools in a row behind the quartz counter that demarcated the kitchen area.

However, owing to the long, sultry days they were experiencing, tonight's meeting had been moved out onto the lawn, with seats arranged in ranks. Aaron had agreed to his mum's request to call at De Silva House so they could walk down together or, in the case of Aunt Norma, wheel, Yvonne having hired her a lightweight wheelchair. Their progress out of Frenchmen's Way, passing Yvonne's rows of hollyhocks and delphiniums before the hedges and cottages of Long Lane to Droody Road was severely hampered by the number of people who stopped to ask after her ankle.

'It's not bad,' she told everyone, looping an elbow over the crutches racked up beside her in the chair. Then she'd launch into a discussion of whether she'd have to wear another cast after she'd returned to hospital for her next appointment at the fracture clinic or might get away with a boot or even a bandage. The meeting had begun by the time Aaron pushed his great-aunt up the drive of Megan's house and up the side of the building.

He parked Aunt Norma and took one of the garden chairs. He instantly identified Clancy's back view at the end of the second row. She'd changed out of the plain white T-shirt she'd been wearing when he saw her at the Roundhouse this afternoon because now thin blue straps ran over her shoulders, through loops each side of her dress, and tied together between her shoulder blades.

He was wondering how she tied the bow behind herself like that when someone passed him an A5 sheet of paper headed 'Parish Meeting 2nd August – AGENDA', which most people seemed to be using as fans or fly swatters. He saw he'd managed to miss 'minutes of the last meeting' and 'matters arising' and now they were on 'Chair's address'. Megan was currently addressing the fact that the village meeting at De Silva House on the 25th of May had no standing and only at Parish Meetings could votes be held and motions carried.

'That said,' Megan went on. 'A very interesting thing came indirectly from that meeting and that's that we have a new resident who's an expert on the internet.' She sent Clancy a bright smile, who grinned back as if amused at the description. 'So I'm going to hand over to Clancy Moss and she's going to talk to us about our options.'

Clancy rose and turned to face the meeting. She looked cool and self-possessed – or, at least, as cool as was possible on a hot, humid summer's evening – and he was reminded of her status as a businessperson. She'd probably addressed meetings and made presentations as part of her daily life.

She began, 'I don't consider myself an expert, but I'm happy to share what I know.' Her gaze snagged on his for a moment and she smiled before plunging into what sounded to him like a well-thought-out lecture on satellite broadband and bonded broadband, where several people could link their signals together for strength, delivered with casual ease. She acknowledged that as the village was in a conservation area satellite dishes could only be placed on the non-road side of houses, and that was if there was no Grade I or II listing to prohibit it, and that the village was in a worse position regarding mobile phone signals. 'Megan's asked me to make a recommendation,' she went on.

'I don't know what all the fuss is about the internet anyway,' Aunt Norma grumbled under her breath. 'We did without it for enough years.'

Aaron leaned over to reply in her ear. 'It allows me to run my business.'

Aunt Norma sent him a sidelong look and pressed her lips together.

Clancy was still speaking so Aaron switched his attention back to her. 'I suggest we research internet providers in other parts of Norfolk, and put together a letter detailing the reasons we need internet access here in Nelson's Bar, and ask for information as to why we've been left out of the party. I'm happy to help Megan with this. Likewise, the mobile phone companies. Later, if necessary, we can make noise with the press and maybe our local MP or councillor.'

Megan put up her hand. 'I was wondering if Nelson's Bar could have its own website?'

Clancy's hair swung as she nodded. 'There are plenty of free or low-cost options, especially if you have a volunteer to create and update the site. Our being an internet "not spot" doesn't mean the village doesn't exist as far as outside internet users are concerned. If Nelson's Bar wants more tourism then a website would be great.'

'We don't need tourism,' a voice said from several rows forward of Aaron's seat. 'There's enough tourists on this coast. Let's keep Nelson's Bar a peaceful place.'

Kaz jumped to her feet and turned to face the meeting, face creased with concern. Clancy stood back to give her the floor. 'Some of us need tourism for our living. I'd better take this opportunity to inform the village that we're putting in for planning permission to build an extension to the B&B. Nelson's Bar doesn't have a hall but Oli and I believe the village could do with more space for socialising. In view of what's been said this evening about tourists, this is a good time to bring this to your attention.' She shot a look in the direction of the earlier dissenting voice. 'The B&B has to bring in business or we won't survive. As well as our tourist guests, people from the village come to us for breakfast or lunch. We don't presently have the kitchen space to offer dinners but both it and our tiny bar will be significantly extended if our plans come to fruition, which would mean an extension to what we could offer all year round. We'd love you to spend your beer money with us instead of at the pubs in Thornham and Titchwell, but if a lot of you hate the idea then please do let us know before we put in a load of work and commit ourselves to the finance.'

She paused, then added in a rush, 'The alternative to the extension could easily be the B&B closing because it's getting less profitable in its current configuration. Oli and I don't want that, or to have to leave Nelson's Bar.'

She took a deep breath and twisted her hands in front of her. 'In fact . . . we wondered how open the village would be to . . . well, to fundraising, really. It could make all the difference.'

'What – like passing the hat round?' someone asked in tones of outrage. 'Why should we contribute?'

Ernie lifted his ever-ready voice. 'Yes, why should we? You'll want us to come in spending our money with you, why should we help you finance the place? We might as well have a village hall and have done.'

Kaz drooped, taking an uncertain step towards her seat.

Then, as a clamour of conversation erupted, Clancy stepped forward once more. Her voice was calm and sympathetic, yet rang with conviction. 'The thing is, Ernie, there is no village hall. There's no pub in Nelson's Bar, or even so much as a playing field. The B&B is the social hub of this village. A village hall would take not only years of fundraising, lobbying for funds and applying for grants, it would take constant financial input from the villagers to maintain it. It would have to be run by volunteers. There's no real need for any of that, if Kaz and Oli can extend the B&B to provide villagers with a bar and a function room. I think it's something we all need to be realistic about.'

Ernie didn't seem to have a reply so Clancy turned to Kaz. 'It's just occurred to me – maybe it would be worth looking at a crowdfunding campaign? You might get something, which would be better than nothing.'

Kaz looked grateful but whispered, 'I'm not really sure what that is.'

Clancy patted her arm. 'We can research it.'

They both returned to their seats and Megan closed the meeting before making a beeline for Kaz to embark on a whispered conversation.

Aaron wouldn't have minded a chat with her himself,

as the presence of the B&B enhanced Roundhouse Row for guests. Roundhouse Row had been, to him, a conflict to be conquered and a pain in the bum, but these days it was a source of regular income in the summer. Under Clancy's stewardship, bookings this year were now solid right up until October half-term.

As if she'd sensed him thinking her name, Clancy rose and turned, her gaze flying to his. With a tentative smile, she began to head his way. He edged behind Aunt Norma's wheelchair to meet her.

At the same moment, Aunt Norma scrabbled for her crutches and tried to stand, obliging Aaron to catch the wheelchair to prevent it from tipping. 'Ta,' she said briefly, then intercepted Clancy. 'This funding research, and the website. Do you get commission?'

The smile that had begun in Clancy's eyes dimmed. 'No, Mrs Farrow,' she replied stiffly. 'If you were about to volunteer in my place, I promise I won't step on your toes.'

Then Ernie was upon them. 'Now, Norma,' he boomed. 'Clancy's a good girl. You leave her alone.'

As Norma turned to answer, Clancy slipped past. Exasperated, Aaron glanced around to check his mother was nearby to manage Aunt Norma's wheelchair and crutches, trying to ignore a grumble from Aunt Norma that sounded like 'Alice could always soft-soap people too', then he headed off after Clancy.

Behind him, Ernie's volume rose. 'Your great-nephew could do a lot worse than Clancy, you know.'

Then an indignant 'What do you mean?' from Aunt Norma. 'Which great-nephew?'

Aaron put on a spurt. Aunt Norma was quite capable of hollering after him as if he were about six and he didn't want to offend her by ignoring her. He spotted Oli moving to intercept him, a frown on his forehead and lips parted on a question, but Aaron dodged with a breathless 'Let's get together to talk soon, shall we? Sorry, got to go.'

It only remained to sidestep Genevieve, with an apologetic 'Sorry! Need to talk to Clancy.' Then he was free to wind his way impatiently through those already leaving the meeting via the path at the side of Megan's house.

A quick glance left and right and he caught a glimpse of Clancy striding between the sunbeams dancing in Marshview Road in the direction of the footpath to the cliffs, chestnut hair flying.

He broke into a run and in moments was beside her, catching his breath as they marched up the path. 'I hope Aunt Norma didn't come across as too irascible.'

Clancy shrugged, not slowing her pace. 'It's OK. I'm aware she blames me for Alice being Alice. I just . . . don't want to have to wallow in it. I didn't mean to rush away from you but it's been an emotional week.'

Her troubled expression caused him rising exasperation. Their relationship forever seemed doomed to going one step forward and two back but he wasn't going to fall into the trap of letting her slip away, just because Aunt Norma hadn't been particularly friendly.

He reached for her hand. It put a hesitation in her stride as she glanced at him, brows up. 'Can we stop galloping so we can talk?' he suggested, giving her hand a squeeze. It was hot. He was hot too. They'd all baked in the past weeks of high temperatures. Even the clifftop grass beneath their feet had become beige and dusty.

Clancy managed a half-smile and slowed down. She

didn't remove her hand, which was a good sign. He managed to ease their pace to a stroll. 'The reason I was waiting on your doorstep like a parcel this afternoon was to talk to you. I'm sorry I had to let Harry take me off instead.'

'How did it go for him with Jordy?' Her brows lifted enquiringly. 'He collared me before the meeting and demanded to know what the hell I thought I was doing taking Harry off to London without telling anyone. I apologised if I'd upset him and trotted out the stuff about Harry being an adult and that travelling with me was safer than hitching. He carried on chuntering though. I seem to have a talent for upsetting your family.'

Aaron frowned. 'Sorry he had a go at you. Want me to have a word with him?' When she shrugged and brushed Jordy's complaints away, he related the scene he'd witnessed in Harry's home. 'And now we're talking about something else again!' he added feelingly. 'I really want to have a conversation about *us*.'

'Oh.' Her gaze flickered and one eyebrow lifted as if she was considering asking, 'What "us"?'

To forestall that, he plunged on. 'I overreacted when you said you were going to London. I wanted to apologise, but Harry and Rory's escapade kept getting in the way.'

Her gaze remained on him. 'Do you want to know how things went while I was away?' She said it as if it were a test but her steps were slowing all the time and she still hadn't taken her hand from within his.

The wind swirled over them, warm and humid. Lilac clouds were gathering in the sky, seeming to press the day's heat back at them. He thought about denying needing to know how things stood with Will, but . . . that wasn't the way he was, so what would be the point? Carefully, feeling his way through a conversation that all his senses

210

were telling him might be important, he said, 'I don't want you to feel interrogated but . . . yes. I would like to know how things stand.'

They'd walked far enough around the headland now to have passed the B&B and be circling back towards his side of the village, looking out over the ocean. The light was leaving the sky and the sea deepening to an oily blue-grey. Clancy drew to a halt, turning so that they were facing each other, and let out a breath. 'When you asked what would happen if the business went bust you made me think,' she admitted, with a wry smile. 'I came to the village full of anger that I'd been treated badly. I felt betrayed. It felt almost too big to cope with. I clung to my pain and saw everything through the lens of righteous outrage. I thought Nelson's Bar would be a convenient place to exist until I knew what to do next. I didn't expect to like it here. Love it, even: the cliffs, the sunsets, the quirky people. I hadn't expected to revel in the freedom from twelve-hour days, from my brain feeling as if it would burst if I forced one more piece of legislation into it, even while knowing that that was exactly what I had to do. Even so—' her voice became husky '—my feelings about Will were in chaos. The switch from him being my fiancé to being Renée's lover was too sudden and violent. I didn't want to love him any more, he didn't deserve me to – but I was scared in case somewhere inside me I did. I didn't want to feel love or loyalty to my erstwhile colleagues either.'

She turned to gaze back at the village, the huddle of cottages turning to silhouettes in the dusk. 'So, I didn't let go of my anger. I told myself it was satisfying to know I'd left those who'd hurt me in a difficult situation. Then, finally, I realised my anger was hurting myself more than it was hurting them. It was preventing me from really moving on. Even though I told myself I was starting my new life, I wasn't quite.'

Seagulls had come to wheel and call above them, the wind rising, rustling along the clifftops in the dusk. She turned back to him and smiled. 'So I've agreed that Renée can buy out my half of the apartment and that Will, Asila, Monty and Tracey can buy me out of the business. It hasn't been a particularly fun week but I feel lighter for putting down all the negative stuff. It was scary though. I was quite glad of Harry and Rory to think about at times.' Her fingers squeezed his and he found himself squeezing back.

'It was scary leaving your life behind?' He tried to put himself in her shoes and understand. Not be jealous that her old life had been exciting and vital.

She looked surprised. 'No, that was just . . . *process*. Agreements to reach.'

A feeling burst over him. Maybe it was hope. But she'd left half-answered the most important question, so far as he was concerned. 'So what about when you saw Will?'

She shook her head. 'Did I love him? No. I didn't hate him, either. I just accepted. We didn't have that flame that only burns when you're with the other person, the thing that makes them more important than anyone and anything in the world. Even though he was careful not to say too much about Renée and the baby, I think she completes him. She is his world.'

Aaron's heart felt as if it rocketed up and burst like a firework in the sky. He felt liberated. He could ask her out to dinner or for a day away from Nelson's Bar to enjoy the summer and each other's company. But his gaze fell to her lips and . . .

212

He dipped his head and kissed her. His arms slid around her body as he felt her lips part beneath his. Excitement flooded him, tingling at the base of his spine. He tilted his head to deepen the kiss, prickling with desire as her tongue stroked his and her hands grasped his T-shirt. Her hair blew against his cheek like silk as the wind buffeted them and she leaned in close enough that his arousal pulsed against her. Her hands dropped to his buttocks to pull him closer and he ran his fingers up her ribs, remembering in the nick of time before reaching her breasts that they were in a public place and any one of the residents of Nelson's Bar could be watching.

Slowly, Clancy disengaged, and Aaron came to his senses enough to realise that rain was falling in large drops, landing on the parched earth and dry grass to leave circles the size of coins.

'It's raining,' she said stupidly, holding out a hand as if her bare shoulders and arms weren't enough to feel the droplets. She glanced up at the sky that was deepening to purple. In the distance, thunder growled.

Aaron grabbed her hand. 'Let's go. My place is closest.' The rain began to fall harder, to pelt exposed skin. Thunder rumbled like Nelson growling in the back of his throat. Clancy laughed as she had to hop when she almost lost a sandal. 'The weather gods must have decided we need a cold shower.'

He laughed back, uncaring that rain was running down his face and neck, that his T-shirt was beginning to cling to his back. Droplets were running over the uppermost slopes of her breasts above the curve of her neckline, making him feel that the weather gods would have to hurl snow or hail at him to affect his level of desire. In fact, he stopped, caught her to him and kissed her again.

If it hadn't been for wanting privacy, he could have stayed there kissing her all night.

Chapter Eighteen

They arrived at his cottage as, out to sea, lightning zigzagged across the horizon. Clancy paused at the back door to watch as it illuminated a thousand white caps on waves racing before the squall. Then Aaron unlocked the door and they fell into the kitchen. 'Whoo,' Clancy gasped, laughing as she wiped rain from her face, aware of the racing beat of her heart.

Nelson flew to meet them with a wildly wagging tail, rearing up to put his paws on Aaron's shoulders. 'Hey, big stuff.' Aaron patted and petted the excited dog until he could persuade him to get down onto the four paws dogs were meant to walk on. 'Say hello to Clancy then you can go out.'

Nelson was happy to plaster his ears back and treat Clancy to a wide doggy smile, but once he'd checked out the weather through the open door he turned tail and headed for his basket.

'Wimp,' Aaron muttered. His wet hair curled into his eyes as he smiled at Clancy. 'At least it's one less of us to dry.'

Her stomach lurched. His gaze was hungry. Intense. She was aware of all of him at once, of the clean line of his jaw and the way his shoulders and chest moved beneath his clothes as he breathed; of him moving closer, damp skin sliding across damp skin as he pulled her close.

'I want to kiss you again,' he murmured. 'But I don't want to stop there.'

He didn't kiss her. His gaze just remained fixed on hers and suddenly she realised what he was asking. He wasn't going to kiss her if that's all there was to it. He wanted . . .

A blush ignited in the pit of her belly and flew up her body to her face. 'Oh!' she gasped, hyper-aware of his hands circling gently over her back as he waited. Her smile felt tremulous and almost not her own. 'I want to . . . kiss you too. And not stop.'

And then he was kissing her. No gentle kiss, as in the garden at Keelmarsh House; no questing exploration of her mouth like on the clifftop; but a demanding kiss, lips hard on hers, his tongue stroking, settling her body against his so snugly she could feel his heartbeat hammering. Or was that hers? If she'd chilled in the rain she was no longer aware of it. Heat from Aaron's body stole around her as if they were in the mid-afternoon sun. She let her palms trace his back and shoulders, the firm contours that came from physical work.

He broke off to give her a long, searching look. 'You know what I'm asking?'

She joked, shakily, 'Is this like data protection legislation – I can't get into your bedroom without a double opt-in?'

His eyes brimmed with laughter. 'You've already ticked all my boxes.'

She cocked her head to one side. 'And met all your terms and conditions?'

'Tick.' He dropped a kiss on her wet hair and began to lead her upstairs. The room he took her to proved not to be his bedroom, but the bathroom. The laughter in his eyes subsided. 'Let's get you out of those wet clothes,' he suggested huskily. First he pulled a thick blue towel from the airing cupboard and gently rubbed her hair, then stroked the softness of the towel over her forehead, her cheeks and chin, pausing to kiss each eyelid. Slowly, he reached behind her and tugged at the tie of her dress, smiling in satisfaction when the bow unfastened. 'I sat behind you at the meeting wanting to do that.'

He unhooked her straps from her shoulders, pausing at every patch of newly bared skin to pass the softness of the towel over it, pushing the dress down over her hips, making her shiver as it dropped around her ankles.

'You're still wet,' she pointed out breathlessly as he flicked her bra undone.

He lowered his mouth to her breasts while he continued to run the towel over her back. 'Ladies first,' he whispered, engrossed in playing with her nipple with his tongue.

Though she dropped her head back at the sensation of his boiling mouth on her cold, wet skin, she demurred. '*Equality Act 2010.*' And began to pull his cold, damp T-shirt over his head.

Taking the towel, she rose on tiptoes to dry his hair, bringing her breasts against his chest, making him say, 'Hmm-*mm*,' deep in his throat and hold her there, while, mirroring his actions of a moment before, she dried the planes of his face, his neck and his shoulders. She slowed her movements across his chest, enjoying both his firm body and his sharp intake of breath.

After drying his arms she nestled ever closer to pass the towel behind him and smooth the moisture from his back.

'That's amazing,' he groaned, swaying slightly so her breasts moved against him.

As she let her fingers drift onto the button of his waistband he began to stroke her bottom through her underwear.

She began to struggle for cohesion, finding herself unequal to unfastening his shorts while she was being caressed so languidly, her breath catching in her throat as her fingers fumbled.

'Let me.' With a rapid change of pace Aaron got himself out of his shorts and boxers, dried himself with a few lightning strokes, whipped off her panties, dried her legs and muttered, 'Anything else can stay wet!' making her snort with laughter as he put both arms around her and walked her backwards out of the room and across the landing.

Thunder growled outside and from downstairs Nelson gave a grumbling bark in reply. 'Good boy, Nelson, quiet down,' Aaron breathed, nibbling the side of Clancy's neck.

Feeling the backs of her legs collide with the bed, Clancy glanced behind her. 'My hair's still wet . . .'

'It's sexy.' He ran his fingers through the damp tresses. 'I like the wild look. You're gorgeous.'

With a squeak of pleasure she allowed herself to be lowered to the cool sheets of his bed, exploring his chest with her lips and tongue while her hands slid down to knead his finely haired buttocks, liking the way it made him groan as his erection pulsed against her. She slid her hand between their bodies to stroke him, making him jump.

His gaze moved between her face and her hand moving on him, teasing him with her fingertips. Then he pulled her further up his body so he could once again bring his mouth to her breasts.

Outside, the thunder crashed as if the storm was angry at sweeping in from the sea and finding this spit of land in its way, as Aaron stroked and explored her, making her melt with every touch of his hands, his body, his mouth.

They hadn't pulled the curtains and flashes of lightning punctuated the thunder. When he finally sank into her she cried out, pulling him harder and harder against her until she convulsed in a burst of joy and pleasure that made the storm outside seem like nothing.

Clancy woke in the morning to the agreeable sensation of a hot body spooned around hers and a hand stroking the curve of her hip. She relaxed with a contented sigh. She could get used to the delicious spread of tingling desire being stoked deep in her belly.

The hand trailed delicately towards her breasts and a deep voice murmured in her ear, 'It's Saturday and I'm taking the day off to—'

Clancy jumped fully awake. '*Saturday?* Crap, it's change-over day! I have to get going.' Lifting the hand from her body and giving it a quick, apologetic kiss, she rolled from the bed and began hunting for yesterday's clothes. She found them, damp and chilly, in various places on the floor.

'Yuck,' she said, wrinkling her nose at the crumpled and clammy dress. 'I'm not doing the walk of shame in that. But I don't suppose anything you've got will fit me.' She glanced at the bed and found herself being regarded balefully. 'Oh, um, sorry to run out on you,' she said belatedly.

He sighed. 'I can't summon up arguments against you doing your day's work, in the circumstances, but let's at least stick your clothes in the tumble dryer while we eat breakfast.'

219

Clancy opened her mouth to protest that there was no time for breakfast on a Saturday but then the sight of Aaron rising naked from beneath the sheets grabbed her attention. He smiled when he saw the direction of her gaze, dropped a kiss on her hair, groped her bottom, took yesterday's damp clothes from her and led her down to the kitchen. Once he'd let Nelson out into the garden to dissuade him from his usual welcome dance, bearing in mind his claws and their nakedness, Aaron set the clothes whirling in the dryer.

It turned out that there wasn't time for breakfast after all. At least, not if they were to share a most enjoyable thirty minutes on the kitchen table. It was Clancy who eventually groaned groggily and said, 'The dryer's stopped. I really have to go or we'll have holidaymakers turning up with no one to give them the key and the cottages uncleaned and beds unchanged.'

'Suppose so.' Wearing a smile and a satisfied expression he helped her slide to her feet. 'I'll take Nelson for his run then come down and help.'

'What, aren't you one of my bosses?' she reminded him, pulling her dress, still warm from the dryer, over her head. It felt a bit too warm for comfort but it was a big improvement on wearing what had looked and felt like a damp paper bag.

He slid his arms around her, which didn't make her feel any less overheated. 'Ulterior motive. I'm hoping to spend time with you later.'

It sounded like a statement but she knew it was a question. She melted a little inside at evidence of this slight vulnerability. They'd spent the night giving and receiving pleasure, but he was still wary of taking too much for granted. She kissed her way up the strong cords of his neck, feeling the scrape of his morning stubble against her lips. 'I would love that.'

'If the sea settles down after the storm I'll show you Secret Beach. It's not high tide until about six.' He moved her hair aside to kiss her neck.

'It's a date. But now I have to go—'

'—because it's changeover day,' he finished for her with a grin. 'I get it.'

The storm had freshened the morning, washing away the dust they'd lived with for the weeks of the heatwave. Clouds of palest grey scurried across the sky as if trying to catch up with their big brothers who had stormed through during the night. Clancy sped down Long Lane towards the Roundhouse, enjoying the edge to the breeze and the scent of the nettles that grew at the base of the hedges. The world felt washed and fresh. It suited her mood, the feeling of beginning a new chapter.

Last night had been . . . She shivered with pleasure as she let herself into the Roundhouse, stooping to pick up the keys on her doormat that indicated the erstwhile occupants of numbers five and four Roundhouse Row had vacated already. Skipping across the flagstones to the central staircase she ran up for a two-minute shower then jumped into shorts and a T-shirt. Getting caught in the rain and an energetic night of sex had given her haystack hair. She twisted it up behind her head, grabbed the cottage keys and her cleaning things and began, belatedly, on changeover day, humming beneath her breath as she worked.

The beds in number four and number five were soon stripped and the first load of laundry chugging around in the Roundhouse's washing machine. The guests from number six had left too with a lot of door slamming and arguing about how best to pack the car. Clancy was madly polishing and vacuuming when she heard a bark that she thought might be Nelson. Peeping through the bedroom window of number four she was able to see that Aaron had paused to chat to Ernie over the front hedge, backing away with that half-smile half-frown people wore when they wanted to end a conversation.

He glanced up at that moment and, catching Clancy's eye, waved. 'Be up in a minute,' he called, his voice squashed small by the glass between them. She waved back and danced back to her cleaning, her heart light and skippy.

In minutes Aaron was running up the stairs to join her, Nelson galumphing happily at his side. Clancy was working near the window and Aaron drew her away so he could kiss her out of the view of anyone who might be passing by outside. 'This changeover day is a total pain in the arse,' he grumbled, rubbing suggestively against her. 'But if cleaning cottages is the only way to spend the day with you then I'll have to put up with it. Give me a job quick before I throw you on that bed and ravish you.'

She laughed up at him. He smelled of shower gel or shaving foam and his hair looked as if he'd let the wind dry it. He felt big and firm and delicious. 'You will not! I've only just changed the sheets.'

Nelson rose on his hind legs, turning his head to regard them out of his eye as if to join in the hug, so they broke apart, Clancy telling Nelson he was sweet and Aaron telling him that he was an interfering bloody hound.

They broke for lunch in the kitchen of the Roundhouse, sharing a few bawdy jokes about missing breakfast, then hurried on with cleaning the final cottage, number six. The sun had reappeared, the newly washed village rooftops almost steaming in its heat, and they worked with all the windows open, finishing just in time for this week's guests to arrive. Aaron stood back, holding on to Nelson's collar as families tumbled out of cars to claim keys, children high-pitched with excitement, demanding to know where they were going to sleep and whether they were allowed to pat the big doggie, attention Nelson bore with a happy wink of his good eye.

'I'm exhausted,' Clancy declared, when she'd shut the Roundhouse door on the last guest.

Aaron cocked an eyebrow. 'Bed?'

She cocked an eyebrow back. 'Would I get any sleep?'

'Not at first,' he admitted, running a hand up over her stomach and onward to her breast.

'Later then. I'm all hot and sweaty after rushing through the changeover and I believe you promised me Secret Beach.'

Aaron's eyes smiled. 'That was foolish of me.'

They took Nelson home, as it wasn't reasonable to expect him to swim around to Secret Beach, then strolled towards the cliff path, fingers linked, swimwear beneath their clothes.

Clancy felt drunk with happiness, happier than she ever remembered being before. 'I feel almost like jumping The Leap,' she declared as they walked past the last of the buildings and a few people gathered in the afternoon sun on the lawn of the B&B.

'Let's do it,' Aaron suggested. 'It's the fastest way to Secret Beach anyway.'

Her heart bounced. 'Really?' She remembered the last time she'd begun the jump, before Aaron and Nelson had got in her way, the anticipated exhilaration after watching Harry and Rory fly off the cliff. And Aaron had done it before. The sea had forgotten its irritability of last night and serene blue waves were flirting with the sunlight. 'Then let's do it.'

They stripped off their shorts and T-shirts and piled them at the foot of a tree. They picked their way to the cliff edge to check the area below was clear. Clancy shivered with a mixture of nerves and excitement as they backed up, the dry grass scratching their bare feet.

'Sure?' Aaron's dark eyes studied her as he took her hand firmly in his.

Clancy's heart began to gallop, making her feel queasy. 'Sure,' she confirmed bravely, gazing out at the glittering sea.

'Then . . . threeeee . . . twooooo . . . one . . .'

'GO!' she burst out, unable to bear the anticipation. And they began to race for the cliff edge. Clancy thought about closing her eyes but then they were airborne and she was screaming with delight as the wind rushed past them, a cacophony of gulls flapping and shrieking from hitherto unseen perches. Flailing, flying, falling . . . then the water rushed up and . . .

Bam!

Clancy hit the surface like a slap. It would have taken her breath away if she hadn't already been holding it, the sting of impact, the freezing cold that made her recoil as they plunged, down, down, much further down than she'd anticipated, her vision a blur of bubbly turquoise blue. Aaron's fingers had been wrenched from hers as they'd hit and she struck out for the surface, her lungs beginning to burn.

Then she popped up with a rush, dragging in her first breath with a 'WHOO!' The whole experience could only have taken seconds but time had seemed to slow to allow her to savour every sensation, every instant, every inch. Her nose and eyes smarted from the salt water but she'd never felt so alive, gasping and laughing as Aaron bobbed beside her, his skin gleaming wet.

He reminded her of some beautiful selkie-like creature with his hair sleek against his head but not wanting to look an idiot by telling him so, she exclaimed, 'What a rush!'

'Want to climb up and do it again?' His arms sculled beneath the choppy surface to negate the sea's inclination to push him onto the rocks. 'Or go straight to Secret Beach?'

'Beach!' she decided promptly, the climb not appealing to limbs growing quickly weary of sculling to keep clear of the base of the cliff after a day's work and a night's fun.

He led the way around the rocks, putting himself between her and them. It seemed for a minute as if they were making no headway and the waves were much livelier when you were in them than they looked from above, but then a current swung them around a rock and they were delivered into the calmer water of a cove.

'Whoa. This is gorgeous!' Clancy trod water while she took it in. The cliffs overhung, dark red-brown at the bottom and rising in stripes of white and lighter red, protecting a tiny triangular beach of silver-beige sand and a scattering of rocks as if someone had rolled them there like dice. There were only twenty metres to swim before Clancy's feet found the sandy sea bottom and she could wade to dry land with water streaming off her, Aaron once more taking her hand as they waded onto the beach.

Awestruck by the natural, cathedral-like beauty around her, Clancy breathed, 'It's like being cut off from the world.'

'It used to be,' a voice remarked drily.

Clancy whipped around to find Harry and Rory sprawled on the sand in the lee of a couple of rocks, gazing up at them with exasperation.

Clancy giggled. 'Oops,' she said. 'Did we barge in? We could leave . . .'

Harry treated her to a huge grin, saying, generously, 'We don't mind sharing if you don't do anything we shouldn't see.'

'What, with all this sand about?' Aaron joked, dropping to the beach alongside the lads. 'How are things?'

Brows clunking down over his eyes, Harry shrugged. 'Dad's bringing university and girls into every conversation. He's said everything but "I know how to set you straight".' He shared a glance with Rory. 'He's being fake and it makes me feel fake. I'll be glad to get away now.'

Aaron made an 'awkward' face. 'It's a tough time. You know I'll support you whatever you decide to say or not say to Jordy.'

'*Not* say,' Harry said feelingly, taking Rory's hand. 'We just want to get out and be ourselves.'

The conversation turned to lighter things, to Secret Beach, jumping The Leap and the village in general. When the conversation moved on to villagers she knew vaguely or not at all, Clancy rolled onto her back, an arm across her eyes. It was so peaceful here, letting the sun dry her on Secret Beach where Harry and Rory felt safe enough for the very minor public display of affection that was the holding of hands. Without opening her eyes, she took Aaron's hand too. His fingers tightened over hers for an instant's silent communication.

The waves hissed rhythmically onto the beach and the gulls sounded far away, high on the wind. Clancy thought about last night in Aaron's bed. And today, working through the chores together, smoothing fresh-smelling sheets and clearing away the combination of dust, crumbs and sand left by every batch of holidaymakers. Being with Aaron gave her a feeling of contentment she never remembered feeling with Will.

Aaron was so much his own man, creating gardens and guitars, things of beauty, with the skill in his hands.

Her life with Will had been so bound up in IsVid, in the industry and intensity she'd come to think of as normal for achievers, the work/life balance tipped firmly in favour of 'work' by long hours and the importance of success.

Here . . . here in Nelson's Bar her existence was different. Just as yesterday evening she and Aaron had run to the sanctuary of his house from the pelting rain, thunder and lightning crashing and flashing, she'd run to the village to shelter from a life-storm.

In the coming months, she thought drowsily, there would be a lot of money coming her way as Renée bought her out of the apartment and the others bought her out of the company. For the first time she let herself really think that Nelson's Bar could provide her forever home. She could buy herself a house, get herself a stake in it.

Her parents had derived huge satisfaction in playing their part in building things that not only changed the landscape of the countries they visited but also left the region enriched by their efforts. Schools. Assembly halls. Transport hubs. Perhaps Clancy was only just discovering a similar trait in herself.

She just wanted to build a place for herself in Nelson's Bar, she thought dreamily . . .

*

Aaron lay on the warm sand and watched Clancy as she slept, her chest rising and falling as she breathed. The black and gold fabric of her swimming costume clung to her like a second skin. It was pretty, but he definitely preferred her first skin, the soft silkiness he'd become intimately acquainted with last night.

He'd have to wake her or the rising tide would splash the soles of her feet and do it for him. Harry and Rory had already slipped off quietly into the surf to swim back to Zig-zag Beach and trek up to the clifftop. The last slope of Secret Beach was shallow and covered rapidly, so it was better to go now than be there to battle the first waves that would hit the cliffs behind them and bounce back to create inhospitable white water. He used to throw himself around in it when he was Harry's age but it didn't hold much appeal now.

He reached out and traced the shape of Clancy's breasts through her costume, watching her nipples peak in response. 'Time to wake up,' he murmured.

Her eyes fluttered open. She stretched and smiled. 'That's your normal waking-people-up technique, is it?'

He dipped his fingers into her cleavage to enjoy the satin of her skin. 'I have a repertoire,' he boasted.

She laughed, fishing his fingers from her swimwear and sitting up. Her expression altered as she took in how little of the beach was left. 'Wow! The tide's in.'

'Time to go,' he agreed. The waves were breaking almost at their feet now.

She groaned, but rolled to her feet and waded reluctantly into the water with a loud 'Brr!' The sun had moved on, making the sea feel a damn sight colder than when they'd arrived. They countered the chill with energetic strokes as they set off to rejoin the rest of the world.

Clancy dragged her feet all the way up Zig-zag Path, yawning. They arranged that she'd call at Aaron's when she'd showered and properly woken up and he'd take Nelson for another run, meantime. He kissed her goodbye when they'd retrieved their clothes and dressed, then watched her traipse past the lawn of the B&B, its brightly coloured parasols snapping in the breeze, to the wide mouth of Droody Road. He turned towards the declining sun and Potato Hall Row bathed in the light from another pink sky.

But once he reached his cottage his feet, as if he'd already arranged things with them, carried him further through the shadows gathering in Long Lane, up to Frenchmen's Way and De Silva House. When he turned up the drive he paused and looked at the red brick, admiring the building's stately lines, so tall and dignified compared to his squat flint cottage. He wasn't sure what he was going to say, but he knew he had to say something. He found his family sitting down to dinner.

Daisy shouted in joy to see him. 'Uncle Aaron! I've been to the beach and on the funfair. I've had candyfloss—' she sent a sidelong glance at her grandmother '—but I'm still going to eat all my dinner.'

Aaron grinned and scooped her up for a hug. 'And did Daddy go on the waltzer?'

Lee sent him a rueful look. It was well known in the family that the more violent fair rides sent him green.

'No.' She pouted, picking up her fork and stabbing a piece of lettuce. 'I'm not big enough yet to go on that and he didn't want to go without me.'

'Nice of him,' Aaron said gravely. As the others ate, he made himself a cup of coffee and chatted with his parents about the car they were thinking of buying, his brother about business, his niece about funfairs and his great-aunt about the likelihood of her emerging from the next fracture clinic without a plaster on her ankle.

When the meal was over he said, casually, 'I've come to give you a bit of news.'

All adult eyes swivelled his way, though Daisy, evidently unimpressed, asked if she was allowed to watch CBeebies. 'Just till it's time for your bath,' Lee agreed.

Aaron drained his coffee cup and looked around the faces turned towards him, the faces of those he loved. 'I'm seeing Clancy,' he said baldly. He watched them closely.

Fergus looked mildly surprised and glanced at Yvonne for her reaction.

Both Yvonne and Norma frowned. 'But she's Awful Alice's cousin,' Aunt Norma pointed out.

'Clancy isn't Alice,' he pointed out gently. 'Alice is long gone. Clancy is here and Clancy is Clancy. So that doesn't matter, does it?'

'That Ernie Romain said there was something between you two and I told him to shut up,' Aunt Norma replied, with an air of Aaron having let the side down.

Aaron waited for his mother's reaction. 'Oh,' Yvonne said quietly. 'You've taken me by surprise.' She looked from Lee to Aaron and back again. 'What do you think, Lee?'

'What am I supposed to think? It doesn't bother me, if that's what you mean,' Lee remarked, though in the voice of one who wasn't sure he was being listened to.

Aaron clapped him gratefully on the shoulder and Lee returned the salute as he got up and wandered off after Daisy.

As soon as he was out of earshot, Yvonne lowered her voice. 'I'm really not sure about this, Aaron, not sure at all. Aren't things going to be awkward?'

Aaron sent his mum a level look. 'Lee seems OK with it, and he chats with Clancy when he meets her. Why don't you try to get to know her a little more? She's a great person and it's not fair to be down on her because of Alice. I think Clancy has tried to be polite whenever you've met so I suppose all it takes is for you to do the same and there will be no awkwardness at all. Will there?' He stooped down and kissed her soft cheek. 'You wouldn't want to be difficult, would you?'

Yvonne sighed, then managed a smile. 'Message received and understood, Aaron. If she's all right with you then that's all the rest of us need to know, isn't it?' She hugged him in the tightly squeezy way that told him she felt he was being exasperating but she supposed she'd have to put up with it.

After clapping his father on the shoulder and kissing Aunt Norma's cheek, he popped his head into the lounge to say goodbye to Lee and Daisy. 'Are we cool?' he asked Lee softly.

''Course.' Lee even summoned up a smile.

Daisy was too caught up with what she was watching to take her eyes from the TV screen as she said, 'Bye! Will you bring Nelson next time?'

'Would you tear yourself away from the telly if I did?' he joked.

He was rewarded by a beaming smile as she pointed at the TV. 'If it's not *In the Night Garden*.'

He set off back to his place with a spring in his stride. He'd sorted things out with Clancy; he'd sorted things out with his family – even if he was well aware that his mother and aunt would take a while to come around. They each shared the trait of staking claims on what they saw as the moral high ground and then taking a while to be convinced if that ground shifted. He knew their attitude had sprung from a wish to protect Lee.

He arrived home and let Nelson leap up and paw the air while Aaron grabbed the lead to take him for a run along the clifftops. Maybe tomorrow Clancy would be free and they could take Nelson for a long walk along Brancaster Beach and find somewhere good to eat.

When a knock fell on his back door, he pulled it open, a smile of greeting at the ready. Then he saw it was Genevieve who stood there rather than Clancy making an early appearance as he'd hoped. 'Oh! Hello, Gen.'

Though she greeted Nelson who, showing no understanding of human dynamics, hurled himself at her with his dance of love, Genevieve smiled thinly at Aaron, holding out a key. 'I thought it would be a good idea to return this.'

Awkwardly, Aaron relieved her of it. 'Thanks. Come on in and I'll get yours.' He didn't lie and say he hadn't thought about returning each other's keys.

She only came in as far as the doormat and didn't close the door while Aaron accomplished the fiddly task of removing her key from his keyring. 'How are you?' he asked as the silence became uncomfortable while he wrestled with the recalcitrant spring with his non-existent nails.

'Disappointed, I suppose,' she replied flatly.

Having no real idea how to answer, when he'd finally wrangled the key off the ring he passed it to her. Did ex etiquette indicate that he should offer her coffee when it really wasn't convenient? He resisted flashing a glance at his watch. Clancy could arrive at any time.

Genevieve said, 'Thanks,' as she looked down at her key. She turned as if to leave. An instant's hesitation, then she turned back. 'I know it was me who broke us up,' she blurted, her eyes large and damp. 'But I regretted it. To be honest, when you didn't ask for an exchange of keys I started to hope that you thought we'd get back together again. Then you rushed out of the Parish Meeting after Clancy yesterday evening and I did something stupid. I followed. It gave me a ringside seat when you two got in a clinch.'

'Ah.' Aaron cast around for the right response. 'I'm sorry if that upset you but—'

'I know!' She held up her hand to pause his flow. 'I *was* the one to end things. But I was hasty. I was under stress with the subsidence at The Mimosas and disappointed you didn't share my view of our future. I regretted it the second you left but . . .' She shrugged one shoulder. 'I understand that you've moved on. I can't pretend that you doing it so rapidly and with someone in the village is comfortable.' She shrugged again. 'And I feel short-changed by Clancy because she'd been quite friendly towards me, but I'll just have to get on with it, won't I?'

Aaron frowned, his good mood soured by Genevieve's evident unhappiness. 'I'm sorry if you're upset.' Something about her air of being hard done by didn't sit well with him though. 'I'm just trying to understand why you're so . . . *disappointed* that I'm seeing someone else when you are too. The guy you were having breakfast with at the B&B, a breakfast that involved a lot of kisses.'

She gave a half-laugh. 'I was being pathetic and trying to make you jealous. He was just some tourist I met in Hunny. He went home after a few days.'

'I see.' He wanted to say, 'So you ended our relationship in a snit, you sucked the face off a tourist at the B&B in a half-arsed plan to make me jealous, and somehow this gives you the right to get all tragic about me seeing someone else?' But he crammed a lid on it. What Genevieve felt, she felt, whether the logic appealed to him or not. He couldn't change her feelings but he could try and draw things to a close gracefully.

'We had a great year,' he said gently. 'Let's part as friends. We've all got to live in Nelson's Bar, after all.'

With a sudden snap to her movements, she lifted her chin. 'Have we?' Then she managed a small smile before she turned away, leaving Aaron reflecting on the fact that telling himself he'd done nothing to feel guilty about didn't stop him feeling guilty.

When you made someone unhappy, you felt bad.

Chapter Nineteen

A lukewarm shower rid her of the last of her drowsiness and Clancy thought tingly, anticipatory thoughts about the evening to come as she dried her hair, bending over to blow air on the roots.

She chose a summer dress from her wardrobe, a 'go-anywhere' number of dusky purple spangled with white shooting stars that would work whether they stayed in or went out . . . and wouldn't crumple if cast off onto the bedroom floor. A few minutes with eyeliner and mascara and she was ready.

It was as she clattered down from her loft bedroom that she heard voices floating up the stairs. She paused in surprise as the sound of muffled laughter floated after it. Was it coming from inside the Roundhouse?

Could Aaron have brought someone round? Or had she forgotten to lock the door and one of the cottage guests thought it was OK to just wander in? Putting on a spurt, she ran down the rest of the flight and then the next, jumping down into the open-plan ground floor and putting on the brakes abruptly to see the front door open and luggage piled on the flagstones.

Then a woman dragged a man in through the front door, saying exasperatedly, 'Behave yourself, Hugo! I'll have you know that this is a respectable village.' The sides of her head were shaved and the remaining chestnut hair hung in several plaits right down to her waist. She wore only a bra with a pair of shorts that were more hole than denim and tattoos of fairies and elves danced up her arms and across her shoulders. 'Clancy, you're here!' the woman exclaimed, espying her and throwing her arms wide.

It took the cogs in Clancy's brain several seconds to mesh. 'Alice?' she enquired uncertainly. The last Alice she'd seen had been significantly more sophisticated and conventional. Tailored, even. '*Alice!*' Clancy shook her head in disbelief not just that Alice had appeared before her so suddenly that there ought to have been an accompanying puff of smoke but that she looked as if she'd dressed from Camden Market and wore *tattoos*.

Alice laughed, making the large tunnel earring in her left lobe shake along with the flesh pushed up by her purple velvet bra. 'Yes, it's me. Surprise! It's so fantastic to see you!' She enveloped Clancy in a big cousinly hug.

Now the first instant of shock was over, Clancy was able to hug her back, a flame of pleasure igniting inside her despite her shock. 'Wow, it's so great to see you!'

'I know!' Alice beamed. 'And this is my husband, Hugo.'

Clancy could hardly believe her ears. 'Husband? You're *married*? Why didn't you tell me?'

Alice squealed with laughter. 'Because I knew I was coming home and wanted it to be a surprise!'

Stunned, Clancy disengaged from Alice to let her hand be shaken by the burly man who was apparently her cousin-in-law. He wore a black muscle vest along with studded combats and his dark beard went down so far that it met his chest hair coming up. A row of rings glinted in his eyebrow.

'Correct,' he said with a small smile. 'She's Mrs Hugo Suffolk now. We've come to see whether she's still allowed into Norfolk.' He laughed at his own joke, which had been delivered in precise Queen's English. He sounded like *Made in Chelsea* but looked like he'd been living on a beach . . . which he could have been, of course. From the beery smell that hung about him and the size of his pupils, what she had no trouble in deciding was that he'd been drinking.

He turned away and prowled around the living space, touching the oak posts beneath the stairs and patting furniture as if giving it his approval. 'Nice property. Authentic.' He paused at the kitchen area and began opening cupboards while Clancy looked on, dismayed at his casual familiarity. He sighed with satisfaction when he discovered a bottle of red wine, taking down a glass and looking around enquiringly. 'Anyone else?' It might have been a polite and hospitable gesture if it had been his house and his wine he was helping himself to.

'I will,' said Alice. 'Just the thing while I have a lovely catch-up with Clancy.'

Clancy tried to gather her scattered thoughts, to align this tinkling, alternative-looking Alice with the smoother and more sophisticated Alice she'd always known. One thing that hadn't changed, evidently, was Alice's ability to spring things on people. 'Not for me.' She turned to Alice hesitantly. 'Sorry to dash when we haven't seen each other for so long but I have plans—'

'Oh, you can spare me an hour.' Alice dismissed Clancy's

schedule with a nonchalant wave. 'For goodness' sake, I haven't seen you for ages.'

'That would be because you've been off on your travels for the last six and a bit years.'

Alice beamed as Hugo brought her a large glass of red. 'You've got me there.'

Hugo grabbed a backpack from the pile of bags with the hand that didn't hold the other glass of wine plus the bottle. 'Where's our room?'

'Your room?' Clancy echoed, a horrible cold feeling landing hard in the pit of her stomach.

Alice put down her wine and bounced up. 'I'll show you.' Then she paused, 'Oh, hang on. Which room are you in, Clancy?'

'The loft.' The feeling grew colder. Alice and Hugo had come to stay. For how long? Clancy had got used to occupying the Roundhouse in solitary splendour and didn't one iota fancy sharing it. An Alice who had changed almost beyond recognition was unsettling enough, but Hugo was a stranger.

Truth was, though . . . the Roundhouse didn't belong to Clancy. It belonged to Aaron and Alice and she could do precisely nothing to prevent Alice moving in as many people as she wanted.

'Fantastic,' Alice sang out, skipping ahead of Hugo up the stairs. 'We'll take the master. Don't run away, Clancy! I'll be back in two minutes for that catch-up.'

Clancy stood rooted to the spot, dismay warring with disbelief as she listened to the voices from the floor above with footsteps trekking to and fro. *Alice was back*. A completely altered Alice with tattoos and an alternative hairstyle instead of the Max Mara and stylish up-do she'd worn four years ago to Aunt Sally's funeral. And Alice had a husband who she was moving into the room she'd once shared with Lee, apparently.

Then Alice was running down again, waving her phone. 'Has this village *still* got no mobile signal? FFS! I feel like I've entered *Brigadoon*.' She linked arms with Clancy's to tow her over to the sofa, collecting her wine on the way. 'So,' she began confidently, tossing some of her plaits over one shoulder. 'How are you finding Ye Olde Nelson's Bar? I couldn't believe it when you moved here. You! I would scarcely have recognised you without your business suits and impeccable manicure.' Clancy glanced down at her hands. They were a little more work-worn than in the past. Alice went on, 'Did Will really cheat on you? What a bastard. I hope you kicked him where it hurt. How long are you here for?'

Clancy, who'd opened her mouth to ask this same question of Alice, was wrong-footed. 'I haven't put a limit on it,' she said eventually. 'As you know, I'm doing the caretaker's job and it's pretty busy at the moment. Every property's booked up.'

'Aces.' Alice took two big gulps from her wine glass, her throat working as she swallowed. 'All dosh welcome, frankly.' She rolled her eyes.

'Right.' Clancy waited for her to elaborate and when she didn't said, 'So where have you been since I saw you last?'

'All over!' Alice waved the hand that didn't hold the wine glass. 'I bought a motorhome to drive around Europe. Met really interesting, rewarding people, you know? Broadened my horizons and made up for all the bloody years in one bloody village or another. I mean, the UK's just one small patch on the world map, isn't it? After Europe, I went over to Morocco, then Algeria and

239

Libya . . .' She gulped more wine, as if just the mention of such hot countries made her thirsty. 'Came back to Europe, left the van with a friend, went to America, met Hugo in the Carolinas, married him in Vegas, came back to Europe.'

Clancy examined the tattoos twining their way up her arms, fairies with pink wings and elves in green hats. 'What did you do in all those places?' she asked curiously, trying to picture Alice in a motorhome rather than a posh villa or hotel.

Alice's eyebrows arched and she lifted a hand, palm up, her shoulders shrugging nearly to her ears while she apparently searched for a suitable answer. 'Hung out,' she declared eventually, 'soaked up the culture, you know? Met interesting people. *Travelled*,' she pronounced, as if that conveyed it all. 'Like your family did.'

'Not really,' Clancy felt the need to point out. 'My parents are workaholics. They build schools and hospitals and government buildings.'

Alice shrugged as if the distinction escaped her. 'So, anyway, Hugo's a bit bloody expensive. Never done a stroke in his life, I don't think, and the Bank of Mummy and Daddy has withdrawn its support so it seemed sensible to come back here. Bit sick of the van and credit card's too full for hotels.'

Clancy's heart began to beat in big, apprehensive thumps, the flash of joy she'd felt at seeing her cousin again fading fast. She licked her lips. 'For how long?'

Alice gave another of those elaborate shrugs. 'I haven't put a limit on it.' Then she laughed at repeating Clancy's own words back at her and glanced round. 'Is there another bottle of wine? Bloody Hugo took that one up with him.'

The possible consequences of Alice's return beginning

to dawn on her made Clancy feel temporarily too heavy to leave her seat. 'Don't think so. You could have a look, I suppose,' she answered mechanically. Her mind was spinning. She wanted to ask Alice why she hadn't contacted her ahead of time but had the feeling Alice would be incredulous at the very notion that she should. Clancy would be the usurper in this scenario, not Alice.

'Actually . . .' Alice leaned towards Clancy confidingly. 'Actually, to be honest . . .' She dragged the final word out through barely parted lips and lowered her voice. 'Hugo is being a pain in the arse. We're not getting on very well. Being shut up in the van with him whinging and freeloading was doing my head in. There's at least a bit more space here. And a spare bed for when he passes out and snores like a pig.'

If Clancy's heart could have sunk any lower it would have.

Alice brightened. 'So tell me everything that's been going on in Nelson's Bar.' Then, before Clancy could answer, dropped her voice to a conspiratorial whisper. 'Is Lee still around? I've been thinking about him a lot.'

'Erm . . .' In a burst of horror, Clancy realised how unwelcome Alice's homecoming was going to be amongst Aaron's family. How the hell was Lee going to react when he realised the breaker of his heart had turned up again? 'Erm . . .' she said again, faintly this time. She was going to have to give Aaron the news.

Crap.

Crap.

And double crap.

Her rosy vision of this evening popped like a bubble.

'Well, is he?' Alice's voice demanded, sounding somehow far away.

Clancy jumped up, casting round for her bag and keys. 'I'll leave you to settle in and . . . whatever. I expect I'll see you soon.' As they were now living in the same house. *Crap*.

In seconds she was outside the front door and, after a moment to check out the motorhome parked outside like a small lorry, hurried away from the Roundhouse up Long Lane. A blood-red sunset was beginning, turning the cottages pink and making the flowers in the gardens glow ethereally, but she barely saw it. It wasn't until she was within sight of Aaron's place that her pace faltered. Then she squared her shoulders and opened the garden gate, circumnavigating the workshop on the side of the house to knock at the back.

A volley of barks followed and the boarded wooden door shook, presumably at the onslaught of a large canine.

Then Aaron pulled the door open, calming Nelson's excitement, his face creased into a smile. 'Am I pleased to see you,' he said, pulling her into his arms and resting his cheek on top of her head while Nelson bounced around them.

She laughed hollowly as her head came to rest on his shoulder. 'You might not be in a minute.'

He pulled away to examine her expression. 'What's the matter?'

It was like ripping off a sticking plaster. The only way was to do it quickly. 'Alice is at the Roundhouse. She's just turned up. With her husband.'

His face went slack with surprise. 'Seriously? Did you know she was coming? *Husband?*'

She felt curiously hurt. 'Don't you think I might have mentioned it if I'd known she was coming?' she asked tightly. 'Particularly with a husband?'

He pulled her close again. 'Sorry, stupid questions. But, shit, this is going to put the cat amongst the pigeons.'

Clancy could only agree. They collapsed onto his big sofa – Clancy accepted a glass of wine this time, feeling she needed its bolstering qualities – while she stroked Nelson's head and recounted the recent arrival at the Roundhouse, describing the motorhome in the lane outside and Alice's extreme change of image. 'Though she's exactly the same insouciant Alice underneath,' she concluded drily. Then she found herself hesitating. When Alice had asked about Lee and complained about Hugo, she wouldn't have expected Clancy to race off and pass it all on to Aaron. Yet Clancy had just taken umbrage that Aaron might think she wouldn't share with him what she knew . . . The spectre of torn loyalties loomed with all the appeal of a rainy Monday.

'I'm beginning to wish Lee had stayed in Northamptonshire. They're bound to meet up, otherwise,' Aaron sighed. 'I'd better talk to Lee. And the rest of the family. For fuck's sake!' he exploded, slapping his hand to his forehead. 'Why did she need to show up now?'

Clancy prickled to hear the exasperation in his voice. 'Because she's half-owner of the house and has every right to?' she suggested.

He tilted her chin up to brush a kiss on her lips. 'I shouldn't have said that. She's your cousin and you were probably glad to see her.'

'I was,' she conceded. Then she was compelled by honesty to add, 'Though we've both changed so much . . . But don't think this only affects your family. I didn't warm to her husband much and now I'm sharing a house with him.'

'Yeah,' he said absently, resting his cheek on her hair. 'Awkward.'

They sat in silence for several minutes.

Then Aaron put his wine glass down on the coffee table. 'I'm going to have to tell Lee and my mum and dad.'

Clancy nodded glumly. 'Suppose.' *Warn them*, she knew he meant.

'That's if Dilys hasn't seen Alice and her motorhome and already been on the phone to Aunt Norma,' he added with a sigh.

She was able to fill in that blank. 'Dilys and Ernie were invited to a Golden Wedding do in someone's house along Marshview Road this evening.'

'Well that's something at least.' He sighed again. 'I told my family we're seeing each other, by the way. I hope that was OK? I didn't want them to think I was sneaking around.'

She turned to look at him, trying to read the steady dark gaze. 'I suppose . . . well, yes, I guess they had to know.' His words gave her an uncomfortable feeling, as if seeing her was something he'd had to confess to, but she could see that he was in a situation. One that he'd have to manage. Just because she wasn't rich with rellies herself didn't mean his large family shouldn't be considered. 'How did that go?'

'As well as it could,' he returned enigmatically. 'But I think I'd better talk to them about Alice on my own.'

She needed no persuading on that score. His family would be forgiven for taking sides and assuming Clancy would be on Alice's. Which she was, of course. The whole scenario was uncomfortable.

As Clancy was definitely in no hurry to return to the Roundhouse, she offered to take Nelson for his evening run while Aaron visited his family. 'Here's a spare door key,' Aaron said, taking it from the kitchen table. 'I'll try not to be too long. Maybe we can salvage something of our evening afterwards.'

Clancy took the proffered key. Aaron sounded as disappointed as she felt at the way the evening was panning out. She tried to rediscover some of the buzz she'd felt before Alice's arrival. 'Hope so!' And, realising he hadn't kissed her properly this evening, lifted her face to touch her lips to his.

Aaron reacted by clamping his arms around her, a hand on her upper back and one on her behind, pressing against her as his tongue caressed hers. The next few minutes passed much more agreeably than the last, though Nelson whined and nudged them with his nose as the kiss got deeper.

When they came up for air, Aaron's usual smile was back in place. 'That's better.' He repeated the kiss before finally quitting the house, turning the opposite way to her when they reached the garden gate.

She left the lane and meandered onto the clifftop, giving Nelson plenty of time to sniff, enjoying the summer evening, noticing a few green shoots and wildflowers nosing through the parched clifftop grass after the recent rain. The glorious deep north Norfolk sunset made everything look as if she were viewing it through a pink filter. The gulls that usually wheeled about the clifftops seemed to have taken the cerise and purple evening sky as the signal to retire to bed and Clancy could hear little but the breeze in her ears and the rasp of Nelson's extending lead winding and unwinding. He glanced back at her from time to time, giving a gentle tail-wag as if to say, 'Oh, you're still there. Good!'

They made their way to the furthest point of the headland, Clancy turning her gaze to the sea and wondering how Aaron's family was taking the Awful Alice news. Clancy would have been thrilled to see Alice again under other circumstances – like before she'd begun a new life in Nelson's Bar herself – but Aaron had only spoken the truth when he'd declared that Alice's arrival would be the cat amongst the pigeons. Pigeon Clancy had flown out of the Roundhouse pretty much as Cat Alice stalked in, swishing her plaits if not her tail.

How would Lee take seeing Alice again? She both was and wasn't the Alice he'd fallen in love with. Her appearance was startlingly different . . . but not unattractive, especially in the kind of skimpy clothing she'd sported earlier, her beautiful, delicate tattoos twining sinuously up her arms and across her shoulders. Clancy could imagine new Alice knocking Lee's socks off just as old Alice had.

Then Clancy was pulled back to the present – literally – as Nelson gave a great tug, trying to head for a figure strolling across the parched grass towards them. 'Genevieve,' Clancy called, letting Nelson tow her closer so he could perform his one-dog welcoming dance.

Genevieve obligingly fussed him, her eyes on Clancy. 'Out without Aaron?' she queried.

Clancy didn't stop to think that as she'd been involved with Aaron less than twenty-four hours this was an odd opening. She just rolled her eyes. 'My cousin Alice has turned up so he's gone to tell Lee, so that he doesn't chance on her unprepared—'

'I might as well say this to your face as I've already said it to Aaron,' Genevieve butted in, not, apparently, interested in Alice or Lee. 'I think you've played a mean trick on me.' Her usually friendly face was shuttered, the corners of her mouth turned down.

'Pardon?' Clancy literally took a step back.

'I suppose you thought it was clever to coach me with all that stuff about women not needing men and the glories of a single life, then bowl in and snap Aaron up for your-self.'

For the second time in a few hours, Clancy's stomach sank like lead. 'Oh, hell,' she said guiltily. 'Is that what you think? It wasn't like that! When I said those things I was recognising the end of my old relationship. At that point, there was nothing between Aaron and me.' A nasty thought struck her. 'You didn't end the relationship on the strength of that conversation, did you? I wasn't giving you *instructions*, for goodness' sake! And I absolutely wasn't plotting to move in on Aaron myself.'

Genevieve's gaze hardened. 'So it was all one big, happy coincidence – for you?'

Put like that . . . 'I suppose so,' Clancy admitted unhappily. 'I'm so sorry. You probably think I'm a conniving bitch—'

But she was talking to a turned back as Genevieve paced deliberately away, chin up and fists clenched at her sides.

'But what about your new bloke?' Clancy called after her, a spark of indignation igniting. 'You'd already found someone else.'

'Jealousy tactic,' Genevieve called back flatly. 'Not a new relationship.'

Clancy groaned, watching her go and feeling an inch tall. She hadn't given Genevieve much thought when she gave in to the pull she felt towards Aaron. After beginning so promisingly, this was turning out to be a sadly crappy day.

Aaron beat Clancy back to his place by a few minutes and was sliding lasagne in the oven as she and Nelson arrived. 'I'd intended to take you on a proper date tonight,'

247

he said. 'This is a poor excuse for one.' Then he hesitated, studying her. 'Are you OK?'

She found it hard to meet his eyes. 'Genevieve had a word with me.'

'Oh.' His hand dropped away from her waist. 'She had a word with me too. Sorry. I meant to tell you as soon as you got here but you had the glad tidings about Alice and I forgot.'

Although she could understand exactly how that would happen, Clancy said, 'Forewarned would have been fore-armed. She obviously thinks we're doing something . . . wrong.'

'But we're not.'

She clasped her hands in front of her. 'It feels as if whatever we've started between us is at a cost to her.' She couldn't help remembering how she'd felt when Will had done pretty much the same thing.

Aaron gently untwisted her fingers, took her hand, opened the back door, and led her out to sit on the bench, the stone cool through their clothing as moths danced in the sultry evening air. 'The facts are that she ended the relationship and I was glad she did. Your relationship with Will was already over. We're free to see each other. We shouldn't feel guilty.'

The dusk was turning to darkness and his garden was a collection of shadows beneath a starry sky punctuated by slices of light from the kitchen door and window.

'But we're hurting Genevieve,' she pointed out. 'And I'll bet your folks aren't any keener on me now Alice has turned up again.'

He made an impatient movement with his head. 'You're not Alice! And I'm not Lee.'

That wasn't a direct answer. She sighed, not even

wanting to know what his family had said about Alice. 'I wish we could have just stayed on Secret Beach. It was sheltered and uncomplicated there.'

He half-laughed. 'It's high tide. We'd be treading water and trying to keep clear of the rocks.'

'Describes us perfectly,' she responded.

They sat together while the lasagne cooked, spilling its rich aroma onto the evening air without tempting Clancy's appetite at all. Aaron squeezed her hand. 'I've agreed to speak to Alice first. Try and get some idea of what she's thinking. It seemed sensible when my mother asked it but as soon as I left my parents' house I began to think it a bad idea. I've committed though, so I'd better do it. It might help Lee out.'

She snorted. 'It seems as if you're like me. You get all the shit jobs.'

He laughed, but he didn't disagree.

Neither of them ate much lasagne. Nelson got the foil trays to lick out and the rest of the meal went into the bin. Then they looked at each other.

Aaron moved close, running his hands up Clancy's arms. 'Whatever I'd thought would happen this evening, I have to say that Alice's exploits didn't enter my mind.'

Her skin tingled at his proximity. She wanted to respond, to slide her arms around his waist, but she felt conflicted and couldn't let his words go unchallenged. 'Does it really come under the heading of "exploits" for someone to come back to live in their own home? I can imagine you feel aggrieved at her doing it without having the courtesy of notifying you as co-owner, of course. And you're worried about how Lee will cope,' she added fairly.

Slowly, his fingers drifted down her arms until his hands hung by his sides, though he continued to occupy her personal space. 'Isn't this where we came in?' he asked sombrely. 'You sticking up for Alice and me worried about Lee?'

She thought back to those early days, a couple of months ago, and searched her heart. 'I suppose so. That's not going to change, is it? It's natural that we should each see things in favour of our loved one. You thinking that I'm dismissing Lee's emotions and me feeling you're demonising Alice's human frailties.'

'Demonising.' He said the word thoughtfully, as if testing its fit in the conversation. 'I'll have to watch out for that. Not going to change . . . ? It could, if we agreed to just leave Alice and Lee to get on with it. Refuse to let it affect whatever's happening between us.' His eyes were solemn and dark.

'Easier said than done. Lee's your brother and Alice is more than a cousin to me.'

His eyebrows rose. 'I suppose I lose sight of that. I never thought you and Alice were remotely alike in personality. Even when Lee was happy with her I found her hard work. She always acted so entitled, expecting everyone to fall in with what she wanted yet constantly changing her mind as to what that was. Always wanting what she didn't have.'

Clancy wrestled with this summary of Alice's character and decided now was not the time to try and create positive spin. So she asked the question that was burning inside her, instead. 'If I'm not like that, what am I like?'

A slow smile spread over his face. 'You're pragmatic and fair.'

'Oh.' That sounded a lot like 'boring and unexciting' Clancy thought.

He lifted a hand to stroke her hair, letting it drift down

onto her neck. 'You're kind. You help other people. You don't automatically put yourself and your feelings to the head of the queue all the time. You're also fun, intelligent, sparky and sometimes do the unexpected.' His hand slid down further, until it cupped her behind. 'You're hot. Just to see you walk across a room makes me want you. I keep drifting off from conversations because I'm thinking about you or watching the way you move.'

Disarmed, she moved in close as his words seemed to slide over her skin and leave goose bumps. 'How lovely.'

But then he spoilt it. 'I'm just worried that Alice will use you.'

Without running her words through her inner censor, she replied, 'In the same way your family's using you to open the conversation with her?'

He blinked in surprise. They moved apart and didn't touch again as they prepared to leave then walked down Long Lane to the Roundhouse, every leaf of every tree and hedge silvered by the moonlight.

Aaron was ultra-aware of Clancy walking quietly by his side, conscious not just of her body, as he was pretty much every time they were together, but of her welter of feelings. They almost hung like captions above her head. *Unhappy. Troubled. Conflicted. Uncomfortable.*

But, also, *protective.* Clancy was protective of Alice. He should remember that. They'd lit a flame together but it had burned for only a night and a day and could easily flicker and die. Their exchange of views back at his cottage had made that obvious.

They turned in at the front gate of the Roundhouse and Clancy let them both inside what was usually a spacious and airy ground floor. She halted. Aaron did too.

251

His eyes needed time to take in what looked like an explosion of possessions in the middle of the floor, from unfastened luggage to musty-smelling tarpaulin and, bizarrely, a saxophone. The TV blared from the lounge area.

A large man was sorting through an open bag. He looked up and said, 'Good evening,' and returned to his task.

Then a flurry of movement and a woman hurried across the floor to meet them, a huge smile on her face, her arms outstretched. 'Aaron! Oh, wow, it's *so* good to see you again! We must have a complete catch-up!'

Though Clancy's description of Alice ought to have prepared him, he was stunned not only by the surprising warmth of this greeting, but the change in her as well. There seemed a lot of Alice's flesh on show, her plaits swinging around her. And the tattoos . . . Clancy hadn't exaggerated the extent of them.

He had an instant to be glad she looked less like Clancy than of yore and then she was trying to envelop him in a hug. The hands he placed on her shoulders served to ensure she didn't get too close. She whirled away, addressing the man searching through the baggage.

'Hugo, come and meet my business partner, Aaron,' she called brightly. 'He owns Roundhouse Row with me. Aaron, this is my husband, Hugo.'

Hugo, smoothing his beard, stepped forward to shake Aaron's hand. 'All right, mate?' he said carelessly. The phrase didn't work with his well-spoken accent and Aaron had a strong impression that he was using language he thought Aaron would understand.

Taking an instant dislike to him, Aaron replied, 'How do you do?' and turned immediately to Alice. 'We need to talk.'

252

'Sure. Later this week,' she suggested, abandoning him in the middle of the floor and turning to pick up the saxophone from the floor. After licking her lips, she began to play. There was a bit of elephant-blowing-its-nose noise, but she did create a tune.

Conscious of a rising fury at her blatant attempt to dismiss him, Aaron strode over and raised his voice over the racket. 'Now, please,' he said.

The saxophone gave a squawk and a squeak as Alice tried to blow harder. Even Hugo had stopped ferreting in his baggage to watch the scene unfold.

Then suddenly Clancy was there too, laying her hand on Alice's arm. 'Might as well get it over with.'

Alice cut baleful eyes Aaron's way for a moment, then she let her bottom lip uncurl from beneath the saxophone reed and stooped to lay it once again on the floor. 'I'm quite tired,' she pointed out, 'but if you're quite sure it has to be now—' she widened her eyes in elaborate exasperation '—then by all means.' She strode to the lounge area, parked her backside on the sofa and folded her arms.

Clancy suggested tentatively. 'I can go upstairs—'

'No, stay,' declared Alice. 'Make us coffee, lovely Clancy.'

'Make it yourself, lovely Alice,' Clancy replied affably, taking an armchair.

Alice looked at her and giggled.

Taking from this that the best way to deal with Alice was simply to be direct when necessary, Aaron took a deep breath. 'I'm keen to avoid as much awkwardness as possible. Lee's living locally right now with my parents and my great-aunt. You introduced me as your business partner earlier, which is true as far as it goes—'

'I would have thought it one of those things that's either true or it's not,' Hugo interrupted, leaving the pile of possessions behind to join them, sitting on the sofa beside Alice.

'OK,' Aaron allowed, wondering whether Hugo was ever friendly with anybody. 'But we ended up sharing property by default, after Alice . . . split up from my brother.'

'Split up from' sounded less incendiary than 'dumped', 'trashed' or 'jilted'.

'Why was that?' Hugo demanded, folding his arms. 'What do you mean by "default"?'

Aaron paused, glancing at Alice. 'You're happy to discuss this in front of Hugo and Clancy?' Obviously, she was, because she'd had enough opportunity to make it otherwise, but Hugo's manner was so abrasive that he found himself wanting to annoy him by questioning his presence.

Alice shrugged.

He turned back to Hugo. 'When Alice left my brother at the altar of Thornham church, he was distraught. He needed to get away from the village. I bought him out at Roundhouse Row so that he could buy a house elsewhere.'

Hugo frowned down at Alice. 'Is that right?'

She traced the shape of a shooting star tattooed on her hand. 'Bit dramatised, but yes.'

From the corner of his eye, Aaron caught Clancy's eyebrows lifting. 'How long have you two been married?' she asked Alice.

'Three months,' answered Hugo.

'Four months,' said Alice at the same time.

Hugo looked slightly surprised, thought for a moment and said, 'Yes, four. Middle of April.'

It wasn't long, but Aaron was pretty sure Alice could have found time before she brought Hugo to Nelson's Bar to explain her history there. He gritted his teeth and ploughed on. 'Roundhouse Row has provided us both with income. Are you intending to request changes?'

Alice regarded him from under her brows. 'I don't feel a need to get involved, if that's what you mean. It's worked perfectly well for the last few years. I'm happy.'

Aaron just bet she was happy with letting other people do all the work. He couldn't resist pointing out, 'But the caretaker has always had the Roundhouse in lieu of a proper wage.'

She frowned at Clancy, picking at the sofa more rapidly. 'Isn't that what you're doing? Caretaker?'

Clancy nodded.

Alice frowned at Aaron then, obviously not getting his point. 'Then that's OK! Clancy's my cousin.'

He clarified. 'The agreement wasn't for you and your husband to live here too.'

Alice giggled this time, obviously feeling he wasn't getting the point. 'But Clancy is *my cousin*.'

Aaron wanted to ask how that was relevant but as Clancy didn't, and didn't look at him to allow him to glean clues from her expression, he set that aside for now. 'I'll be straight with you, Alice. Your being here has the potential to upset my brother. I'd like to think that you'll consider his feelings, and those of my parents.'

At that, Hugo got up, rolling his eyes, and took himself off up the stairs without a word.

'Of course.' Alice gave one of her over-elaborate shrugs as if she hadn't noticed Hugo's departure. 'It was all a long time ago. I'm sure Lee has moved on from all that . . .' She waved a hand in the air in lieu of finishing the sentence.

Aaron felt it better not to comment. His brother's mental health wasn't something he wanted to discuss with the woman who'd prompted the problems. Who knew? She might get a power kick out of it. He got up, feeling ruffled and dissatisfied at Alice's I-don't-get-what's-bugging-you manner. Clancy turned to watch him but her expression was remote and she made no move to see him to the door. He had no idea what she was thinking or what she wanted, so he said goodnight.

He wished heartily that Princess Awful Alice had remained safely wherever she'd been instead of turning up to spoil everything.

But once he was in the porch and about to open the outer door he heard footsteps behind him. When he turned, though, he found himself in the company of the wrong cousin. Alice was there, playing with a plait and regarding him with caution. 'Erm,' she began hesitantly. 'How is Lee?'

'OK.'

She twirled the plait faster. 'Is he married and everything? Having a lovely life?'

The nervous titter that followed grated on Aaron's nerves but he decided to share minimal facts with her. She was bound to bump into Lee. Nelson's Bar was tiny. 'He moved away, was in a relationship and had a daughter. Now he's a single dad and he's moved back.'

'Oh.' She looked thoughtful as she turned and went back inside.

As he marched back up Long Lane, Aaron wished he could have told her that Lee had found the love of his life and would probably say hello for old times' sake at some point, but he was very busy with the happy business of living.

Her presence was like a snake in the village grass.

He reached home in a few minutes, so deep in thought that when he rounded his building and a shadowy figure on the garden bench moved, he nearly jumped out of his skin. Then Lee's voice said, 'Evening.'

Aaron took refuge in brotherly ribbing. 'What are you doing littering my garden?' He sat down, having a fair idea of what was coming.

'Have you seen her?' Lee asked.

Aaron joked no longer. 'Alice? Yes, just came from there.'

'And?' Lee kept his gaze on where the sea could be heard but not seen.

Heart aching for his little bro, Aaron answered as fully and honestly as he could, softening his voice when he mentioned Alice's husband and feeling Lee's recoil. He described her traveller-chick image and the lack of apparent change to her personality. 'She asked about you,' he concluded, because Lee had the right to know.

Slowly, Lee nodded. 'Thanks.' He clasped Aaron's shoulder and left without giving any indication of how the news bulletin had been received.

Aaron sat on for a long time, hoping Alice Nettles – or whatever her name was now – would clear off ASAP.

Chapter Twenty

By ten on Monday morning, Clancy could not *wait* to exit the Roundhouse. The less than forty-eight hours she'd shared the place with Alice and Hugo felt like a month. Hugo, however, stopped her on her way out. He'd put a little plait in his beard this morning, evidently determined to look anything but mainstream. Clancy was surprised he hadn't painted daisies and rainbows on the motorhome.

'May I see the accounts of Roundhouse Row? Alice said it's OK,' he mumbled so quietly that Clancy was pretty sure Alice had said no such thing. Accounts went to Alice via her solicitor so if she wanted Hugo to read them, she could show him herself.

Clancy dodged the bullet by replying, 'Aaron has them, I'm afraid.' Clancy had them too, but Hugo didn't need to know that. She paused, unease suddenly making her stomach feel hollow in case Alice, despite showing no inclination so far, at some time decided to take over the Roundhouse Row reins. If she did, there would be nothing to keep Clancy in Nelson's Bar.

Except Aaron . . . And who knew where things were going with him? One fantastic night together and then all the things that had stood between them in the past had returned with a vengeance. Or Alice had, which was the same thing.

'But—' began Hugo, frowning blackly.

The front door knocker clattered and Clancy was pleased to have an excuse to interrupt him. 'I'd better see who that is.' She made a beeline for the front door before Hugo had a chance to complete his sentence. There she found Genevieve, a square white box in her hands.

'Oh,' they said in unison.

Genevieve recovered herself first. 'Sorry to bother you,' she said stiffly, 'I'd like to see Alice, please. I've made her a cake to welcome her back to the village.'

Clancy debated whether it was worth seizing the opportunity to try and sweeten things between her and Genevieve but, as if reading her mind, Genevieve dashed the hope. 'Look, I don't want to be awkward but I really would appreciate it if you'd get your cousin.'

'Come in.' Clancy led Genevieve indoors, where Alice and Hugo's possessions still cluttered the floor. 'This is Hugo, Alice's husband. Hugo, Genevieve's come to see Alice. They knew each other when Alice lived here before.' Then she made good her escape to do the gardens of the holiday cottages, taking tools with her from the Roundhouse shed.

There was little breeze for once and though the sky was overcast, she was soon sweating as she trimmed shrubs, tamed climbers and mowed lawns. With no inclination to return to the Roundhouse, she worked right through lunch, swatting away bugs as her mind circled dismally over the past couple of days. If Alice *didn't* take over the reins then Clancy could be stuck sharing with her and Hugo indefinitely.

Hugo respected no boundaries. He took what he wanted from Clancy's groceries, he hogged the TV remote and his personal habits were less than fastidious.

Presently, she heard voices and laughter from the garden of the Roundhouse and rap music began to blare.

With a sigh, she moved into the front garden of number four, where she was soon approached by Dilys hurrying along in orange floral flip-flops.

'What's all that blimmin' racket?' the older woman enquired irritably. 'And whose is that blimmin' big camper, clogging up the lane? Have you moved a rock festival to the village?'

Clancy continued doing battle with a rambling rose that seemed to let her close in on it with the sole aim of scratching her arms and depositing earwigs in her hair. 'Alice is back,' she muttered, snipping grimly, and went on to explain about Hugo. She thought she was doing a pretty good job of keeping her voice neutral but then Dilys put a gentle hand on her shoulder.

'You poor girl,' she said sympathetically. 'There's a chocolate cake in my fridge. Why don't we go inside where it's cool and you can help me eat it.'

'That sounds wonderful!' Clancy abandoned the rose bush and dumped her secateurs with the rest of the tools.

Before long she was seated at Dilys's tile-topped table eating moist chocolate cake with a teaspoon and drinking a large glass of orange squash. Dilys disposed of her slice of cake by picking it up and munching it. She frowned. 'To look on the bright side, I suppose it's lovely for you to see Alice again.'

'Mm,' Clancy said through a mouthful of cake, feeling

sheepish that in the shock and surprise of Alice turning up and moving her husband and a muddle of possessions into what Clancy had come to see as her space, she'd failed to entirely appreciate the return of her cousin. Her conscience gave a twinge as she remembered the years they'd been close and that Alice was entitled to marry whom she chose. Clancy ought to be making more effort.

Still, it was peaceful in Dilys's house, so she lingered to help pick apart a mess of embroidery silks that had tangled themselves in Dilys's work basket, then allowed herself to be persuaded into another slice of cake with a cup of tea. Finally, she said, 'I'd better get those gardening tools put away and go back I suppose.'

Dilys gave her a big hug. 'Don't worry, pet. Things will work out.'

By the time Clancy arrived back at the Roundhouse she'd given herself a talking-to. All she had to do, she decided, was to ask if they could put a few boundaries in place to enable everyone to live comfortably together. Boundaries about possessions and tidiness would be a great starting point. She let herself in through the back door.

And found the mound of possessions larger than ever.

It looked as if Alice and Hugo had brought in the entire interior of the motorhome. Large flat cushions teetered in piles, pans cluttered up the sink and the whole place smelt musty and sour.

Hugo was lying on the sofa, staring at the TV. He lifted his head slightly to gaze at her as she came to a sudden stop at seeing Possession Mountain. 'I'm afraid we've run out of wine,' he said. If his tone had been apologetic, Clancy might have summoned up a smile and a light remark. Instead, he sounded accusatory, as if this were a hotel and he was about to review it on Trip Advisor.

261

She did just about manage to count to ten while she crossed the room to seat herself in the armchair where he could see her from his supine position. 'I'm going to have to ask you not to take my food and drink,' she said politely. 'Alice knows where the supermarkets are. You'll have to buy your own wine. Also,' she ploughed on, trying not to give him time to object, 'I'm hoping we can sort out some boundaries about tidiness. Your things are everywhere. If we try and be fair to one another—'

'It's Alice's house.' Hugo treated her to a big fake smile.

'Half hers,' said Clancy, after a shocked moment. 'I know, because I've been looking after her half for years. But not one bit yours.'

'Have you heard the marriage service lately? That sharing of worldly goods thing? What's hers is mine.' He rolled his eyes and turned back to the TV.

In furious silence Clancy marched up to her room in the loft, gathered up clean clothes and went down to find a bathroom on the middle floor. One bathroom door was shut and judging from the noise of a running shower emanating from it, Alice was inside.

The other bathroom was a disgusting mess. Clancy's towels were soiled and wet, dumped on the floor in pools of water. Even the toilet hadn't been flushed, to her utter disgust. After a few seconds to take in the awfulness of the scene, she stowed her clothes inside the airing cupboard, which was about the only place they'd remain clean and dry, and set about bleaching the whole room with angry movements and a simmering hatred for the situation in which she found herself.

Finally, she took out clean towels and her clothes and showered away the sweat and dust from her day's gardening. The anger and disappointment inside her refused to be washed away though.

As soon as she was dressed she set out to corner Alice but was distracted by the sound of footsteps above her. In her bedroom? It was an invasion of privacy too far. Flinging down the towels and clothes she'd intended for the washing machine she flew up the stairs, quite expecting to find Hugo poking around in her things. When she flung open her bedroom door, however, it was Alice she found, gazing out of the window.

'Haven't you made it nice up here!' Alice half-turned. She was wearing a cerise bandeau from which her boobs threatened to jiggle free at any moment.

Clancy tried to keep a rein on her temper. 'Yes, it is a nice, peaceful oasis. As you're here, may we have a chat?' There was a bigger battle to be fought than Alice coming into her room. She guided her cousin over to the bed so they could lounge on it in an echo of when they'd been teenagers sharing a bedroom and tried her speech again. 'I'm hoping we can sort out some boundaries, as we're all living together. Like, you buying your own groceries. And about tidiness. Yours and Hugo's things are everywhere. He seemed to think I should sort it out with you.' It was a blatant misrepresentation of what Hugo had said, but Clancy was not in the mood to be scrupulously honest if a fib would serve her better.

Alice gurgled with laughter. 'That's Hugo,' she agreed. 'Isn't he a pain in the arse? He does *not* know the meaning of the word "tidy". He's a teeny bit spoilt, I'm afraid. Some of the people we met in the States christened him "Hugo Fuck-up" instead of Hugo Suffolk.' She pealed with laughter. 'We get on each other's nerves all the time when we're in the van.'

Gritting her teeth, Clancy persisted. 'I am going to have to insist on these boundaries though, Alice. Hugo's drunk all my wine—'

'Oh, come on, Clancy! I'll get you more wine, if that's all that's bothering you.' Alice pushed herself up from the bed.

Clancy put a detaining hand on hers. 'It's not. I'm bothered by the bathroom being left like a tip, I'm bothered by being treated rudely, by you coming into my room without a by-your-leave, by you stinking out downstairs by using it as a rubbish dump, by my things being taken without permission.'

Alice withdrew her hand and drifted serenely towards the door. 'Gosh, aren't we Miss Bossy? You can't have everything your own way, Clancy. That's not fair now, is it? We all have to learn to get along together if we're going to house-share. You need to learn how to chill.'

Clancy listened to her cousin's footsteps starting down the stairs and lifted her voice to follow them. 'If I have no option but to abandon ship it might adversely affect the income you receive from Roundhouse Row. Someone would have to do all the changing of beds and cleaning. Dealing with Aaron . . .'

The footsteps returned. 'OK, OK,' Alice said, laughter in her voice. 'You've been a star looking after things for me while I've been away and now doing the caretaker job. You deserve some consideration. I'll have a little word with Hugo. OK?' Then she withdrew once again.

Clancy rolled down on the bed and gazed at the ceiling. Everything was far from OK. She felt uneasy, uncomfortable, wound up and put upon. She indulged in a wistful fantasy that Alice had returned alone, the old Alice rather than this stranger Alice, and that the two cousins could have shared the Roundhouse in harmony. Living together could have been fun. Like the amicable sharing of opinions, gossip, films, books, friends and family whenever they'd been together in the old days.

Though she loved her cousin, the old Alice seemed just a memory.

And even if she didn't agree with Aaron that Alice was all about herself she did feel uneasy that Alice hadn't seemed one bit worried over how her return to Nelson's Bar might affect Lee who, after all, she had hurt badly. The subject of Alice and Lee was causing tension between Clancy and Aaron. He hadn't contacted her today. If he was going to become aloof every time some challenge came along then Clancy was going to be disappointed in him.

She remembered the research she'd agreed to do – was it only three days since the Parish Meeting? – about broadband and mobile signal in Nelson's Bar and also the subject of crowdfunding for the B&B. Could she justify strolling up to Aaron's cottage and asking to use his satellite broadband? If she stayed in the Roundhouse this evening her choices seemed to be skulking up here alone or suffering the company of Hugo downstairs . . .

She jumped up. As the only landline phone was on the wall in the kitchen area where Hugo and Alice could listen in, she decided to stroll up to Potato Hall Row without first checking whether Aaron would be at home. She grabbed the hair dryer and blow-dried her hair smooth, applied a squirt of perfume, then she was ready to run down both flights of stairs to the living area.

'See you later,' she called, trying to sound affable, although Alice had now joined Hugo on the sofa watching some action movie exploding across the TV screen, despite

Possession Mountain still cluttering up the place. Clancy closed her eyes to the mess and hurried out into the freshness of the evening, where moths danced in the halos around the streetlights that were just coming on.

Her pace slowed as she rounded Aaron's workshop, her attention stolen away by the beauty of the silver-pink sky and the sun sinking into the sky's silver-pink reflection. Then a quiet *diddle ing-ding, ing-ding, ing-ding ding* from a guitar came from behind her and she turned to see Aaron sitting on the bench smiling at her, a guitar across his lap. 'Hey,' he said, rising, holding the guitar with one hand so he could hug her with the other arm. 'I've been waiting for you to call me back. I left a message with Hugo this morning.'

Nelson suddenly raced out of the house, performing a little shadow box in front of Clancy before dropping down to let her fuss him. 'Did you? He didn't pass it on.' Her heart lifted to know Aaron had tried to reach her. 'Honestly, he's a waste of space and even Alice admits he's a pain in the arse . . .' She halted as a movement caught her eye and she realised that Lee, Yvonne and Norma were seated in garden chairs in amongst the long shadows by the back door. Heat flashed into her cheeks. 'Oh, sorry. I didn't realise you were with family. Hello,' she finished feebly, wishing she hadn't just said 'arse'.

Lee, Yvonne and Norma returned her greeting.

Clancy fell silent at the sensation of so many eyes upon her, eyes that belonged to people who were not pro-Alice. Perhaps she should gracefully extricate herself. If Aaron had phoned her this morning and he'd just hugged her in front of his folks, she could probably be reassured that he wasn't withdrawing from their . . . whatever it was. 'Well,' she began.

'Well,' Yvonne got in ahead of her and jumped to her feet. 'We should be getting back. We've left Fergus babysitting Daisy. Ready, Norma? Careful with your crutches. It's not far to the car.'

'About the same as it was in the other direction,' Norma responded testily, rising to her feet and steadying herself.

'I didn't mean to chase you away,' Clancy said uncomfortably.

'You're not.' Yvonne gave Clancy a wintry smile, then glanced at Lee, who hadn't moved. 'Coming?'

He raised his eyebrows, looking more like Aaron than usual. 'I wouldn't want Dad to think I didn't trust his babysitting capabilities. I'll see you later.'

After a still moment, Yvonne kissed the cheeks of each of her sons and gave her arm to help her aunt to depart.

'Oh, dear,' Clancy said unhappily when the two women had made their way out to the lane, soon followed by the sound of a car starting up. 'Sorry.'

'Don't be.' Aaron wiped away a frown and looped an arm about her waist. 'Have a beer with Lee and me.'

'OK.' Clancy tried to hide her dismay because Aaron was clearly uncomfortable at the chilliness of his family. She felt unwelcome everywhere at the moment.

Lee wasn't chatty. When Aaron came out with a fresh supply of Becks he drained the can in his hand and took two more. They were large cans too.

While Lee stared out to sea like a sad grey cloud, Aaron told Clancy about the garden he was working on, one that had been beautiful once, full of winding paths and native flowers. The new owners wanted the whole lot ripped up and laid to lawn with a massive blue gazebo in the middle. He'd told them he couldn't lay turf in the present dry spell unless they were prepared to water it well every day and they'd said, 'Can't you pop by and do it?'

Clancy sipped her beer. 'I heard on the radio that we have rain coming soon.' They were seriously talking about the weather? Where was the easy way they'd developed between them over the past three months?

'How do you feel about me hooking up to your internet to research broadband and crowdfunding?' she asked brightly, taking out her phone. At least if she brought up her supposed reason for being here they'd have something real to talk about.

'Sounds a great idea. It might be easier if we use my laptop.' Aaron got up and went indoors, glancing at Lee as he passed. Lee continued to watch the last of the sun sinking below the horizon.

When Aaron returned, he and Clancy sat together on the bench over the laptop screen. It didn't take them long to discover that Nelson's Bar's copper telephone lines were ancient, the village was a long way from the exchange, they had none of the vital modern 'cabinets' – those green boxes you scarcely noticed in urban streets – and the village, on its headland sticking out to sea, was not within mobile signal mast range.

'No surprises there,' Clancy observed. 'Let's look for crowdfunding information for the B&B.' Clancy tapped rapidly at the laptop keyboard, feeling better now that Aaron's knee was rubbing against hers and his right hand had settled cosily on her thigh. It was like a private hug.

'I'll bet crowdfunding will be a hard sell to Kaz and Oli,' Aaron observed. 'They seem to be pretty conservative to me.' His thumb was drawing slow circles on her thigh and Clancy was beginning to find it distracting. Especially when his hand drifted slightly higher. Even in the last of the light, she could see by the expression in his eyes that he was absolutely aware of where his hand was. To the millimetre.

Lee's voice emerged from the dusk. 'Anyone for another beer?'

Clancy jumped. She'd considered him lost in his own thoughts. 'I haven't drunk this one yet,' she said, surprised Lee had apparently drunk two beers in the short time she and Aaron had been internet browsing. Although she'd never got to know him very well, he'd never struck her as someone who drank much. But then, she'd never considered the easy-going, slightly reserved man she'd known when he was Alice's partner likely to be beset with depression, either.

Aaron gave her thigh a parting squeeze before he moved his hand and turned his attention to his brother. 'Maybe we should make some pasta or something to soak it up. We've all got to be up for work tomorrow and you'll need to be up to get Daisy's breakfast.'

'All right.' With a shrug, Lee let himself be shepherded into the kitchen and together the three of them made pasta with a jar of sauce and whatever vegetables they found in Aaron's fridge.

When they sat down to eat, Lee took yet another beer – the fifth Clancy had seen him with, let alone whatever he'd drunk before her arrival. Aaron didn't say anything, but Clancy noted his quick frown.

Lee ate morosely, gazing at a spot in the middle of the kitchen table as if it held the secrets of the universe. Aaron and Clancy talked over what the evening's research had shown them, trying and failing to draw Lee into the conversation. He'd shrug or give yes/no answers but then return to staring at the table top.

When he took a loo break, Aaron put down his fork in favour of lifting Clancy's hand from the table and kissing it. 'I'm going to see if I can get him to go home before he drinks any more, which I think will mean me walking along with him. Do you mind?'

'Of course not,' she replied, though conscious of the sinking knowledge that she did mind a bit. 'I gate-crashed your evening.'

He carried on as if she still needed to be persuaded. 'I think Alice being in the village has knocked him for six.'

She sighed unhappily. 'Much as I love her, her appearance has definitely caused issues.'

When Lee returned, Clancy was already on her feet. 'Got to go,' she announced. 'Loads to do.'

Lee managed a smile as he wished her goodnight. He remained in the kitchen as Aaron saw Clancy out, Nelson padding at their heels as if checking they weren't going anywhere good without him.

Once they were out in the darkness of the patio, Aaron drew her into his arms. 'Thanks for understanding. It's just that he's so . . .'

'Sad,' she finished for him.

He stroked her hair and caressed the back of her neck. 'I was going to say as down as when Alice first left, but, yes, sad.' Then he lowered his head to trail kisses along the side of her neck and she closed her eyes to enjoy it.

Letting Clancy go with a goodnight kiss didn't hold a candle to taking her upstairs to his bed, but, after walking her out to the lane, Aaron went back indoors.

As Lee was still table-gazing, Aaron filled the kettle and spooned coffee into mugs. 'All right?' he asked, when he'd set down the mugs and sat down opposite his brother once more.

Lee answered drearily. 'Alice living here again makes me feel as if someone's tossed my life up in the air. I'd just got it sorted out. Bringing Daisy back to the village. I'd made up my mind to find somewhere to live in or around Nelson's Bar, then suddenly . . . *Alice*. With a *husband*. I feel like running a million miles away but at the same time I'm fighting an urge to go and see her.'

Aaron's heart sank. 'You've never seen her since she left, have you? What would be your purpose in seeing her now?'

Lee snorted. 'Beats me. Probably not to talk over old times and agree to be friends. It's just . . . she was so beautiful and fun. I keep remembering how I felt about her. Urges can be bizarre.'

Even without bizarre urges, there were a fair number of possibilities, Aaron thought. Anything from committing murder to begging for another chance on bended knee. Immediate short term, his best course of action was to see if he could deliver his brother safely home. He yawned. 'I want a word with Mum so I'll walk along with you, shall I?'

Lee looked incredulous, obviously seeing through the thin excuse. 'You're seeing me home?'

Recognising that putting Lee's back up and maybe destroying his trust wasn't helpful, Aaron laughed. ''Course not! But I have to speak to Mum and Nelson needs his bedtime walk. And I have to be up early tomorrow.' He took down Nelson's lead and the big dog leapt from his basket, his whole body a-wag.

Lee argued no more. He rose from the table, his movements loose, and he had to pause to achieve the change of direction required to get through the back door. They ambled down through the golden light spilled by the streetlights in Long Lane, peeling off right into Frenchmen's Way. Glancing left, Aaron thought he could distinguish which of the illuminated windows down the hill would belong to the Roundhouse's loft. He pictured Clancy getting ready for bed – sliding out of her clothes and brushing her hair.

Lee halted so suddenly that Aaron travelled on a few steps without him. 'I bet I can have a beer with Jordy. See you later.' Lee turned and began to jog down Long Lane.

Helplessly, Aaron stared after him. He could scarcely order a thirty-four-year-old home. In the light from the street lamps he was able to follow his brother's progress, relieved when he swung left onto Droody Road rather than angling right towards the Roundhouse, as Aaron had half-expected. Muttering an oath, he completed his own short journey and was soon letting himself into his parents' kitchen where he found them seated in easy chairs at the end of the room, watching a small TV. They had an enormous lounge with an enormous TV but they generally seemed to prefer the everyday cosiness of the kitchen.

They both looked up in surprise to see him. 'Where's Lee?' Yvonne asked immediately.

It was logical that they should expect the brother who currently resided at De Silva House, but Aaron was feeling prickly and kept his answer short. 'He went to Jordy's.'

Yvonne blinked and he knew the tone he'd used wasn't the one he usually used with his mother but all evening, through Clancy showing up at his house, even when he'd been sitting pressed against her, smelling her shampoo and watching the way her hair swung, he'd been gently simmering underneath.

In fact, maybe being even ruder might be the way to add weight to what he was about to say. He picked up the TV remote and turned off the darts match they'd been watching. 'So what was that with Clancy?' he demanded of his mother.

Fergus glanced enquiringly between Aaron and Yvonne. Yvonne looked uncomfortable. 'What?' she asked defensively.

Aaron pulled up a chair and folded his arms as if prepared to sit there all night. 'If you want it spelling out, I told you that Clancy and I were seeing one another. I got the impression that you were going to make an effort not to blame her for the actions of her cousin. Then you're in my garden, she walks in and you and Auntie Norma march out. That's what. You were rude to the girl I'm seeing, in my own home. I think I'm due an explanation.'

He watched his mother's face, reading the expressions that flitted across it – doubt, sheepishness, irritation – and refusing to fill the silence. His dad, he noticed, was waiting too, his expression one of frowning enquiry.

'If you put it exactly like that, I suppose I can see why you're miffed,' she allowed at length, smoothing the fabric of her trousers. 'I just felt that it would be hypocritical of me to sit there without saying anything.'

'About?' He was bewildered.

Yvonne sighed, meeting his eyes with the kind of expression he was used to seeing when he'd transgressed in some way. 'I've tried not to interfere but Genevieve's a lovely girl and we've known her a long time. I suppose I let her colour my judgement. You're my son and I shouldn't have. It's just that it all seems a bit two-faced to me.'

Aaron shook his head. 'This conversation's like plaiting jam. What are you talking about?'

273

His mum's gaze darted away again. She pushed back her hair. By the end of the day it always defied whatever styling product she'd used to tame it and hung defiantly in her eyes. 'I met Genevieve in the village. You know we always got on well so she invited me for coffee. She told me Alice had asked her about Lee and she said she hoped I wasn't too worried "now Clancy's asked Alice back". I didn't realise that Clancy had *asked* Alice to come back and when I saw her tonight, with Lee having been so quiet and sad since Alice turned up like a bad penny, I had trouble biting my tongue. I thought it was best I leave before I say something I'd regret.'

Aaron, who'd listened to this with mounting disbelief, kept calm only with an effort. 'Clancy did not invite Alice back and her turning up out of the blue, complete with a husband and her usual blithe disregard for anybody's wellbeing but her own, has put Clancy in a seriously uncomfortable position. Gen sounds as if she's making mischief! Both of you seem to be conveniently disregarding the fact that the house belongs to Alice as much as to me – though I sometimes wonder whether buying Lee out of the property to allow him to start again was really doing him the massive favour I thought at the time.'

A silence stretched out. Yvonne's eyes began to turn pink. 'Then I should say I'm sorry,' she said in a small voice. 'I shouldn't have taken Genevieve's word for it.' She turned a beseeching gaze on him. 'But do understand, Aaron. It's hard to stand back and do nothing when a situation might affect your son.'

Aaron made his voice soft because, although annoyed, he knew she was misguided and impetuous rather than mean or stupid. Her heart was soft and he could imagine Genevieve finding it just too tempting to utilise that to put in a bad word for Clancy. 'You have two sons.' When Yvonne's lip trembled he sighed, reaching out to lay his hand over her soft-skinned one. 'I understand you feel protective of Lee. I've been overprotective of him myself but you *have* to remember that Clancy is not the enemy here! If you decide to be offhand with the woman I'm seeing then I'm going to be deeply disappointed.'

At the sound of the kitchen door opening behind him he stood up, assuming it would be Lee coming home and seeing that as his cue to leave. 'I didn't want to believe young Harry when he said that the only way to have the relationship you want is to move away from this village, but right now I can see what he means.'

From behind him, Jordy's voice suddenly rang out, dangerous and deep. 'What do you mean about Harry? What relationship? You obviously know something I don't.'

Aaron's head swivelled so quickly that he almost cricked his neck. Lee had let himself into the kitchen all right, but he had Jordy in tow.

Thinking fast, Aaron gave a credibly impatient shrug. 'Why do you always sound so suspicious of him? It's what you've been saying yourself, isn't it? He needs to get out of the village and go to uni. Meet new people.'

'I suppose so,' Jordy said slowly, his eyes fixing narrowly on Aaron as if not a hundred per cent convinced.

But then Lee, looking a bit unfocused, clapped Jordy on the shoulder and mumbled goodnight, and Jordy fell silent until they'd heard his uncertain footsteps mount the stairs. Then he said, 'Lee came looking for beer. He looked like he'd had plenty so I thought I'd better see him back.' He'd assumed the slightly worried expression Aaron realised had become the norm for them all when talking about Lee.

Yvonne rubbed her forehead as if it ached. 'Thanks, Jordy.'

Aaron echoed the thanks and said his goodnights, giving his mum the kind of hug that he hoped told her he loved her, then took Nelson for ten minutes on the clifftops, breathing a sigh of relief that the awkward moment with Jordy had passed. For a horrible moment there, he'd thought he'd outed Harry.

Chapter Twenty-One

Over the next couple of weeks, Clancy began to wonder whether someone had messed with the clocks. The August days seemed to pass so slowly – especially any time she spent in the vicinity of Hugo, who seemed glued to the Roundhouse sofa, his chief activities there being TV-watching, snoring and farting.

Alice seemed to be quite liking life back in Nelson's Bar, a situation Clancy would not have anticipated when Alice fled her own wedding day, or at any point in the intervening six years, though she had lived in the village for three years before that, as she reminded Clancy. Now, Alice skipped from the house regularly, walking the cliffs, she said, or driving the motorhome somewhere with Genevieve, with whom Alice seemed to have easily renewed her old friendship. The majority of these outings seemed not to involve Hugo.

When Clancy mentioned these expeditions to Aaron he furrowed his brow and responded, 'Hell. I hope Lee isn't missing at the same time,' which made Clancy wish she hadn't said anything. It was annoying that the Alice–Lee situation was a spectre between Clancy and Aaron, and she once again wished Alice hadn't come back to upset things. Should she feel guilty about that?

Her own relationship with her cousin was hard to categorise. At times they chatted with the affection she remembered, but they were unfortunately overshadowed by longer periods where Clancy's chief emotion was exasperation. Had Alice always been *quite* so blithe about the needs of others? Though she routinely stigmatised her husband as 'a pain in the arse', Alice dealt with his selfish, parasitical ways by pretending there was no problem. She certainly didn't seem prepared to remonstrate with him when he continued to help himself to Clancy's food and drink.

In the end, repressing a desire to ask Alice what on earth she'd ever seen in Hugo, Clancy gave up any hope of that boundary being respected and suggested an arrangement whereby Clancy ordered grocery deliveries for them all using Aaron's broadband and Alice gave Clancy money to cover their share.

Aaron had invited Clancy to use his broadband whenever she wished, so, to give her an excuse to be out of the Roundhouse as much as possible, and to Megan's delight, Clancy took on the creation of the Nelson's Bar website as well as to make good Friday's promise to Kaz and Oli to do some research about funding. August had turned wet, raining off Aaron's gardening for almost a week, so he helped with information and ideas for the website. Sometimes he worked on a telecaster-style guitar he was making in his workshop and she moved her laptop in there to chat while they both worked.

Then they'd end up wrapped around each other, their respective projects ignored.

Clancy got a splinter in her buttock from sex on his workbench. It was worth it. When they were alone, everything was fun and/or hot, they laughed and loved together. His cottage became the haven that the Roundhouse had initially been to Clancy.

But even inside Aaron's four walls, real life began to intrude.

'Mum and Dad have invited us to go out to lunch with them,' Aaron said after taking a phone call one Sunday in mid-August.

As sunshine had returned to the north Norfolk coast that very morning, Clancy had gone outside to watch the sea and give him privacy during the call. Now she felt guilty that her stomach shrank at the thought of being included in a family outing. 'Both of us?' she asked extra-brightly so he wouldn't be able to read her misgivings.

'That's right.' He slid his arm around her and cosied up to nibble at her neck. It hadn't taken him long to work out that she was one large nerve-trembling erogenous zone from tips of her ears to the crook of her neck. 'I think we could view it as an olive branch.'

His casual manner didn't fool Clancy, though she would have loved to concentrate on what he was doing with his mouth rather than decoding the thread of tension in his voice. 'Then we should certainly accept.' Her voice became brighter still.

He stopped nibbling and stroked her cheek with a fingertip instead. 'It'll be fine. You all got on together before the wedding-that-never-was. If my family has been touchy with your family since then, I apologise on behalf of us all. But if you all avoid each other it leaves me in a tricky spot.'

She touched her lips to his hand, instantly wanting to

279

ease him out of said tricky spot. 'I'll go back to the Roundhouse and shower and change.' She'd taken extreme care not to try and move any of her possessions into Aaron's cottage. It was his space. He'd been clear enough to Genevieve about that and Clancy was all too aware how it felt to have the possessions of others thrust upon you.

As it turned out, the Sunday lunch experience wasn't too bad. Clancy picked Aaron up in her bright blue BMW and they met Fergus and Yvonne in a pub garden in Old Hunstanton. If Fergus and Aaron were the ones to keep the early conversation going, Yvonne and Clancy did relax a little after a while and join in.

They talked about Aaron's work, then Yvonne contributed some funny things Daisy had said and Fergus recounted a story about a stag do at the hotel where he worked. The groom's surname was Smurfit so his mates had painted him blue. Clancy told them about the website she was making for the village, then Yvonne wondered aloud whether Lee would buy his own place in the village when his money came through from his house in Northamptonshire.

Clancy didn't mind everyone not mentioning Alice. It was less stressful that way.

When lunch was over, Aaron agreed to stop in at De Silva House and help Fergus move things around in Aunt Norma's annexe – hoping to abandon her crutches and plaster soon and move on to sticks – because she'd bought a new reclining chair to watch TV from and Lee was already out with Daisy. Clancy happily offered to take Nelson for a run. Aaron's parents were important in his life and it gave her a warm feeling that he was the kind of son who'd willingly give a hand, but that didn't mean she felt the need to overstay her time in their company.

After stopping in to change into jeans and a cardigan, she fetched Nelson and set off along the clifftop, the wind making Clancy's hair writhe around her head. She tried to imagine what Nelson's Bar would be like in winter, with grey skies and a roiling sea. The wind would probably feel as if it was trying to snatch you off the cliff. She even let herself imagine that she would still be living in the village then.

'Clancy!'

Her daydreams interrupted, she turned to see Harry and Rory running towards her from the direction of the village. 'Hiya!' she called. 'How's everything going?'

Harry pulled a face. 'Dad's gone a bit weird again. Always seems to be on my back about something. Get a summer job, get prepared for uni, go out more, stay in more . . .'

'Get a girlfriend,' Rory contributed, and they looked at each other and burst out laughing.

Glad to see them again, Clancy invited them to join her for cake and a drink at an empty table outside the B&B. They crossed the grass and ordered from one of the plastic menu cards. Nelson had a slurp from the water bowl left out for dogs then settled himself beneath the table, an ear and eyebrow cocked as he nosed around for stray particles of food. Clancy munched her way through chocolate cake, Harry coconut and Rory lemon drizzle.

Kaz came to their table to clear their empty plates. 'Haven't seen you for a while!' she said to Clancy, her skin crinkling around her eyes as she smiled. 'I wanted to tell you that we're making progress! Informally, the planning people see no problems, though we haven't done the formal bit yet. I don't know about the finance though. The bank only seems to want to lend to people who don't need to borrow. We've got an application in but I'm not holding my breath.' She laughed, though it sounded forced. 'Thing is, we'd really like to start the building in November, and be all ready for next spring.' Kaz balanced her tray on one hand so she could cross the fingers of the other. 'These outside tables are OK in a good summer but not too popular when the cold weather comes.'

Clancy agreed. 'The B&B needs an equivalent indoor space where villagers and tourists could be fed and watered.'

Kaz's attention was taken by customers at another table and Harry and Rory soon went on their way too, thanking Clancy for the snack and patting Nelson's shaggy back before they left.

Clancy sat on, pondering whether Alice and Hugo might find a Norfolk winter bleak and bugger off in their motorhome to Morocco or Timbuktu. She couldn't count on it. After October, her caretaking responsibilities at Roundhouse Row would be minor too, though it was apparent from the records that she might expect the occasional walker or birdwatcher booking.

Would she want to be a caretaker forever?

Probably not, though she didn't miss the buzz of working at IsVid as she'd assumed she would. She didn't miss the stress and the long hours either. The feeling was growing inside her that she should seriously consider rooting herself in Nelson's Bar, this tiny windswept village up on the headland with its stripy chalk cliffs. She was going to have a chunk of money. What she wanted was something absorbing and worthwhile to do with it. Something that would attach her to Nelson's Bar.

Contemplatively, her eyes followed Kaz as she emerged from the B&B with a fresh tray crowded with tea and scones and delivered them to a table nearby. Impulsively, she stopped her as she passed on her way back inside. 'I've done some research for you about funding, if you're interested in hearing it.'

Kaz promptly sat down opposite Clancy. 'Yes,' she said simply.

'Right.' Clancy gathered her thoughts. 'Leaving aside traditional bank borrowing, which you're already investigating yourself, there are lenders who specialise in lending to rural businesses. They might be more approachable but they're no more affordable.'

'Oh,' sighed Kaz, gazing down at the table top. 'What about that crowdfunding thing you mentioned at the Parish Meeting? I googled it myself but it seemed more to do with causes and charities than business.'

'There's definitely organisations where people invest to lend to businesses exactly like yours,' Clancy hastened to assure her. 'It's all done online and it's perfectly reputable. It can be cheaper than traditional borrowing too, but your most likely investors come from your community. And you might have to give investors a slice of the business. And a campaign takes up to three months.'

'Our community didn't seem that keen on helping at the meeting,' Kaz pointed out. 'The whole thing sounds airy-fairy. Oli wasn't at all keen when I told him what I'd read.'

Clancy took a deep breath to steady herself, recognising that this might be a life-defining moment and not wanting to miss the chance. 'Have you thought about taking a partner in, instead of borrowing the money? A single investor?'

Kaz's eyebrows shot up. 'We haven't, but only because we wouldn't know where to start. I don't think there would be enough profit for a sleeping partner. It would have to be someone who'd want to shoulder some work. Like who?'

Another breath, even deeper, then Clancy blurted, 'Like me.'

Slowly, Kaz raised enormous eyes to her. 'Are you serious?'

Clancy felt excitement bubbling inside her. 'Absolutely, yes! It would be a big commitment and there would be a lot to discuss but I'm being bought out of the business I used to be part of in London and I'm looking for something else. I could do all your marketing as well as play a role in the day-to-day running.' She barrelled on, suggesting aspects to her role, then, collecting herself as she realised Kaz was wide-eyed and stumped for words. 'Talk to Oli. It would be a massive step for you guys. Just let me know if you want to open the conversation.'

Kaz's face blazed with a sudden grin. 'I'm pretty sure he'll want to! We'd be bonkers not to. Oh, blimey, Clancy, you could save us! Give me a few days to discuss it with Oli, then I'll come back to you.'

Clancy beamed. 'And it could be *stupendous* for me if I love the B&B even half as much as you do!' She left a little later after a further, excited outpouring of ideas from both her and Kaz. Nelson pranced on his lead in joy that the walk had resumed while Clancy's mind whirred. Had she really just taken a step towards buying into Nelson's Bar? It didn't fit with her citified life since uni. But it felt *great*. Her heart soared right up into the blue summer sky.

Nelson's Bar could be her home.

Aaron had been back for a while when Clancy returned to his house. Nelson greeted him, then yawned and went to bed. 'Did you take him for an especially long walk?' Aaron opened his arms to receive Clancy, who showed more enthusiasm in her greeting.

In fact, her eyes were sparkling. 'We went twice around the cliffs and down and up Zig-zag Path too,' she admitted. 'I needed to blow off steam.' She fairly hummed with nervous excitement. 'I haven't done anything that can't be undone. And I don't want you to think I'm taking anything for granted about you and me. And if things didn't work out, I'd try really hard not to make you feel guilty.'

He dropped a kiss on her forehead. 'I haven't the first idea what you're talking about.'

Her eyes searched his. She took a deep breath then burst out, 'I might be buying into the B&B.'

Surprise washed through him. 'Are you serious?'

She laughed, shifting from foot to foot as if unable to keep still. 'Exactly what Kaz said!' Then she danced away to make coffee. 'I'd work alongside Kaz and Oli to some extent. Though I'm wondering if it could be part time and I'd take on some kind of other work online,' she went on, forgetting to switch the kettle on. 'The idea kept coming into my mind all the time I was looking into funding for Kaz and Oli. I thought out their ideal investor and then I realised . . . well, it was me! I love it here and Kaz and Oli need capital to expand, but then I began to wonder if you'd feel a bit . . . hunted.'

A huge grin stretched itself across his face that Clancy was thinking about Nelson's Bar in the long term. 'If hunting me is what you've been doing for the past couple of weeks then I'm not tired of it yet.' He watched her pacing in the limited area between the table and the white pot sink.

But suddenly apprehension won control of her expression. 'But, seriously,' she said, pausing, 'it has only been a couple of weeks. If I buy into the B&B then I'd be around indefinitely. What I don't want—' she hesitated, obviously choosing her words '—is for me to do something either one of us later regrets.'

'Right.' He processed her words, watching her continue to fidget. *Either one of us* she'd said . . . so this wasn't necessarily about him feeling 'hunted'. His grin faded a notch. She was still trying to extricate herself from one man, Will, with whom she'd shared not just a home but a business as well. Back in July it had taken an emotional toll on her to return to her old life specifically to tear it apart. He'd focused on the positives of that, particularly the positives that affected him, but it must have been hard and stressful. He didn't blame her if she was now wary of tying herself to anything. Or anyone.

'Am I overthinking?' she demanded, when he said no more.

'Of course not. It's a huge decision and I don't think you should take it lightly.' He wanted to catch her to him but her continuous pacing was putting distance between them. Was he supposed to sweep her into a happy dance because buying into the B&B would mean she'd stay? Or remain neutral while she made the best decision for her, regardless of him? He watched, hoping for a clue.

She stopped pacing to stare into his eyes. 'Decisions can be easy to make but hard to overturn.'

So it *was* the enormity of reversing out of her London life that was on her mind. He tried the neutral thing. 'I think you should do what's best for you.'

She dropped her gaze. 'That's sensible. I suppose I don't even know there's a decision to make until Kaz has talked to Oli, so I can just shelve it for now.' She smiled. 'Thank you for your input,' she added brightly.

He frowned. He'd already learned to distrust her bright

voice. It was what she used when she didn't want you to know what she was thinking. 'Input? I feel as if you were all enthusiastic and I brought you down to earth,' he said hesitantly. This time he did slip his arms around her, pulling her to him and stilling her restless movements, wanting to feel her against him, as if she'd be able to absorb all his questions through her skin and give him reassuring answers.

She leaned her cheek on his shoulder so he couldn't see her face. 'I'm a down-to-earth person,' she said resolutely. 'Both feet, firmly planted.' Then she freed herself to return to working on the village website on her laptop.

He wished he understood whether it had been his reaction that had quenched her sparkle. Or her realisation that she was moving dangerously close to jumping out of the frying pan and into the fire.

Chapter Twenty-Two

As evening neared, Clancy returned to the Roundhouse. Aaron had a long-standing arrangement with Mick, Nick and Rick to go to the Princess Cinema in Hunstanton to see a live streaming of the Flow Festival in Helsinki. He'd be back by eleven, he'd said, and made her welcome to stay and await his homecoming. But she couldn't settle to work on the website.

The day's events were on her mind. Buying into the B&B would anchor her in Nelson's Bar and . . . and . . . and . . . what? She wished Aaron's reaction had been easier to read. Nothing he'd said was *wrong*. Buying into a business *was* an enormous decision and it *did* have to be the right one for her.

She would have welcomed a beaming smile or maybe even, 'It would be so great if you stayed!'

Her feet slowed as she squeezed up to the hedge in Long Lane to let a car nose past, exchanging nods with the woman behind the wheel. OK, think this through.

She and Aaron were sleeping together. Sleeping with someone wasn't a decisive tie. People had sex all the time.

You found someone who made you feel desire, you used a condom and bingo. The deed was done.

It wasn't a commitment unless you made it one.

And they hadn't talked about what their relationship was. They'd talked roundabout it, and that was a different thing. That was what people who *didn't* want to commit did. It didn't matter if a couple set fire to the sheets . . . if that was all they wanted then that was all they wanted.

Aaron hadn't committed to Genevieve. In fact, she hadn't asked him the direct question and so Clancy didn't know that he'd ever committed to any girlfriend in a joint-future way. He might not want to commit to her either.

She arrived back at the Roundhouse feeling dispirited. Just to cheer her up, she found Genevieve there with Hugo and Alice. Genevieve and Alice were curled on the sofa, chatting and screaming with laughter, a bottle of wine in a cooler beside them, an empty on the table. Clancy didn't recall Alice even mentioning Genevieve when she'd lived in the village previously but here they were acting like lifelong best friends.

Alice waved her wine glass when she saw her. 'Clance! It's wine o'clock! Grab a glass.'

Clancy debated. By the looks of things she was about four glasses of wine behind but here was an opportunity to mend a bridge or two with Genevieve and perhaps recapture some of the old relationship with Alice. Even Hugo seemed to be making an effort, sitting upright in a chair instead of lolling on the sofa. He was even smiling, although that could have been because he was the only one drinking red, which gave him a full bottle to himself.

'OK, thanks,' Clancy agreed. Maybe a glass of wine and a giggle would set her on an even keel. Allow her to relax and let the future take care of itself.

She grabbed a glass from the kitchen area and then a new bottle of white, as she saw Genevieve upend the last one over her own glass, giving Clancy a smile she didn't know how to take. Clancy smiled back though, and tried to initiate a conversation.

'Is the work finished at your cottage—'

Genevieve turned to talk to Hugo as if Clancy hadn't spoken.

Irritated, Clancy tried to talk to her cousin but the wine seemed to have made Alice feel combatant as she kept breaking into the conversation between Genevieve and Hugo to snark at Hugo.

Hugo, perhaps to pass the snark on, turned to Clancy. 'Where do you go when you're out so much? You can't spend all day making beds and cutting lawns,' he demanded loudly.

Clancy bristled. 'No,' she said, briefly.

Genevieve turned her attention to Clancy too. 'Is it true what Alice told us?' she quizzed her. 'That you found out your last boyfriend was cheating by seeing video of him having sex on the desk in your office?'

Alice clapped her hand over her mouth. 'Genevieve! I told you not to say anything!'

'Sorry,' said Genevieve, sipping wine with no sign of repentance. 'Forgot.' But she cocked her head at Clancy as if still hoping for an answer.

'His office, not mine,' Clancy corrected her stiffly, glaring at Alice, hurt she'd over-share like that.

Hugo snorted a laugh, scratching his beard. 'Will lost control of the head he doesn't think with, eh?'

Resisting the temptation to throw her glass of wine over someone, Clancy picked up her bag with her laptop in it, made sure she had her purse and car keys, and excused herself, thinking dismally how much she'd loved the Roundhouse before Alice came back.

She spent the evening in a pub in Brancaster, eating alone and working on her laptop. It was a pleasure to have a fast, reliable connection, she thought, then reflected ruefully that it was only a day or so since she'd been happy that Nelson's Bar was so cut off.

She emailed her parents, putting on a chatty front, enthusiastic about the possibility of investing in the B&B. *When my dosh comes through I'll have plenty of money,* she wrote. *There's not much in the way of business opportunities in Nelson's Bar so while I don't want to rush into anything, I don't want to miss out either.* She went on to tell them about Alice, not saying anything about the ripples her return was causing or that Hugo was a knob.

Or that she'd been spending a lot of time naked with Aaron but she wasn't sure whether it would go anywhere.

Or that he'd turned cagey today when she'd talked about the B&B. Or that his mother was chilly. Or that his ex-girlfriend was hostile.

Or that she was afraid she was coming to feel more for him than he'd ever be able to reciprocate.

Her parents loved her, she knew that, but when they'd brought her up to be self-sufficient and independent they'd done it for a reason and she never cried on their shoulders. Instead, she signed off, *Hope you're having a great time in Namibia. Lots of love, Clancy xxxxx*

Finally, after a luscious salad that she hardly tasted and a glass of wine to make up for the one she hadn't drunk at the Roundhouse, Clancy shut down her laptop and prepared to drive home through a starry evening with a bright half-moon scooting across the sky half on its back. In no hurry, she looked about her as she drove sedately through Titchwell, then turned right through the pinewoods, tree trunks flashing past in her headlights. Enjoying the peaceful purr of the engine as she rose up Long Climb, she eased into the elbow bend that led into the village.

Illuminated, as she straightened the vehicle up, were a man and woman, barely an inch between them, her face turned up to his.

Luckily, Clancy was able to react fast enough to spin her steering wheel to the right and jink wildly around them, braking to check back shakily in her rear-view mirror, not sure she'd seen what she'd thought she had.

But now both faces were turned her way and it was unmistakeable.

Alice and Lee.

She completed the final hundred yards to the Roundhouse, parked and beeped the car locked, wishing she could unsee what she'd seen. Because then she wouldn't be put in a dilemma about whether to keep it from Aaron.

Under her breath, she cursed Alice.

She went straight to her room, casting a disdainful look at Hugo sleeping on the sofa in front of a reality show. It was barely ten minutes later when a gentle tap fell on her door. She'd put off undressing in the expectation of this moment. With a sigh, she opened the door and let her cousin inside. She didn't ask Alice why she'd come because they both knew.

Alice's cheeks were pink, her eyes glittering, apparently over her tipsiness of the early evening. 'Lee doesn't want his family to know yet,' she whispered, wearing a beseeching puppy-dog gaze.

Clancy sighed. 'I don't suppose you want Hugo to know either, do you? What the fuck are you doing, Alice?'

Alice tried to stroke Clancy's arm. 'Don't be angry. We're only talking . . . at the moment.'

Clancy pulled away, crossing to the window, staring out at the inky black sky with its spangling of pinprick lights and wishing life were simpler. 'So you're asking me to keep a secret from Aaron? Not very fair, Alice.'

'But you and I are cousins!' Alice sounded faintly shocked. No doubt she'd thought this little interview was a formality, that Clancy would unhesitatingly see things her way.

'You only remember that when it suits you.' Clancy lowered her gaze to the street lamps that curved away up Long Lane in the direction of Potato Hall Row. 'Seems as if you've been talking about my private affairs freely enough.'

'Sorry,' Alice said in a small voice. 'Genevieve had promised not to say anything about what Will did.'

'So had you.' Clancy was aware that Alice had moved closer but refused to turn around. For one thing, her eyes had begun to burn. Was it only this morning she'd been so full of hope about making a place for herself in this little village on its headland? It didn't take much to topple a few dreams. Aaron's muted response to her idea. Genevieve's hostility. Hugo's knobbishness. Alice and Lee . . . again.

'I'm going to have a shower before bed,' she said, moving away from the window, deliberately not giving Alice the assurance she wanted. Without looking at her, she pulled her towelling robe off its hook and went down to the bathroom.

By the time she returned to her bedroom, Alice had gone.

*

Aaron liked to watch Clancy sleep, especially when it was so warm that she pushed off the bedclothes and lay naked in his bed, as she was this Tuesday morning, the 6 a.m. sunlight outside lighting up his bedroom curtains. It wasn't that she ever hid from him the soft roundness of her breasts or the sweeping curve of her hip, but in sleep she brought a smile to his face, her limbs relaxed and thrown wide, her expressive eyes hidden but her face peaceful.

She wasn't asleep now though. She was lying too tidily, her breathing too fast, and she was frowning.

He inched closer, so that his front lay against the smooth, warm skin of her side. He kissed her temple. 'You OK?'

'Mm.' The frown smoothed itself away as if she didn't want him to see it.

'Something worrying you? I can almost hear you thinking.' He wished she'd open her eyes. He couldn't have a meaningful conversation with eyelids. She'd spent Monday evening and night with him. He'd tried a couple of times to ask whether she'd had her talk with Kaz and Oli about investing in the B&B, because it had felt like an elephant in the room. Both times she'd distracted him by smooching up with her beautiful body and soon they'd been making love, not conversation.

'I have to get ready for work soon,' he went on. 'Make the most of the dry weather. Mrs Edge in Holme-next-the-Sea's waiting for me to create a stone waterfall water feature beside her patio. She's hosting a family barbecue for her Silver Wedding anniversary on Sunday and she's hassling me to get it done.'

Clancy turned and slid her arms around him, burying her face in his shoulder, one hand drifting down to his hip. 'I could walk Nelson for you after you've gone. Then we'd have time to . . .' She ran her fingertips over the

294

morning erection that was a reliable result of waking up next to her nakedness. 'It's a shame to waste this.'

His focus changed to what her hand was doing and he allowed himself, once again, to be distracted by sex. He couldn't make her talk if she didn't want to but, by giving her pleasure, he could try and take her mind off whatever was bothering her. Not very selfless, he knew.

By the time they finally parted he'd only time to say, 'Will I see you tonight?' as he opened his back door, half of his mind already on the day ahead.

'I have the interim Parish Meeting about broadband and the website at eight,' she reminded him. She was standing in his kitchen with Nelson's lead in her hand and Nelson staring fixedly as he waited for her to connect the lead to his black leather collar.

'I'd forgotten. I'll see you there.' He blew her a kiss and hurried out to his truck to raid his stash of cereal bars to breakfast on as he drove the few miles to leafy Holme.

A day of slog followed as he tried to get the stonework for the water feature finished so the lime mortar that held the stone together could be going off in the next day or so. Mrs Edge was ultra-conscious of the Holme conservation area and had commissioned him to build her water feature of the same materials as her house – red and white chalk or 'clunch', mixed with flint. Getting the mix of the three stones right was vital, because he sure as hell didn't have time to knock it apart and start again if she wasn't happy. He'd got the hole in the ground dug, and the mound for the waterfall lined with sand and a waterproof liner before the weather turned wet.

It was past seven when he drove back into the village, pleasantly exhausted but content in the knowledge that Mrs Edge had approved her several-stepped waterfall and pool with shining eyes. Tomorrow he could get the planting done around the stonework and then on Friday afternoon he could call in to fill up the pool and set the pump so the water would splash gaily down the waterfall.

Nelson was there to greet him when he got home, though there was also a note on his kitchen table in Clancy's flowing handwriting. *Took Nelson to Old Hunstanton beach for a good walk this morning. Cxx*

He gave the big dog a fuss, knowing how he liked to be appreciated when they'd been parted for several hours. 'The beach, eh? Lucky old dog!'

Nelson put his ears back and panted, tail waving.

'I'll feed you before I go out,' Aaron promised as he stuck a chicken leg and a jacket potato into the oven to cook while he went up to shower away the dust of the day. 'The meeting should only take an hour.'

In fact, the meeting must have speeded by as it was almost over by the time he arrived at Megan's house, going around the back to find the French doors open to the warm evening. He entered with a whispered apology.

He could see Clancy sitting at the front. It seemed she'd already said her piece as Megan was summarising the action to be taken now the Village Committee had voted to consult a company Clancy had unearthed who provided broadband via platforms on church spires as there seemed no realistic hope of major providers seeing Nelson's Bar as a commercial proposition.

As this was an interim meeting, attendance was sparse. Apart from the committee members and Clancy, only eighteen villagers were present. Aaron's parents were there, he was unsurprised to see, as Yvonne liked to involve herself with village matters in every way save actually standing for the committee herself.

And, seated behind his parents, sat Genevieve and her mum and dad, Viv and Warren. He registered the fact with the familiar inner sigh about the awkwardness of your ex living in the same tiny village as yourself, and your families inevitably knowing one another.

Still, when the meeting ended and everyone began getting ready to leave, he made sure he greeted Viv and Warren, who responded briefly before turning to say goodnight to Genevieve with big hugs.

It gave Aaron the opportunity to head in Clancy's direction. As his parents moved towards him at the same time, the four of them converged. He was glad to see Yvonne making an effort with Clancy, complimenting her on the village website. Though it was a work-in-progress, Clancy had apparently projected sample pages onto Megan's lounge wall for everyone to see. Clancy seemed more relaxed than he'd seen her around his parents and she wore a natural smile as they talked.

Genevieve came up to congratulate Clancy too, and he saw Clancy's green eyes cloud, though she murmured polite thanks. Then Genevieve hugged each of his parents, which he suspected was an effort to discomfit Clancy. *Look how friendly I am with Aaron's parents. We have real history.* Yvonne flicked him an uneasy glance, though Fergus, who was so laid back he was almost horizontal sometimes, simply appeared to take the gesture at face value and began to ask Genevieve about the work at her cottage.

Aaron had actually put an arm out to see if he could casually usher Clancy away from the group when he heard Genevieve say, 'So what do you think about Lee and Alice? I suppose you'd have preferred her to be separated from Hugo first, but it would be amazing if he finally got his happy-ever-after with her, wouldn't it?' She beamed around the group as if expecting answering smiles.

Yvonne's eyebrows shot up, her lips parting in shock. Even Fergus looked stunned.

Genevieve's smile faltered and her hand flew to her mouth. 'I hope I haven't spoken out of turn,' she said, looking mortified. 'I thought that as Clancy knew . . . Wow, I'm so sorry!' Then she turned and scurried away. As she stepped through the French doors she glanced back, then vanished in the wake of everyone else leaving the meeting.

Beside him, he heard Clancy sigh. When he turned back to her she was pink with embarrassment. She met his gaze levelly and then glanced at his parents. 'I'm sorry. Genevieve has given you the wrong impression. I did see Alice and Lee talking together in the lane a couple of evenings ago and Alice must have told that to Genevieve. I don't know what they were saying and they weren't in a clinch or anything. Alice later told me they'd only been talking. I didn't ask any more because being stuck in the middle of everything again was exactly what I didn't want.'

'But Genevieve seems to think something's going on,' Yvonne said sharply, a furrow between her eyebrows.

Clancy didn't drop her gaze. 'Does she?'

Yvonne's frown deepened. 'Didn't she just say so?'

'Not sure,' Fergus contributed doubtfully. '*Is* that what she said? Or did she just hint?'

'Well . . . I don't know.' Yvonne looked confused. 'It sounded as if they were doing a lot more than talking. Not that I knew they'd even exchanged a word since Alice came back!' she added with asperity.

Aaron watched Clancy. Her gaze switched between his

parents as they talked. What she didn't do, he noticed, was meet his eye.

'You know,' he said, suddenly seeing no reason not to acknowledge a frailty in his old girlfriend. 'Genevieve can put a spin on facts when she feels like it.' It at least made Clancy look at him. Her expression was . . . contemplative. But cautious.

He took her hand and bid his parents goodnight, dropping a kiss on his mother's cheek.

Outside the light was fading. Aaron strolled across the village, still in possession of Clancy's hand, aiming towards his place. He felt her hesitate as they hit Droody Road, as if she might decide to peel off for the Roundhouse, but then she continued with him.

Soon they were in his kitchen. He left the door open so Nelson could have a good sniff around the garden. The moths could fly in but the conversation he meant to have with Clancy wouldn't be interrupted by Nelson scratching to come in again.

Her expression was shuttered but she was the one to speak first. 'Alice said they'd only talked but Lee didn't want his family to know. I said it wasn't fair to ask me to keep a secret from you and I ended the discussion.'

'When did you see them?' he asked, noticing the way her beautiful mouth had turned down at the corners. She was not enjoying this.

'Sunday night.' She tangled her fingers with his, her gaze steady. 'Alice was adamant that nothing had happened. She's my cousin.'

'But I'm your lover,' he reminded her neutrally.

She nodded. 'A lover who takes his brother's part whenever Lee and Alice are discussed.' She moved in closer so that he had to combat the urge to slip his arms around her. Her gaze was both apprehensive and mutinous. 'Do they really have to stand between us all the time? They're adults. If they get back together there's nothing you or your parents can do about it. If Alice decides to end her joke of a marriage it's her decision.'

He squeezed her fingers, wishing heartily that Genevieve had kept her mouth shut. 'I was here to see Lee crumble when Alice left before – left him in the cruellest of ways – and I worry about his sanity; what will happen next time they break up. I can't pretend it's not a concern.'

Nelson ambled in, bringing the fresh scent of outdoors with him, and put his head between Aaron and Clancy to gaze up, ears back, and give a big doggy smile. Absently, Clancy tousled his ears. 'I've never made it clear to Alice how badly Lee was affected by her leaving. I don't know whether he'd want her to know. It would be interesting to know what, if anything, he's told her himself, wouldn't it? I think I'll go back to the Roundhouse tonight. I need to get my head round things.'

Reflexively, Aaron tightened his fingers around hers. 'Don't go home—'

Her smile was strained. 'I don't have a home.' She went up on her toes to give him a peck goodnight but turned away before he could catch her to him and kiss her properly. She slipped out into the evening, leaving him nursing a hollow feeling as he examined her final words.

I don't have a home.

The Roundhouse probably didn't feel like home now Alice had restaked her claim, installing Hugo to act as if he owned the place. Clancy's portion of the home she'd shared with Will was being transferred into the ownership of his new wife and soon Will's baby would live there too. The first eighteen years of her life had been spent transferring from country to country as her parents' careers dictated. They'd flown home from Oman in time for her to be born in a hospital in London, she'd told him once, then they'd returned as soon as an airline would have her on board.

It was a far cry from being born and brought up in one small village. That was home. It always had been.

He thought about going after her, but then decided to respect her decision to be alone. And, since that initial meeting with Alice, he hadn't felt much like visiting the Roundhouse or Roundhouse Row. Maybe he ought to change that; establish his right to be there. He could offer to help Clancy again on changeover day. It hadn't seemed like work to breeze through the cottages in her company, watching the way her shorts clung to her rear as she hoovered and polished and changed sheets.

Meantime, he'd had a hard day in the sun after expending a lot of energy in bed with Clancy. He'd give Nelson a run because Aaron feeling knackered was not the dog's fault, and then he'd go to bed.

As he was reaching for the door keys the phone on the kitchen wall began to ring, but he waited for it to go to the answering machine because he could think of several people he didn't want to talk to right now. Then he heard Lee's voice come down the line. 'Oh, shit, aren't you there?'

Instantly, he reached over and picked up. 'Yeah, hi, what's up?' He didn't have to be told something was up because Lee's emotions were usually on show – in his body language or, in this case, his voice.

Lee groaned. 'I'm going to ask you a huge favour. I know you're not going to want to say yes but I'm asking you not to say no. It'll only be temporary.'

Aaron's heart began a slow descent towards the canvas shoes on his feet. 'Go on.'

'Can Daisy and I come and live with you until I can find somewhere else?' Lee asked miserably.

Aaron sighed. 'I don't think I have to ask why.'

'Yeah. Mum heard something about Alice and me and came home to give me a good telling off. Thirty-four is too old to be under the parental microscope and I told her to butt out. I'm mega-aware that you're not keen on sharing your house but I promise it's only until I can either find a rental or I get a completion date on my old place and buy somewhere else. Maybe in Hunstanton,' he added, 'because Daisy will go to school there and I've never been that thrilled about the village kids going on a minibus.'

Aaron could do little but agree to his brother's request. That strained note was in Lee's voice again and if Lee lost his shit, the consequences could be major. 'But you need to tell Mum and Dad.'

'Already discussed.' Lee's voice hardened. 'Mum's agreed to continue to look after Daisy while I'm at work in the short term, maybe until I get a childminder sorted out in my new place. We'll be civil to each other and everything but I just can't live here any more. I've already spoken to the guy I'm supposed to be working with to say I'll be missing tomorrow while I move our stuff over – if that's OK – and make sure Daisy feels as settled as she can be. She's asleep now, or I'd come straight away.'

'Right.' Aaron made sure he didn't sigh. 'There's always a key to my place hanging in Mum and Dad's kitchen so just come and take over the two spare rooms. I'll be working till late afternoon tomorrow but you know where everything is. Make yourself at home and maybe we can talk in the evening.'

'Thanks, mate.' Lee sounded relieved but not noticeably happier. He hesitated. 'Will it kind of . . . make things awkward between you and Clancy?'

Biting back the impulse to say, 'You and Alice are always making things awkward between us,' he said instead, 'That's one of the many subjects I suppose we're going to have to discuss. Don't worry. We'll work it out.'

When the call was over, he clicked his tongue to Nelson and stepped outside, feeling exhausted yet a long way from sleep. He was sorry for Lee, who was not resilient, but he was sorry for their mum too. She loved her kids, but she'd obviously gone in too hard with Lee and alienated him in the process. She saw Alice as wrong for Lee – Aaron didn't disagree with her – and a married woman. Going into protective mode must have caused her to fail to treat Lee like an adult.

As the wind blew through his hair, Aaron watched the clouds moving across the moon and acknowledged that he'd sometimes fallen into the same trap himself.

He, like his mum, had to learn to let Lee live his own life, mistakes and all.

Chapter Twenty-Three

'Alice has *what*?' It was Wednesday morning and Clancy was staring across the lounge area of the Roundhouse at Hugo in horror. 'But I was only talking to her a few hours ago!'

'Talking' was one way of describing the way Clancy had flown at Alice about what she'd shared with Genevieve.

'She's left me!' Hugo repeated, white and visibly shaken. 'While you were out chatting with one of your precious holidaymakers we had a few words and suddenly she was packing a bag. She said our marriage was over, jumped into the motorhome and drove off.'

Wordless, Clancy could only gaze at a Hugo who looked even less appealing than usual in shorts and T-shirt that Clancy suspected were actually pyjamas. She didn't doubt his story that Alice had packed her things and gone. Nobody could manufacture Hugo's hit-by-a-truck look. She'd seen a similar expression in her mirror after catching Will and Renée with their respective pants down.

Hugo sank down onto the sofa, rubbing his hands over his face. 'I didn't think she'd really go,' he mumbled. Then he lifted his head sharply, glaring at Clancy. 'I expect you're pleased!'

'No.' Clancy felt as if the truck that hit Hugo had given her a glancing blow. If Alice had gone . . . it left Clancy with Hugo. *With Hugo!* Caretaking duties or not, it would be untenable to share the Roundhouse with him. She had to suppress a shudder at the mere idea, not having it in her, at that moment, to feel sympathy for Hugo or concern for Alice. In fact, though she knew she had only to drive out of the village and she'd stand a good chance of ringing Alice in privacy, she disregarded the idea.

'Did she say where she was going?' she demanded.

'I think it was "anywhere but here",' Hugo snapped.

Eyes pricking with tears, Clancy marched out of the front door. At first, she walked blindly, mind churning with this latest development, feet carrying her down the familiar route towards the cliffs. Once there, she slowed, tossing back her hair and gazing out at the sea shining merrily on what now seemed an inappropriately beautiful day.

Slowly, her initial feelings of panic and hurt began to settle. OK, so Alice had gone – again. Leaving Clancy with an uncomfortable situation to resolve – again. But she could do it.

It was possible that Hugo wouldn't stay, though Clancy would be surprised if he'd give up a house easily. He had no real means of support, from what Alice had said. No, Clancy had already begun to consider the future and this merely accelerated the process.

As Kaz had promised to come back to Clancy on Oli's reaction to her going into partnership with them Clancy hadn't pressed for an answer, especially as only three days had passed, but, feeling slightly better at making up her mind to do something positive, she decided to go to see them now. She turned inland. The parasols were open above the tables in front of the B&B and Clancy could see Kaz bustling outside with a tray. Heartbeat steadying, she hurried across the grass, smile at the ready. Kaz had served some people clustered around a table and was heading indoors by now, empty tray swinging from her hand. When she caught sight of Clancy, she paused.

'Hi!' Clancy summoned up a smile, hoping 'anxious for news' wasn't written on her face. 'May I have a cappuccino, please?' She dropped her voice. 'But really I'm here to ask if there's any progress? Did you talk to Oli? I know you said you'd need a few days to think but I couldn't wait any longer.'

'Why don't you take a seat? I'll join you in a minute.' Kaz gave her a quick smile and turned away, leaving Clancy to choose one of the two empty tables, suddenly nervous. This was a turning point. If Kaz and Oli went for her idea then it could tie her to Nelson's Bar for years to come, though she'd still have to find a temporary home until the deal was done. Then she'd buy a place and have a home and a business again, but one that was about as different to the last as was possible. If things went the right way with Aaron then she'd have a man who was a good deal different to the last, too. Aaron was stronger, more reliable, and more interested in adding beauty to the world around him than Will.

It was early days for them, of course, but if/when things went wrong, she decided stoutly, she'd be prepared. She was not Genevieve. She wouldn't lean, need and expect as Genevieve had.

Her thoughts were interrupted by Kaz arriving with the

cappuccino in a white cup with a saucer and sitting down across the table.

'So what did Oli say?' Clancy demanded, tearing the top off a sachet of brown sugar.

Kaz fidgeted awkwardly. 'Sorry, Clancy, but I didn't ask him. I realised your idea wasn't really a goer.'

Shocked, Clancy stilled, sugar sachet in hand.

Not quite meeting her gaze, Kaz went on. 'I'm sorry if you're disappointed but when I really thought of someone else owning a part of this, I realised it's not what I want. The B&B came from Oli's family and we're building it up. The two of us.'

Clancy couldn't unfreeze to pour the sugar into the cup. 'Oh.' Her heart slowed to a sad, heavy beat. 'I see.' She managed to sound composed. Experience had taught her that when you went into business boundless enthusiasm was a key ingredient. If Kaz had gone so cold on the idea that she hadn't even discussed it with Oli then it was never going to happen. 'Thanks for being honest,' she said, trying to sound bright. She finally tipped the sugar into the cappuccino and stirred it in.

'I am sorry,' Kaz said again, levering herself to her feet quickly, as if relieved Clancy wasn't trying to force the issue. 'No hard feelings?'

'Of course not,' Clancy responded automatically. 'It was entirely your decision.' Then, as Kaz turned away she said impulsively, 'How much would it be if I asked to book a room here for a while? Now Alice and her husband have moved into the Roundhouse—'

But Kaz was already shaking her head. 'We couldn't have anyone full time until about the middle of September. We're pretty booked till then. That cappuccino's on the house, by the way.'

Clancy sat, gazing out to sea. It was lunchtime but she was too full of disappointment to eat. Her chances of making a home in Nelson's Bar had taken a serious hit and the prospect of staying on in the Roundhouse had taken on the proportions of a nightmare.

Briefly, she considered asking whether Dilys would take her as a lodger as a stopgap but quickly realised that living next door to the Roundhouse wouldn't be much more fun than living in it.

She absolutely wasn't going to expect to move in with Aaron. They hadn't been together long enough; they hadn't even discussed what form their relationship was taking.

As she sat there, staring into thin air, Lee and Daisy hove into view, Nelson on his extendable leash, cantering up to dance in front of Clancy. If you could harness his tail's energy, it could provide electricity, like the offshore wind farm did, Clancy thought absently, rubbing his hairy head. He gazed at her with one bright eye.

'Hi.' Lee followed Nelson over. He looked worn out.

'Hello. Hello, Daisy,' Clancy greeted them.

Daisy was looking unusually glum. 'I'm sulking at the moment,' she advised Clancy. 'I'm going to be a good girl later.'

'Right. Good to know.' Even feeling as low as she did, Clancy had to smother a grin.

Lee rolled his eyes. 'I've taken the day off to move from Granny and Grandad's house to Uncle Aaron's and I'm afraid Daisy's not keen on the change.'

While Clancy gazed at him in astonishment, he went on, explaining in the awkward way parents did when they were conscious of childish ears listening, that Daisy was still going to see lots of Granny and Grandad because she'd go to their house each day while he was at work until she started school in September, but Aaron had very kindly said Lee and Daisy could live with him and Nelson for a while.

Clancy nodded along, trying to hide her dismay. Despite her resolution not to expect to move in with Aaron, utilising his Wi-Fi to create the village website had provided her with a refuge. She'd been at his place *a lot*. It would be completely different with a brother and a four-year-old niece in residence. The tops of her ears felt hot just to think about people being elsewhere in the house when she and Aaron . . .

Lee looked uncomfortable, as if reading her thoughts. 'I hope we won't cramp yours and Aaron's style—'

Daisy tugged his hand, evidently tiring of adult conversation. 'Come on, Daddy, we promised to take Nelson down onto Zig-zag Beach.'

Lee murmured a gentle reproach about interrupting when he was talking, but Daisy was already turning away. 'Bye, Clancy. Can I hold Nelson's lead, Daddy?'

Clancy pinned on a smile as she waved. 'Bye, Daisy. Have a lovely time on the beach.'

When she got up to go a few minutes later, she left four pounds on the table for the cappuccino. She found she didn't want it on the house.

Despondent, she drifted across the clifftop grass, gazing at all the different houses and cottages of the village like a cutesy picture on a jigsaw puzzle. She turned in to Long Lane, wandering into Aaron's garden to hook up with his Wi-Fi and check her email. She wasn't sure whether it was reasonable to hope he'd sent her a message explaining the Lee and Daisy situation, but somehow she'd feel better if he had.

He hadn't.

Clancy gazed at the garden he'd made between his back door and the sea. The plants he'd called 'architectural' in geometric-shaped beds amongst the paving. The bench that he'd made from the back doorstep of a falling-down cottage. The bank of wildflowers he'd grown to blend his garden in with the wildness of the clifftop. She had to swallow very hard. She thought about taking advantage of being on his Wi-Fi to ring him. Hearing his voice might make her feel better.

But, no, he'd be working. She was *not* going to make her happiness and wellbeing his responsibility.

It was as Clancy was leaving the garden that she bumped into Yvonne coming in. 'Oh,' they both said, halting.

A variety of emotions flitted over Yvonne's face. 'I was looking for Lee.'

'I saw him and Daisy walking Nelson,' Clancy said, not feeling equal to a conversation with Aaron's mum. 'I just stepped into the garden for the Wi-Fi.' She made a tentative move to edge past Yvonne who, she thought, was not a bad person. Just guilty of a monocular view of any situation involving her sons.

Yvonne moved too, making it harder to pass. 'Clancy, can I ask you something?'

'Of course,' Clancy answered politely, hoping it wasn't going to be anything about the present whereabouts of her cousin. In her current low state, a conversation about that would just about reduce her to tears.

A smile from the older woman. 'You're aware of what's going on between Lee and Alice?' She said 'Alice' as if she didn't even want the word in her mouth.

'I don't know,' said Clancy. 'It depends what is going on, I suppose. If anything is.'

Yvonne looked wrong-footed, her complexion pasty,

lines of anxiety gathering around her eyes. 'Well . . . I know Alice is your cousin,' Yvonne said, at length. 'I just thought that maybe, as you're seeing Aaron now, that you might feel—' She paused, as if hoping Clancy would fill in the gap.

Clancy stayed stubbornly silent.

'—you could tell me what's going on,' Yvonne finished in a rush.

Clancy turned sideways and made a more determined attempt to edge past. 'It's not my business,' she said flatly. 'Sorry.'

'Oh, I'm not trying to interfere,' Yvonne called after her. 'I didn't mean to suggest that.'

Clancy hesitated. Stopped. Went back. 'I know you're only looking out for your son,' she said, trying to be reasonable and pleasant. 'But Alice is thirty-four. I suppose Lee's around the same age. Even if they're heading for disaster, I'm afraid I can't help you because I don't know anything.'

A tear trembled on Yvonne's lashes. 'I know what you're saying,' she muttered. 'But you're not Alice's mother. It's easier for you.'

'Is it?' asked Clancy tiredly. She took her leave from Yvonne politely and walked back down Long Lane towards the Roundhouse. She was so sick of the day that she got into her Beemer without going indoors, did a U-turn in the lane and drove out of the village, swooping down Long Climb with a belly like lead.

She parked at the side of the road at the top of the hill in Old Hunstanton and walked down through the gardens into Hunstanton itself. She bought a cup of coffee from a catering van and jumped down onto the beach to sit with her back against the concrete wall to drink it, watching children build sandcastles and gulls wheel over tourists to see who they could mug for a muffin.

When the coffee was gone, she climbed a few steps and walked along the promenade until she reached the caravan park beside the funfair, and then she just carried on, all the way to Heacham. At a loss what to do when she got there, she walked back again, flopped into her car and drove back to Nelson's Bar, her mind no more settled than when she'd started out.

The village waited beneath an endless blue dome of early evening sky. When she'd parked the car by the hedge she went inside.

Hugo was sitting on the sofa staring blankly at the TV. Clancy didn't look at him. He didn't look at her either but said, offhandedly, 'Lover boy rang for you.'

'Thanks.' Clancy felt a small lift of her heart and went over to the phone, not caring that Hugo was there to listen.

The ring tone sounded six times before Aaron answered.

'Hey,' she said. 'It's me.'

'Hey,' he said, sounding distracted. 'Can I ring you back? Mum's really upset—'

'Sure.' She waited to see if he'd say anything else, wondering whether her scratchy conversation with Yvonne earlier was what had upset her. When he didn't add anything she said, 'Speak to you later,' and replaced the phone in its cradle. Realising she hadn't eaten since breakfast, she crossed to the fridge for the chicken breast she'd put there. Miracles, it was where she'd left it, and she wrapped it in foil with a slice of onion and shoved it in the oven. She'd make a salad to eat with it when it was cooked.

Before she could go up to her room, the landline rang again, burbling from its holster on the wall.

Clancy picked it up quickly. But, rather than it being Aaron calling back as promised, a strange noise came down the line. 'Hello?' Clancy said tentatively. Then she thought she caught her name. 'Sorry, I can't make out . . .' Then her stomach did a slow flip-flop as she recognised that the strange noise was crying. And she knew the voice. 'Will?'

A quavering sob answered her.

'Will,' she said again, more urgently. 'What on earth's the matter?'

'Hospital,' he choked out. 'Renée's really bad. Monty and Asila too. This moron in a lorry . . .' He gulped, let out a high-pitched keening noise. 'I was driving, Clancy. We were coming off the M11. He just changed lanes and left me nowhere to go. I'm at the hospital and they're all more hurt than me. I don't know what to do.'

'Hang on,' she found herself saying, because she always knew what to do. The hard shit. 'I'll come. Which hospital? Homerton? I'm on my way.'

Chapter Twenty-Four

Aaron had walked into his garden after walking Nelson to find his mum there in tears.

'Oh, Aaron!' she sobbed as soon as she saw him. 'Whatever's he done?'

'Who?' he demanded sharply but he didn't really have to ask. It must be Lee. A cold sweat broke over him. 'Come indoors and tell me what's happened.'

He had to get Yvonne a glass of water because she was crying so hard she couldn't form words he could understand. Nelson sat in his basket, looking worried and unhappy. When the phone rang, Aaron picked it up in case it was his brother. Clancy's voice spoke to him and he rapped out, 'Can I ring you back? Mum's really upset.' Though he would love to have talked to her because he'd been ringing the Roundhouse to try and tell her about Lee and Daisy moving in, he obviously had A Situation to deal with first. He replaced the phone, aware she'd put down at her end too abruptly for comfort.

He put an arm around his mother. 'So, what's going on?'

'This note,' Yvonne gulped. 'Lee's not here and I'm worried to death.' She wiped her eyes. 'I was cleaning his room at our house, after he'd packed up and moved here. I found this under his bed.' Dully, she held out a crumpled sheet ripped from a spiral notepad.

Aaron, heart sinking, plucked the sheet from his mother's fingers, reading its few lines in Lee's loopy handwriting.

I am tormented. Feel hopeless.
Hopeless.
Hopeless.

Slowly, he folded the sheet up again, noticing, absently, that now his fingers were shaking. 'And you haven't seen him?'

Yvonne shook her head. 'His van's not here and there's no sign of him or Daisy. He's not answering his phone. Oh, Aaron.' She lifted a tear-stained face. 'It's not . . . it's not a *suicide* note is it?'

'There's no need to think that,' Aaron reassured her automatically, even though his stomach was burning with dread because he'd wondered the same thing. 'It doesn't say anything to that effect. I think—'

Then the kitchen door flew back on its hinges, making Nelson erupt from his basket with a cacophonous protest. When he saw Jordy in the doorway, Nelson paused, though he continued to growl in his throat.

Aaron put a hand on his collar. 'What's up with you, dog? Don't you recognise Jordy?'

Jordy stepped indoors, shutting the door with a bang, his dark eyes fixed on Aaron. 'You knew all along didn't you?'

'What?' demanded Yvonne, looking from one to the other.

Aaron met his cousin's glare, pretty sure he knew what was coming, but he still asked, 'About what?'

Jordy took a step nearer, making Nelson growl again. 'That Harry thinks he's gay with that damned Rory kid.'

Nelson's growls rose and Aaron stroked his head. 'It isn't the right time for this, Jordy. Have you seen Lee today?'

'Did you?' Jordy shouted, his face red and sweating.

Obviously, Jordy wasn't going to answer Aaron's question until Aaron answered Jordy's.

'Yes. Harry is what he is, just like you're what you are and I'm what I am. He has a lot of feelings for Rory. There's nothing wrong with it.'

'If there's nothing wrong with it then why's he been hiding it?' Jordy spat.

Aaron considered his answer. 'Because he knows you're homophobic' didn't seem right. He chose a different gambit. 'He's still the kid you've always loved. You don't want to lose his respect, do you?'

Redder and angrier than ever, Jordy snapped, 'Haven't seen Lee for days,' and slammed back out, leaving Aaron shaken and Nelson hurling himself at the door with a volley of barks.

'Oh, dear,' sniffed Yvonne. 'I've got to say it's crossed my mind about Harry and Rory. Now Jordy's found out I'll bet he's had a go at poor Harry.'

'Yeah.' Aaron ran his fingers through his hair, exhausted by the dramas enacted in his kitchen this evening. He had the urge to speak to Harry but the youngster could be anywhere and Aaron had a crisis to deal with. 'Let's try and track Lee down.' Aaron began to ring around, drawing a blank with Mick, Rick and Nick and everyone he could think of. He rang the Roundhouse, because Clancy might know something. She could have been to the cottage to work on the website and seen Lee and Daisy. And then there was another Roundhouse occupant who might know something too. Alice. He got only the engaged signal. He tried again.

Engaged again.

And again.

He looked at his mum. 'I'm going to go down and see if I can talk to Alice. If they have been seeing each other she might know where he is.'

Yvonne couldn't become any paler, but she almost visibly stiffened her upper lip. 'I suppose so.' Then, quietly, 'Thank you, Aaron.'

Aaron picked up his keys. 'Is Dad on evening shift? I'll walk you home so you'll be with Aunt Norma, OK? Then I'll come back to yours when I've been to the Roundhouse.' He had high hopes of Clancy being there. He should have managed to make the scale of the situation clear to her before letting her hang up. What he'd said must've sounded like a brush-off.

'I can walk home on my own. You just go ahead.' Yvonne gave Aaron a hug. He clipped on Nelson's lead, which made the dog look cheerful for the first time since all the human drama, and then he strode out of the door behind her.

Before long he found himself jogging, Nelson extending his stride like a little pony to keep up. Aaron was so keyed up by the time he reached the Roundhouse that he rang the doorbell and used his key to go in without waiting to see if he was welcome. Then he paused and stepped back to look out at the lane behind him.

Clancy's blue BMW wasn't there.

He hurried in to find Hugo eating a pie from a plate on his lap in front of the telly.

'Is Clancy here? Or Alice?' Aaron demanded, noticing that, behind Hugo, the phone hung from its wall holster, which would explain the constant engaged signal.

Hugo stared at him balefully. 'What do you want with Alice?'

Aaron strode in, grabbed the TV remote from where it lay beside Hugo and switched off the set. Then he took Hugo's plate off him and deposited it on a nearby table. 'This is important!' he snapped. 'I need to talk to Alice.'

To his disbelief, Hugo's face began to crumple. 'Alice has left me,' he said pathetically. 'She's packed up and gone.'

For several seconds, Aaron just stared at Hugo in horror. If Alice had gone and Lee and Daisy had gone . . . the obvious conclusion was that they'd all left together. Sooner or later, it would blow up in Lee's face and who knew what would happen? Aaron dropped down into an armchair. 'Shit.' Then, with compunction, 'Sorry, Hugo.' He wasn't sure if he was commiserating about Hugo being left or apologising for storming in.

'Thank you,' Hugo said morosely.

For a minute, Aaron's thoughts were taken up with how he was going to break the news to his mother. Then they circled around. 'I presume Clancy's not here? I see her car's gone.'

'She got a phone call and went,' Hugo replied.

Aaron rose. 'I might be able to get her on her mobile if she's left the village. Do you know where she's gone?'

'To be with Will.' Hugo turned his small dark eyes on Aaron. He had pie crumbs in his beard. 'She packed a bag and went. It's been quite the day for it.' Then, perhaps seeing by Aaron's expression that now was not the time to muck him about, he expanded his explanation. 'There's

318

been an accident. Clancy left to be with him. I heard her say Homerton Hospital. Some of the friends she used to work with were in the crash too.'

'Right,' Aaron said numbly. His stomach felt as if he were tumbling down a lift shaft. After taking his leave from Hugo, he jogged back up Long Lane, pausing only when Nelson dragged at his lead in a polite hint that he'd actually like to stop and cock his leg.

When he reached De Silva House he went straight in, finding Yvonne and Aunt Norma drinking tea in the kitchen. Yvonne leapt up as soon as Aaron appeared.

'Hugo says Alice has left him,' Aaron said, slipping an arm around his mum. 'I don't think we should read too much into it but . . .'

'But Lee's vanished with Daisy at exactly the same time.' Yvonne sat back down suddenly, lifting piteous eyes to his. 'What are we going to do?'

Aaron sat down across the table. 'I don't think there's anything we can do. In a way, I hope he *is* with Alice.'

Yvonne's eyebrows shot up. 'Why?'

Aunt Norma was the one to answer. Her plaster cast had been taken off now but she was still walking with sticks. 'Because if he's run off with Alice, then presumably he's not feeling suicidal, despite that note.'

Yvonne made a strangled sound, clamping a hand over her eyes. 'I just want to know he's safe.'

'Me, too.' Aaron patted his mother's arm. 'I'll keep trying his mobile, and if I don't get him I'll send a text asking him to get in touch with one of us ASAP.'

'Thank you,' Yvonne sniffed.

As soon as Aaron got home, he called Lee's mobile, receiving an 'unavailable' message and an invitation to leave voicemail. He waited impatiently for the beep. 'Lee, this is Aaron. Can you get in touch with me, or with Mum or Dad, as soon as? It's important.' He decided not to say that everyone was worried about him in case that made him remain silent. He texted a similar message for good measure, then he abandoned everything Lee-related for a moment and called Clancy's mobile.

That call went to voicemail too.

All of a sudden, his legs felt like lead. He tried again with exactly the same result, then sent a text. *Are you OK? Hugo tells me there's been an accident. Please contact me as soon as you're able. xxx*

He fed Nelson and fetched a guitar, settling at the kitchen table, his mobile phone in front of him and close to the landline phone too, waiting for one of them to ring. It was hard to play with sweaty, trembling fingers though.

Later, at Homerton University Hospital, Clancy was exhausted. Several members of staff had suggested that she could go home and rest, that her friends were in good hands, but still she continued to sit on one of a collection of chairs just inside the main door. Over the past hours she'd acted as the information hub for the families of Will, Asila, Monty and even Renée. Now her energy was leaching away and it was dawning on her that she had no obvious place to go. She couldn't make her tired mind work around the logistics of booking a hotel room online now it was past midnight on Wednesday, in case it resulted in her getting a room for Thursday night, not tonight.

She needed a hotel that had a night staff so she could telephone and sort it out person to person. She kept shying away from the option a bruised, battered and subdued Will had given her, which was to use her key to the apartment and sleep there.

Maybe she'd just continue sitting here instead, not making the decision.

Her mind drifted. Aaron had been trying to contact her. She'd read his text several times but by the time she'd finished talking to Will's parents, who were in a different time zone on holiday and were trying to change flights, and reassuring Asila's husband, who was haunting the hospital corridors in tears and seemed totally incapable of retaining any information the nursing staff gave him, it had already been late. She was reluctant to risk waking Aaron with a call so had left a text: *I'm OK but Will, Renée and some of my erstwhile colleagues have been hurt in a car crash, some quite badly.* She felt unequal to the task of explaining why she'd travelled to be with Will – she'd been wondering about it herself and her only conclusion had been that he'd caught her at a low moment and provided proof that there was somewhere she was needed and wanted – so she just added: *I'll be in contact. xxx*

While she'd been sitting here, she'd thought of Aaron a lot: his ready smile, the way he moved, the heat of him when he made love to her. The odd mixture of reliability and free-spiritedness that was him, living in his cottage on the clifftop.

Was there a place for her in his life? Or in Nelson's Bar at all?

She'd been careful not to be presumptuous about moving in on his space but he'd apparently agreed to share his home with Lee and Daisy. They were his family and she was not, and she was trying not to feel it was a reflection of the scale of her importance to him, but it *was* making her consider alternatives. The Roundhouse was out; the B&B was out. A house in Thornham or Titchwell, just a few miles from Nelson's Bar, would be her best option. It would be an easy drive to perform her caretaking duties, or they could advertise for someone to take over at the end of the summer. Clancy could get a different job or throw herself into another business. Then, if things didn't work out with Aaron, they wouldn't be falling over each other in the village or having to deal with each other at Roundhouse Row.

It was a slightly odd thing to realise, but it might be that having a life that was easy to separate from Aaron's would be the key to keeping him in it.

Having a plan of sorts woke her up a bit. She stirred herself to get up and leave, grabbing her car keys as she left the hospital in search of her car, then she drove to the apartment and let herself in to fall on the blue velvet sofa that a few years ago she'd chosen with Will.

As she tried to sleep, she remembered telling Aaron about her relationship with Will, about how their supposed love had been something that built up gradually, over time, and that she found it hard to believe in the kind that took you by surprise in a month or a week. Sleep seemed to get further away instead of closer as she suspected that the empty feeling in the pit of her stomach was nothing to do with missing dinner. It was missing Aaron.

Chapter Twenty-Five

Tense and apprehensive, Aaron was up early on Thursday. His first job was to check his mobile for messages from Clancy or Lee.

Nothing from Lee but his heart hopped to see the text from Clancy. Then he was disappointed to see how brief it was. *I'll be in contact.* Did that mean she didn't expect him to contact her? A glance at his bedside clock told him it was early for a call but he replied to the text: *Sorry to hear about the accident. Are you at a hospital? Let me know when I can ring you. xxx*

He checked Lee and Daisy's rooms but was unsurprised to see them empty and undisturbed. He was equally unsurprised that when his landline rang at seven, his usual breakfast time on a workday, that the caller was his mother, voice hushed with strain. 'Have you heard anything from Lee? When Dad came in after his late shift he said to wait until he woke up at lunchtime and we'd talk then, but do you think we should call the police?'

Aaron's heart turned over at even discussing that prospect.

'Surely Lee's too devoted a dad to have taken Daisy with him if he meant himself harm?'

Yvonne sniffed. 'So . . . does that mean Lee and Daisy are somewhere with Alice?'

Then Aaron heard Fergus's calm voice in the background, regardless that he could have had very little sleep. After a few moments he came on the line. 'It's too early to panic. Let's give him time to contact us at least.'

Aaron agreed. He tried ringing both Lee and Clancy, to no avail, and then rearranged his work so he could be at home today. He had a plan to put together for a prospective customer and he could do that at his kitchen table, keeping close company with the phones.

It was actually approaching lunchtime when his mobile finally rang and *Clancy* flashed up on the screen. Warmth raced through him. He burst out, 'Clancy?' just as Lee and Daisy walked through the door, smiling and looking relaxed, backpacks on their backs.

'Where's Clancy?' demanded Daisy, letting go of Lee's hand so she could skip up and down on the floorboards yodelling, 'Clanceeeeee, Clanceeeeee, Clanceee-eee-eee.' Nelson joined in with a few skips of his own, barking.

Though relief thundered through him at the sight of his brother and his niece quite obviously safe and well, Aaron was not going to put Clancy off this time. He pointed at Lee and hissed, 'Stay there!' then stuck a finger in his ear to try and hear Clancy on the phone. 'Are you OK?'

'Yes.' She sounded reassuringly familiar and composed. 'Sorry I didn't get back to you last night. I was up till all hours and then I overslept. Will escaped the accident with cuts and bruises but Renée and Monty are still unconscious. Asila's come round but has concussion. They've all got upper body injuries – ribs, shoulders and clavicles. Monty has a broken leg, too.' She dropped her voice. 'They hope that Will and Renée's baby is going to be OK. There's a normal heartbeat, the baby's moving and there's no bleeding but they're going to keep her under close observation. At least she wasn't behind the steering wheel. They were all in the car together because they were coming home from some shindig Renée's company had put on. Hang on.'

Her voice receded while she spoke to someone. It was muffled but sounded like, 'Yes, I will, but just give me a minute.' Her voice returned. 'Will's in shock. His parents are on holiday but they're trying to get flights home. His sister Mel's just rung to say she's walking from the tube station and I said I'd drive her to the hospital. Asila's husband got to the hospital last night, and Monty's mum. Tracey was the only one from IsVid not involved because she's on holiday too.'

'I hope everyone recovers quickly,' he said automatically, his stomach dropping at picturing Clancy with Will – even a Will who was probably going out of his mind about his wife and baby. He and Clancy used to share their lives and Aaron felt jealousy creep across him. Vaguely, he was aware of Lee taking Daisy out of the kitchen, followed by the sound of the TV in the sitting room.

Clancy was still speaking. 'Will was trapped in the car with everyone bleeding and unconscious. It must have been horrific.'

He agreed, hating himself for minding the caring note to her voice, the familiarity when she talked about Will's family and her old friends and colleagues. He wanted to check she was coming back from London but now was not the time to turn possessive, even if he did think, in the circumstances, Will was frigging lucky that Clancy would drop everything to support him.

'Anyway, I have to tell you something before Mel arrives,' she went on. 'I'm afraid I've got Harry and Rory again.'

'Why?' he asked blankly.

She half-laughed. 'Crazy, right? I was throwing my bag in the car when they came up. Harry was upset. He said someone suggested to Jordy that Harry's gay so Jordy asked him outright. He said yes.'

'Cue Jordy to explode,' Aaron sighed, running his fingers through his hair in exasperation at the dramas going on all around him. 'I discovered last night that Jordy had found out, but not the details.'

'Jordy's explosion was pretty comprehensive, by Harry's account,' she said sombrely. 'Lots of shouting and slamming about. Poor kid was crying, with Rory trying to comfort him. When he heard I was going to London Harry pleaded to come so I gave them ten minutes to grab their stuff. They did it in eight. I'm sorry,' she added. 'I feel as if I'm sticking my oar in with Harry and Rory but I just felt they needed someone.' She sounded almost defiant.

'Thanks for being that someone,' Aaron said. 'But I'm worried what will happen to them next.'

'Me, too!' she agreed. 'In the immediate short term they're OK because they're in the spare room of the apartment. They were very helpful last night finding their way here to fetch clothes and stuff for Will and Renée. It gave them something to focus on other than Jordy's pyrotechnics.'

Aaron leaned on the kitchen wall, feeling its coolness through the fabric of his T-shirt. She'd said 'here' so did that mean she'd stayed in the apartment too? He was shocked by the weakness that sent a tremor through him. 'Do you think Harry will come home with you?' he asked experimentally.

'I don't know.' She sighed. 'Home's got to be more than just a roof over your head. Harry has that in Nelson's Bar but it doesn't make him happy. Here, he's got nothing but Rory, but that seems enough. Although,' she added, when he didn't immediately come up with a reply to that, 'I'm not suggesting it would be fun for them to be home*less* in London. Let's just see what the next few days bring.'

'Has Will been discharged from hospital?' Aaron wondered just how many rooms the apartment had and where Clancy was sleeping.

'Not yet,' she said briefly. Then, 'Mel's just coming in. Can you do me a favour and let Harry's parents know he's safe and with me again? Rory's rung his mum, who's mega pissed off at Jordy, I understand, but I can't get Harry to ring home.'

'Of course. Thanks for looking out for him when you're helping others through their crises too.' He tried to imagine her day yesterday, miles away in a hospital he'd never seen with people who used to be very important to her. 'And look after yourself—'

'Sorry, I'm getting a beep, someone else is trying to get through,' she broke in. 'You look after yourself too.'

Then she was gone.

Slowly, Aaron replaced the handset. It was only when he turned and saw Lee was watching that he remembered he had anything else to deal with. He shook his mind onto a different crisis. 'You're obviously OK,' he said to Lee, crossing the room to give him a hard, brotherly hug. 'We've all been worried sick at you doing a vanishing act.'

Lee looked sheepish. 'Sorry. I did the diva thing again.

Mum rang here to check on me once too often and so I got a late booking at a guesthouse in Wells and took Daisy to build a few sandcastles while the sunshine lasts. I was anxious so I turned my phone off. I overreacted but I felt everything closing in on me. I should at least have left you a note.'

Aaron nodded, knowing with sick certainty that 'everything closing in on me' was Lee-speak for 'I was perilously close to completely losing my shit'.

'Problem is, Mum did find a note,' he said gently, and filled his brother in about its contents.

'Crap! That must have fallen out of my stuff when I was moving here. I haven't felt like that lately. I think it's just a bit of venting left over from when I'd realised Beth wasn't bothered about being part of Daisy's life. I am such a fuck-up.' Looking helpless, Lee ran a hand over his hair.

'There's something else.' Aaron hated to complicate the delicate situation but didn't see any option. 'Apparently, Alice has left Hugo. When you vanished at the same time . . .'

Lee's hand dropped. 'Alice has left Hugo?' he said blankly. 'So where's she gone?'

Aaron could only shrug. 'I didn't have a chance to ask Clancy if she knew anything before she rang off just now. She's coping with her own dramas.' Which there was no point in heaping on Lee at this second. 'You ring Mum. I want a word with Jordy and Anabelle.'

He pulled on a sweatshirt over his T-shirt and, deciding to leave Nelson behind in case Jordy got loud and Nelson met aggression with aggression, he let himself out into the bright and breezy day and set off across the village.

As he strode along the dusty footpath that took him through the jumble of tiled cottages that was Trader's

Place as a short cut to Droody Road, he replayed the conversation with Clancy. *Home's got to be more than just a roof over your head. Harry has that in Nelson's Bar but it doesn't make him happy.* Then something about Rory. In parallel, he heard her making a remark in relation to herself. *I don't have a home.* It wasn't hard to join up the dots but he wasn't sure he liked the picture.

He arrived at Jordy and Anabelle's place, half hidden behind the green crinkled leaves of a hornbeam hedge, and knocked at the kitchen door. He was answered in a second, Jordy throwing it open, expression turning belligerent as he saw Aaron. 'Oh, yeah, getting involved again, are you?'

He stumped back into the house, leaving Aaron to follow him into the kitchen where Anabelle stood by the table, her skin a contrasting pallor to Jordy's angry, dull red.

Aaron went straight to the point. 'I thought you'd like to know that Harry's safe. He's in London again. With Rory and Clancy.'

Jordy slapped the kitchen worktop, lips thinned and teeth gritted. 'What the fuck is it with her? She gave him a lift last time he sneaked off.'

Opting not to address that, Aaron kept on speaking. 'The main thing is he has a roof over his head, at least for a few days. I'll keep in touch with Clancy—' would he ever '—and tell you if that changes.'

With a bellow, Jordy bulldozed his way across the kitchen to grab Aaron's arm. 'That bitch Clancy—'

'Careful,' Aaron hissed, feeling his fists clenching at his sides.

'But what's she got to do with Harry?' Jordy bellowed, though he loosened his grip.

'She cares, I suppose.' Aaron kept his temper with diffi-culty. He wasn't a parent and felt unsuited to the job of mediator. Clancy had asked him to do this though, and Harry saw him as an ally. 'He's your son, man. You can't only love him if he's exactly what you want him to be.'

Anabelle spoke for the first time since Aaron had entered. She gazed at Jordy. 'It's time we called it a day.'

'Called what a day, Belly?' he demanded in the impatient voice Aaron had heard him use with her so often.

Anabelle drew herself up. 'Us. We've reached the end of the road, Jordy. I'm leaving you.' She sounded perfectly composed.

Jordy stared at her in shocked, awful silence, the colour draining from his entire face, even his lips as Aaron watched helplessly, unsure if he should go or stay. 'Is there another man or something?' he managed at length.

'Yes,' Anabelle answered with a firm nod. 'It's a man who cares about me. Living with him will be different. He won't call me Belly.' She gave a tired smile. 'He'll call me Mum. I'm leaving you for my son. He's my *son*. He's entitled to be whoever he is. I've been thinking about doing this for ages,' she added, 'and now you've completely chased Harry away you've made up my mind. I'll rent a house in Leicester. Harry and Rory can come to live with me, at least for a while, and then they'll be safe. Harry can go to uni and Rory and I will find jobs.'

Though he appeared to have brought the situation down on himself, Aaron suddenly felt sorry for Jordy, whose mouth opened and closed as his brain refused to supply him with the words that would keep his wife, keep his life.

Even Anabelle was gazing at Jordy with compassion. 'All you had to do was accept your own son,' she said.

330

Then she hugged Aaron hard and thanked him for bringing them the news. She patted Jordy's shoulder as she passed. 'I'm going to pack. It won't take long.'

After several long moments, Aaron cleared his throat. 'Do you want me to stay, Jordy? If you want to talk or anything—'

'No.' Jordy turned and looked up the hallway after his wife. 'No. No. Just leave me be.'

Chapter Twenty-Six

Will was discharged from hospital on Friday morning. His sister Mel had slept in his bed at the apartment then left this morning when his parents had returned from holiday in the Maldives to the welcome news that Renée had regained consciousness. The baby inside her had been declared safe, so far as could be determined.

Still, Will seemed unable to leave the hospital. It was as if he felt that the moment he took his eyes off Renée she'd slip away.

Renée's and Will's parents were in with Renée now but, barring complications, it was expected she'd be discharged in a couple of days, as would Monty and Asila. When the parents came out from Renée's room and Will could go in, Clancy planned to slip away. The accident had happened on Wednesday afternoon so she'd been hanging around holding people's hands in waiting rooms and corridors for the better part of two days. She felt as if she must smell like a hospital.

Beside her, Will stirred, as if sensing her withdrawal. 'I can never thank you enough for being here, Clancy. Most women would have told me to get knotted, after what I did.'

'You can get knotted if you like,' Clancy offered generously, giving him a quick smile. 'It won't change who you're in love with.' Black eyes and a broken nose had temporarily marred his looks but he'd barely mentioned his own injuries in his anguish over Renée and the baby.

He smiled, crookedly. 'I did love you, Clancy, in a way.'

The words didn't even cause her a pang. 'And I loved you, Will, in a way. It's not the way you love Renée though.' She knew that now.

'No.' He kissed her cheek. 'I can see Mum and Dad coming so that means I can go in now. Sure you won't stay a bit longer?'

She rolled her eyes. 'What? In the apartment with you? That would be seriously weird. You get your girl home and live happily ever after.' She kissed him gently on his forehead in return.

Then, over his shoulder, she saw a figure coming towards her along the hospital corridor. A tall, well-set figure, a familiar figure, who faltered for an instant, then strode on. 'Oh!' she said in surprise. She pulled away from Will, her cheeks heating even though the embrace was only a friendly one.

Will turned to see what had caught her attention. 'Ah!' he said, glancing between Clancy and Aaron with a small smile. 'Sometime, you need to update me on what you've been doing since you left. Thanks again, Clancy. You're a star.' Then he gave a wink and vanished through the double doors to Renée's ward.

Aaron continued towards Clancy, although his eyes followed Will for several moments.

'What are you doing here?' she asked, suddenly breathless.

He halted, his dark eyes switching to her. 'I came to see if you're OK. Phone calls seemed too distant. I would have come yesterday but Lee took Daisy off for a break without telling anyone. Until they turned up again, Mum panicked.' He hesitated. 'Lee and Daisy have moved in with me—'

'Lee told me.' It seemed a long time since the discovery of that fact, on top of Alice leaving her with Hugo and her B&B plans foundering, had pitched her into the doldrums. Then a thought occurred. 'Had Lee been with Alice?'

Aaron shook his head. 'Apparently not, though she seems to have taken off again.'

'Hugo told me. I haven't had time to worry about getting in touch with her.' In fact, she'd all but forgotten, overtaken, as she'd been, by other events.

He sat down on the seat next to hers. 'So, are you OK?'

She felt herself flushing. Had he come all this way to ask that? 'I'm fine. I was just saying goodbye to Will. Indications are good that Renée and the baby are going to be all right. Monty and Asila too. They'll all go home to be looked after by their loved ones in the next few days. The crisis is on its way to being over.'

His gaze didn't waver. 'Are you coming back to Nelson's Bar?'

She managed a grin. 'I suppose it is changeover day tomorrow so I ought to.'

He didn't smile and she felt as if he saw right through her, heard everything she wasn't saying. 'That sounds as if you're not sure you're ready.'

Her gaze slid away from his without her meaning it to.

334

'One thing I've had plenty of time to realise, hanging around waiting areas, is that there's a lot of stuff to sort out.' A tiny sigh escaped her.

'What?' he murmured, sliding an arm around her. 'Talk to me.' Then, before she could try, 'Actually, not here. I'd like to see the area where you used to live. We can talk over lunch.'

She looked at him in surprise, but agreed. 'It would certainly be nice to be outside.'

They had to move both their vehicles and find pay-and-display kerbside parking in Chalk Farm, which, as usual, was tiresome and took time. It was nearly two by the time they were standing on Prince of Wales Road.

'So the apartment is up there, on the corner,' she said, feeling self-conscious. Aaron didn't *look* out of place because he didn't have hayseeds in his hair or anything, but she suspected he was feeling out of place without the sea on one side of him and windy lanes and cute cottages on the other. 'I slept there the last couple of nights but packed my bag and put it in the car this morning. Will should be taking Renée home soon.'

He turned to gaze at her. 'Does that make you unhappy?'

'No,' she said, honestly, not even having to think about it. 'I'm ready for it to be her home now. But it's been a godsend for the boys to use the spare room. Did you know Anabelle's taken them off to live with her in Leicester?'

'I knew she was going to. I feel sorry for Jordy but . . . you can't keep someone who doesn't want to be with you.'

She nodded. 'Harry was so sweet when he said goodbye last night. Got all mushy about me helping him and Rory out. The pair of them and Anabelle went to a Travelodge in Leicester while they find a house to rent. He's got really conflicted feelings about his parents splitting up.'

'I've talked to him on the phone. It's a lot to cope with for him.' Aaron glanced back at the apartment building on the corner. 'So were you on the sofa?' He didn't justify the question or look embarrassed. He just asked.

'Had to, really. The boys were in the spare room.' She watched his eyes carefully and saw them flicker.

Then she decided to change the subject, taking him at his word that he was interested in her old stamping ground. 'This is Prince of Wales Road, NW5. If you go down Crogsland Road to Haverstock Hill you'll see the tube station. In more or less the opposite direction is Malden Road where we could find somewhere nice for lunch. Would you like to have a wander around first?' It seemed very different to striding around the clifftops of Nelson's Bar but he'd expressed an interest so she felt she ought to offer a tour.

'That would be good.' He took her hand and brushed a kiss on the back of it, then paid attention as she took him around the neighbourhood she'd once called home, raising his eyebrows to see so much living accommodation over shops.

As he didn't look impressed, she joked, 'Or you can live in a nine-bedroom house at the Belsize Park end if you have five million quid or so.' He looked pained.

She showed him Talacre Park and the gardens, and he studied the benches full of people eating lunch in the sunshine. He kept glancing at the sky, she noticed, as if checking it was still there. She found herself trying to make up for his lack of enthusiasm, or perhaps her old choices in living here, by listing all the great advantages to living and working in London. He seemed to listen.

They ate lunch at a pavement café in Malden Road on wooden tables and benches similar to those outside the B&B. That was the only similarity. Here the traffic was a constant presence. They had to raise their voices over its noise and they could taste exhaust fumes along with their paninis.

He said suddenly, 'You're not sure about Nelson's Bar, are you?'

'My things are there,' she said, unguardedly, but logically.

He put down the last of his panini. 'Is that your only reason for going back?' He was using his stolid, unemotional voice.

She paused to drink from her coffee mug, ultra-conscious that she actually yearned to return. Mainly because of him. And it might not be what he wanted to hear. OK, so she was intelligent enough to realise that him being here now, with her, out of his milieu, was because of her, but the memory of how hard he'd fought to keep his own space when he was with Genevieve was pin-sharp in her memory. What if, one day, Clancy too wanted more than Aaron was able to give?

'I thought I'd fallen in love with Nelson's Bar,' she said slowly, watching a delivery lorry stop outside a shop causing the traffic in both directions to have to squeeze into the remaining room with horn-blowing and hand-waving from irascible drivers. 'But I'm not sure how Nelson's Bar feels about me. Alice and Hugo arriving changed everything for the worse. If Hugo stays with Alice gone, the Roundhouse will be a torture chamber and he's Alice's legal husband so I have no power to chuck him out.'

'I probably could,' Aaron observed, 'but it might take time.' He waited for her to go on.

'My B&B idea fell through. Kaz and Oli can't even accept me as a long-term guest.' Like the IsVid situation all over again, she'd realised, she'd begun to feel squeezed out.

Being wanted was important.

A sigh escaped her. 'So I've been thinking about alternatives.' She didn't tell him that the alternatives were mainly driven by her trying to create conditions in which their relationship would flourish. 'I thought maybe Thornham or Titchwell, until the end of October when bookings drop off at Roundhouse Row. Then my money should be through and I can think about starting up a business and buying a place.'

The frown had remained pinned to his forehead. 'But not in Nelson's Bar?'

'I don't think so.' She blinked, because being pragmatic wasn't always joyful.

'How does being back here in London feel?' he asked, after a minute.

'Weird. Familiar. Good. Bad. As you know, I was towed along in my parents' wake in my childhood. Going back instead of forward hasn't cropped up much.' She screwed up her face in thought. 'Will asked me if I'd return to IsVid on a temporary basis until everyone gets back on their feet, but I'm not really needed because they'll all be working from home on their laptops in no time. That part of my life is over. The agreements will soon be ready to be signed.'

'Right.' He gazed around himself, taking in the constant traffic noise, the endless stream of passing people.

She could almost see him hating the noise, the fumes,

338

the bustle. 'Do you think it would be a good idea to leave soon? This is a very late lunch and if we hang on much longer we'll get caught up in rush hour.'

Slowly, he nodded. 'OK. If you're sure you're ready to go, I'll follow you up. Your Beemer's a racer and my truck's more of a cart horse.'

Clancy dawdled on the final leg of the journey, but Aaron's truck never appeared in her mirrors.

Soon she was driving into Nelson's Bar, through the dappled sunlight of the pinewoods, up Long Climb and curving down sharply into the final dip. When she pulled up in front of the Roundhouse she stepped out of her car with some ambivalence, glad to be back in Nelson's Bar but not looking forward to interacting with Hugo again. Stretching out the kinks of the journey from her back and legs, she pulled her bag out of the boot and let herself in through the front door.

For once, Hugo wasn't lounging on the sofa. He was asleep – or passed out – on the floor with three empty wine bottles for company.

Her nose wrinkling, Clancy coughed at the sour smell, leaving the door open to let in some much-overdue fresh air. Hugo roused, blinking blearily as he heaved himself up on one elbow. 'Oh. It's you.'

'Alice hasn't returned then?' Clancy asked, as she headed for the stairs, determining that her next job would have to be finding a new, however temporary, abode.

'No.' Hugo sounded pitiful. 'Genevieve has been here looking for her so she's not with her either. Where have you been? Have you seen her?'

'Nope. Looks like she's gone.'

He fixed Clancy with an ugly look. 'Don't know what

you're looking so pleased about. Alice doesn't really like you, you know. She laughs at you behind your back about this shithole little village.' Then he added, with evident triumph, 'And Alice and Genevieve queered your pitch with the people at the B&B.'

Clancy halted, her knees suddenly turning to water.

'That's right,' Hugo jeered, satisfaction thick in his voice at having brought her up short. 'They've been egging me on to be obnoxious to you too.'

Clancy's heart pounded so heavily the blood roared in her ears and she thought she might actually have toppled over if an arm hadn't snaked around her waist. 'You really are slime, Hugo,' said Aaron's voice. He must have drawn up just behind her after all. He turned Clancy to look into her face. 'He's not necessarily a reliable source of information.'

'I don't know,' she gasped, the air feeling too thick to breathe. 'It could be true, couldn't it? Genevieve tried to make mischief with your parents right under my nose. It would have been easy to work on Kaz behind my back.'

Aaron stroked Clancy's back. 'I'll speak to Genevieve—' he began grimly.

With an effort, Clancy straightened her backbone. 'Thanks. But I don't care about Genevieve. It's time I tried to get hold of Alice.' She took an instant's strength from his warmth, then gently disengaged herself and squared her shoulders. She could cope alone. It's what she was good at. 'Can I ring you in a bit, when I've had time to sort myself out?'

Disappointment and doubt warred in his voice but he released her. 'Come and use my Wi-Fi to make your call then. I have an errand to run, so you can have your privacy.

I'm not leaving you here like this.' He glared at Hugo over Clancy's shoulder.

She didn't argue. The possible scale of the betrayal from Alice was just too much. She muttered, 'Thanks,' took out her car keys and trailed outside. In moments she was pulling away again, driving drearily towards Potato Hall Row. Realising that Aaron was no longer in her rear-view mirror and seeing Lee's van outside, she got out of the car and found she could pick up the Wi-Fi if she positioned herself halfway around the workshop, out of sight of any of the windows. She didn't feel like talking to Lee just yet. He was way too entangled in her issues.

She rang Alice's number. The call was declined.

Enraged, she sent a rapid text, her finger ends hurting she stabbed the screen so hard. *ANSWER THE BLOODY PHONE!!!!* She gave that a minute to be delivered, then tried again.

Alice answered. 'Hi, Clancy! I've been meaning to get in touch with you.' She sounded guilty.

Clancy cut straight to the chase. 'Did you and Genevieve tell Kaz something that made her pull back from accepting my offer to buy into the B&B?'

A shocked silence, possibly at Clancy's voice emerging like a death-metal roar. 'It wasn't me,' Alice protested. Then, more reluctantly, 'I think Kaz mentioned your idea to Genevieve and Genevieve sort of hinted . . . Well, she said . . . Y'know, a bit gossipy.'

'No, I don't know!' snapped Clancy. 'Suppose you tell me?'

A pause, then Alice went on, sounding suddenly remorseful and uncertain. 'It was . . . well, just like . . . there must be a reason you'd been dumped by your old colleagues and Will at the same time.'

Clancy could hardly believe her ears. 'So she painted me as someone nobody wanted to be tied to?'

Alice's voice got smaller. 'Sorry. I didn't really think how shitty that was. Wine was involved when she told me and she made it sound a bit like a joke she was playing on you because she was upset about you and Aaron. Then I wasn't sure how to tell you. And then I left anyway.'

'You're my cousin.' It was the phrase Alice had used so often, *too* often, to justify requests for help or treating Clancy unfairly. Clancy closed her eyes and leaned wearily against the wall, tipping back her head and closing her eyes against the sun. 'I've taken a lot of responsibility on your behalf over the past six years.'

'I know.' Alice sounded genuinely distressed.

'You never gave a thing back.' Clancy's voice strengthened as she realised just how sick of it she was. 'Not a thing. When I was on the way to creating a nice new life here, you came back and ruined it, bringing your awful, crappy, bastard, obnoxious husband with you. And now you've run off and left him behind like a turd in a swimming pool so I have to find somewhere else to live at no notice.'

'Oh! I never thought—' Alice began to cry.

'You must have *thought*, Alice. Even leaving aside whether you fully appreciated the effects of Genevieve stabbing me in the back about the B&B, the business I'd hoped would give me roots in Nelson's Bar, you could see and hear Hugo being horrible to me on a daily basis.'

Alice cried harder. 'I did ask him to stop.'

'Big deal.' Clancy felt so exhausted she could almost have dropped the phone and slept on the floor. 'Find someone else to run Roundhouse Row for you in future.

I'm going to be busy.' She ended the call and stumped back to her car, intending to find somewhere to sit in the sunlight and try and work out what to do with her life.

Chapter Twenty-Seven

Once Aaron had seen Clancy drive off to his place to use the Wi-Fi, he climbed into his truck and drove the short distance to Trader's Place and Genevieve's cottage, her garden still bearing the scars left by her builders. It was late enough in the afternoon for her to be home from work.

He knocked. 'Gen,' he said when she answered, ignoring the smile that blazed across her face when she saw who her caller was. He looked into her blue eyes, sorry that it had come to this between them but having not a single qualm about what he was about to say. 'I've just heard a worrying allegation that you might be making mischief for Clancy, specifically with Kaz and Oli at the B&B.' He watched the smile vanish and apprehension slide into her eyes. He went on grimly, 'I hate to think that it's true, because we both understand that we're over. Don't we? No going back, whatever happens, so you know there's no point. No. Point. At. All.'

Her eyes filled with pain, but she gave him a querulous smile. 'I just . . . I . . .'

He'd been in a relationship with this woman for a year, so he bit his tongue on the anger he wanted to bellow in her face. 'I can't be what you want. You're not what I want.'

She nodded jerkily and he turned away without trying to soften his rejection, Clancy's hurt and bewildered face in pin-sharp focus in his mind's eye.

When he'd set out early this morning he'd drawn castles in the air about Clancy coming back to Nelson's Bar and them both living happily ever after. But did that make sense?

How could he expect things to change for him and Clancy if everything else remained the same? If Lee and Alice's situation put them in opposition, if Genevieve made mischief, if even his own mum was cool to the woman he loved? He got into his truck and paused to lean his arms on his steering wheel for a moment, expecting to have to absorb the impact of hearing the L word, even in his mind. But, no. It settled there quite happily.

When he pulled up outside his cottage a few minutes later, there was no sign of Clancy's car so he could only assume she'd been and gone. He got out of the truck and went indoors. Nelson fired at him like a missile, tail a blur, whimpering far back in his throat as he did when he'd sincerely thought that his owner might never return – which seemed to be any time they were apart for more than twenty minutes.

Daisy jumped up from the kitchen table. 'Uncle Aaron! We's painting, 'cos Daddy had today off!' she yelled, displaying painty hands and a piece of paper bearing a colourful collection of swirls and smudges.

Lee grinned from the other chair, looking less excited by the painting treat. 'I missed the start of a job erecting a conservatory so I've taken today and Monday,' he said. Then he nodded in the direction of the wooden-armed chair in the corner. 'Uncle Jordy's here too, but he doesn't want to paint, does he, Daisy?'

Aaron hadn't noticed Jordy, huddled in the corner, his hair in need of washing, new lines delineating the contours of his face.

Daisy sent Jordy a reproachful look. 'But painting's fun, Uncle Jordy.'

Jordy uncoiled himself from the chair. 'That's why I've left it to you, Daisy. I want you to have all the fun.' He glanced at Aaron. 'I was hoping to have a chat with Uncle Aaron.'

Aaron suppressed a sigh. Seriously? He wanted to think, to work things out, to find out where Clancy was now. But Jordy looked as haggard as if he hadn't slept for days. So, ''Course,' Aaron said. 'Let's go into the sitting room.' He dropped a hand on Lee's shoulder as he passed, glad to see his brother looking OK. In fact, of all the three men, for once it was probably Lee who looked most at peace.

Once in the sitting room, Aaron closed the door. He and Jordy dropped into chairs at angles to each other. 'What's up?' Aaron asked.

Jordy rubbed a hand over his eyes. 'Did you see Harry?' Aaron had already told him he'd be driving to London today, in case Jordy had wanted to give him a message for his son. He hadn't.

'No, mate. Anabelle took them off yesterday. Clancy saw her. They were all OK then.' He hoped Jordy hadn't assumed Aaron was somehow going to bundle Harry – with or without Rory – into his truck before he came home. For all the deep affection he had for Harry, Clancy had been Aaron's focus today.

'Shit.' Jordy rubbed his hair this time as a change from his eyes. 'I don't know what I can do.'

Aaron thought hard. His mind was tired but no one with any decency could sit opposite the tortured countenance of Jordy and feel no sympathy. 'I suppose you could rethink your approach,' he said, eventually. 'Shouting and hollering hasn't made Harry un-gay or out of love with Rory. It hasn't made Anabelle want to see things out with you.'

With a muffled sound, Jordy hid his eyes. 'I've screwed up. But I'm frightened. Life could be hard on Harry. You hear so much about gay-bashing and hate. I couldn't stand to think of him hurt. Beaten up.'

Aaron watched sombrely as Jordy disintegrated into tears. 'Was *that* why you were so crappy about Harry's feelings for Rory? You're frightened that being gay will bring him into contact with hate crimes?' He'd assumed Jordy's stance had sprung from blind prejudice.

With a huge sniff and blow, Jordy nodded. 'I don't want that for him.'

Aaron reordered his thoughts. 'Well. Maybe you could tell this to Harry? Because I don't think he knows. I take your point but there must be advice for how to manage the kind of horribleness you're talking about. The lads met with a youth worker in London – maybe someone like that could provide guidance?' He added gently, 'He can't choose who he is and he can't help who he loves, Jord. And if you love Anabelle . . . well, if you love someone you're mad to let her leave you if she loves you back. That's all I can say. Want a beer?'

Jordy nodded, wiping his tears roughly on his sleeve. ''Bout time you offered.'

When the beers were drunk, Jordy left by the seldom-used front door so Lee and Daisy wouldn't see his red eyes. Aaron sat on alone for a while, his own words echoing in his head. *If you love someone then you're mad to let her leave you if she loves you back*. If. If . . .

After a while, he got Nelson and the lead. Daisy instantly jumped off her chair. 'Are you taking Nelson for a walk, Uncle Aaron? Can I come?'

Aaron smiled at the little girl. 'Not this time, sweetheart. Sorry. I have to have a talk with Granny on my own.'

'Awwwwww, pleeeeeeeease,' Daisy wheedled, her face slackening with grief that her favourite – and only – uncle wasn't going to be wound around her little finger on this occasion.

Lee came to Aaron's rescue. 'I think *we* should offer to take Nelson for a walk and leave Uncle Aaron and Granny to talk.' He glanced at Aaron. 'Is that OK?'

Daisy was instantly distracted. 'Oh-*kay*!'

Aaron felt a flood of warmth. 'I'd appreciate it.' He was acutely aware that Lee had barely mentioned Alice leaving her husband and the village, or whether Lee knew where she was. But what happened next was Lee's decision, not Aaron's. Aaron had been overprotective-slash-interfering for too long. It wasn't until others began to interfere in his life that he realised how frustrating and undermining it could be.

A few minutes later, Aaron was facing his parents across their kitchen table. It took resolve, because he knew there was no way he was going to be able to say what he had to without causing them dismay, but he began by explaining how Clancy had begun to feel unwelcome in the village. 'She told me something important – that home isn't always a place,' he went on. 'Harry's going to make his home with Rory and that's all he needs, even if it means leaving everything he knows in Nelson's Bar when both he and Rory have lived all their lives in this village, like me. So I've come to explain to you that, although I have no idea what the future will look like, I want to be with Clancy. Nelson's Bar has always been important to me but now . . . I might leave the village.' He patted his mum's hand, because he knew she'd take it hardest.

'Where will you go?' Yvonne looked stunned.

'Good question.' He raked his fingers through his hair. 'If she decides she has to be in London, maybe I can make roof gardens for people there.' Aaron shoved away an image of himself working with the fumes rising all around him from the nose-to-tail London traffic.

'But you'll be like Crocodile Dundee trying to live in New York!' Yvonne protested.

Aaron gave a wry smile at his mother's words because *Crocodile Dundee* had been a favourite film when Lee and Aaron had been little, but it was an uncomfortably evocative analogy. 'When two people from different backgrounds want to get together, someone has to change. It might have to be me, that's all. It would get us out from under Genevieve's eye. I'm not OK with what she's been doing.' He gave an outline of what that seemed to be.

Fergus drew in his breath sharply. 'That's not on.'

Yvonne thrust her fingers into her hair, making it stand on end. 'Genevieve did that? I can hardly believe it.' A guilty look stole into her eyes. She hesitated. 'I suppose she's said one or two things to me too . . . Oh dear. I don't think I've made Clancy feel very welcome.'

Aaron hated to hurt his mother but there was no point dissembling. 'It would be great if you could make more of an effort,' he agreed.

'Leave that with us,' Fergus said firmly. 'If she's important to you then she's important to us.'

Aaron left a very quiet mother behind him, though he got a reassuring smile from his dad.

When he arrived home, he forced himself not to ring the Roundhouse. Clancy had said she'd ring him so he should respect that. He checked his answering machine. Only a message from Mrs Edge awaited, asking why he hadn't come to get her water feature going. Guiltily, he rang back and asked if he could come now, in the last of the daylight, pleading a 'bit of an emergency' had taken him out of Norfolk today.

Rather than turn the truck in the lane he followed the curve of Long Lane until he could turn into the other end of Droody Road.

Just before he made that turn, he saw the figures of Lee and Daisy with Nelson crossing the clifftop towards Zig-zag Path.

And Alice.

He slammed his foot on the brake.

Then, smothering a sigh, hoping Alice wouldn't play football with Lee's heart this time, he drove on. Whatever did happen, he resolved not to interfere. It was between Lee and Alice.

As he drove out of the village, Clancy's bright blue BMW was outside the Roundhouse, and his heart lifted to see it.

She hadn't gone anywhere yet.

Clancy's car might be outside the Roundhouse but Clancy herself was in the B&B, facing Kaz and Oli across their lounge, in the worn but private quarters of the B&B. It had a view over the rooftops and trees of the village and she supposed they reserved the sea views for the guest bedrooms.

On the sofa opposite Clancy's chair, Kaz was fidgeting and Oli frowning.

'I just want you to know the story of why I came to Nelson's Bar,' Clancy began. Though it was a story she hoped she could one day leave completely behind, she didn't see why she had to put up with Genevieve's snide version being received as the truth. As she told them about her fiancé getting caught with his trousers down and the following rancour with her colleagues, she watched Oli's eyebrows shoot up and Kaz look embarrassed and shame-faced.

'I'm very sorry to hear all this,' Oli said tentatively, when she'd finished. 'But is there a reason you're telling us?'

Clancy nodded and looked at Kaz.

Kaz began to wring her hands. 'Genevieve made it sound . . . quite different.'

'I know. That's why I wanted to set the record straight,' Clancy said softly.

Oli turned to his wife. 'I'm bewildered! What's been going on?'

Slowly, having to sniff quite hard at times, Kaz explained. 'Clancy offered to invest in the B&B. But then Genevieve made it sound as if Clancy was really bad news so . . . I told her we didn't want to go ahead.' Then she looked at Clancy and choked, 'I'm so sorry.'

Oli shoved back his thinning hair. 'You turned down an investor without consulting me?' he thundered.

A tear leaked from the corner of Kaz's eye. 'I realised after that I should have asked Clancy herself about what had happened. But when I went to the Roundhouse the man who answered the door said she'd gone back to London.'

After glaring at his wife for several silent seconds, Oli turned back to Clancy. 'I don't suppose you want to pick up the conversation with us again now, do you?'

Clancy rose. 'I'm not sure,' she said as kindly as she could, considering. 'I can't see it happening now but I am still thinking about what to do next.' Then, seeing Oli's shoulders slump in disappointment, she said, 'I did gather a lot of information about funding, though, so I'll send that to you.'

After listening to further apologies from Kaz, Clancy returned to the Roundhouse.

Simply ignoring Hugo as she thought about the B&B and wondered whether she should have listened to Oli a little more, she occupied herself with laundry, cleaning down the kitchen and making herself a sandwich.

Some of the shock of what Genevieve, and possibly Alice, had done in putting in a bad word for her with Kaz, wore off as she worked. She paused, sandwich in hand, to realise on a wave of dismay that by reacting as she had, making Aaron leave her alone, she'd actually let Genevieve come between them.

The last thing Clancy cleaned was herself, standing for ages under the hot shower, washing with her favourite jasmine shower gel and wondering why she felt so hoppity-skip about ringing Aaron.

When she'd first seen him at the hospital this morning she'd been so shocked she'd forgotten to kiss him. Was that why he'd been odd all day, looking as if he had things to say but not saying them? Being distracted and absent as they walked around the streets of Chalk Farm?

She dried her hair, then hearing Hugo moving around

in his bedroom on the floor below, she took the opportunity to skip downstairs to the landline and dial Aaron's number, feeling as if her heart was vibrating at the back of her throat.

She got his answering machine. Sod it. She didn't leave a message because she couldn't say, 'I don't really know what's happening. But whatever it is, I want to find some way to be with you.' That wasn't the sort of thing you said to someone's machine. You said it when you were face to face with the person and could see their expression and read their reaction in their eyes.

When Aaron finally got back to Nelson's Bar that night, it was as the passenger in the front of a breakdown vehicle, his truck having expired suddenly on him on the way back from completing the work for Mrs Edge. He'd waited more than two hours for the tow vehicle to take his truck to the garage at Brancaster and then deliver him home.

The Roundhouse had been all in darkness as they passed, otherwise he would have asked the breakdown mechanic to drop him there.

He thanked the driver and went indoors, surprised to see Lee downstairs watching TV, looking dragged down and exhausted.

Cautiously, Aaron said, 'You OK?'

Lee's smile was pained. 'I saw Alice.'

'Oh?' Aaron said, as if he didn't know.

Lee shrugged. 'We've been talking a bit recently. I've been trying to understand all the passion I had for her, I suppose, but tonight I finally admitted to myself that she's not the woman I remember being in love with. I don't mean the way she's wearing her hair or the hippy-dippy clothes. She's just . . .' He shrugged and shook his head as if searching for words. 'She's got no depth. No conception of what other people feel. My rose-tinted glasses must have been pretty powerful if she was always like that. She asked if we could try again but I said it wouldn't work.'

Relief made Aaron's knees go funny. 'That must have been tough,' he said, thinking of all the years that Lee had wasted pining for Alice, sunk into depression and anxiety.

'Yep.' Lee turned back to the TV. 'At least it's made me feel ready to move on with my life. I'll start looking for somewhere for Daisy and me to live in Hunstanton soon.'

'That's great.' As Lee seemed to have said all he was going to, Aaron went to check his answering machine. One hang-up and when he checked, it had come from the Roundhouse's number. His heart lurched but there was nothing he could do at this time of night, so he went to bed.

Chapter Twenty-Eight

Saturday. *Again*. Changeover day sure came around quickly.

Clancy would rather have taken a walk along the cliffs to calm her fizzing thoughts. She tried to ring Aaron, but frustratingly, got the busy signal. As she stood there glaring at the handset, the front door of the Roundhouse opened and someone walked in.

'Alice!' Clancy gasped, her call, for the moment, forgotten.

Alice stood just inside the door, her many plaits swaying around her tattooed shoulders and the straps of a floaty summer dress. 'I'm sorry,' she said gravely. 'I've come to make amends.'

Clancy stood still. It would be too, too easy to just accept whatever olive branch Alice held out, to forgive and forget. To carry on exactly as before. Although a lot of her ire had subsided, she still felt as if Alice had punched her in the face. In fact, she thought she'd rather have received a punch in the face than a stab in the back. 'How?'

'Just leave it to me. Hugo upstairs? I'll start with him.'

Alice gave Clancy a quick hug, though Clancy stood unresponsive, then she ran upstairs.

Clancy hovered. She'd tugged on cropped jeans and an old T-shirt, ready to set to as soon as the first guest drove away, but now she wasn't sure she should leave.

After fifteen minutes, during which she heard raised voices but not what was said, Clancy's patience was rewarded by the sound of footsteps on the stairs. Hugo came down first, carting along a well-stuffed holdall and treating Clancy to a filthy look as he passed.

Alice was on his heels. 'Hugo needs to make a phone call,' she said to Clancy, still in the solemn tone she'd used when she arrived.

Clancy nodded. By the way they both stood gazing at her, privacy was required. 'OK, I'll begin changeover day.' With a last look at Alice, who was looking unusually serious, Clancy made for the door.

'I'll come and find you soon,' Alice called after her.

Clancy slipped off to number four, clutching her cleaning materials and cloths, flung open windows and began stripping beds. She was shaking duvets into clean covers when she glanced out of the window and halted. Down in the lane, Hugo could be seen ferrying a substantial segment of what had gone to make up Possession Mountain into a heap by the front gate.

Fumbling her way through making up the beds, Clancy was unable to take her eyes off the scene unfolding outside as a taxi appeared. Alice, arms folded, looked on as Hugo heaved his bags into it. Then the taxi turned in the lane and drove away.

Alice turned as if to make for the cottages, pausing to have a word with Dilys and Ernie, who had appeared like pop-up dolls. The three conferred, Ernie gesticulating, Dilys with hands on hips, Alice nodding apologetically. Finally, she must have persuaded them back indoors as she set off again towards the holiday homes.

Realising that Alice wouldn't know which cottage she was in, Clancy ran down and opened the door of number four.

Alice dimpled when she saw her, stepping over the threshold and closing the door behind her. 'I think I've got rid of him but it would be sensible to change the locks.' Her eyes were hopeful.

Clancy folded her arms. 'How? What have you done?'

'Hugo's mum is an MP,' Alice said casually, though her eyes sparkled. 'Her seat's tenuous at the moment and she can't afford for any hint of scandal like, say—' she puffed out her cheeks in an elaborate show of thinking hard '—a son hitting the skids financially, and it coming out that she'd withdrawn financial support. So she promised to bring Hugo to heel by supporting him again if he left the Roundhouse. And I promised not to get any journalists I happen to know to investigate Hugo to see what skeletons he's left in cupboards as he travelled the world.'

'Alice!' Clancy breathed. 'That's blackmail.' And who would have thought blackmail could leave one feeling so relieved?

The fine eyebrows that were so much like Clancy's own shot up into Alice's hair. 'I prefer to use the word "negotiation".' Then she grinned and took one of Clancy's hands tentatively. 'Have I done enough for you to forgive me a bit? I do also have good news. At least, I think you'll think it's good news. Let me tell you and then you can decide.'

Clancy didn't really hesitate. Although Alice had let her down, she was still her favourite cousin, and she had got rid of Hugo, ruthlessly, but efficiently. 'Go on then. Tell me.'

When she'd listened to what Alice had to offer, Clancy thought it was *fantastic* news. At least for her. She wasn't so convinced how it was going to turn out for Alice.

'You're absolutely sure?' she kept asking. 'Because it's a big step.'

Alice's eyes filled with tears then. 'I'm sure,' she said. 'I need to leave the village again and it's absolutely the best way to pay you back for being the best cousin in the world.'

Then Clancy's eyes filled with tears too.

Alice left soon after that. She carted the remainder of Possession Mountain into the motorhome, though Clancy couldn't help her because she still had two more cottages to service. Alice said she didn't want Clancy to wave her off anyway, because it would be too sad. From the front bedroom window of number six, Clancy watched sadly as the big vehicle's roof passed above the hedges and turned the elbow bend before sinking steadily out of sight on the steepness of Long Climb.

Wiping her eyes, she tossed the final armload of used bedding over the bannisters – just too late to warn Aaron, who was coming up.

He swore and tripped as the fabric billowed over him, banging his elbow on the handrail as he fought his way out.

Clancy tried not to laugh. 'Oops, sorry!' she called, as he craned around to look at her. 'I've been trying to phone you but a lot's happened this morning and I'm running miles behind.'

'Was that Alice in the motorhome?' he demanded, taking the remainder of the steps two at a time.

'It was.' Clancy met him on the landing, her heart picking up pace. She regarded him uncertainly.

But not for long. He pulled her into his arms, his lips descending firmly on hers in a kiss that both set her senses ablaze and settled her nerves as it went on and on. 'Can we go somewhere to talk?' he said eventually, when they came up for air.

Her heart gave a little anticipatory hop, because she was desperate to share the good news Alice had given her, but she glanced at her watch. 'There's still the rest of this and number five to clean and change—'

'Sod them!' Aaron planted his hands on his hips.

She wound her arms around his neck and kissed him again. 'So you're going to stay here and tell three families they have dirty sheets and their holiday homes aren't ready?'

Aaron heaved a sigh. 'OK. Let's get it done.'

With both of them working furiously they finished before the first guest hove into view. Clancy led Aaron into the Roundhouse to dump the cleaning things. 'We could stay here because—'

But he was already grimacing. 'No! I want to go where no cousins, brothers, parents, guests, exes, pets, phones or emails can interrupt.' Then he grinned. 'Get your swimming costume.'

Giggling, Clancy hurried into a one-piece and threw her clothes back on over it, then she grabbed towels, and they hurried along Droody Road, onto the grass of the clifftop to The Leap. Once they'd stripped off their clothes – Aaron to his boxers in lieu of trunks – he took her hand. 'Ready? Let's go!'

They raced towards the cliff edge, yelling as they launched themselves into nothingness, scattering gulls in the wind as they plummeted through the air and crashed stingingly through the waves into the near-silent world of underwater. As before, the swim to the surface seemed a couple of seconds longer than was comfortable, but then they broke the surface together.

'Come on.' Aaron led the way around the rocks to Secret Beach, empty today. Clancy felt a twinge of sorrow that there was no Harry and Rory hiding out from the rest of the village so they could show their love for each other. Then Aaron was pulling her to her feet in the shallows, helping her over that bit where the waves played at sucking the sand out from underneath your feet as you tried to walk.

Finally, he pulled her down on the beach beside him, kissing her so suddenly and thoroughly that she didn't know if she was breathless from the swim or from the kiss. Then he broke away. 'I love you,' he said firmly. 'I'm not sure if that's been completely obvious but I want to make sure you know.'

Her heart flipped like a giddy pancake. 'That's good,' she murmured breathlessly, reaching up to touch his cheek, slippery with water. 'Because I love you too.'

Relief blazed in his eyes. 'If you don't want to live here then I'll be at home wherever you are. There must be some kind of gardening business I can get off the ground in London.' He looked struck. 'I was thinking of specialising in roof gardens and I could call it that, couldn't I? "Off the Ground Landscaping".'

Clancy shivered, and not because of the spray from waves breaking nearby. 'You hate London,' she said in astonishment. 'I don't know who'd be more miserable, you or Nelson.'

He tried to shrug her words off. 'But if you can't be happy here—'

Cautiously, she bit back an assurance that she could be ecstatically happy in the tiny little village high up above the sea. There were other hurdles to be cleared. 'I talked to Oli and Kaz about the B&B yesterday and now they know the truth about what happened with IsVid, Oli wants to talk again about me investing with them.'

Aaron's hands tightened on hers. 'Will you?'

She shook her head. 'Can't now, because . . . um, have you spoken to Lee about Alice?'

He brushed his brother away with an impatient shrug. 'They're not going to try again. He told me last night. But, listen—' he gripped her still more fiercely '—I'm not going to let them get inside our relationship any more, whatever they do.'

Joy blossomed in her chest. 'Me, neither. Or me, too – whichever's right. Alice came this morning. I think she's upset about Lee but trying not to show it. I can't promise she'll stay away though because I think she suspects Lee was The One, and she let him go so there would always be a chance she'd pop back up.' She turned to face him squarely. 'I think she'd genuinely hoped . . . Anyway, she's gone travelling again. And I have sole possession of the Roundhouse because she's manipulated Hugo out of the way too.' She told him about her cousin's insouciant blackmail.

Instead of looking pleased, though, Aaron frowned. 'Even if Alice comes back to the Roundhouse sometime, it doesn't have to matter. You could move in with me.'

It was such a shock that she had to pause to get her breath before she answered. 'I'm not sure that's the best idea—'

'Lee and Daisy are going to move to Hunstanton,' he added persuasively. 'We'll be alone.'

'Yes, but Genevieve—'

'Forget what happened with Genevieve,' he broke in, knitting his dark brows over the bridge of his nose. 'I didn't want her moving in because she was the wrong woman. You're the right woman.' And he closed in for a hard, hot kiss, as if to prove it. 'I've talked to Genevieve and I'm pretty confident she won't try and make trouble for you any more.'

'*But*—' Clancy said loudly, intent on getting a word in '—Alice has taken Genevieve travelling with her! Apparently she stayed at Genevieve's cottage last night after talking to Lee and she's persuaded her that she needs a break from Nelson's Bar.'

Aaron's jaw dropped. 'Seriously?'

Clancy nodded, freeing a hand to stroke seawater droplets from his arm. 'Alice and I had a row yesterday. I told her she took from me but didn't give and that I wasn't going to look after her half of Roundhouse Row any more. She was so shocked she came up with a plan to rebalance the scales.'

He looked bemused. 'And that's taking Genevieve away for a bit?'

Breathless all over again, but this time with joyful anticipation, she laughed. 'Only partly. Alice has offered me something else. Something really valuable in my opinion, and not just in money. Something that will – if you agree – make me very happy and settled, here in Nelson's Bar.'

Silently, his eyes searched hers.

Clancy took a big breath. 'She's offered to let me buy her out of Roundhouse Row,' she said in a rush. 'If you're up for it. It will have to wait until my money comes through but we'd be partners. We could live in the

Roundhouse. It wouldn't be my space or your space. It would be our space.' She waited, hardly daring to breathe.

Then a slow smile broke across his face. '*If* I'm agreeable? *If* I think it's a good idea? I think it's just about perfect! Fancy Alice doing something so generous in the end.' Then he grabbed Clancy to him, rolling on his back so she was completely supported by his body and he could drag her head down to his to kiss and kiss while the waves broke, the gulls called, and they were covered in a great deal of the sand of Nelson's Bar.

And, Secret Beach being called 'secret' for a reason, they held a *very* secret celebration.

roundhouse, it would not be impossible; only, she would be careful to choose what hydraulitique he was. Impression came before ever he could ... we were ... until there was a good deal ... near about ... I hope that it all went duly to question in the ... to the good old change ... Since the ... it was in no way correspondingly appreciated to look back ... during that day. So the ... to take ... conventry ... consult a little could and may some granted to a ... cannot be said of many others.

And so it ... that ... and ... a ... they had ... seemed to take up ...

Epilogue

August, the next year

Bridegroom Aaron stood at the front of the function room at the Duke of Bronte, which had dropped the label B&B now Oli's brother had become a partner in the business, bringing with him enough capital to finance the extension that allowed the celebration of weddings. Best man Lee stood beside Aaron. A piano was playing gentle background music while the congregation, which filled the room and spilled over into ranks of red velvet seats on the lawn, waited for the bride.

Then there was a stir at the back and he turned to see Clancy Moss walking towards him up an aisle edged with sprays of flowers.

Her dress was cream, flowing around her as she walked, and tiny ivory narcissi were pinned in her hair. Her arm was linked chummily with her father's, her parents having torn themselves away from their busy lives long enough to attend. Aaron didn't think they completely appreciated what a wonderful, warm, intelligent, funny woman they'd given to the world in Clancy, but he was fine with that.

It meant she was all for him, which was just how he liked it.

Walking importantly at the other side of Clancy and holding her hand was Daisy, dressed in yellow and carrying a basket of matching roses.

The music swelled and the celebrant and registrar, both ladies with neat navy suits and benevolent expressions, stepped forward to greet the bride. Clancy beamed at Daisy as they neared where everybody waited and whispered, 'I have to take a step forward now, remember.'

'And I have to stay behind you and be quiet,' Daisy whispered back.

Unlinking herself from both Daisy and her father, Clancy moved to Aaron's side without waiting for any formal, dated gesture of being 'given away'. She took Aaron's hand instead, at the same time mouthing 'You OK?' at Lee. Beside Lee, a well-brushed Nelson, wearing a black bow tie on his collar, wagged his tail, giving a tiny whine. Lee had him on a short lead to prevent him from jumping up at Clancy's wedding dress.

Lee, who now agreed that Aaron had got the best cousin, grinned and whispered, 'Glad you could turn up.'

Aaron laughed softly and gave his little bro a playful nudge, appreciating that he'd made the effort to joke and smile. They all knew that somewhere amongst the guests lurked Alice, who'd left Genevieve picking grapes in Italy to fly home. No one had thought it would be a good idea to invite Alice to be a bridesmaid, but Clancy hadn't been able to exclude her altogether. Happily, Lee was seeing a woman called Elaina, seated alongside Yvonne and Fergus. Elaina worked in an amusement arcade in Hunstanton and had a little boy in Daisy's class at school. She'd transformed Lee into a much happier man than he'd been in the Alice years.

Clancy turned to check out the front row, where Gerry had joined Clancy's mum, Brenda, sitting beside Aaron's own mum and dad. All four parents beamed back at her. He could only marvel that Clancy had so open-heartedly forgiven certain members of his family for their chilliness in the past. Yvonne and Norma had almost worn a path between De Silva House and the Roundhouse in the past year.

In the row behind, Aunt Norma, Dilys and Ernie beamed at Clancy too. Harry sat next to Rory, both looking incredibly handsome in suits. Harry's first year at uni was behind him and Rory was well into an apprenticeship as a passenger transport driver. Anabelle and Jordy had never repaired their marriage but got along well enough to sit together, alongside the lads, for the wedding.

Finally, Clancy turned to Aaron and winked.

Aaron winked back and blew her a kiss.

The wedding celebrant cleared her throat, or possibly smothered a laugh, and murmured, 'Is everything OK?'

Clancy took a last look at everyone, then beamed. 'It's absolutely perfect. Welcome to Nelson's Bar. We're ready when you are.'

Loved

A Summer to Remember?

**Then why not try one of Sue's
other sizzling summer reads
or cosy Christmas stories?**

**The perfect way to escape
the everyday.**

What could be better
than a summer spent basking
in the French sunshine?

Grab your sun hat, a cool glass of wine,
and escape to France with this gloriously
escapist summer read!

Available in all good bookshops now.

In a sleepy village in Italy,
Sophia is about to discover
a host of family secrets . . .

For Ava Blissham,
it's going to be a Christmas
to remember . . .

Countdown to Christmas with your must-have author, as you step into the wonderful world of Sue Moorcroft.

Available in all good bookshops now.

It's time to deck the halls . . .

Return to the little village of Middledip with this *Sunday Times* bestselling Christmas read . . .

Available in all good bookshops now.

One Christmas
can change everything . . .

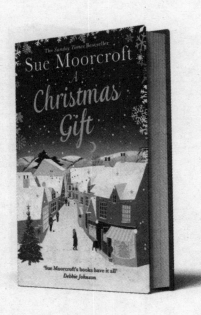

Curl up with this feel-good festive
romance, perfect for fans of Carole
Matthews and Trisha Ashley.

Available in all good bookshops now.